PAPER FATHER

By D. Todd Deeken

Dear William,

I hope you enjoy this novel like I did. The author, Todd, has been a very big role model and inspiration to me over the years creating my favorite car TV show/podcast "EveryDay Driver" and working on the Lord of the Rings films. The story is equally inspiring as it is entertaining. Hope you enjoy!

— Henry
5/13/2021

Copyright © Todd Deeken 2020

For my son.

ZERO

Samuel Kerr sits alone in the dark with his back to a small fire. With the nub of a pencil he scribbles on the pages of a small notebook. His face is in the shadows, concealed by darkness and a tangle of stubble. He's writing to his son.

> *Danny,*
>
> *One more day now and I'll get to see you again. I can't wait to tell you who I am and hear who you are. I know you'll never read this, and I'm glad. There's so many things I could tell you about the life I've lived these last few years. But I know you're only seven and I'd rather forget it all anyway.*
>
> *So, when I see you I'm gonna give this up. No more writing down all the things I never got to say, because we'll be together again. You have a question, you just ask me. I have a thought, I'll tell you. I'm sorry I haven't been around. I hope you remember me.*

He stops and thinks. Then he turns the page, noticing that the notebook is not only full, it's falling apart. He closes the back cover and starts writing something else.

> *Ariel,*
>
> *I know you're still mad about what I did to our little family. I know I've missed out on a lot of special years with Danny. I know how much you probably hated hunkering down with my parents, but there's a lot of terrible things out here now and I'd rather you stuck it out with them. The devil you know… or whatever the saying is.*
>
> *I've been counting the days for a long time. I hope you have too. But I bet you found someone. Or you're*

looking. I can't say I blame you.

I still miss you. I miss us. And I hope we can go back, even though so much of the country has gone to shit. I want to find a place of our own again. You. Me. And Danny.

He closes the notebook and drops it into a stretched and filthy plastic grocery bag. Then he glares at his tiny nub pencil and tosses it into the fire. There's a large kitchen knife in the dirt beside him as lays down. He keeps his back to the fire and looks for movement. The knife is in easy reach.

Part 1

Going Home

1

Heat waves rise from a long, straight stretch of blacktop, crumbling and scarred with potholes, spearing up the side of a rolling ridge. It's been a while since anyone walked here. Thick trees flank the road, standing leafy but still in the stagnant and stifling summer afternoon. Given enough time, nature will swallow this road completely.

Sam walks alone up the center line of the ruined asphalt. He's scruffy, his clothes dirty, and a tattered plastic bag hangs over his shoulder. An unkempt beard clouds his face, dirt cakes his boney cheeks and a pair of ratty goggles covers his eyes. It's hard to tell what he looks like.

A trail of dust kicks up behind him, rising into the still air. The disturbance can be seen for miles in this sleepy part of the world. And on a nearby ridge, someone watches through binoculars: Sam is an intruder, and he must be dealt with.

Sam turns off the main road and works his way down a long dirt driveway. Vine-like weeds reach across the ruined gravel and grass shoots fight up between the stones that crunch under his feet. He keeps his head down, exhausted, but still moving.

He stops at a mailbox dangling from a post. The name "Kerr" is barely legible in the dents and rust on the side. He takes a deep breath and looks up slowly, allowing himself to see the house just beyond the mailbox.

Sam stares at the simple structure with a wraparound porch. It stands in a clearing on the hillside, with a view of the valley below. Shutters hang askew. The paint peels in the sun. The doors stand open. Abandoned.

He slides his bag off his shoulder and grips it like a weapon. His eyes never leave the open front door as he pulls the kitchen knife from his belt. A moment of utter stillness passes as he stares some more. Bag in one hand, unsheathed knife in the other.

Then Sam surges toward the front door, closing fast, tense and alert. Boards CREAK on the porch as he dodges the steps in a quick leap.

One step past the threshold he stops.

Tension drains from his body, and he sinks to his knees. He slumps as if his skeleton were melting. He lets the bag fall away amid the rubble of the entryway. His knife CLANKS to the floor as he shoves the goggles up into his hair. Tears collect in his blue eyes. He bows his head, pained and reverent.

A body lays on the floor: an elderly man, on his back and deteriorated beyond recognition. But the hole in his chest is still clear.

Sam stares at the corpse before him. Tears cling to his eyelashes. His mouth hangs open as if to cry out, but nothing comes. Utter silence.

Then he forces himself up. He leans against the wall, stepping past the corpse and deeper into the house. His knife and bag lie forgotten.

In the little kitchen he finds an elderly woman face down on the tile floor. Her housecoat shoved aside and her body even more shriveled than the man's. A chunk is missing from the back of her skull.

Sam gropes for the counter as tears cloud his eyes. His knees buckle, and he sinks into a fetal ball on the broken, dirty tiles. Tears come like waves, and he surges with his own weeping.

No words. Overwhelming sadness. He's lost in spittle, wailing and uncontrollable grief.

2

Now the sun hangs low in the sky. Sam casts a long shadow as he stabs at the crusted earth. He tosses dirt over his shoulder without looking. The second of two graves takes shape at his feet. The bodies lie nearby, side by side, awaiting their graves.

He's stripped to his waist and sweating. His thin sinewy frame suggests he's strong and fast, but undernourished. He digs on methodically: the blade of the shovel dives in and tosses out, over and over in a steady rhythm.

Then Sam stands and cocks his head, listening. The rhythmic thudding of an engine rises from the distance. It's getting closer. Whatever is coming will be at the house in a moment.

Sam suddenly feels very exposed. He grips the shovel by the shaft and slinks into the back of the house. The engine is close now, right outside when it coughs to a sudden stop. He leans against the wall of the kitchen, listening.

He hears footsteps on the driveway. Then the **CREAK** of the porch.

The sweat on his forehead goes cold. He tries to control his breathing as he raises the shovel like a bat. His eyes dart across the hallway, toward the master bedroom of this little ruined house.

In the entryway, a thick man stands in the doorframe. He's wearing desert camoflauge, contrasted with plates of black body armor. There's a name on his chest, **HOLLIS**, in military block text. His short black hair glistens with sweat, but his eyes are cold.

He nudges the plastic bag at his feet. Then his eyes drift to the discarded knife and the dusty silhouette where a body once lay. The drag marks through the dirt pull his gaze toward the kitchen.

Around the corner Sam stands in the kitchen, leaning flush with the wall and still holding the shovel. He can't see Hollis, but he curses himself for not keeping his knife with him. He waits, taking shallow breaths and listening, unsure what to do next.

Then he hears the unmistakable sound of a pistol being drawn and cocked. Hollis holds it low and ready, eyeing the corner of the kitchen wall.

"I got your stuff here," Hollis says. "Why don't you just show yourself."

Sam sighs, and Hollis aims his pistol toward the sound.

"Who are you?" Sam asks.

"Now, I think I better ask the questions."

"Why? You a cop?"

Hollis looks at himself. He smirks. "I'm the closest thing I guess."

"What the hell does that mean?" Sam growls back.

Hollis looks around, thinking of sight lines and ways to ambush whoever is in the kitchen.

"Think of me as the neighborhood watch."

Sam looks around as well. He has to get to the master bedroom. But there's no way to get there without revealing himself.

"So you knew the Kerrs?" Sam asks.

Hollis shifts the grip on his pistol. Uneasy. "Yeah. You?"

Sam looks down at the mark on the floor where he found the elderly woman. His eyes rise in the direction of the graves. "Well enough."

He makes a decision and steps into view, turning the corner in one fluid motion. The shovel hangs loose in his hand, and he's face to face with Hollis.

Hollis trains his pistol on the lone man and eyes the dirt-caked shovel.

"Awful nice of you to bury them, but that don't make you friends," Hollis says flatly.

"Yeah. Seems like something the 'neighborhood watch' would have done."

Hollis doesn't like that. He raises the pistol further.

"Who are you?" Hollis growls.

Sam just stares at the pistol in Hollis' hand.

"That's a unique pistol."

Hollis eyes his own gun. Then he snaps back to the moment. He studies the thin, filthy man before him.

"German, right? Walther," Sam says, as if he were seeing it in a gun-case instead of pointing at his head.

"Congratulations, you know your weapons. Now who the hell are you?" Hollis asks.

"That doesn't look like a nine-mil," Sam continues.

"Forty-five. Leaves a big hole. You'll know first-hand if you don't start talking," Hollis says.

Now Sam knows for sure he's seen the gun before. He saw it years ago, through a plexiglass wall in a prison.

3

An elderly man with thinning gray hair sits behind the plexiglass wall of a prison visiting station. He fumes to himself, squeezing the handset with white knuckles. Sam sits down on the other side of the glass in his prison jumpsuit. He's almost unrecognizable, doughy and pampered compared to the dirty, stick-like figure in the abandoned house. This younger, softer version of Sam picks up his handset and looks at the older man with concern.

"Everything okay?" Sam asks.

"They took my Walther pistol, Sam," his father replies.

"Dad. No one's going to let you bring a gun into a prison."

"I got it bored out. I was going to show you," his dad says, apologetic. "It takes a forty-five shell now. Probably the only one in the world like that – punch a hole right through a wall."

"They'll give it back to you when you leave," Sam reassures him.

"I have permit to carry," his father says.

"It's not a free country in here, Dad."

The two men stare at each other. The old man turns sad now, really taking in the sight of Sam, his son, in prison clothes. In this moment, neither of them knows he'll be dead before Sam is free again.

***

Now Sam is standing in the hallway of his parents' dilapidated house, staring at the barrel of his father's one-of-a-kind pistol.

"Where'd you get that?" Sam asks Hollis.

"Let me see your arm," he responds, ignoring Sam's question.

Sam doesn't move. Hollis stiffens, eyeing Sam's thin, bare shoulder. He points at the bulbous line of scar tissue just below the deltoid of Sam's left shoulder.

"You're a damn con, aren't ya?" Hollis snarls.

"I did thirty-eight in the debt system. I'm square," Sam says.

"I don't care what you were in for, we don't want you around here."

Sam sighs and looks toward the master bedroom. Hollis watches him, the pistol still aimed at his chest.

"This is where I'm supposed to be."

"Alright, fine. We'll do it this way…" Hollis sneers as he digs into a pocket of his fatigues.

Pulling out a worn-out cell phone, Hollis steps toward Sam. He grips the pistol tighter.

"You so much as twitch…" he warns.

Sam stands still as Hollis scans his shoulder scar with the phone. The device BEEPS affirmative, and Hollis pulls the screen to his face.

A mug shot of the thicker, softer Sam from prison appears on the phone. His name is clearly visible below the image: SAMUEL JASON KERR. Hollis' eyes go wide. This is not what he expected. He turns to look at Sam and

SMACK! Sam swipes Hollis with the blade of his shovel. The big man goes stumbling backwards and CA-THOOM, blasts a hole in the ceiling. Sam drops the shovel and sprints for the master bedroom.

Hollis tries to recover, blinking his eyes and regaining his balance as he levels the pistol again. CA-THOOM! The Walther blasts away a chunk of the doorframe just as Sam darts out of sight.

Still reeling from the strike, the big man touches the side of his face and sees blood on his hand. Now he's angry.

In the master bedroom, Sam darts into his parents' closet. It's been scavenged clean of everything but the bare shelves on the back wall. He grips the shelves as if to tear them off, and pulls. With a terrible scraping shriek the wall pivots and arcs open, revealing a hidden door.

There's an old combination dial on the door. Sam spins it as fast as he can, praying he's right.

A bullet ricochets into the closet as Hollis rounds the corner and fires. Sam tugs on the huge safe door; it swings open, and he leaps through. Hollis steps into view as Sam heaves the door closed behind him. Another bullet clangs against the thick metal, but now the door won't seal. Sam knows Hollis will kill him in seconds.

Sam looks around him, seeing the supplies and weapons of a fully stocked panic room. He grabs the nearest pistol and turns to face his attacker. Hollis pulls open the safe door in time to see Sam pull the trigger.

CLICK. The pin snaps on an empty chamber. Both men freeze for a second. Their eyes dart to the boxes of unopened ammunition stacked on shelves. The guns aren't loaded.

Sam hurls the pistol at Hollis just as the big man starts to fire the Walther again. CA-THOOM. The slug splinters the gun rack a few inches from Sam. Cornered, but moving fast, Sam grabs a box of ammo and hurls it at the shelf above Hollis' head. Dense stacks of canned goods cascade off the high shelf and rain down on Hollis. He cowers on instinct.

Sam has only a second to turn back to the gun rack and pick a weapon. He sees long, thin hunting rifles and a thick pump-action shotgun. The shotgun is the most like a club, so he snatches it from the rack and turns to Hollis as the cans stop their tumble.

Sam swings the shotgun like a bat, smacking Hollis across the jaw with the wide, flat stock. Hollis stumbles back into the door, his finger twitching on the pistol. CA-THOOM. This shot tears a chunk of flesh from Sam's side, his blood splattering the back wall.

Both men stumble now, with Sam falling against a counter. Through a spike of pain he sees a line of shotgun shells. Snatching one quickly, he raises the shotgun and turns to face Hollis.

The big man gets up, bleeding from both sides of his face but rising on adrenaline and anger. With no time to load the shell, Sam swings the shotgun again. Hollis drops the pistol as he takes the hit to his chest and wraps his arms around the shotgun, trapping it. Sam can't pull it free, and Hollis pulls him closer. The big man head-butts Sam with brutal force, and Sam stumbles back in a daze. Hollis now has the shotgun. He hefts it like a bat and smiles at Sam, thinking about payback.

Hollis swings the shotgun in a huge arc. Sam ducks at the last second, and the stock whistles past his head to break another shelf of canned goods. Hollis keeps his feet and steps back to swing again. Sam waits until the big man raises the shotgun for the deathblow.

When Hollis lifts the shotgun, Sam pounces and shoves a shell into the load flap. In a blur of motion he traps the shotgun vertically over his attacker, pumps it once and drives his thumb at the trigger.

BA-BOOM! The blast thunders through the tiny space, sending a 12-gauge slug straight down into Hollis' upper chest. His lower back explodes in a rain of blood and flesh. Sam falls back into the gun shelf. Hollis stands motionless, stunned.

Then Sam kicks Hollis hard in the chest. The big man's body careens out of the panic room and lands in a heap on the closet floor. Blood pools under him as it quickly drains through the massive hole. Death comes in seconds.

Exhausted, Sam sinks to the floor of the panic room. He looks at the thumb-sized dent missing from his oblique. It's bleeding and hurts like hell. He sees first-aid supplies on a shelf, tears open a package of gauze and staunches the bleeding. He's alive.

4

As the last light of day fades away, Sam drags Hollis out of the master bedroom and to the back door. The body leaves a smeared trail of blood across the house. Dumping Hollis into the dirt yard, he strips off the big man's holster and body armor. He wonders if leaving the body in the open will attract attention. It's a risk he'll have to take, as he's too tired and scared to dig another grave in the dark.

Sam rounds to the front of the house and finds Hollis' transportation, a beat-up customized ATV with holsters, brush guards and extra gas cans. He kicks the transmission into neutral and pushes the ATV into the darkest corner of the open garage. Darkness has come quickly, but in the morning he'll have to find a better hiding place.

Inside the unlit house, he picks his way through the rubble and back to the panic room. There's a skylight in the roof, with light trickling in through an elaborate series of mirrors. He can see just enough to find a large flashlight on a shelf. It clicks on instantly, and he recoils from the brightness.

When his eyes adjust, Sam inspects the door of the panic room, trying to figure out why it wouldn't close. He sees a bullet from the Walther pistol lodged into the doorframe. Finding a pair of pliers among the supplies, he picks it out of the seam, and then the heavy safe door seals once again.

With the flashlight balanced on the floor and pointing at the ceiling, Sam can see most everything in the panic room. The ten-by-ten space has the familiar feel of his old cell, but these walls are stacked floor to ceiling with supplies he never imagined while in prison. The shelves on one wall create two tightly stacked bunk beds. He can't imagine his parents getting any kind of sleep or staying sane locked in this space together, but he still wishes they'd had the chance to try.

Among the canned goods, Sam finds an opener. He opens the first thing he can reach, some kind of beans. He eats in silence, letting his exhaustion settle over him.

Sam's mind drifts to his long and dusty walk from Chino to this house he so hoped would be a home. Now he's locked away in another cell, with few options and none of the family he hoped to find. He knows there will be work to do and big decisions tomorrow. His side aches, and he takes a look to see it already crusting over. His shirt and his plastic bag of supplies are out there somewhere, but he's not going back through the house in the dark.

The tight bunk has clean sheets. This is the first real luxury he's had in a long time. Sleep comes quickly.

5

Sam awakens as the growing light of dawn warms the skylight. He lays in the bed for a while, looking slowly around at the stockpiles in this tiny fortress. In addition to the canned goods and gun rack of weapons, he can see some much needed clothing, a pair of backpacks, paper, pens and an additional small fireproof safe.

He sits up, staring at the safe.

"Why the hell did you put a fireproof safe inside a panic room?" he wonders aloud.

He shakes his head at his own father's paranoia and goes over to the keypad lock. It blinks six stars at him, awaiting a code. With no electricity anywhere in the house, this safe's lock must be battery powered, and he has no idea of the combination. He tries the numbers for the panic room. No luck.

His father liked to talk about the "reckoning" coming to the United States. Sam always discounted these theories as the rantings of an increasingly paranoid old man. But now, standing in his parents' ransacked house in a world gone to hell, he has to admit his father was right. The country's whole financial system has fallen down around them. People like him went to prison to cover their debts. People like his parents hunkered down to fight off the inevitable squatters and scavengers.

Sam smirks at the irony of his father preparing for a world like this one, only to be struck down in his own entryway. And now his unbelieving son reaps the benefits. His father is dead and gone, but the safe stares at him as yet another parental lesson. Another secret stash he would have mocked only three years before.

He knows his parents were never good with passwords. They stayed staunchly out of touch with technology and suspected anything or anyone trying to access their personal information. As a result, they had few passwords, most of which were terrifyingly simple.

He types: 1,2,3,4,5,6. It fails, but he sighs with relief that they didn't fall prey to the most basic passcode.

Next he tries his parents' anniversary. Then their birthdays entered as two-digit days, two-digit months, two-digit years. The safe locks itself into a secure mode after these attempts and begins a fifteen-minute countdown before he can try again.

While the numbers tick down, Sam scavenges the panic room. Grabbing an old denim shirt folded neatly on a shelf, he realizes this was once his shirt. He'd given it to his father when it had gone out of style, and now he claims it back. There's a thick, puffy down jacket complete with stuffsack for easy packing, and he peels it from a hanger and tosses it on the bed. Some day soon, that jacket will be a godsend. He pulls down the bigger of the two backpacks and finds empty water bottles in the side pockets and a water filter in a front pouch. Whenever he moves on, he'll be far better equipped than he was when he walked out of the prison with just the clothes he was wearing more than three years before.

The timer on the safe finishes its countdown, and Sam stares at the waiting stars. He tries his own birthday. It fails. Then, with a deep breath he tries a date only seven and a half years prior: 030423, the birth of his own son. The safe CLICKS.

Swinging the door open, Sam sees almost every square inch crammed with paper and keepsakes. He pulls out a wad of paper, folded over twice and as thick as his wrist.

"Seriously?" he marvels when he realizes this stack is a huge printout of emails. He always laughed at the fact his parents kept printing out emails even though their account was deeply archived. Now it serves as a record of conversations otherwise lost forever. He sets the stack aside, knowing he should go through it to glean any helpful news from the last three years, and continues unloading the safe.

The safe is only eighteen inches square, and yet almost everything inside is square-shaped and shoved in with only millimeters to spare. There's a box of ammo on one side, hollow point shells made illegal more than five years ago. This hundred count of .45 ammo is worth almost as much as gold now, but could be worth even more in the Walther during a crisis. Underneath the shells sit four bars of actual gold, a fortune for anyone living outside the sparkling walled cities. The rest of the available space is crammed with two ratty-edged photo albums, and Sam struggles to lever them out.

He opens the cover of the older book and sees photos of his parents in college and shortly after they married. The hairstyles and fashions of the late 1980s seem every bit an era from another century. In a few pages, he's seeing himself as a child and his spoiled exposure to technology and the rise of the internet. What were once simple pictures now look like the decadant abundance of an only child in an upper-class home. Standing here under a skylight in a fortified room, with that world all but gone, makes these photos less like a time machine and more like the snapshots of a parallel universe.

Sam knows the other photo album before turning the cover page. His wife made this book and gave it to his parents when their son was born. Inside, he flips the pages he knows all too well but never imagined he'd see again. The hospital photos with "Daniel" written on cards. A picture of Sam with his newborn son asleep on his chest, still so tiny that he only reaches from Sam's neck to navel. Sam flips through to find more pictures on more pages, with balloons and goofy graphics on each page. Then he stops on a picture of an older Daniel hugging his mother in a moment of laughter.

He stares at his wife, the mother of his child. She's beautiful, and he knows others think so as well. Her high cheekbones and sharp jaw attracted many men before he came along, and Ariel had always used her good looks and flirtation to move through the world. The boy looks like her in this photo, and Sam hopes he always will.

When he walked to this house after his release, Sam expected to find Ariel and Danny here with his parents. Now he's relieved to know they weren't here to be killed alongside the rest of his family, but he knows they are lost to him. Ariel couldn't cope with his arrest and the stigma of waiting around for him to work off his tab. It was *their* tab, of course — they'd run up the debt together. But Ariel treated money as an always-available necessity instead of a finite commodity. Her patience for stark hideout living with his parents would have worn out in weeks.

Flipping pages, Sam passes Danny's birthdays and watches his son grow up again in memories from long ago. Then, just after the boy's fourth birthday, the images become sporadic and altogether different. They are loose-leaf pictures, printed poorly from a digital file. Instead of a celebration, they are now a record taken in quick moments in a world gone back in time. The boy isn't as clean or well fed. His clothes aren't as well kept. Ariel has vanished from the photos, relegated to photographer. Sam has never seen any of these moments, and it brings tears to his eyes to see his son growing beyond his own memories.

Then the pictures stop altogether, and Sam imagines how difficult taking or printing photos would have become as the nation's infrastructure retracted further and further. He remembers the internet access at the prison changing from easily available to wildly expensive and restricted. He remembers the rumors of hunger turning to looting and occasional power outages turning to whole cities living by candlelight.

He fans the rest of the pages, seeing only blank paper pass until the back cover. There, inside the hardback is another photo, tucked into the seam. Danny looks well, and years older than when the photos stopped. Ariel kneels down beside him in the frame, smiling broadly and looking years younger and happier. It seems like a picture of his family in another life and place. Except Sam knows this means they've made it inside one of the shining cities. He can only imagine what his wife did to get them entry, but they are clearly enjoying the spoils.

The photo must be recent, as Danny looks at least six years old, and the city opulence behind him seems familiar to Sam. He looks at the huge pile of printed emails and knows any information about where they've gone will be found there. Pulling the photo out of the book, Sam snatches up the stack of papers and begins reading.

6

Sam scans through the printed email pages, looking for something from his wife. But as the contents of the emails turn from casual to cryptic discussions of the failing infrastructure, it dawns on him that her latest correspondence might have been from another account. He has no way of knowing when his parents lost power or their internet connection. Some areas held on to a vague normality for the better part of a year when the accounts were reconciled. Eventually though, most everyone outside the cities lost all services. Internet, water, and power ceased, and only those with self-sufficient homes resisted enduring a world of candles and outhouses.

***

He remembers walking with his father on this property. The day was so hot he could feel sunburn in real time. Danny shuffled and wobbled in front of him, living up to his toddler stage. Little pants bulged over a big diaper, and his long-sleeved shirt arched over his baby stomach. The tiny cap on his head covered his face from the scorching sun. Sam wished he had a hat.

"It's right down here," his dad said from the bottom of a small hill on the scrub-brush land.

"He's exploring," Sam said.

"Pick him up, I want you to see this," his father said.

Sam looked at his dad and then beyond to the large above-ground reservoir. A tangle of pipes snaked off the side and dropped into the earth.

"I see it, the pipes go into the pump," Sam said dismissively.

"It's all solar," his dad said with pride. "We'll have power and water when no one else does."

Then Danny stumbled over a rock in his path. He fell face first onto the ground, his cap knocked away.

Sam dropped down to Danny's level. He stood him back on his feet and wiped off his clothes as Danny stared wide-eyed and gasped for breath.

"You're okay, little man," Sam said in a soothing tone as he put the cap back on Danny's head. "Fell down. But okay!"

Sam raised his arms over his head and repeated himself triumphantly, "Okay!"

Danny almost smiled. He started to lift his little arms up in triumph.

"Is he okay?" Ariel called from behind Sam. Danny could see her, and with Mom coming to comfort, he melted down. Sam dropped his head as Danny cried out and reached for Ariel.

"He was," said Sam as Ariel picked him up.

"It's okay, Danny. Mama's got you," Ariel said as she comforted her son and turned back to the house.

Sam watched her go.

"Come give this a look now," said Sam's dad.

Sam sighed and turned to his father. "It's pretty cool, Dad."

"We can go on almost indefinitely," Dad said. "If I keep the propane tank filled, it will be like nothing happened."

"Has something happened already?" Sam asked.

"We get an outage now and then," he said, as Sam reached the reservoir and looked back at the solar panels on the house. "Last one was nearly two days."

"Well, I'm glad for you," Sam said.

"You guys should get it, too."

"Dad. We never have outages. Our HOA doesn't like solar panels anyway," Sam said, hoping to move on.

"You're always welcome here," Dad said. "Let me show you something inside."

***

Sam stands in his parents' panic room and wonders if it's safe to step out and turn on the lights. This self-contained house is like an oasis right now, and he's surprised no one was squatting here when he arrived. When Sam knew he'd be one of countless people imprisoned to work off their debt, he'd put Ariel and Danny on a bus and sent them here to wait for his return. His dad never said how long they stayed.

Reading these emails helps him fill in some of the timeline, but it tells him almost nothing about Ariel's whereabouts or how long she stayed here. He wonders how she was able to travel to any of the shining cities built by mass prison labor. The big metropolitan areas were allowed to decay and provide crumbling shelter for those who couldn't go anywhere else or had no ambition to try. Meanwhile, places that were once small, destination spots became fortresses of wealth and security.

Sam flips rapidly through the pages, looking for any mention of Carmel, the closest of the shining cities. He finds no leads. Frustrated, he picks up the photo again. The background offers no clues, as it looks like the overly manicured streets of any shining city. Absentmindedly, he glances at the back of the photo and starts to set it down before he realizes what he's seen.

Aspen, 2029.

This description written in his mother's handwriting makes him shake his head at the absurdity. For years he'd teased his parents for continuing to print out digital photos sent to them by email. He couldn't ever seem to explain the ability to tag or title a picture with the information his mother normally scribbled on the back. But now, her habit of printing and captioning gives him the only clue about the remains of his family.

How on earth did Ariel and Danny get to Aspen? This first question rises and then fades away as a hundred others flood his mind. His brief moment of triumphant discovery turns to suspicion and concern. He looks around the panic room and finds a few maps on one of the shelves. He unfolds the pages, remembering how easy it used to be for him to look up a location and scroll through the maps with the tip of his finger. Now he smoothes the folds of this giant paper map and searches for Aspen in the tiny print.

Scribbling and calculating in the margins, Sam estimates the distance to be around one-thousand miles. Going that far required serious commitment in the days when he had a car. But now, one-thousand miles across this broken country would be farther than most people traveled over the course of their entire lives. He knows he's already come a few hundred miles since he got released. But a trip to Aspen would dwarf even his hardest moments getting here. The location of his parents' home lived in his memories, and he had no danger of getting lost or caught by the wrong information. Venturing to an unknown place would be a far harder journey.

Sam looks around the panic room, with its stocked shelves and heavy door. He knows he could survive a long time in here, hidden away and safe. Leaving invites constant insecurity and probable death. He touches the blood-crusted bullet scrape on his side. He looks at it, knowing it will scar. Getting to this tiny fortress nearly killed him.

"Aspen," he sighs. "Why not Carmel, or Tahoe?"

He wonders how many closer shining cities he will pass on the way to Aspen. Though he's heard of some of them, he knows he was kept out of touch these past three years. There's no way to guess why she ended up in Aspen. He only knows her disdain for him and their financial situation must have overpowered her loyalty to family.

When their possessions were "reconciled," like so many others, they'd already done the math and knew their assets would fall thirty-eight thousand dollars short of their debt. Before the authorities came to incarcerate Sam for the required thirty-eight months of labor, he and Ariel had planned for his return. She'd agreed to go to his parents' home to survive the coming years while he worked off their debt.

Part of Sam hates her for moving on, but he knows they'd be dead if she had stayed. His son is still alive. The family he worked to return to has gone on without him, but at least he can say they've *gone on*.

Now he needs to take an inventory. He has to imagine what he'll be up against and whom he might encounter. He looks at the pile of body armor tossed in the corner. Some of it is still splattered with Hollis' blood. The Walther pistol lies on the floor where Hollis dropped it. When Sam picks it up he notes dried blood along the side and barrel. He'll have to clean it — something he's never done, but vital to him learning this weapon.

Carefully laying the Walther on the workbench below the gun rack, Sam grabs the shotgun from the hooks and turns toward the thick metal door. He cocks the shotgun, tensing at the cacophonous sound echoing in this tiny, quiet room. Spinning the lock, Sam swings open the door and lowers the shotgun at the empty closet. The cool fresh air of the morning washes over him. He can hear birds, but nothing else.

With a deep breath, Sam steps out of the panic room and creeps through the house. Daylight reveals everything of value has long been ravaged or removed. Strangely, the family photos still hang on the walls, neglected and covered in dust, but remaining as artifacts from the home's better years.

Sam moves toward the back door. Birds chirp outside, and a breeze blows through the broken windows and out the distant front door. He can see a cluster of birds picking at Hollis' exposed corpse. Slamming the door open only sends a few scattering off. The larger birds, two huge carrion crows and a vulture, continue picking at the body until Sam is only a few feet away. With a sudden movement they take to the sky, and he watches them go.

Only after the birds are well out of reach does Sam think they could have been a fresh meal. He'll have to find a hunter's instinct if he intends to survive.

Hollis has been picked and pulled by a dozen beaks. Sam rolls the body with his foot and digs carefully in the big man's back pockets for any treasures. The smell overwhelms him when he turns Hollis onto his back. Stumbling away, Sam pukes on instinct. Luckily, he keeps the shotgun out of the way and then goes back to checking pockets.

Sam finds a small palm-sized LED flashlight, a multi-tool and the cell phone Hollis used to scan his shoulder chip. Standing, Sam considers stripping off Hollis' pants, but decides they are too blood-stained and probably ten inches too big in the waist. He needs to dig another grave and bury the corpse before it attracts any more attention or scavengers. But for now, his inventory is more important.

Shoving the new finds in his pockets, he holds the shotgun at the ready and walks around to the front of the house. He stands, perfectly quiet and still, watching and listening. He can feel the heat already rising, and knows the day will be still and stifling. Satisfied he's not being watched, Sam steps into the garage and walks to the back corner to inspect the ATV.

The four wheeler is a large AWD model with huge fenders Hollis converted to storage areas. Two large gas cans hang on the cage-like storage rack along the back wheels. A brush bar with spotter lights turns the front into a menacing snarl. An ancient hunting rifle hangs in a long holster by the driver's seat. Sam lifts the rifle into view, takes one look at the rusted and wrecked shaft, and knows it deserves the trash. Thanks to the panic room, Sam has plenty of great weapons to fill the holster.

Sam slides the shotgun into the holster and unfastens the gas cans. One of them is full, but the other seems less than half. He opens the ATV's tank and finds it nearly full as well. He guesses this heavy rig might get him a quarter of the way to Aspen if he used every drop of gas on a flat, straight road. This quad will make a great start, but he'll be ditching it if he can't find more gas. Hollis probably stole every gallon here, but Sam needs to not make enemies. He knows gas might be too expensive to be worth the ride. No matter what, there's a long walk in his future. Thinking he can drive all the way to Aspen is a pipe dream.

7

Sam can't escape the fact he's broke. More than three years in debtors' prison may have cleared his financial slate, but it left him without a penny. He stepped back into the world at complete zero, no debt and no assets. He couldn't sell the clothes on his back. The possessions he brought to his parents' house had all been scavenged. Anything and everything he'll need must be taken from the panic room or bought along the way. Sam knows he could kill and steal if he wanted, but the thought of incurring any kind of debt makes his stomach turn. Burning through credit already ruined his life and splintered his family.

***

"There has to be more," he remembers her saying.

On the front step of their little suburban house, Sam stood in the doorway with Ariel looking sullen as Danny leaned against her leg.

"That's everything. And as much as they'll allow," Sam said to her.

He looked beyond her to the two carry-on sized suitcases in the front hall. They stood out in the otherwise empty house. No furniture remained. No evidence they lived here. One small suitcase per person, filled with whatever you could fit. The only loophole in the "reconciling" program remained in the dimensions of "one small suitcase."

"Front zipper," he reminded her. "Be sure you split it up soon."

She nodded, walling off her emotions as she looked beyond Sam to the nondescript bus idling at the end of their lawn. Plain-clothes men sat inside, depressed and watching this scene they'd each lived already. A huge bouncer of a man waited at the open door of the bus, patient for Sam to climb in, but clearly ready for this to turn for the worse. A small bookish-looking man waited just behind Sam, holding a stack of paper.

Sam squatted down to his son's height. He forced a smile.

"Dada gotta go to work," Danny said to Sam. But the boy knew this was something more.

"Something like that," Sam said quietly. He reached out for a hug, and the boy stepped close. Ariel wiped a tear away, angry it existed at all.

"They'll take you in. They'll keep you safe. It'll go quick," Sam said as he stood. But it felt permanent. Thirty-eight months may as well have been thirty-eight years.

He turned and stepped to the man with the stack of paper. As the little man pointed, Sam signed in various places. His possessions vanished with each pen stroke. His debt consolidated with thousands of others. He promised to work off the remainder: thirty-eight thousand dollars, earning him thirty-eight months in one of the new "Federal Infrastructure Facilities." Work camps, building the new financially balanced America on the remnants of the bankrupt one.

It could have been thirty-six months. When they first heard of the crumbling system, Sam had stepped to the nearest ATM and pulled as much cash as his cards would allow. Just under two-thousand dollars was stashed in Ariel's suitcase. Sam would pay it off, of course, but he hoped it would get them to safety before even paper money became suspect.

***

Now standing in his parents' ruined garage, Sam knows paper money has become worthless. He wonders how long it lasted and whether Ariel used it to get to Aspen. Sam served an extra two months just to give them that head start, and now has no idea where they went. At least they weren't here when his parents were killed.

Then he remembers the bars of gold in the fireproof safe in the panic room. Though he hasn't sensed a person since Hollis, Sam suddenly feels very exposed and runs back into the house. He charges into the panic room and pulls the door closed behind him. The gold bars are right where he left them. He feels like a child again, having free access to clothes, food, money and even weapons because his parents provided them.

The insanity of this trip to Aspen settles into his thoughts. Traveling a thousand miles through mostly lawless wilderness. Hollis — with all his body armor, swagger and easy thievery — will prove a tiny challenge compared to a mob or a well-armed survival group living in the forests or abandoned towns.

He will pack from the supplies in this room and be better prepared than most. He knows a lone man riding an ATV and carrying high-end weapons invites attack. Going out to find his family guarantees he'll look death in the face.

He could live behind the panic-room door on this dilapidated property, but the memory of his son giving him that last hug and trying to understand destroys any chance of staying put. Sam's missed three years of being a father — half of his young son's life. Sam knows he has nothing to offer. Yet he can't silence his need to guide Danny and try to equip him for the strange life they are all now living.

He looks around the panic room, and it strikes him anew how similar it is to his cell. Live or die, Samuel Kerr is now a free man and hunkering down in this cell isn't an option. He will pack for a journey he must take, but can't begin to imagine.

8

"What if I never find him? What if I die first?"

Sam stops in the midst of loading the larger of two backpacks. It takes him a minute to realize he's just asked these questions out loud. The thought overwhelms him.

A moment before he'd been thinking about the most important things to take on this thousand-mile trek across the country. There are two major mountain ranges between here and there, a dozen roads, and no telling how many clusters of strangers. He's already missed three years, and the thought of any more had put him in a trance of preparations.

Sam's betting his life and plans on a computer-printed photo with a scribble on the back. Ariel and Danny could be anywhere now, and this is his only lead. There's a real chance he'll die somewhere along the way and never see his son. Or he'll survive and simply never find him.

What would he say to Danny? Now that he's seven. Or at seventeen. Or twenty-seven. Standing here in a room prepped by his own father, Sam realizes he may never get the chance to say anything else to his son. His influence may have ended when the boy was three.

On a shelf above the fireproof safe is a new pack of five legal pads. He must have looked past them a dozen times. But now, he grabs them, peels back the plastic and pulls out three of the pads. He places two of them in a large top pocket of the backpack. Then he grabs a pen from the coffee mug of random utensils.

Setting the third pad down, Sam poises the pen over the first line for a long time. What should he say to a boy he doesn't really know anymore and may never get to know again? It hurts to think this way, but it also frees him. He can be candid without consequence. If he sees Danny again, these words will go unread. But if the boy's only lessons from his father will be on these pages, then cutting through the bullshit and niceties seems quite necessary.

So he starts a new notebook of stream-of-consciousness scribblings to his son.

> *To my cute, smart, inquisitive son, Danny Kerr.*
>
> *There's no telling if you'll ever read this. I hope for both our sakes you never do. I hope you have good memories of me and don't think of me as the guy that got on a bus and left you and your mom with nothing.*
>
> *I always think of you and that hug we had before I had to go. You deserve more than some absent father, but if I never make it to you and this somehow gets through, then I want you to know that I tried. I wanted to tell you all this stuff myself. But I gotta try to offer you something more than I did so far. Maybe something in here will help you out.*
>
> *Your mom did the right thing. Never doubt that. She took you someplace safe, because your grandparents' house got really dangerous after you left.*
>
> *Your grandpa, my dad, left me this paper and a bunch of other stuff so I could try and find you. He was always there for me, and I hope you can say the same about me — even if you only have these pages to prove it.*
>
> *I'm headed to find you, Son. Aspen's a long way away, but either me or this paper will get there. Somehow.*

Sam stops. His handwriting is lazy and unpracticed. He wishes he still had a smartphone to dictate, but he may as well wish for the whole world.

When he writes these first words, Sam has no way of knowing these pages will make it to Aspen. His wife will read them and have to decide if she wants Danny to know his father through these written words.

For Sam, these pages will prove to be his conscience during the journey and a lifeline to sanity and catharsis. His musings will be his only constant travel companion.

He opens the top zipper pocket again and shoves the third legal pad and a fistful of pens into the hole. With a struggle, he zips it closed and goes back to packing. He selects a few canned goods, clips the empty water bottles to low hanging exterior loops and lays the gold bars carefully inside the zippered pouch originally designed to hold a water bag.

He looks at one of the bars, shifting the weight of it in his hand. These are the first gold bars he's ever seen. How things have changed.

Sam sets the bar down in front of him and pulls out the pad again. He knows he has to train himself to write down his thoughts as if Danny were standing beside him.

> *I don't know what you've been told about money. But we used to use little flat plastic rectangles to pay for everything. It might seem silly now, but back then everyone used them. These rectangles had codes on them, and banks would trade the codes back and forth to pay for things. We paid the banks, and sometimes we used a second rectangle to pay for the first one.*
>
> *That's kinda why the whole thing collapsed. There wasn't any real money anymore. I have to admit, it feels pretty dumb now. Somebody somewhere asked to be paid everything they were owed in real money, and the whole system started to unravel.*
>
> *Now we all use the metal system. Gold and silver have always been used to buy stuff. But these days titanium and steel are worth a lot,*

*because the machines that used to dig it all up
don't work anymore.*

This mention of titanium washes over Sam, and he realizes there's more money here than he first thought. His father had another stash of wealth, but claiming it will be messy.

It's midday, but he digs back into his father's grave as fast as he can. He senses that the longer he stays here, the more chance he'll get discovered. Now the thought of burying Hollis feels like an enormous waste of time. If he's wrong about his father, he might regret this dig as well. But he keeps shoveling.

His father's torso starts to appear under the dirt, and he works to uncover the body's left leg. When he's pulled away most of the big chunks of dirt from hip to knee, he drops the shovel and picks up an axe.

"I'm sorry, Dad," he says, as his fingers flex on the axe handle. "I hope you understand."

With a huge arc over his head, the axe swings down into the rotting flesh of his father's body. After a few big blows, he's shattered the pelvis and severed the leg from the torso. The knee splits with only two hacks, and Sam blinks back tears from the stench and the guilt. He reaches in, barehanded, and lifts his father's severed left thigh out of the grave. Then he quickly shovels the dirt back over the rest of the body. It's grisly work, and when his father's body is mostly covered again he knows he'll leave Hollis to rot and be scavenged.

Sam carries the leg into the house and lays it down on the floor of the master closet. He steps into the panic room and takes a large knife from the wall rack. Standing over the leg, he steels himself for the smell and task to come. Then he drops down and plunges the knife into the rotting flesh. Tearing, cutting and prying, he peels the flesh from the bone like a giant chicken leg.

The sight causes Sam to nod with satisfaction. As he hoped, this isn't bone, but titanium. His father's left hip, femur and knee joint are all high-grade surgical titanium and worth almost as much as gold in this broken world. Peeling the last of the flesh away, Sam leaves it to rot on the closet floor and carries this trophy into the panic room. He wraps the two-foot beam in a towel and hides it along the back corner of his pack, away from the bars of gold.

> *There are many difficult challenges and terrible things in the world, Danny. And you'll decide real quick which ones you can do and which ones you can't. But the truth is you're a lot stronger than anyone will ever tell you. Give a person enough good reasons, and they can commit themselves to awful things. Belief is stronger than your stomach or your limits.*
>
> *I never thought I could work with my hands, but I did more hard labor than most when I was on the inside. Turns out it was good for me.*
>
> *Then I got out of prison and didn't have any clothes except the ones I'd worn inside. And without any money I didn't have any options to buy something else. I believed I'd find someone to trade with, but the only people I saw were dead. I used to throw up at the sight of sickness, and your mom can tell you I've been worthless near blood and death.*
>
> *But when you've got nothing, you'll try anything. You might even surprise yourself.*
>
> *So, don't decide what you can't do. Go see for yourself. If you've never done something, it only means you've never had to try.*
>
> *Whatever you need to do. You'll do it well.*

Sam begins making trips back and forth to the ATV. He packs all the ammo but only some of the canned goods. He straps a sleeping bag to the back storage rack but leaves the tent behind. He fills both the rifle holsters of the ATV, placing the shotgun along the right rear fender and the biggest hunting rifle on the left.

On his last trip into the panic room he takes a final look into his backpack. It has his water bottles and a filter. Below that, he has stuffed it to the seams with clothing of various materials and weights. The gold and titanium remain hidden in pockets, and the legal pads and pens are in easy reach in the top.

Closing the pack, Sam pulls it over his shoulder. Except for ammo, he's left quite a bit behind. But he knows he's already overpacked, and once he ditches the ATV he'll have tough decisions to make.

Stepping out of the panic room, Sam closes the thick door behind him. He spins the lock, and closes the secretly hinged closet door to cover the entrance. Though he doesn't expect to ever see this place again, he feels compelled to leave it hidden. The knowledge that it sits here providing a refuge gives him a surprising sense of security.

> *Don't waste. Waste can mean letting things you don't need get destroyed instead of used. It can also mean taking more than you need. If you don't know how you'll use something, then don't keep it. Trust me, you'll never use it.*
>
> *We used to keep things we hadn't used in years. Everyone did. We filled our oversized houses with enormous piles of things we weren't using. And when it all got taken, it's easy to see how much of it never really mattered.*
>
> *It hurt your mom to see all our stuff get taken away. She might have told you about some things she missed, but the truth is that we kept the really important things. That tiny suitcase you were allowed to keep helped us figure out the things we really needed. You'll be pleased to know that a lot of that suitcase was filled with pictures of you.*

Sam straddles the ATV and thumbs the ignition. The engine spins a few times and burbles to life. Then he realizes he doesn't really know how to ride one of these and ends up sitting in the garage for a few minutes punching buttons and changing gears. Eventually, he kicks the quad into reverse and rolls out into the afternoon sun.

Pulling his goggles back down over his eyes, Sam pats the Walther pistol now holstered to his hip. As his eyes scan the forest he practices reaching for the shotgun. Then he switches hands and reaches for the hunting rifle. The shotgun requires him to take his hand off the throttle. So he tries to draw the shotgun with his left hand crossing over the enormous gas tank. This reach is awkward, but might save his life if he has to run and shoot.

Reaching into the inside pocket of his light jacket, Sam pulls out the picture of Ariel and Danny along with his widely marked-up map. He slides both pieces into the clear, plastic map sleeve on the ATV's gas tank.

"Aspen," he whispers, shaking his head. "Hope you're still there."

With a twist of the throttle, Sam bumps down the potholed driveway and heads for the main road.

Part 2

The Lonely Road

1

The first day of his journey seems more like a vacation than a pilgrimage through a nearly lawless land. Sam steers his ATV down paved roads winding through a former national forest and over a mountain range. Weeds and grass scar the pavement, but there are few obstacles. The loaded-down quad bike trundles along faster than he could run and steadily conquers some of the worst elevation changes ahead of him.

As the late daylight fades, Sam marvels at the thick pine forests and untouched beauty around him. Nature has reclaimed this area in grand fashion, and he spooks multiple animals away from the road. Somewhere in the back of his mind he knows the howl of his engine echoes through the park like a homing beacon. But for now, he keeps the throttle high and tries to take in the scenery rushing past.

After seeing his third group of deer, Sam realizes it would be wise to kill one and keep the meat. But he's never killed anything larger than a squirrel and has no idea how to carve an animal carcass or cure the meat. He reminds himself of the survival handbook he found in the panic room, and smiles that he was smart enough to slip it into a pocket of his pack.

He decides not to kill an animal on the first night. Sam knows the canned goods will keep him fed and allow him to focus on finding his first night's camp. Hopefully he can read the guidebook before he actually has to field-dress an animal that weighs as much as he does.

Darkness and cold descend quickly once the sun dips behind the ridgeline. Sam avoids turning on the ATV's lights and lets his eyes adjust to the moonlight. Speeding along in darkness is a great way to get ambushed, but nothing gives away an exact position like a set of headlights. The rising moon gives off enough light to navigate the winding forest road, but he knows future camps will need to be set up in the daylight.

After hours of riding and a headlong charge into nighttime travel, Sam breaks out of the trees and onto the untouched grass of a high meadow. In the full moon he can see in every direction for at least a half-mile. He speeds across the giant meadow and eyes a stand of medium-sized pine trees forming an island of cover in this open sea of grassland. With visibility in all directions and no other cover, Sam knows this cluster of trees will make the perfect spot for the night.

When he kills the engine, the silence feels as though it has weight. Sam stands listening for a long time, straining to hear anything strange or sudden on the wind. He imagines there are others surviving in this wilderness and knows someone will be tracking the sound of his ATV.

Sam pulls out his sleeping bag, the shotgun and the ATV's keys before climbing up one of the largest pines and sitting on a low-hanging branch. From here he can see an almost panoramic view of the deserted meadow. He tries to wriggle into the sleeping bag and keep his eyes open, but sleep catches him quickly.

A strange sound jerks Sam awake in the predawn hours. He can't quite place the strange crunching grumble until he looks down to see a large black bear leaning on the ATV and biting through a can of food lashed to the rear.

"Hey, get out of there!" he yells.

The bear only looks up at him for a moment before turning back to the can and pulling it from the ATV. The huge beast bites the can in half, sending juices spattering everywhere.

Sam slides off the tree limb and then half-drops, half-falls to the ground. Still tangled in his sleeping bag, he raises the shotgun. The bear puts both front paws on the back of the quad bike, and the suspension compresses under the weight. Sam steps out of his sleeping bag, leaving it behind as he steps closer. The bear looks up.

BAM! Sam unloads a round of buckshot into the bear's chest. The animal starts, surprised more than injured, and retreats from the ATV. It turns back, chest bleeding while it sniffs all the food it's leaving behind. Sam now loads a slug into the shotgun. If the bear charges, the next shot will gut it horribly. The animal lumbers a little farther away, and Sam steps with it, keeping the shotgun leveled.

When he steps out of the trees and into the open, Sam realizes the bear is the least of his worries. The animal turns and lumbers away, bloodied and limping. But somewhere in the back of Sam's mind he senses eyes on him. He's being watched, and the bear created the perfect diversion for him to be hunted.

PAAF! A bullet strikes the trees behind him, followed a split-second later by the crack of a long-range rifle. Sam crouches, runs back into the trees and hides behind his ATV. Another shot takes off some bark near his head. The shooter is refining their distance sighting, and the shots are getting closer.

He drops the shotgun and pulls out his own rifle. Ducking behind the rear wheels of the quad, he loads the chamber and then lays down to shoot from under the ATV. He scans the distant tree line, looking for the shooter.

Then he sneezes, and it saves his life.

Just as Sam wrenches his neck to the side and his eyes close to sneeze, he catches a glimpse of movement behind him. As his eyes open, he turns and sees three men approaching across the open meadow and nearly upon him.

The lead runner can tell Sam has seen him and abandons stealth for brute force. He raises a wicked-looking axe and screams like a warlord. With no time to change weapons, Sam shoulders the hunting rifle and hopes for the best.

CA-CHOW. The hunting rifle slams back into his shoulder as the bullet catches the runner in the neck when he's less than thirty feet away. The left side of the runner's neck shreds and splatters the pine trees. His feet keep pounding forward in a strange mix of determination and residual motion. Then he's off balance, bumping a tree, and pinballing forward as the axe is knocked from his hand.

Sam drops the hunting rifle and snatches the shotgun from the ground in one motion. He turns to see the two other men sprinting through the trees. One has a machete but still hasn't passed the axe-man's corpse. Sam can't tell what weapon the other man has because he's a blur of movement barely ten feet away.

With more instinct than aim, Sam turns toward the closest attacker and pulls the trigger. As the shotgun bellows, he can see the man raising a well used short sword. The shotgun slug almost misses, hitting him on the left side of his waist and tearing a chunk from his side as it decimates half his pelvis. He is spun by the force of the blast, stumbles off course and runs face first into a tree trunk. Sam turns toward the last man as he cocks the shotgun again. The man stops suddenly and drops his machete.

"Wait, don't kill me!" he pleads.

Sam hesitates, watching for this thin and filthy attacker to make the next move. Then that same part of Sam's brain speaks up again. This guy isn't surrendering, he's stalling. His eyes flicker past Sam.

Dropping to the earth, Sam feels rocks and stumps leave future bruises. A new long-range shot tears into the tree above him. Sam looks up to see the thin attacker has retrieved his machete and is stalking through the trees. This guy and the distant shooter are closing in from both sides, and one of them is going to end this.

Staying hidden from the sniper shots, Sam watches the trees for the machete attacker and feels for the ignition of the quad bike. He slides the hunting rifle into the seat holster and hears a SPANG as a bullet ricochets off some part of the ATV. The longer he stays here the more chance he's dead.

Sam buries a finger into the ATV's start button and hugs the side of it as the engine comes to life. He grips the throttle with one hand and holds the shotgun with the other. The machete attacker charges, and Sam thumbs the throttle to lurch away.

Sam clings to the side of the quad bike as it barrels into the open. He remembers all the pictures and stories he loved as a boy that showed Indian braves shooting arrows under their horses as they rode clutching the side. When he fires at the machete man and only blasts a chunk of turf off the ground, he realizes he's no skilled Indian brave.

Releasing the throttle, Sam tosses the shotgun away and grabs the butt of the hunting rifle. Then he lets go of the ATV and rolls into the grass with the rifle hugged to his chest. When he stops, he tries to shake off his stunned daze and look for his targets.

The machete man is easy to see, but he also catches his first glimpse of the long-range shooter in the forest. An obese woman stands leaning against a tree and already sighting toward him. Sam army-crawls through the tall grass toward a boulder mostly buried in the meadow.

A bullet trenches through the dirt a foot from his elbow. Sam realizes whatever rifle she's using must be in poor shape and require huge amounts of compensation. He prays his father kept this hunting rifle in top condition as he leans around the boulder and peers down the sight.

The woman retreats deeper into the forest, but she's still a large target. Sam sucks in air, aims for the center of her back and fires. He misses, but catches her shoulder. Her shooting arm goes limp, and she spins around in the force of the shot.

No time to shoot again, Sam hears from his survival voice, and rolls over to look for the machete man. He's changed weapons, having found Sam's shotgun, and running into can't-miss range.

Reloading as fast as he can, Sam knows this is as close as he'll ever come to a real-life quickdraw moment. He lowers the rifle into position as the thin attacker levels the shotgun. Sam stays prone and pulls the trigger. The shotgun bellows, sending a slug into the ground right in front of Sam and blasting dirt and grass into his eyes. He winces, recoiling backwards and not seeing his attackers chest absorb the rifle blast just before his back expels it out of a softball sized hole.

The sun finally breaks the horizon, sending long streaks of orange light across the high meadow. Sam digs at his eyes like a child, trying to clear his vision. He looks around, red-faced and still blinking away dirt and tears. His attackers are dead, but the woman trying to snipe him is probably still watching. He forces himself to scan the edge of the forest. He can't see her, but his eyes water too badly to see anything for more than a second.

Crawling through the grass, Sam retrieves his shotgun from the machete attacker. The man gurgles his last breaths, his lips trying to form words Sam doesn't stay to hear. He crawls quickly through the grass with the rifle in one hand and the shotgun in the other.

The ATV hadn't been rolling very fast when he bailed off the side, but now it seems a world away. He takes the risk, stands and runs for the vehicle. His survivor mind already hears the shot that will ring out, and he wonders with sick irony how close to the quad he'll get before he is cut down. But the shot never comes.

Sam reaches the ATV, shoves the rifle and shotgun into their fender holsters and roars the engine to life. He wrenches the throttle and rumbles through the meadow and back to the nearby road.

He'll be nearly three miles away when he discovers the bullet hole in the leaking gas tank. Later still when he realizes he never went back for his sleeping bag.

2

Sam knows he doesn't have anything to properly patch his gas tank. He wishes for a stick of chewing gum in some forgotten pocket. The hole is only a third up from the base of the tank, so he'll have to stop and fill it regularly. And any kind of off-road tilting will dump gas in a steady stream.

He nabs a branch from a tree and carves the tip into a point. With effort, he shoves the point into the hole, making the branch into a makeshift cork. This is far from perfect, but at least he's filled the gaping hole in the tank. He knows what he really needs is another vehicle.

After putting more gas in the ATV's tank, Sam looks down the abandoned road to the distant valley below. He hopes he'll find an abandoned car on the highway, but he knows better. He pulls out the legal pad and a pen, the reasoning coming to him as he writes.

> *I used to watch movies that showed the world ending in one way or another. They were always based on some rapid disaster, and as people fled the cities they left cars and supplies all over the highways.*
>
> *Maybe it's cause this happened slowly, but the roads are empty. Without money to go anywhere, people just stayed put and tried to survive. Cars sat parked cause no one dared use their gas.*
>
> *Once everyone realized that they were going to have to answer for all their debt, people quit going anywhere or buying anything.*
>
> *And when the tally was done, there were still those with plenty of money. They wanted the comfort and mobility they were used to, and they had the money to pay for it. That's why most of the shining cities have small airports inside their walls. Private planes are still flying, bringing*

them into the cities where they don't even need cars anymore.

Most of what we used to get around will eventually rust to the ground inside some locked garage.

Sam rolls down the steep incline of this mountain pass. He keeps the ATV in a low gear and lets the engine brake his descent. At this angle, gas seeps out of his twig-patched tank, but at least it isn't pouring.

He can see for miles in the clear mountain air and early morning light. There's no one around, and his eyes catch any new movement. Around one blind corner, he comes upon a line of deer in the road and slams on his brakes.

The deer scatter, and it takes Sam a beat to realize he has to go after them. He'll need the meat before long, and he needs to learn to dress a deer without getting shot at or attacked. Somewhere in these forests there are more people like those he battled this morning. But for now it's quiet, and he's in a place with great sight lines.

He shuts off the ATV and grabs the hunting rifle. The deer haven't gone far. They amble up a nearby hillside following a game trail. They're beautiful, and it breaks Sam's heart a bit to realize he'd much rather be stalking them with a camera than a rifle. But looking through digital photos on a computer in a well-lit office now seems so foreign and frivolous he nearly laughs at the absurdity.

Survival trumps everything else. Sam must hunt and camp and live in ways many people used to think of as novelty vacation pastimes. His three years in prison taught him to embrace whatever it takes to survive. And the mountains and rugged surroundings tap into a childlike, outdoor-loving part of himself he thought had died.

Five deer work their way up the path. Sam targets a doe and has to stop himself from overthinking the moment. With a CRACK of the rifle, the doe falls and the others scatter. Sam climbs to the fallen animal, thankful and a bit sad. He's gasping for air when he reaches the body. He struggles to get it down the hill, surprised by the weight.

At his ATV, Sam pulls out a survival reference book taken from his parents' safe house and begins dressing the animal. His inexperience makes the process far more bloody and inefficient than it will ever be again. Hours pass, and the doe yields more meat than he can pack or treat. He cooks a fresh chunk over an open fire, and for a moment he feels very free and blessed.

It dawns on him that he's never killed and eaten a meal in his entire life. He'd caught fish and downed small animals, but they were always the carnage-filled adventures of a boy. Now he has killed with purpose and benefitted directly from the results. Sam likes this feeling, and pulls out his notepad again.

> *You may never know how much this world has changed us all, but necessity has forced us to adapt. My father taught me about guns, and I mostly hated the experience. I liked watches and stainless-steel appliances and things that were clean and modern.*
>
> *But today I killed to survive, and it felt more real than anything I'd ever bought or experienced.*
>
> *I don't like killing animals. It always seems a cruel surprise to a creature with no concept of a higher intelligence planning its end. I always imagined the fear in the last moments of a hunted animal. But when their meat or skins might keep you alive, there's something primal and natural in the moment you step up to the top of the food chain.*
>
> *Bigger, faster, smarter animals kill the lesser ones for food. The lesser animals know this, but I don't think I ever realized that until today.*
>
> *Killing another man is far different…*

Sam stops writing. He wonders if he should continue this line of thinking. If his son does read these words, will it warp him to know his father killed a man? Three men. Maybe more by the time Danny gets these pages.

Then a darker thought strikes Sam. He wonders if a record of killing men could be used against him later. There are now so few shining cities and places of law. Even in prison he heard of large sections of the nation being ruled by a western-style justice. Prosecuting from a man's writings seems impossible in this disjointed nation. But he stops anyway, and seals the pages inside his backpack.

The fire dulls to embers, and the moon dominates the sky above. Sam spreads the coals to let it burn out. He puts on every piece of clothing he has, hating himself for leaving his sleeping bag behind. He lies beside the ATV on the dirt shoulder of this abandoned road. Exhausted, sleep takes him.

He awakes to the sound of rockfall and a distant yell. Stumbling to his feet, he looks around, bleary-eyed in the predawn. Sam spins quickly, the motion tearing the scabs on his side. The sound of falling rocks ceases as he figures out its direction. There are dark shapes coming down the ridge above. He can see at least three people, and one of them tumbles to a stop after their fall. A rush of adrenaline makes Sam hyper-awake, and he lifts his pack and lashes it to his ATV in one quick motion.

Stealing another quick look toward the approaching group, Sam now counts five people descending. He fires the ignition on the ATV and jumps on. Slamming it into gear he lurches downhill, accelerating quickly. Someone yells behind him, but he doesn't look back again.

The road is empty and dark. Sam has to slow down and fears the ATV might topple in the sharp corners. The deep shadows force him to turn on the lights. With the headlights blaring, he can navigate the road but can't see the people he passes on the ridges above him.

The lights flash on something metal in the road ahead. Sam swerves to avoid it, but the loaded ATV responds slowly. The right rear tire hits the metal. Then Sam swerves the other way, avoiding another. As his right tire deflates, Sam realizes what he saw in the road: a makeshift spike strip.

The quad shudders as Sam hits the brakes as hard as he can. The right rear tire shreds with a rhythmic thump as he pulls to a stop. He looks around the fender and sees the damage. Then he looks at the edge of the road and sees a burned and stripped-out car. Whoever set this trap has done it before.

Desperate for the sun to rise, Sam hits the throttle and starts downhill again. The ATV wobbles and fights him, but he refuses to stop. Over the thumping tire and the sound of the engine, Sam thinks he hears people coming onto the road behind him. He keeps driving, limping the quad down the road faster than he could walk, but still painfully slow.

An hour later, the sun rises in his eyes as Sam's ruined ATV rumbles to the base of the canyon and into the valley. He looks both ways down the empty road. There's a gas station with a huge store nearby. It looks abandoned, and he knows it's probably been picked clean already. But he can't fight the urge to look, and his ATV is about done.

Sam pulls into an abandoned gas station and kills the engine. A nearly crushing quiet takes hold, with no birds and no wind. He looks west, back up the valley, and can't see any movement. Whoever was hiding in the canyon is now many miles away. He's alone.

Looking east, the sunrise casts gorgeous colors across the valley floor. For a moment, Sam thinks this beautiful view was probably the same long before the rise of civilization, and it remains. He's alive to see it, and he pulls out his legal pad again.

> *I never got into fights growing up. I talked my way out of a few, but never just threw down with a classmate or bully. Then I went to prison, and feared I'd wind up in an animal brawl. But almost all the guys around me were just indebted middle-class softies like me.*
>
> *Some guys actually got softer in prison, finding every chance to lay around and do as little as possible. It was the opposite of the fights and power plays I expected. But being in there away from you and your mom made me want to do something with that time.*

And leaving better than I came in seemed like a good goal.

I worked hard. Got strong. Improved my reflexes and stamina beyond anything I could remember, even as a kid. I left that place in better shape than I've ever been, but no more of a bad seed or criminal than I'd been before.

Except now I'm a killer. I've killed people that tried to kill me. I ran when I could, but I killed when I had to.

I never would have thought I could kill anyone. And as your dad, I would tell you it is possible to get through most arguments without any violence. I did it. I grew up just fine without fighting. So, strive for that.

But know this, Danny. If someone really comes for you, you'll know it's not just a stupid schoolyard fight. And if that happens, don't hesitate for a minute.

Live, son. Whatever it takes.

Sam looks at the abandoned gas station. Then he steps off his ATV and examines the bits of tire still clinging to the dented rear wheel. Putting his pad away, he draws his shotgun and looks around the parking lot. There isn't a single vehicle in sight. It seems strange.

3

Sam levels his shotgun as he eases toward the general store. It was once a large one-stop shop for tourists in the area, but now the shelves are empty, some collapsed, and the aisles themselves stand askew. A mix of blown-in sand and dusty neglect covers the floor, the bits of trash and the ruins of the shelves. It looks like the last people in this building left months ago, maybe years.

One look says there's nothing here for Sam, but he steps in anyway. His injured side seeps blood into his shirt, and the pain causes him to leave mismatched prints in the dusty floor. Sweeping with the shotgun, Sam inspects all the corners of the store. The roof is intact, and most everything gone, but he realizes this large room is definitely smaller than the building's exterior dimensions. There's something else here.

Making slow and careful steps along the outer edges of the store, Sam looks carefully at the walls. His parents' panic room has forever changed the way he thinks about buildings. He knows a place like this would have had storerooms and maybe even a safe, hidden from plain sight. He keeps looking, leading with the shotgun and inspecting the wall.

After two times around the room, Sam nearly gives up. He steps to the center of the space, ruined empty shelving all around him. Letting the shotgun dangle from one hand, he looks at the footsteps he's left all over the room. He spins slowly, reviewing the emptiness one more time. The kitchen along one wall has been cleared of anything valuable. The bathrooms in the opposite corner stand open, and he can see wrecked porcelain and stolen stall walls probably scavenged to build some ramshackle lean-to in the mountains. The office in the corner is equally bare, with the security glass long broken and the door torn away. Only the tourist posters remain, with dust covering the epic views of Yosemite that used to attract visitors but now are only seen by the cowering locals.

Sam's eyes stop at the enormous poster along the back wall. It stands seven feet high and at least four feet wide between two shelving sections. He can't imagine anyone wanting to buy a poster of Half Dome this large, and the oddity of it almost overrides the more important realization.

"Why there?" Sam says to no one. He speaks without thinking, and now the question actually filters through his consciousness. The break in the shelves seems especially odd to him now.

Raising his shotgun again, Sam limps closer. He holds the weapon at the ready as he reaches out and pulls back an edge of the giant picture. The poster is heavy, and it takes a good amount of careful strength to peel it back to see the wall behind.

Except it isn't a part of the wall. A door hides behind the poster. The handle and framing have been removed, leaving a secret one-way portal flush with the wall. Sam smiles at the simplicity of this hidden doorway, and he wonders how many scavengers never found it.

With the butt of his shotgun, Sam pounds on the thick door. He can hear empty space behind it.

"Hello?" he asks.

Sam leans close, holding his breath and straining to hear any kind of noise from inside. Anyone alive would have heard his banging, and even if they were asleep they'd be moving by now. He almost thinks he hears something, but concludes it's in his head.

He starts away from the door, letting the poster fall back into place. If anyone else comes here soon, they might notice his fingerprints in the dust of the picture and wonder what's behind the poster. Then again, it doesn't seem like it would matter much.

Limping back outside, Sam inspects the outline of the building. He approximates the placement of the interior wall with the poster and concludes that a full third of the building must be hidden behind the door. He walks around the back of the building and finds only a small delivery roll-door and simple cinder-block construction. Grabbing the bottom of the roll-door, Sam tugs upward. It holds fast, even though the track and surface seem clear of any obstructions.

"Please lower your weapon and step away," comes a crackling voice through an ancient speaker box above the roll-door.

Sam steps back quickly and aims up at the box on instinct.

"I don't mean you any harm," Sam says, as he stares down the barrel.

"You're the one aiming a weapon," the voice crackles again. It's hard to make out exactly what he's hearing, but Sam thinks the voice belongs to a man.

"I'll lower it, but I'm not putting it down," Sam says to the speaker. Then he takes a step back and points the shotgun back at the ground.

There's a rattle from behind the roll-door, the distinctive sound of locks and chains clanging together. Then there's a long pause. Terrible scenarios rush through Sam's mind, but he keeps the shotgun at his side. This takes effort, but he breathes slowly and watches the door.

Suddenly the door rolls open, almost in one instant move. It reveals a lean, elderly man in a thick, clean flannel shirt and jeans. He watches Sam, while Sam eyes the long pistol on the man's hip.

"Come in," the old guy says as if he were welcoming a long-time friend who was late for dinner. No fear, no formality, and a bit of impatience.

But Sam hesitates. His hand flexes on the dangling shotgun. His eyes dart around looking for others and expecting to be ambushed.

The guy sighs. "Come on, kid. You look like shit, and you're bleeding through your shirt... I don't think you're gonna hurt me."

Sam limps closer. Nothing about the guy seems threatening or strange, and that actually makes Sam even more on edge.

"I'm just looking for a place to crash. Maybe a few supplies. I can pay you," Sam says flatly.

"What the hell am I going to do with money?" the old man snorts.

They stare at each other, standing firm on either side of the doorway.

The man now looks past Sam to the cliffs and forest behind him. Sam can see candles burning inside the cinder-block room. There's a gun rack on the back wall and a lot of supplies.

"So what do you want?" Sam asks.

"Look, kid. I'm not gonna stand here with you and write a constitution. You been looking awful hard at this place... better than most. So if you wanna come in so bad, then get in here. But I'm not leaving the door open 'til you get up the nerve."

Sam limps a step closer, and the man steps aside. Another step and Sam crosses the threshold into the storage room. With a WHOOSH, the old guy pulls the door closed and goes to work on his locks.

Sam watches the man refortify the entrance with no concern for Sam. He keeps his back to his armed visitor as he shoves an unhinged metal door into the back of the roll-door and locks it down with two steel cross-beams. This is as fortified as a roll-door has ever been.

As his eyes adjust to the candlelight in the windowless room, Sam can see the shelves of the store's former storage area neatly arranged in half of the space. They are covered with a horde of salvaged and organized items. Sam realizes the majority of the pillaging done in the store was probably done by this guy. The destruction was likely done by the angry folks that followed.

"Put your gun down," the old man says.

Sam whirls on instinct, bringing the shotgun up as he focuses on the guy's voice. But the man just stands there, unafraid, his pistol still on his hip.

"Oh... so you're gonna shoot me now, hmm?" he says, almost amused.

"You're not taking my gun."

"Wouldn't think it. I've got plenty. But unless you're gonna kill me, I suggest you set it down somewhere before you pass out and blow another chunk out of yourself."

Sam sits in one of two folding chairs beside a card table. He sets the shotgun down on the table but keeps his hand tight around the stock. He notices dust on the other chair, and wonders how long it has sat unused in this strange fortress. Somewhere in the back of his mind Sam hears the old guy ask him another question.

Then he blacks out.

4

Pain brings Sam back to consciousness. His eyes pop open, and he sees he's lying on his side on a cot. The old guy has just finished pouring alcohol into the missing bloody chunk on Sam's side. Sam sits up as the man tries to place a fresh square of gauze over the wound.

"Easy there, you're gonna set it to bleeding again," he says.

As his mind clears, Sam realizes he's wearing only his boxers. He sees his filthy clothes and body armor stacked to the side.

"I passed out, and you undressed me?" Sam asks.

"Of course I did. You're bleeding through your clothes."

Sam stares at the man, indignant.

"Whadda you think happened here?" the old guy asks flatly. "You think I lured you in here 'cause I wanted your pants off. Damn, boy, you don't know people much, do you?"

Sam looks at his side and sees that this stranger has cleaned and dressed the wound better than he could have done.

"It's starting to get infected," the old guy says, raising the bottle of alcohol. "This stuff hurts like hell, but it will help. You need stitches."

Sam sees a needle and thread on the floor. It's clear the old guy was about to do more. Sam knows he never dealt with the wound properly, and this guy seems to know what he's doing.

"I'm sorry," Sam whispers. He lays back down on the cot, exhausted and embarrassed.

"You want me to finish?"

Sam takes a deep breath and rolls back onto his side. The man looks at him and then at the wound again.

"You a doctor?" Sam asks.

"Nah," smiles the old guy. "Wife was a nurse, and she stitched up our boys plenty of times. I was always her lovely assistant."

Sam can see the good memories playing on the man's face. It makes him smile too.

"Where are they now?" Sam asks.

"My wife died a couple years ago. She wasn't made for a world like this. One of my boys is in the debt system. The other… I just don't know."

"I served in the debt system," Sam offers before thinking.

"I know," the old guy nods. "I saw your scar."

Sam senses no judgment from this man, and no malice. He looks at the weathered hands prepping the thread and heating the needle with a lighter.

"This is going to hurt," the old guy says.

Sam nods and tenses. It does hurt, but the man works fast. The tightening of the stitches sends fresh burning up Sam's side. He breathes in gasps, then lets out a yell as the line of thread is pulled tight and tied off.

"You okay?" the old guy asks as he sits back.

Sam takes a deep breath, then sits up and sticks out his hand.

"I'm Sam. Thank you."

The old guy looks at the hand and then at Sam's face. He slowly finds a smile, and then they shake.

"Patrick Harmor. Most folks called me Pat."

"Glad to be here. I'm still amazed you let me in."

Pat gets up and wonders through his little compound. He disappears behind some shelves and rummages through something.

"It's been a long time since anyone took a good look around this place.

No one's actually looked behind the poster in years."

"You were watching me?"

"I've got the old security system hooked up to some car batteries. I only turn it on when there's something worth seeing."

"That's pretty ingenious."

Pat steps back into view carrying a new pair of camo pants and a clean T-shirt. He tosses them toward Sam.

"I was a solar installer before the world went to shit. Keeping this stuff running is about the only thing that's easy."

"How long you been here?" Sam asks as he carefully pulls on the shirt.

"About three years now, I guess. More than two, anyway. We were on vacation, just the two of us, and quickly realized we weren't getting home. Drove as far as we could in our shitty little car, but eventually…."

Pat trails off as if the story lost interest. No mention of what happened to his wife. No details on how he wound up here hoarding a bunch of supplies. Sam just watches him moving through the cinder-block room.

"I can't imagine what you've had to do to survive out here this long," Sam offers. Pat glances at Sam, and then turns back to whatever he's doing. No response.

Sam realizes Pat is arranging food and utensils around a hotplate. He grabs a simple metal lever and switches it from one side to the other. Tracing the wires, Sam can see them split power from a bank of car batteries to different appliances around the room.

The light on the hotplate comes on. Pat puts a simple skillet on top and pours in a can of something.

"Chicken Noodle," Pat smirks. "Cause you're sick…."

"Sounds good," Sam says. He stands up gingerly and starts putting on the new cargo pants. "What can I do to help?"

"Tell me what brings you thundering out of the mountains on some beat-to-hell four wheeler. Who'd you piss off?"

"Everyone, I think," Sam says. "They liked my gear."

Pat stirs the soup, and his expression doesn't change. "You kill them?"

Sam doesn't answer. Pat nods, getting his answer anyway.

"Why didn't you kill me?" Sam asks.

Pat doesn't answer; he just stirs the soup. He adds salt without tasting it first, then stirs again. Sam knows he's gone one question too far. He starts to step away.

"I killed a few. But it's been a long time since anyone's come by," Pat says quietly. "Figured it might do me some good to talk to someone for a change."

"You could leave. Find your way to one of the cities."

"And do what?"

"They'd love having someone who knows solar."

Pat shakes his head. "All my knowledge is about ten years too old at this point. I wouldn't know where to begin. Plus I can't leave Carol anyway."

"Carol?" Sam asks, and then wishes he'd kept quiet.

Pat looks at Sam for a long time. Sam feels incredibly stupid for saying something before realizing Carol must be his wife.

"She's got a nice little spot looking down on me and the lake. Left it unmarked so the lookie-loos don't come calling. She wanted me to burn her like the others, but after nearly forty years I just couldn't go through with it."

Sam can't help but wonder about the "others" Pat just mentioned. He suspects the people he saw and killed in the last couple days may be part of the same group. How many could Pat have seen or killed in more than two years?

"Where's your wife?" Pat asks, and the question snaps Sam back to reality.

"Did I say I was married?" Sam asks, wondering when he'd said anything.

"A man don't wear a wedding ring in and out of prison just for fashion."

Sam looks down at his left hand. His once-thin fingers are now calloused and thick, trapping his ring in place. It has become a part of him, and he'd even forgotten about it until now.

"I'm not sure. Aspen I think," Sam says.

"Aspen? You're not gonna drive to Aspen on that shitty thing that limped in here."

"I know," Sam sighs.

Pat looks at his watch and shakes his head. "Damn. I meant to hide that piece of yours before dark."

"I should get my gear," Sam remembers.

"Awful dangerous after dark. Hopefully most of it will be there in the morning."

"Most of it? You have people watching you?"

"I dunno. But I try not to advertise."

"Well I can't hope that no one's watching and wait until morning. There's stuff I can't replace in my pack, and the meat's going to go bad."

"You've got fresh meat on there?"

"A deer. Part of one, anyway."

Pat thinks for a moment. He switches his electricity away from the hotplate and back to the security system.

"I'd love some venison. We gotta go quick."

Sam expects to push the ATV over to the roll-door, but Pat insists they move it away from the station. The vehicle limps on its ruined tire, and Sam's side blooms with pain as he pushes.

He tries to do a quick inventory of all the supplies on the four wheeler, but he can't see much and ends up doing it from memory. The building's exterior lights remain dark. Pat refuses to turn them on and seems able to navigate around this hideout in the moonless blackness.

They push the ATV, one on each side of the handlebars. At the edge of the paved lot, the earth appears to roll away.

"Grab whatever you're taking," Pat says.

"It's probably a couple of trips worth," Sam admits.

"Whatever you and I can get in one load. That's the limit," Pat insists.

"The gas cans will take their own load."

"Don't need 'em. Just the meat and your gear."

Sam shoulders his pack and grabs his hunting rifle from the fender holster. Pat grabs the legs of deer, sniffing one of them to see if it's gone sour.

"We just leaving it here?" Sam asks about his ATV.

Pat puts a foot on the back of the frame and shoves with all he can muster. Sam watches, unable to realize what's about to happen. He reaches for the machine too late.

"Wait, what are you doing?!"

The ATV dips off the paved lot and turns down the incline. Sam can't see it drop, but he hears the tires thudding the dirt as it rattles out of sight. Then, with a crunch of metal, it goes silent.

"Lots of other stuff down there," Pat says flatly. "No one would know any of it works."

Sam fumbles for words, unsure if this odd old man has just destroyed his transportation or offered him more. He hates the darkness and wishes for morning, so he can see what's really going on beyond the pavement.

Pat walks back toward his roll-door, already a good distance away. Sam follows, hauling his pack. Pat turns back in the doorway, watching Sam impatiently and scanning the surrounding area.

Just as Sam clears the threshold, Pat slams the door down again. He reinforces it as before and then goes to his cameras. Sam can't tell anything odd from the bank of monitors, but Pat studies them carefully. Eventually satisfied, Pat flips the power back to the indoor hotplate.

"Bring me that," he orders, pointing at one of the deer legs. "Let's live a little."

Sam knows he's had well made venison before, but he can't remember when or how it happened. On this night, the meat tastes different. Pat only has a few spices, and the cooking takes a near eternity. But in the end, the meal is worth the trouble and worlds better than his half-cooked effort the night before. Sharing Sam's kill puts them even more at ease with each other, and Sam wonders how long he would have lasted without some help. Now, he lets himself think he might actually make it all the way to Aspen.

5

Sam wakes before Pat. The small frosted skylight in the ceiling gives the room enough light for him to tell the sun is rising. He sees Pat sleeping on his cot like a man recovering from a hangover. Sam scans over his pile of gear and wonders again about the ATV. He goes to his pack and retrieves his pad and pen. Pat snorts in his sleep, but doesn't wake.

> *As you grow up, you're gonna be tempted to think you've figured things out. Whatever's happened to you will become your rule book for what will happen next time. Everybody on the planet does this. It's survival, and it's important. Some people are great at it, and that's what folks call "street smarts" or common sense. It seems to me it's not that common anymore.*
>
> *But there's a problem in thinking you know what's going to happen next. You can get too sure of yourself and be unprepared for those times when the world does something you never expected. Move too quick and you can ruin it, like startling a timid animal.*
>
> *So sometimes you've gotta just react with the situation as it happens. Be in the moment, and forget all the stuff you "know" is going to happen. It's tough. I'm terrible at doing this. But, if you can't figure out how to be in the moment and be raw or open or ready to be surprised, then you'll miss some great stuff and probably ruin some generosity.*
>
> *Always remember it's okay to be wrong. Every now and then you'll find yourself completely lost, and it's tempting to act like you know what you're doing. Don't pretend. Ask questions. Be*

surprised and teachable. Believe me when I say that honest ignorance and a willingness to learn will gain you respect faster than acting like you know something. I know this seems insane, or backwards… but trust me.

There's so much you don't know. Don't get ahead of yourself.

"Writing a book?" Pat asks behind Sam's back.

Sam jumps, half-hiding his pen and notebook on instinct.

"My apologies," Pat says, standing from his cot and holding his hands up in surrender. "Didn't mean to startle you, shoulda made a racket first."

"No, it's okay," Sam recovers. "I should've paid more attention."

Sam gets up and returns the notebook and pen to his pack. Pat watches him, but doesn't ask again. Sam looks up and catches Pat looking.

"It's not a book," Sam starts. "It's like a long letter to my son. Telling him stuff I think he should know."

"Grand idea," Pat smiles. "But if you get all the way to Aspen, then why not just tell him yourself?"

"I hope I can."

Pat watches him for a long second. It starts to make Sam uneasy.

"You're leaving a record," the old guy says suddenly. "Like carving a tree or breaking a mountain in two. Something that will live on with your soul inside it, even if you're lying dead on the side of the road."

Sam looks at Pat now, wondering if this is about to turn bloody.

"You don't think you're gonna make it, do you?" Pat asks.

Sam bristles, standing straighter, but Pat continues before he can reply.

"Now don't get all bent outta shape. I'm not saying you don't wanna make it. I'm just saying a man who's writing down his thoughts in case he dies is starting to think he's gonna die."

"I've been in prison for more than three years. May as well have been dead. I sure as hell didn't think I'd be chasing my family across the country. And every day I'm just dodging people trying to kill me. You're the first halfway-sane person I've met!"

"Halfway?" Pat smirks. "You flatter me."

"Look, I'll just go, okay. Thanks for doctoring me and cooking the venison."

"Wait a damn minute, son."

"I'm not your son."

Sam shoulders his pack and looks around to see if he's forgetting anything. Pat steps in his way.

"Sam. I didn't mean nothing by it. You don't need to leave. You need to rest."

Sam has his shotgun in one hand and his rifle in the other. He looks like a hitchhiker who will never get a ride.

"At least let me help you fix your rig and resupply. That's why you came looking anyway."

Sam looks at Pat, unblinking. The old guy has honest eyes and a soft, fatherly demeanor that makes Sam trust him. He lays the rifle and shotgun on the cot and lets his pack slide off his back and onto the floor.

"I need gas and at least one tire," Sam begins. "Where you gonna dig those up?"

Pat smiles and goes to the hotplate and turns it on.

"Breakfast first, then we'll figure out the rest."

The water boils quickly, and Pat makes a fast, dense oatmeal from an instant packet. Sam takes his tin-cup portion, even though he hates oatmeal. This time is no different, even with an unnecessary helping of sugar. It tastes like the chunks are sticking to his insides, but with the unknowns ahead, that might be a good thing.

"How old's your son?" Pat asks, breaking the silence.

"Seven. Almost eight," Sam replies.

"I liked that age with my boys. I think five to about ten was my favorite. Seems a long time ago now."

"When's the last time you talked to them?"

Sam looks at Pat as he finishes this question. He feels the bite of oatmeal tumble down this throat, sticking the whole way down. Pat says nothing, looking at the floor and taking his time.

"My wife and I liked to RV. We had a small coach, and we'd seen almost every national park since we retired. I love Yosemite, so we'd found a campsite at the back of Tuolumne Meadows and unplugged for a while. No news. No phones. Just walking, reading and eating. Then we noticed the campsite getting all tense. Lots of whispers in the bathrooms, but I paid them no mind. People started clearing out, and we had the place to ourselves.

"Then one morning the camp manager came and asked if we were planning on leaving. That was the first time we heard about what was happening. There was half a tank of gas in the RV and a full tank in the little hatchback we pulled behind. So, I turned us toward San Francisco and decided to see how far we could get."

Sam nods, knowing where this story is headed.

"You never made it, did you?"

"No. We made it. I abandoned the RV somewhere along the way, and we hypermiled the hatchback. We finally found a gas station with a reasonable line, and I topped it off before we got to the airport. Seeing all those planes grounded and the people roaming the terminals… that's when I knew how big this was."

Sam nods. When Pat remains silent he says, "I was at my desk, reading some stupid email about a conference call, when my cell phone rang. My wife asked if I'd seen the news. I pulled it up online, and it was like everyone was reading at the same time. Then everyone got stupid."

"So you know exactly what I mean then," Pat says quietly. "The minute people were reduced to the cash in their pocket, and the prospect of paying their debt, they had no idea what to do next. We had lots of cash and traveler's checks, and those worked for a while. But the plastic wasn't worth keeping as an ice-scraper!

"We tried driving back east to find our boys. I figured the traveler's checks would hold out. But by the time we got out of San Francisco and back into the Sierras, the gas stations were already cash-only, and the attendants were holding shotguns across their laps like this was the apocalypse.

"I-80 East was the Wild West — people stealing gas and driving like it was the Autobahn. Someone was gonna get killed in no time, so we headed south to find a more deserted way east. My wife couldn't get a cell signal anymore, and we didn't know if it was too many folks trying to get on, or if the whole thing had just gone down."

Pat looks around his makeshift home. Sam waits for him to continue.

"By the time we got here, there'd already been some sort of showdown," Pat says. "There was a guy in the office lying across his desk in a pool of his own blood. All the gas cans were gone, and the pump heads had been hacked. No telling how much gas had been stolen. Anyone who'd come along had taken all they could."

"So why'd you stay?"

"We were running low ourselves, and I had no idea how to hack a gas pump. There were a couple of abandoned cars parked here, but they already had their caps open and been siphoned dry. I figured it was probably convoys of folks consolidating, but it didn't help us any.

"Carol, my sweet wife, she just didn't have the heart for running any farther. She found this room and asked me if we could stay the night. There was this cheap little radio in the office, and we thought we'd get some info on emergency channels."

Pat points at a worn, yellow-plastic emergency band radio sitting in the corner.

"That was the first thing Carol ever took that wasn't hers." Pat gives a pained smile at the memory. "We huddled around it the first night, hoping for something to make sense of what was going on."

Pat gets up, takes Sam's cup and rinses both cups in water pumped electrically from some underground source. Sam marvels at the many systems Pat has made work with his solar expertise.

"Then she discovered that the phone in the office worked. It was intermittent, but it was the first chance we got to talk to our boys. We stayed, trying to reach them, and finally got through.

"It was clear pretty quick that even if we got home there wouldn't be much we could do to help them. Grown men at that point with their own debts... and spending habits I certainly couldn't cover. Everything they told us — and everything on the emergency channels — just said getting back was useless. We were bound to lose our house and a lot of the stuff inside. And when we thought about all the things we'd never see again, we only really cried about Carol's memory boxes. Stuff in there we couldn't ever buy again...."

Pat moves as he talks, walking down a back aisle of his little storage facility, and returns brandishing a menacing hunting rifle. Sam bristles, suddenly feeling very exposed, but Pat keeps moving casually around the room.

"We kept staying here. Gathering more stuff into this room. Scouring the place and making a home like it was our new RV. And the news kept getting worse.

"About three days in, I stood on the roof for the better part of an hour trying to see what else might be around. Landline had gone dead. No luck with the cell phone. But I found a few panels mounted on the roof, and realized I could rework them to get us some juice.

"Didn't change what happened to Carol, though."

Pat starts gearing up. He hangs the knife on his belt and ties on some heavy hiking boots. Sam watches him for a moment, wanting to ask what Pat is planning. But instead he decides to watch and keep the old guy talking.

"What happened to Carol?" Sam asks.

Pat glances at Sam quickly, but keeps moving. He slips into a light jacket and a wide-brimmed hat. He pulls on two belts of ammo, bandolier style, and finds his rifle. Sam smiles when he sees Pat hang the long rifle across his back on a home-made sling between the bandoliers. In another time, Pat would have been the perfect guy for some strange reality show. But then, in that other time, Pat wasn't this guy at all.

Walking to the fortified door, Pat now collects a toolbox and a torque wrench. He slips a pair of sunglasses down over his eyes and looks expectantly at Sam.

"Let's go see if we can find you a tire," Pat says flatly, as if he never heard Sam's question.

Sam jumps to his feet. He moves a bit stiffly from his healing side, but he grabs his shotgun and begins to open the door.

6

The sun glares in as Sam raises the roll-door. He recoils and looks to Pat. The old guy just stands there, staring unflinchingly at the nearby hills. He scans them slowly from behind his sunglasses. Then he hands Sam the toolbox and draws his rifle with his free hand.

"You better have some shades, or you won't see shit today," Pat says, and Sam goes to his pack to grab them.

Pat walks across the barren parking lot as if the world were still completely normal. Without the rifle and shells, he'd look ordinary. Sam follows, toolbox in one hand and shotgun in the other. They head for the place where they'd pushed Sam's ATV into the night.

They stop at the edge of the lot. Sam looks down the hill below them to a tangle of cars and metal. Vehicles of all sizes have been rolled down this grade into a rotting and rusting scrapyard. Sam realizes they were all probably pushed here by Pat and his wife. Sam's ATV stands out as the highest vehicle on this end and the newest-looking, in spite of its damage.

Pat looks at the surroundings again, hesitant. He raises the scope to his face and scans the hillside.

"Alright. Go on," he says, holding the torque wrench out to Sam.

"What?"

"I'll stay here and watch. There's at least two other ATVs down there. Bound to have the same size wheels. Take any other parts you want. I don't need them."

A chill runs down Sam's back. He knows the minute he steps down this hill Pat could end him. Even after the old man's hospitality, Sam doesn't like this. His survival instinct and mistrust of others has only grown in recent days, and everything about this seems wrong.

"Keep your shotgun ready. If they come for us, you'll have to have my back."

"Who's... *they?*" Sam asks.

Pat keeps watching the hillside.

"Well, I don't have their first names or nuthin!" Pat snorts. "You met plenty of them in the last few days, didn't you?"

Sam nods at this. Pat's paranoid to be outside, and he can't blame him for it. Taking the wrench from Pat, Sam works his way down the hill to his crumpled ATV. He looks back up to see Pat still scanning the area with his rifle.

Setting his shotgun on the dusty trunk of a nearby car, Sam inspects the ATV. In spite of the sickening sounds he heard when they'd rolled it down here, the brush bar seems to have taken the impact. The problems remain the leaking gas tank and shredded tire.

He looks across the mangled cluster of vehicles and sees another ATV. It's standing on end and crushed between two cars. Its front wheels hang limp, and the gas tank seems just clear of the bent wreckage below.

It takes Sam an hour to crack the two front wheels and gas tank from this discarded vehicle. He struggles with the socket wrenches and a maze of hidden screws that secure the tank. All the while, Pat stands at the edge of the parking lot, looking around for signs of movement.

Once Sam clambers back over the cars to his own ATV, he's sweating and baked by the midday sun.

"I can't get these wheels on with it sitting here like this," Sam realizes aloud.

"Will it start? Can you back it up the hill?" Pat asks, barely looking.

Sam shakes the ATV, hearing a thin layer of gas roll around the tank. He lashes the salvaged wheels and tank to the back, secures the tools and slides his shotgun into one of the fender holsters. He looks at the shredded back wheel with concern and hits the ignition. The fuel pump searches for gas for a few seconds, and then the engine coughs to life.

Pat tenses above him. He raises his rifle to his face again and scans the ridges with his scope.

Sam climbs onto the ATV and puts it into reverse. It struggles to pull away up the hill, spinning its useless rear tire and rocking more than climbing. Sam decides to stand beside the ATV and push it while he hits the throttle. Once it moves clear of the wreckage, the vehicle climbs slowly back up to the parking lot.

Pat is already halfway back to his cinder-block room.

"Bring it in!" he hollers over his shoulder. "We can't fix it out here."

Sam clunks the ATV into gear and limps it back to the door, praying it has enough gas to make it. Pat stands in the doorway, rifle aimed high. Just as Sam kills the engine and coasts inside, the old guy quickly chambers a round and fires up the hillside.

Sam ducks at the sound, but Pat pulls the door closed and pushes the fortified backing into place.

"Who'd you see?" Sam asks, concerned.

"Mighta been one of them. Mighta been nothing. I ain't taking the risk. We've been easy targets for a while, but if they hadn't seen us yet the engine woulda called them in."

"I'm sorry."

"Keep your sorry. I said I'd help ya."

Their eyes have adjusted to the darkness again, and they take off their sunglasses and put aside their weapons.

Together they lift the front of the ATV onto a cinder block and swap out the big front wheels on Sam's ATV for the smaller ones he salvaged. Then they replace the ruined tire with one of Sam's front wheels and leave Sam with one knobby spare. Sam expects he'll have to use it somewhere along the way.

This seemingly simple project has now taken most of the day. The ATV sits just inside the door on four usable tires, but it now leans forward onto the smaller front wheels. Sam looks at it suspiciously, hoping it lasts at least through a full tank of gas in the new tank. The tank seems to be connected properly, but they've had to lash it to the bodywork with wire and zip-ties. The result makes the ATV look even more ramshackle and undermines its once-menacing black with a bright red accent.

Sam fastens the tank storage pocket onto the new one, keeping his map and photo in easy reach.

"Where can we get some gas?" Sam asks, really wanting to test their repairs.

"There should be some left in the reserve tank, but we can't check it now."

"Why not?"

"You have to hand-pump it…. Might take an hour just to get the line primed. It's too close to dark to start now."

Sam scoffs, shaking his head. This strikes a nerve in Pat.

"Look, Sam, when you leave you're welcome to do things however you want. But it seems to me you ain't been too cautious up to this point, and you been through a lot. So you're gonna have to trust me…. We go out there now, we're liable to get shot at. And I ain't doing that again."

Again? Sam thinks to himself. But he just nods, deciding not to push Pat any further.

"Okay, Pat," Sam says finally. "You're right. You know what you're doing here, and it's helped me so far. We'll do it your way."

Pat nods, satisfied. He gets up and heads over to his stores of canned and powdered food.

Sam follows, wincing from the day's work and his healing side.

"Thank you," Sam says, as Pat pulls down some powdered lasagna. "The last few years I've had no one looking out for me, so I've only done things my way." He motions to his side and smirks: "You can see how well that's worked."

Pat smiles at him. "Lasagna good by you? I'll add some venison."

Sam nods, and the old guy heads over to his makeshift kitchen.

They tinker with the ATV into the night. Sam's stories of debtor's prison make Pat feel closer to his distant sons. And Sam misses the technology that Pat describes from his lifetime of work. It's a time of bittersweet nostalgia and a much-needed tune-up for the ATV.

In the morning Sam awakens and cleans and inspects his wounded left side. The red signs of infection seem reduced, and the stitches are holding. The flesh around the wound is now a mix of purple and green from bruising. He fights the urge to scratch it.

"Does that itch?"

"Jeez!" Sam jumps, startled as Pat breaks the silence.

"Sorry," Pat grins.

"You need to wear a bell or something," Sam teases. Then he looks back at his side. "Good morning, and yes… it itches like a son of a bitch."

Pat gets up and moves toward one of the shelves.

"Let me guess, you've got something for it," Sam marvels.

"Well, I've got stuff for bug bites and poison ivy," Pat says as he opens a small box. "Can't hurt, right?"

He pulls a small tube from the box and tosses it to Sam.

"Keep it clean and don't scratch."

"Yes, mom."

They settle into the same routine as the day before. Pat makes oatmeal, and then they gear up to venture outside. Sam wonders if this was Pat's routine even before he arrived. He suspects it was, and wonders how long Pat will maintain this schedule. And what happens when Pat runs out of oatmeal.

Once armed and outdoors, Pat shows Sam two small manholes set away from the main gas pumps. They lead to a reserve tank, and with a handpump and considerable trial and error, the two of them eventually get a stream of fuel. Sam slowly fills his four gas cans. Combined with the small fuel tank, the four wheeler is now carrying nearly thirty gallons; the weight sinks the ATV low on its suspension. It's enough fuel to take Sam most of the way through his trip. But it won't.

It's late morning, and Sam realizes he's as ready to move on as he'll ever be. He double-checks the gas tanks on the fenders and turns to retrieve his pack.

"Before you go…" says Pat, trailing off.

Pat doesn't say anything else; he just turns toward the foothills and motions for Sam to follow. The old man moves steadily toward the same hills he's been scanning for the last two days. This must be important. Sam looks between the cinder-block room and his ATV. Pat isn't waiting for him. Sam follows.

Reaching the end of the pavement, Sam finds a path through the scrub-brush and hurries to catch up. Pat moves well, unhindered by the weight of his weapons. It's obvious he has climbed this many times. Sam struggles to close the distance as the trail switchbacks and steepens. He's breathing hard and finally getting close enough to question Pat when the trail levels out on the hilltop. Pat stops.

Before he can ask where they are going, Sam sees the subtle rise in the earth at Pat's feet. A few stones frame the edges of a grave. It would be easy to miss unless you knew exactly where to look. The old guy hangs his rifle across his back and kneels, running his hands softly through the dirt.

"We used to walk up here every day," Pat says without looking at Sam. "She loved the view, and the way the colors of the sunset played out on the lake."

Pat looks to the east, away from the mountains to the lake in the distance. Sam looks too. It is a great view, and a great vantage point for the gas station complex below.

"We got pretty good at it. Fast. Stronger than either one of us had been in years. So we started exploring farther and farther up the mountains. But we'd always stop here.

"I didn't know anything about hunting. But we saw all the deer piles on these trails and knew they were using them too. So I started carrying a rifle, and every few days we'd get some fresh meat.

"I wasn't a very good shot. Sometimes it would take me two or three to really get the job done. And those gunshots would thunder off the hills, echoing for miles. It never crossed my mind as a problem, 'cause I didn't think there was anyone listening.

"We chased this one doe way up in these hills. To where the brush is gone and it's nothing but pine trees. We loved it. It was exhilarating. Like we were newlyweds on some adventure.

"Finally I got a decent shot, and the doe fell. Carol drew her knife and closed in to finish it off and start cleaning it… ya know." Pat stops. He looks at Sam, and he nods back.

"And they came outta nowhere. Six or seven of them. I don't know that I ever got a clean count, but it was men and women looking awful, like cavemen. They had spears and axes they'd made themselves, and only one gun among them.

"They said they wanted the deer. Carol said it was more than we could carry, so we'd be happy to share it." Pat smiles. "She says this real matter-of-fact while holding her big knife covered in blood. But these folks, well… they don't want some of the deer. They want it all. And they want my rifle, too.

"I told them the deer was one thing, but since I had the rifle I was going to keep it. For a second I almost thought they would back down. Everyone was just standing there like they were frozen. So, Carol left the deer and started toward me. She got halfway, and the one with the gun just seemed to snap out of it and fired all of a sudden. Carol spun but kept on her feet.

"I didn't even think. Or aim. I just lowered my rifle and fired back. Hit the shooter right in the chest. He smacked off a tree and went down. Carol stumbled into me, and I shot at the next closest person I saw. I don't even know where I hit them, but they went down in a red flash."

Pat looks down at the grave for a long time. He breathes, blinking back tears, as his voice goes flat and staccato.

"Carol was begging me. *We have to go. Stop shooting. Forget the deer.* I wrap my arm around her. I feel the blood on her shirt and wetting my hands. *Run*, she says. Over and over, like it's some sort of metronome. *Run. Run.* For a while I think we're gonna get home. She won't stop to check the wound, but we're moving well. She keeps saying *run*. We keep running."

Pat sits down by the grave. Sam stands listening, but Pat stares out at the gas station and the lake as if he were all alone. "She said *stop*. Right here. And we sat side by side. I finally got a good look at her. Blood everywhere. And none in her cheeks. I said I'd carry her, but she said my back couldn't take it. Worried about me even then. The sun was starting to drop. Her favorite time. And we sat here… I don't even know how long. I held her. She cried. I cried. I said I loved her. Over and over. I don't know how many she heard. Sometime during that sunset, she slipped away."

Then Pat goes quiet. Sam watches him, scared to break the silence, and with no idea what to say anyway. The wind whistles down from the peaks above. The shadows grow longer. It seems a long time before Pat speaks again.

"I started watching for those folks after that. Shooting first if I saw something. No idea how many are still out there, but I'd know them if I saw 'em again."

Now he looks up at Sam. "I knew you weren't one of them. But I think you saw them."

"I'm sorry," Sam offers. "Thank you for taking me in."

"Been good to have the company," Pat smiles. "And I thought you oughta meet Carol."

Pat stands, and looks up higher into the mountains. Raising his rifle again, he stares through the scope. Sam can see that he's eyeing specific places in a practiced sweep.

"Let's get you on your way," Pat says, as he lowers the rifle and starts back down the trail. Sam looks off into the mountains and then down at the grave. After a moment, he follows.

They move slower on the descent. It's mid-afternoon when they reach the parking lot. Sam grabs his pack and straps it to the back of the ATV. Then he shoves his shotgun into one fender holster and the rifle into the other. Pat watches him, silent. Sam almost wants the old guy to ask him to stay. He can think of a handful of excuses to stay another night. Having someone to look after him and help navigate this strange new world has been invaluable. Pat has given Sam the first comfort he's felt in years, but he knows it won't last. He's stalling.

"Thank you, Pat," Sam says, extending his hand.

Pat gives his hand a firm shake and keeps hanging onto it as he looks Sam in the eyes. "You find your boy. Don't let nothing stop you. Shoot first, you hear me?"

"Will do."

Sam swings himself into the saddle of the ATV and hits the start button. The engine settles into a healthy idle.

"You're welcome anytime," Pat offers.

"Take care of yourself, Pat."

"I'll watch out for you as long as I can. Hope you put down some miles before dark," Pat says.

Sam wills himself to go, feeling sorry for the old man somehow. He rolls away and looks back to see Pat climbing the ladder on the side of the building, rising to a lookout position.

The ATV runs more smoothly than it ever has, and Sam rolls down the long hill from the gas station to connect with the nearby highway. A mile later, he's turning east, following an old empty two-lane vanishing into the distance.

The road is straight and free of traffic. Grass sprouts through cracks in the pavement, but Sam can see ahead for miles. Stepping up through the gears of his quad bike, Sam climbs to full speed. He knows this isn't fuel-efficient, but it feels like making up for lost time.

Back at the gas station, Pat watches through the scope and sees Sam rushing down the highway. Even with the scope's high magnification, the ATV quickly shrinks to an indecipherable dot. Pat braces the rifle and watches as long as he can. Then he lowers the scope and sits in silence.

The shadows grow across the valley floor. He can't see or hear Sam's ATV any longer, only the wind.

Pat spins his rifle and stares through the scope at the hills behind his compound. He checks a series of trails and the edges of clearings in a specific and practiced order. Everywhere is empty. He really is alone.

He puts the rifle butt on the ground and turns the barrel toward him. Staring out at the lake and valley, he blinks back tears. Then he puts his mouth over the end of the barrel and reaches down its length to put his thumb on the trigger. His breath comes in gasps. Tears break and roll freely down his cheeks. He's hyperventilating, with the barrel still in his mouth.

7

Danny, there's a lot to learn about love. And it's a lifelong process, so there's no way to rush it or stop learning.

But know that you have to be careful. I'm not saying don't love, or don't be open... because you must be. But loving someone, or loving anything, is just about the most powerful thing you'll come across, so you can't take it lightly.

Get love from the right person, and you will feel stronger and better than you ever felt alone. It gives you a power and a confidence that doesn't make sense.

Put your love in the wrong place, and it can drive you to destruction before you even realize how far you've gone. It will hold you back, it will make you ignore obvious warnings, and it will keep you from growing into the man you should be.

Men have fought and conquered for love. But men have also died futile deaths in the name of love.

I hope you love mightily. I hope you feel it overwhelm you.

I also hope... if love ever holds you back, that you'll see it for what it is: obsession, dependency or a stumbling block. Leave those behind.

Sam sets his pad down. He looks past the small fire he built right on top of a concrete picnic table. His eyes scan the dilapidated rest stop around him. No other lights or movement out here on the plains. He can hear the wind whipping down the concrete roadway, scattering debris.

He thinks about Pat, wondering how the old guy is holding up all alone again. Sam can't imagine how painful the man's vigil must be, and wishes Pat would move on.

The night grows cold and cloudless, but the waning moon won't rise for hours. Sam cooks himself a tasteless dinner of dehydrated food warmed by his camp stove. The cooking and drinking drains one water bottle and half of another, making him realize he isn't carrying enough. He looks at the half-empty bottle on the table, knowing only one full bottle remains in his pack. The known scarcity of gasoline caused him to weigh down his ATV with plenty of gas, while he somehow assumed he'd find enough water. This will be a problem.

Now as he peers across the dark, barren scrub-brush of this high-plain desert, he knows water will be as precious as gasoline. Before leaving Pat he'd found maps of his route and scouted a way across Nevada using small highways. At the time he'd believed this to be wise, but it will make supplies harder to find. The wind picks up again, and Sam shivers. The fire has burned down to embers.

Sam unfolds a new sleeping bag Pat gave him. Spreading it out on another of the concrete tables, Sam zips himself inside and lays his shotgun down beside him. He stares up at the stars, marveling at dense clusters like flower-dust across the sky. Even on his long walk from prison to his parents' house, Sam can't remember ever seeing stars so clearly. He pulls out his pad of paper.

> *Take your chances to go away. The older you get, the more you'll find reasons to stay close to everything that's part of every other day in your life. And you'll meet plenty of people who'll shake their heads at the thought of going off by yourself.*
>
> *I know everyone spends time alone. But for a long time before everything crashed, very few people spent time without entertainment. We looked at our phones or watches or reading*

devices, and never just sat and let thoughts flow through us.

Get out. Get away from everything and sit in the darkness all by yourself. You'll learn things. About your heart and mind. About what's really important. And you'll see that once you strip all our connections away, there's a lot of time and effort required to just stay alive.

Other people will try to talk you out of going alone. Some will be convinced that if you go off by yourself without a screen to keep you company you'll go mad or walk off a cliff, or both. Let them believe that, but don't let it keep you from walking off one day and seeing what you can learn from it.

In your seven years, there's a good chance you've already been outside and alone more than I have in my whole life. Maybe what you really want is a nice indoor bed and all the comforts I always had but took for granted. If so, I can't blame you. But I wish I'd been there for your first night outside. I'd like to see your blue eyes staring into a campfire.

I wish you were here. I've been alone for years.

Sam thinks of his father as his tired mind starts to drift. He remembers how much his dad had liked to watch the stars, and how many times the old man had complained about light pollution and the constant flood of screens drowning out God's creation. Sam smiles at the memory and the thought that these stars were here long before man invented his first screen, and remain now that most of those screens have gone away. Strangely, this thought helps him sleep.

The sandblasting scrape of dust awakens him. There's a faint blue glow in the east, but sunrise isn't close. The wind has destroyed the night's clarity, pulling the fine silt from the high desert floor and scouring everything in its path.

Sam rolls off the table, still in his sleeping bag and trying to hide from the wind. He unzips the bag and stumbles free, shielding his eyes as he goes for his goggles. Tugging them from a pocket on his pack, he pulls them on and looks around at the sand tearing through his campsite.

His notebook flaps, the pages tossing while wedged against the table. His sleeping bag rolls in the wind, collecting sand in the crevices. The cloud of dust grows dense, blocking out the sky above.

Sam shoves the pages into his backpack, grabs the bag and struggles toward the small brick building enclosing the rest stop's bathrooms. The stench overwhelms him as he opens the door. Trying to recover, Sam steps inside. The wind smacks the door shut behind him.

Sam emerges after dawn. The wind storm has passed and left a hot and clear morning, with everything covered in a layer of white silt. It seems like a thin snowfall, but the sand falls away at Sam's touch and the temperature is already climbing.

It takes nearly an hour to find all the pieces of his wind-tossed stove, utensils and sleeping bag. The bottle of water he'd left on the table is now empty, having been tossed into the weeds. The inside of the bottle is covered in dust. When he tries to compress his new sleeping bag into the stuff sack, he feels the grit inside and out. He dreads the next time he will use it.

Inspecting his ATV, some of the edges have sand damage on the already worn paint. He straps his pack onto the rear rack between the four gas cans and climbs aboard. The fender holsters seem to have protected the rifle and shotgun, but Sam knows they'll need a thorough cleaning. With concern, he thumbs the ignition and the quad rumbles and spits for a moment, as if shaking off the dust, and then it kicks to life.

Slowly, Sam pulls away from the rest stop, headed further east down the thin, empty highway. He's already sweating. This road may be empty, but more sandstorms and a lack of water could be his end. For now though, he's got gas and an open road. He drives at full speed, hoping for a town somewhere on the horizon.

At top speed the loaded ATV can do over forty miles an hour, but Sam has to concentrate. The mismatched tires and soft suspension create a drifting float, even on the straight and smooth pavement of this deserted highway. In less than an hour, the vibration and constant corrections cause his joints to ache and hands to cramp. Of course, it's better than walking.

Driving past mile after mile of nearly identical high plains scrub-brush, Sam thinks how impossible this journey would feel if he were on foot. He rumbles toward distant mountains that never seem to get closer. But in an hour, he's gone farther than he could in one day of walking. Plus he knows the ride allows his wound to heal faster. A part of him fears he'll lose this advantage at some point, but he pushes the thought away. Every day has been different than he expected, so there's no point in trying to plan.

Two hours in, he rumbles to a halt in the middle of the road. He kills the engine and sits up straight, stretching. Rubbing his wrists in pain, he climbs off and walks around the ATV in circles, still feeling the vibration through his whole body. On the side of the road, he unzips and pees into the scorched earth. He peers at the horizon absentmindedly, shaking his head. It all looks the same.

As he zips up, he turns to look in every direction: scrub-brush, sand and the occasional small hill. It all looks so similar, he doesn't notice the distant shapes at first. Then suddenly he grabs his rifle and stares down the scope to the south. There was something out there. Someone, or maybe two, walking through the brush.

Sweeping with the scope, he looks where he saw the specks on the horizon. Now he can't find them. Another sweep to the south, slower this time, is no more successful. He wonders if it was an optical illusion, or his mind offering a flicker from his subconscious. Stepping up on the pegs of his quad bike, he stands on the seat and looks again. He's determined to find something and prove himself sane.

A spurt of dusty sand leaps up a few feet away from the ATV, followed by the skittering sound of a pebble. Before Sam can wonder what it is, he hears the following thunder from the gunshot. He drops to straddle the seat and shoves his rifle into the holster. Now he knows there's someone out there, and they're already shooting from a long way away. The more time he gives them, the more chance they'll have of hitting him.

Firing the ignition, the ATV jumps to life, and Sam realizes he's taking a gamble every time he shuts it down. He tells himself he'll leave it running during future breaks. If it hadn't started now, he'd probably be dead. Clunking the ATV into gear, he punches the throttle and speeds away.

Within moments, the ache returns to every joint and muscle plagued by the vibration, but Sam ignores it and drives on. He hopes that when he stops for the night he's too far away for those shooters to catch up.

He rolls through the tiny town of Benton, Nevada, without stopping. He doesn't see anyone, but never slows down to find out.

Hours later, he stops on the road and draws his rifle again. Idling in the middle of the street, he braces the weapon and peers through the sight. Amid the heatwaves rising off the blacktop, he can see the first real town straddling this highway. He looks at his map and then the buildings again. Tonopah, Nevada, he concludes, a small town before the world crumbled. Now it looks deserted, at least from this distance.

He still needs water, and he's burning through his gas supply. Going into any town could be helpful or disastrous. Sam hopes that people in a place of civilization won't be as desperate to steal his supplies as those he'd find in the middle of nowhere. But there's no way to know.

Putting his rifle back in its holster, Sam clicks into gear and rolls on toward the town. The cluster of buildings seems to rise from the high-desert scrub as he approaches. The highway opens to three lanes each way as it enters town. He peers back and forth at the old stone buildings and Western-tinged main street.

Nothing moves, and there are no cars on the street. Quick glances down side streets reveal some cars parked at curbs, but no movement. No people. Tonopah seems less like a ghost town and more like a city on pause, ready to come back to life at any moment.

Sam knows anyone in town would have heard him by now. In spite of the deserted look, he's certain some still live here. As he rolls past the old hardware store, he can see all the windows have been destroyed and the shelves stripped clean. The novelty Western-wear store even looks scavenged. Just off this main road stands a Shell station and large convenience store. He rumbles into the parking lot, seeing the store windows boarded up and the pumps smashed. He passes slowly, rolling to the far end of the parking lot and finding the small reserve-tank opening like the one Pat used.

The town drops into an eerie silence when Sam kills the engine. He stays seated on the ATV, and draws his shotgun. Cocking it loudly, he chambers a slug and swings off the dust-caked four wheeler. Resting the shotgun skyward against his shoulder he unfastens a tangle of hose from the gear on the back of the ATV. It's a smaller version of the hoses and handpump Pat used to fill all the gas cans. Squatting over the small reserve-tank cover, Sam opens it and drops a pebble inside. It lands in the darkness below with a faint splash. There must be very little gas left in the tank, but Sam lowers his hose, hoping to get lucky.

As he unstraps one of the gas cans from the back of the rack, Sam stops and stares. He watches a teenager crossing the street with his rifle lowered and a pistol on his hip. Steady and confident, Sam puts the can on the ground, two-hands his shotgun and takes a step behind his ATV.

"Afternoon," Sam says cordially.

The teenager stops, as if surprised to be seen. He holds his rifle waist-high, but white-knuckled. Sam can see the boy is nervous, in spite of his firepower.

"What are you doing?" the boy spits out.

"Just need a drink for me and my ride…. Thought I'd try the reserve tank, but it seems like I'm not the first."

"That's not your gas."

"Is there someone I can pay for it?"

"You're not going to pay for shit." The teen stands between Sam and the store, doing his best to look menacing, and failing.

"Are you the owner?"

The boy loses his focus at this question. "No, I... uh." It's clear he's never been mistaken for the owner before today. "It's not yours, okay. So, go on."

"How about water?" Sam asks as he looks past the boy to the boarded-up store. "Is there any left in there?"

"Not for you. Just go on now."

Sam takes a step toward the teen. The boy tenses. He seems to know his weapon but can't find any real aggression.

"I'm happy to pay for what I need."

"What the hell are we going to do with money?" the young man scoffs.

Sam nods, knowing the kid has a point. He rests his shotgun on his shoulder again and looks around the deserted town. He's drifting closer to the young man, but his moves are so casual they don't draw suspicion.

"Some day you're gonna need some supplies. You'll have to pay for them with something. I'm guessing gold will work for that."

"Fuck you and your gold."

In a blur, Sam snatches the end of the young man's rifle with one hand and lowers his shotgun with the other. Now the kid stares down the shotgun and finds his rifle pointed at the ground.

"Water. Now. I'll still pay you for it if you'd like. But if you refuse me, I'll turn your head into a birdbath."

Sweat blooms on the young man's forehead. He looks at Sam's chapped and cracked lips and then to his cold and serious eyes. Blood drains from the kid's cheeks along with his confidence.

Sam tugs, and the rifle comes out of the boy's hands. Sam lets it clatter to the ground and then pulls the pistol from the boy's hip holster.

"Let's go in the store. Slowly."

"Mom!" the young man calls out.

Sam tenses, two-handing the shotgun now and crouching over the rifle. He sees the door of the store swing open, and a squat, middle-aged woman steps into view past the plywood inserts on the door. She holds a wicked-looking knife, but doesn't seem quick or deadly.

"We don't want trouble," she says.

"I want water," Sam says as he trains the shotgun at the boy's head.

"So I heard. But we don't have any to spare."

"This town's gotta have a well or a treatment plant. Something."

"The well was contaminated. And since most people left, we've been down to bottled."

"We've only got a few left," the boy offers. "Until my dad get's back."

The mom gives the boy a withering look. He's said too much.

"Where'd your dad go?" Sam asks without lowering the shotgun.

The mother and son trade glances. Should they tell him?

"Ely," Mom says. "For supplies."

"They have everything. If you can pay," the boy adds.

"So you do have a use for money," Sam growls. "I'll give you half an ounce of gold for six bottles of water and whatever gas I can pull from your reserve."

"You can get ten times that in Ely," the mother replies.

"I gotta get to Ely first."

Mom lowers her knife. She motions for her son to come closer. Sam nods for him to go, and he watches Sam as she whispers in his ear.

Then he slinks away into the store, looking defeated.

"We can't give you six bottles. We only have five left 'til my husband gets back."

"How long's he been gone?"

"A week."

"Walking?"

"No, he took our little car."

Sam remembers having pored over the maps of this area, putting distances to memory and calculating supplies until his head hurt.

"Ely's about 200 miles. A car could do that in no time."

Mom just lowers her eyes, as her son comes back with five bottles.

Sam doesn't take his eyes off the boy's mother. "You don't think he's coming back?"

"He's coming back," the boy says.

"He always has before," Mom says, but she doesn't sound convinced.

Sam backs toward his ATV. He picks up the rifle and pistol as he goes. He gets to his gear and lays the guns on the seat. Then he zips open his backpack.

"Hey, kid, how many bottles do you have left?"

"Just one more six-pack," he says, before Mom can grab his wrist to be quiet.

"Ma'am, your son is one terrible liar," Sam smiles. "Not a thing wrong with that, I suppose, but it does make it hard to keep secrets."

He reaches down to the base of his pack and feels the hard, rounded corner of a gold brick. He lifts it almost into view, then reaches in with his pocketknife and shaves off a corner. The gold sliver is the size of a dime, and an ugly hack-job shape. Sam knows it's worth far more than what he's asking.

Then taking strides toward mother and son, Sam retrains the shotgun on them with one hand and rolls the gold in his other palm.

"I'll take four of those bottles. And a gas refill. When I leave, you can have your guns back."

The boy stands statue-still. Sam turns his palm and lets the gold fall to the concrete. Then he squats, grabs four bottles and steps back to his ATV.

Mom leans down and picks up the gold. She bites a tip of the odd shape and can't believe what she's holding. She looks up at Sam in disbelief, but he's already working the gas handpump with his shotgun laid across his knees.

"Let us help you," the woman offers, and this time her son tries to silence her.

"Nope. You just go inside and stay there until you hear me pull away," Sam orders.

The boy does as he's told, even taking his mom by the hand and pulling her toward the door as if he were four, not a teenager. His mom follows reluctantly.

Sam sweats as he works the pump. He only gets a trickle. These tanks are dry. He knows he should try stations for refills, but if every stop is a stand-off, he'd rather take his chances. Knowing he has enough gas to get to Ely, he now wonders what he'll find there.

Maybe he'll find the boy's father. Sam suspects he's wrecked on the side of the road somewhere between here and Ely. Without water, this desert scrub-brush wouldn't even need two-hundred miles of open country to kill someone. This standoff for water and gas is only a glimpse of things to come, and Sam suddenly feels he's been in this town far too long.

Sam straps the can and pump onto the ATV. He places the water bottles in his pack, makes sure it's secure, and then lays the boy's rifle and pistol on the ground.

Firing up the ATV, Sam turns out of the station at full throttle. He slams up through the gears, peering back once to see the boy running into the parking lot. At this speed, Sam is already too hard a target to hit.

> *Wherever you are in your life, have confidence. Good self-confidence can get you most anywhere. Knowing who you are and what you're capable of gets respect, friends, and opportunity in a way self-doubt never will.*
>
> *But don't be cocky. There are few things more repulsive than some guy who's cocky.*
>
> *There is a difference, and I struggled with it for most of my life. In fact, I don't think I learned how to be confident until I went to prison and realized that everyone around me was looking for weakness. Confidence can be a shield. And sometimes I needed its protection.*
>
> *Guys that are cocky never shut up about how amazing they are and talk about their greatness in every setting. Most of the time, it's just covering up the fact they can't do much of anything and don't want to be alone. It's hard for a cocky guy to prove why he's worth caring about, but he talks like everyone loves him.*
>
> *With confidence, you know what you can do and what you can't. This frees you up to state your strengths with a matter-of-fact calm. And if anyone presses you on it, you'll be able to answer any questions because you're gifted.*
>
> *You are gifted. I have no doubt. You have things you can do better than anyone else. When you*

find those things, keep your head high and look people in the eye about your strengths.

The strange thing is, once you learn how to speak clearly and confidently about your strengths, you'll find you have no problem claiming your weaknesses either. When someone is truly self-confident, they can admit weakness without ever seeming weak.

A man armed with only his confidence can defeat an armed man plagued with self-doubt. And when two people face off with guns, the more confident one will win.

I'm not just saying this, either. I was in a stand-off in a parking lot, and I won. I didn't succeed because I'm a better shot or a trained killer, or even all that comfortable with a gun. I won because I was more confident than he was.

So don't brag about things you can't do.

And never apologize for things you can.

Sam closes the legal pad and zips it back into the lid of his pack. He takes a sip from one of the four water bottles and looks around his makeshift campsite. He's off the highway among low hills, with his back to a stand of bushy trees. The night is clear and cloudless, with none of the wind from the night before.

To the east, he can see an outline of low mountains, even in the black of night. Their backlit silhouette tells him the lights of a town lie behind them. That must be Ely, but he can't guess how far it is from here. He figures he'll be there tomorrow.

Part 3

Desperate Towns

1

The sun breaks over the same mountains as Sam rumbles back onto the deserted highway. He settles in for a long day of riding, the constant vibration rattling his arms but lulling him into a trance. The miles pass, uneventful and indistinguishable. The road is empty, and the scrub-brush all looks the same. He rattles down the center line as the road curves north to reveal a dark shape on the horizon. The city of Ely.

As Ely grows closer, Sam eases off the throttle. He sees something across the road at the edge of town. A blockade. Standing on the foot pegs, Sam lets his ATV rumble to a halt. He pulls his rifle from its fender scabbard and looks into the scope. He stares at the strange shape stretching across the highway.

Parked buses and semis make up large sections of the barrier, with scrap metal and lumber plugging the holes. Signposts have been repurposed as perimeter spikes. There's no road around the town. The highway leads directly to the fortified city and is swallowed up by the wall.

If he had more fuel or water, he would strike out across the desert and give this town a wide berth. But in this heat and desert scrub he would be out of water in less than a day. His gas might last two.

Sliding his rifle back into its holster, Sam stares at the city. He sighs, knowing he has no choice but to go in for supplies. He hopes he'll be able to get out again.

Easing into the throttle, Sam rumbles toward the walls of Ely. He's still too far away to hit anything with his rifle when he sees the wall open. An armored bus pulls off the highway. Two ATVs streak out from inside, and their riders quickly split to opposite sides of the road. They arc out, as if deterring any thoughts Sam might have of darting around the city. He watches them, easing off the throttle but continuing toward the wall as the bus closes it again.

The guys on ATVs get closer. He can see their makeshift body armor of motocross padding and sporting goods. They don't look official or uniform, but Sam bristles just the same. It takes real concentration to not reach for one of his guns.

The ATVs pass and then turn back to drop in behind him. Sam glances over his shoulders to see them settling into a formation in his blind spots. He can't help but look at his shotgun, but by now he can see people standing on the wall. Some of them are armed. Sudden moves could get him killed now, so he drives on and tries to be casual.

When Sam gets less than a block from the fence, a guy on top of the wall raises a hand for him to stop. Sam hits the brakes, and the two guys behind him do the same. They stay mounted and silent just over both his shoulders. He can feel their stares, but wills himself to look straight at the leader on the wall.

"Good morning," Sam smiles.

"Same to you," the leader answers. "What brings you all the way out here?"

"I'm headed to Aspen."

The leader looks around at others on the wall.

"From where?"

Sam can't see any benefit in lying, so he continues. "I started in California."

The leader sizes him up for a moment, then looks at his companions again.

"That's a long way."

Sam scans the wall, counting seven he can see but knowing there are more eyes on him.

Now he looks over his shoulders, trying to be casual and nodding at his escorts.

"I need some gas and supplies."

"You and everyone else," the leader scoffs back.

"I can pay for it."

"We'll see about that. Right now I need you to hold still and let us do our jobs."

"What jobs?" Sam asks, as he hears the guys behind him climb off the ATVs. He spins to look at them, and they tense, reaching for sidearms.

"Hold on, now," the leader yells. "It's just a scan."

Sam sighs, suddenly knowing where this is going. He's outnumbered. There's nowhere to run. He turns straight ahead, sitting slouched on his ATV.

One of the escorts approaches him. The other stands with his hand on his pistol. The one on his left pulls a cell phone-sized scanner from his pocket and waves it over Sam's arm and shoulder. It beeps with recognition.

The escort steps back and turns toward the leader on the wall.

"He's got a file," he says as he holds the phone aloft.

"Alright, let's bring him in."

The bus-gate in front of Sam rumbles to life, spitting black diesel smoke into the air as it eases into motion and opens the barricade.

The leader steps down off the wall and into the open space. He waves for Sam to come inside. Cautious, Sam eases on the throttle and slow-rolls through the gate. His two escorts follow. When they've cleared the opening, the bus coughs and reverses back into place. The escort with the scanner hands it to the leader, who looks at it for a long moment.

"Samuel Kerr," he says. "You go by Sam."

Sam nods.

"How much of this stuff is yours?"

Sam looks down at the ATV, then back at the leader.

"Most of it."

The leader smiles at that.

"An honest man. I like it. How about that pay you mentioned? That yours?"

"Yes."

There's a group of guards circling them now. They carry a mix of weapons, from pristine rifles to oversized clubs made of household items. They brandish them with the ease of things wielded daily. Sam can't imagine many travelers come down this road, but the faces around him look hard and cynical.

The leader unfastens Sam's pack from the rear of the ATV. Sam glowers at the man, unable to contain his distrust.

"Leave the bike. Come with me."

Without waiting for a response, the leader turns and walks away, carrying Sam's backpack over one shoulder.

Sam kills his engine and looks at the faces around him. He looks at his shotgun and rifle in the fender holsters. His Walther pistol is in the backpack, and there's no way to draw these weapons without getting himself shot. Reluctant, he climbs off and follows.

They walk a block up the highway, with people eyeing them as they go. A golf cart pulls up, three open benches on a long wheelbase. The leader motions Sam into the middle bench behind the driver and passenger. As Sam sits, the leader and one of the ATV guards climb onto the bench behind him.

"Let's go," the leader says.

The cart rolls out, emitting a whine from its electric motor and a thrum from the knobby tires. They turn off the main road and weave down side streets.

"How long were you inside?" the leader asks, as Sam notices the buildings around him getting cleaner and better maintained. Things improve as they move toward the city center.

"Thirty-eight months," Sam replies.

The leader scowls as he does the math in his head. "So you've been in the whole time. This probably seems like another world to you, huh?"

Sam doesn't respond, but he can feel the leader watching him.

"I was here before," the man says. "I stayed as things turned to shit, and we figured it out again. It's just different, that's all."

"Where are you taking me?" Sam asks.

He looks over his shoulder, waiting for an answer. The leader smiles and points ahead. Sam looks to see the City Hall building they're approaching.

"The mayor will want to see you," the leader says. "Think of it as an honor."

They roll down the middle of the clean and empty street. The cart parks directly out front.

As Sam steps out, still flanked by the men, he notices a dusty Toyota Yaris parked alone in the City Hall lot. It must be the one that left Tonopah before he stopped there for gas. He wonders if whatever happened to that boy's father is about to happen to him.

The building looks like a well-manicured plantation house, strangely well kept in comparison to everywhere Sam has been so far. He looks around as they move up the front walk. Every house or building in view looks the same, or better, than it likely did before the world changed. If not for the armed men all around him, Sam would describe this town as idyllic.

Inside City Hall the building is clean and quiet. The few people they pass all look up and watch Sam go by. His escorts guide him silently up the main stairs to the mayor's office. The leader from the wall taps on the open oak door as he leads them inside.

"Here's our visitor, Boss," the leader offers as he steps to the large desk and sets down the phone scanner with Sam's information. The mayor, a thick, Black woman with a wide face, looks at the file and then up at Sam.

Sam watches her rise from the high-backed desk chair. She's tall, over six feet, and moves with a surprising grace. With a smile, the mayor extends her hand toward Sam. When they shake, Sam feels like a child greeting an adult.

"Welcome to Ely, Sam. Pardon the escort, but caution is safety these days."

"I understand," Sam says, cool and flat. "I didn't get your name."

The mayor glances at the leader and then back at Sam. She eyes her visitor, studying him.

"My name is Michelle." Then she points to the leader. "That's Gordon. We could go around the room and introduce everybody, but you'd probably forget half their names anyway."

She returns to her chair and drops into it with a sigh.

"Have a seat, Sam." She points to the two facing her desk. "Gordon. Give us a few minutes, please."

Gordon nods, smiles at Sam and exits. Sam watches the rest of the men file out after him and wonders about that smile. It didn't seem friendly.

The door closes as Sam sits in the chair and looks at the mayor. The big woman scans down Sam's file on the phone, nodding as she speed-reads.

"You were inside a long time."

Sam doesn't say anything.

"I only did eight months," the mayor continues. She slides the phone away and looks up at Sam, gauging his response.

"If you're an ex-debtor, why are we talking?" Sam says. He expects a trap.

"It's not that you were inside. It's that no one comes through here. We don't get visitors, so when someone rolls up — especially with a record — I want to know their story."

"It's all on your scanner."

"That's your record. Not your story."

"Gordon and his boys have all my stuff. You can find out whatever you want."

The mayor stares at Sam, a long silence passing between them.

"You're not making this easy, Sam. I hoped we'd be friends."

"I'm not looking to stay. I just want fuel and supplies, and I'll be gone again."

"That's what everybody wants these days. It's hard for us to find it, so we've gotta be selective."

"I can pay. Unless your boys have already taken it."

"You don't have a lot of trust, do you, Sam?"

"I've learned the hard way."

"Tough time inside?"

"It's been worse outside."

The mayor leans back in her chair, a faint smile creeps across her lips.

"What'd you do inside?"

"Rec," Sam answers instantly, knowing only a debtor would know what that means.

"Reconstruction Crew? Wow, that's impressive."

Sam nods. They do have a shared experience.

"What were you?" Sam asks.

"Oh, the system took one look at my CPA and put me with the paper-pushers."

"You're an accountant?" Sam asks, disbelieving.

"It's a small town," Michelle grins. "I've done a bit of everything here. I fixed people's cars, and their taxes, and even did some time as the librarian."

"You must have done more than that to wind up as the mayor."

"People see me as a fixer. These days, that's valuable." Then the mayor switches back to Sam: "If you were on the Rec?, you must have done a lot of construction before you wound up inside."

Sam shakes his head. "No, I built websites, did some programming and stayed inside a lot. I had no usable skill. But I was healthy and didn't have any back pain."

"The Pyramids, right?" Michelle asks, waiting for Sam's response.

Sam nods, knowingly. "Slave labor. Get's shit done."

They both relax a little.

"The boys radioed me when you were on your way in. Said you're coming from California and headed all the way to Aspen?"

"I've got family there."

"You sure they want you?"

Sam bristles, but the mayor raises her hand before he can protest.

"Hold on, I don't mean to offend," the Mayor says. "All I'm saying is if they're in Aspen then they landed on their feet. Maybe even fell upwards, if you know what I mean. Lots of families have been split up by the shining cities. Most won't risk the good life to bring more folks in, even if they're related."

"It's my wife and son," Sam says, his voice cold. "They'll want to see me."

"Well, it's a long way to go. I hope you're right."

They sit and look at each for another long moment.

"So, I can go?" Sam asks.

"Probably tomorrow," the Mayor smiles. "I've got to talk to a few folks and make sure they can spare what you're needing. And then we'll have to confirm you can pay for it."

"I can pay for it," Sam says, his anger beginning to show.

"Sam. It's a formality. I'm sure you can." Then she turns her head toward the door. "Hey, Gordon!" she calls, and the door opens instantly. Gordon enters, wearing Sam's backpack over one shoulder.

"Sam will be staying the night with us," the mayor informs Gordon as if Sam weren't in the room. "Find him some accommodation downstairs."

Gordon nods and turns for the door. "Come on," he motions to Sam.

Sam doesn't move. He just looks at the mayor.

"I'm sorry, Sam. What we have for you isn't great, but we're at capacity everywhere, so it's the best we can do."

"You're gonna put me in a cell," Sam growls.

"Open door. Think of it like an uncomfortable hotel room."

"The door doesn't matter. If I can't leave town, it's a cell."

"You're welcome to sleep outside," the mayor says flatly.

"I might."

The mayor nods, deciding she really doesn't care how this ends. "Gordon. Give Sam his backpack and show him what we have."

"There's a pistol in here," Gordon announces to the mayor as he takes off the pack. "And a few bars of gold."

Sam snatches the pack and pulls it close, fuming. He digs into the top.

"It's all still there," Gordon says. "We just had to know."

Sam pulls out the Walther pistol, checks that there's a round in the chamber. Gordon puts a hand on his own pistol and looks to the mayor for help.

"Sam," the mayor says with amusement. "If you go and shoot somebody, you're not getting any gas."

Sam shoves the pistol back into his pack and digs down to the bottom. He feels the gold bars and counts them without pulling anything out. They are all there.

"Alright. Show me this cell," Sam says as he shoulders his pack.

Sam passes Gordon and walks out of the office. Gordon looks to the mayor, and she shrugs. He turns and goes after Sam.

In the hallway, all of Gordon's men stiffen to see Sam walk out unattended. Gordon catches up, and starts to lead Sam to the stairs. Sam stays with him, his eyes scanning all the faces they pass. They reach the large central staircase and descend into the basement. A line of Gordon's men follow behind, and Sam starts to feel trapped.

Sam stops suddenly at the bottom of the stairs and turns around. The man behind him nearly falls trying to stop without getting trampled by those behind him. Sam slides off his pack and glares at the cluster of men on the stairs.

"If you're gonna ambush me, why don't you get it over with," Sam says as he dives his hand into his pack.

They don't say anything, but Sam can hear Gordon hurrying back toward him.

"Gordon, you tell these guys to back off unless you plan to kill me," Sam says over his shoulder as he pulls his Walther into view.

Sam takes one step away from the stairs and puts his back to the wall. He steals a glance at Gordon and then back at the guys on the stairs.

"Take it easy, Sam," Gordon says as calm as he can summon.

"You guys have been on my ass since you first saw me," Sam says. "You better either ask me out or give me some space."

"Alright, guys," Gordon orders. "Go back upstairs. I've got this."

The men don't retreat.

"Go. It's alright."

The one closest to Sam risks a look between Gordon and the end of the gun. Then he takes a step back. The guy behind him backs up as well. Sam lowers the gun a few inches. The guys turn and trudge up the stairs. Now Sam lowers the pistol and turns to Gordon.

Past Gordon, he can see a narrow hallway leading to four cinder-block cells.

"I'm not staying down here," Sam says.

"There's nowhere else, I promise you," Gordon replies.

"I've got all I need, I'll sleep out on the grass."

"You do that, and I've gotta assign somebody to stand out there and watch you sleep. This isn't great down here, but at least you'll be on your own," Gordon says as if it were an apology.

"Fuck you," says a voice from down the hallway.

Sam bristles, his gun up again. *Who was that?*

Sam walks past Gordon and down the cell block with his Walther leveled. When the last cell comes into view, Sam sees a middle-aged man sitting inside on a cot and leaning against the back wall.

"Shoot me. Go on," the man says, daring Sam.

"Who are you?" Sam asks.

"Nobody. Ask your friend Gordo."

Sam pulls at the cell door. It's locked. He turns to Gordon.

"The mayor said the door would be unlocked."

"Your door… sure. Not his."

"First one's free!" hollers the man in the cell.

"This is Andy. He and the mayor had a bit of a disagreement."

"Left me here to rot," Andy mumbles.

"What'd you do?" Sam asks.

Andy just glares at him.

"It was called stealing even before things went to hell," Gordon says, folding his arms.

"I can pay you back!" Andy yells.

"Credit's what got us here, remember?" Gordon smirks.

Gordon turns and starts down the hallway toward the stairs.

"Take your pick of rooms. I'll have a guy at the top of the stairs if you need anything."

"I need some things!" Andy hollers after him.

Gordon ignores the comment and keeps walking. Sam watches him go. Gordon hits a light switch at the bottom of the stairs, and the basement drops into near-darkness. Small corner bulbs and high, small cell windows offer just enough light to see.

Confused and suddenly exhausted, Sam walks to the first open cell and drops his pack. He pulls out a holster from one of the side pockets and hangs his pistol in easy reach. After a series of zippers and shuffling, Andy speaks up from the distant cell.

"Got anything to eat?" he asks, his voice now quiet and hopeful.

Sam stands still for a moment. Listening and thinking.

"Hello?" Andy says, his voice picking up some desperation.

"Yeah. I'm here," Sam answers as he unzips a side pocket and pulls out a few strips of beef jerky.

Draping the pistol holster over a shoulder, Sam rounds the corner and walks to the front of Andy's cell. He tosses the jerky through the bars and onto the man's bed. Andy snatches it up and begins tearing a piece with his teeth.

"How long have you been down here?"

"Couple days," Andy mumbles between bites.

"Is that your Yaris out front?"

Andy stops eating. He looks at Sam, his eyes growing darker. But he doesn't answer.

"You're from Tonopah, right?" Sam asks.

Andy gets off the bed. Jerky still in one hand, but laser-focused on Sam.

"Have we met?" Andy growls.

"I met your wife…."

Andy leaps to the bars with astounding speed. He reaches through, but Sam ducks away.

"What did you do?!" Andy shrieks. Sam takes another step away from the cell and resists the urge to draw his pistol.

"I met your son, too," Sam says, trying to be calm.

"You fucking asshole, fuck!" Andy spits. "If you touched them I will fucking—"

"Your son's got your mouth," Sam says, as Andy flails his arms helplessly through the bars. "And your way with people."

Sam draws his pistol, unable to fight the instinct any longer.

Andy lowers his arms, his angry outburst giving way to a depression that seems to shrink him right before Sam's eyes.

"What the hell is wrong with you?" Sam asks.

"Please…," Andy whispers as he sinks to the floor. "Please tell me they're okay…."

"They're fine. Your son seemed scared. Your wife seemed worried. They still believed you were coming back."

Andy puts his head in his hands. He stares at the floor for a long time. The unmoving silence lingers until Sam starts to leave.

"I can't," Andy says flatly. "I can't go back empty-handed."

"Looks like you aren't going back at all," Sam answers.

Andy snorts at that, finding it funnier than Sam thinks appropriate.

"I've been coming here for years. They know me, and they know what I need."

"That probably made it harder to get away with stealing anything."

"I didn't steal it," Andy insists, as he looks up at Sam again. "I was gonna pay them back."

Sam nods. "How much did you take?"

Andy thinks about the question. It looks like the effort is straining him. Sam's regretting asking more about Andy's situation.

"I filled the car with gas. The trunk with supplies. We would have been good 'til spring."

"Why don't you just bring them here?" Sam asks.

"Fuck no. I'm not living under the mayor's rule. She and Gordo can go fuck each other sideways."

Sam shakes his head. No wonder this guy wound up in a locked cell. Andy reminds him of the outbursts Danny had as a toddler. With more swearing.

"Getting by is hard enough now," Sam says. "Why make it harder on yourself?"

"You haven't heard all their rules. And their ways of making you pay," Andy grumbles back.

"You're right. Maybe I'd agree with you if I knew," Sam says as he walks back to his cell.

"Don't placate me, you asshole," Andy says.

Sam shakes his head, glad that Andy can't see him. He sits on his bed, and it squeaks at the disruption.

"Oh. Silent treatment now, huh?" Andy starts again. "Lotta fucking help you are!"

Sam pulls the pen and pad out of the top flap of his pack and starts to write.

> *You're gonna get in a lot of arguments in your lifetime. It's unavoidable. There's no point in trying to please or get along with everyone. Some people just want to bitch and fight no matter what life hands them.*
>
> *But you need to learn how to respond to people. Honesty and emotion are great things until you use them in the wrong moment, and suddenly you can find yourself far worse off than a moment before.*
>
> *Be careful with what you say. Learn when to keep your mouth shut or only share pieces of the truth. I'm not saying lying is a good thing, but instant truth can get you in a fight, a cell, or killed. Pay attention to the people around you and pick the right moment to share what you know.*
>
> *This takes practice. You'll screw it up. We all*

do. Just don't offer anyone an easy target for their anger.

2

"Hey, sleeping beauty!" Andy suddenly yells loudly. "You better get before they lock that door!"

Sam startles awake. He's slumped against his backpack with the legal pad in his lap and his pen dropped somewhere. It's an awkward position, and neck pain greets him.

Footsteps echo down the stairs as a group of people descend into the cell block. Sam looks at the small, high window and can see it's morning. Still groggy, with no idea the time or how long he slept, Sam sits up with a wince and shoves the legal pad back into his pack.

Standing, he finds his side wound aches and his right leg is asleep. With a shuffle, Sam grabs the holster hanging nearby and pulls the pistol just as Gordon and the Mayor step into view with three armed men behind them. Sam points the pistol at the floor but keeps his eyes on the guys with rifles.

"Good morning," says the Mayor with a smile. "I'm glad you got some sleep."

Sam imagines he must look like hell. He can feel the sleep crusting his eyes, and the throb in his side is even more distracting than his leg. Tensing his hand on the pistol, he tries to focus.

"So now what?" Sam asks.

"Well, I wanna talk about that," the Mayor answers.

"Is that why you brought a bunch of armed guards?"

The Mayor looks at the men behind her. They keep their eyes on Sam.

"To tell the truth, I wasn't sure what I'd be walking into down here. I knew you were armed. And I figured you'd be a bit worked up after being down here with Andy."

"I tried to warn you, Sam!" Andy shouts from the next cell. "You're shit outta luck now."

The Mayor takes one step deeper into the cell block and looks into Andy's cell. She doesn't say anything, but her eyes show she's out of patience.

"What're you gonna do, Michelle?" Andy taunts her. "Lock me up? Starve me? You're running out of options."

"Andy," Sam says with a tired edge in his voice. "Every time you open your mouth, you dig yourself deeper. I'm starting to think you don't want to go home at all."

"What the fuck do you know?!" Andy yells.

"I know your son needs you," Sam says.

"You don't know a goddamned thing about my son or what he needs. I ain't taking parenting advice from some idiot too stupid to know when he's about to be double-crossed."

The Mayor eyes Sam as she steps back in front of Sam's cell.

"Is that what this is?" Sam asks her.

"This is just a conversation," Michelle says.

"At gunpoint," Sam grins.

"I'll tell you what," the Mayor says. She waves away the guys with guns, as if trying to shoo them from the room. "Go on, boys, wait upstairs. Gordon and I are fine here with Sam."

They glare at Sam but turn to go. Sam waits, letting the silence settle in around them.

"Gas is expensive these days," the Mayor begins. "And while we know you don't need much, I'm sure you can understand the position I'm in if I let some stranger get a bunch of supplies without the town seeing a real benefit."

"How much?" Sam asks.

The Mayor eyes Sam's pack.

"Half of one of your bars."

"Half?" Sam blurts out. "You could buy a whole tanker with that."

"I hope so," she answers.

Sam stands there, silent and thinking. His fingers squeeze the handle of the Walther, then relax, then squeeze again, as if his tension is breathing.

"We could have just taken them," Gordon says, low and matter-of-fact.

The Mayor glares at Gordon, and Andy starts laughing from his cell.

"I know," Sam nods at Gordon. "You've been honest and mostly fair to this point. So here's what I suggest."

Sam digs into his pack with his free hand. He pulls out one of his four gold bars. It's as long as his palm and half as wide — a small fortune of indisputable currency in this current world.

"I'll give you half of this," Sam says as he holds it up, "if you fill all my tanks. Get me enough food to last a couple weeks. And you let Andy take his car full and go."

"What?" Andy hollers in surprise before anyone else can respond.

The Mayor startles, her reply stolen, but her surprise remains.

"No way in hell!" Gordon barks.

"Why would we do that?" Mayor Michelle asks.

"I don't want your fucking charity!" Andy curses through the wall.

Sam smiles at the Michelle and tilts his head toward Andy. "Do you really want to keep him down here?"

Michelle almost allows a smile. Of course she doesn't.

"Half?" the Mayor confirms.

"Half. And I want to be gone by lunch."

Michelle extends her hand. Sam lays the gold brick on his pack, switches his pistol to the other hand, and shakes. A deal.

Andy is strangely quiet.

Sam lifts up the gold again. "You have some way to cut this?" he asks. Gordon nods.

"Grab your stuff and come with me," Gordon replies.

Sam shoves the brick into his pack and swings it onto his shoulders. As he holsters the pistol, he realizes his leg has almost returned to normal. In spite of the lingering pain in his side and the stiffness in his neck, he manages to step in behind Gordon as they follow the Mayor up the stairs.

"Nice knowing you," Andy grumbles as Sam's footfalls fade.

Even though he overheard Sam's plan, Andy is still surprised when he hears footsteps a half-hour later. He tenses, watching the edge of his cell to see who will appear at the bars.

Sam steps into view and stops. He's alone, his pack fastened and gun holstered. The two men stare at each other.

"This isn't for you," Sam says as he reveals one-quarter of a gold bar. "This is for your family."

He tosses the chunk of gold through the bars and onto Andy's bed.

"Go back. And when you run out next time, you should bring them here and play nice."

Andy starts to say something, but Sam puts a hand on his pistol and glares at him.

"Your son deserves to know there's more in the world than some shitty ghost town and a father who hates everyone. He should have some choices," Sam says.

"I didn't ask for your help," Andy says.

"Yes, you did. You just couldn't do it like a normal, civil person.

You're hell-bent on being the most insufferable and difficult asshole I've encountered in years. And I was in prison!"

Sam's gun is drawn, but he doesn't remember doing it. Andy is wide-eyed and silent.

"Your son is on his way to being just as much of a prick as you are. My guess is he won't live to see twenty unless you get your shit together."

Sam points at the gold with his pistol. "I told the Mayor you'd hand them that when they let you out. They thought I was insane to bring it down to you. It's a fresh start. Don't fuck it up."

Turning, Sam shoves the pistol back into his holster and marches down the hall out of sight. Andy picks up the chunk of gold and stares at it. He looks half-sized, shrunken inside himself at Sam's reprimand and generosity.

"Thank you," he breathes.

Sam doesn't hear him. He's already out of the basement prison and stepping into the sunlight.

Gordon and Mayor Michelle stand outside by a golf cart.

"My boys are gassing your ATV," Gordon says.

"What about supplies?" Sam reminds him.

"Climb in, and we'll take you over there," Michelle offers. "It's not much, but you can probably find something."

Sam climbs into the back row of the golf cart. The Mayor settles in just in front of him.

"You gave it to him?" she asks.

Sam nods. "You'll get it later today, I'm sure."

"You wasted your money," Michelle sighs. "He'll be back here and locked up in a couple months."

"Maybe," Sam says, really hoping for the best. "Either way, you get paid."

An hour later, with the sun high in the sky, Sam finishes loading all of his gear onto his ATV. He shakes the full gas tanks and his pack to make sure they are secure.

The Mayor and Gordon stand a few steps away, watching. Farther back, others stare at him with a mixture of suspicion and awe. They can't believe he's leaving. Some hold weapons and peer down from their place along the wall. Others watch from alcoves and alleyways. All are silent.

"I just want to be clear," Michelle says, repeating herself. "We can find a place for you here. It wouldn't be elaborate, but we'd be happy to have you."

"I understand. And thank you, but no."

Sam swings his leg over the ATV and feels a familiar twinge in his side. It hurts, but he knows it's healing well thanks to Pat's work. Those few days feel like months ago.

"You've got a great little oasis here, Michelle," Sam smiles. "I might come back. But I can't stay until I know."

He fires the ignition, and the ATV coughs to life. Sam revs the engine, and it settles into a rumbling idle.

"Open it up!" the Mayor hollers toward the wall.

With a spit of diesel smoke, an ancient Greyhound bus clatters to life. It creaks as it backs away, opening the wall and revealing an open road on the opposite side of Ely from where he entered. Sam stares at the desolate, nondescript ribbon of decrepit road spearing southeast into the distance.

With a CLACK, Sam snaps the ATV into gear and begins rolling forward. He nods at the Mayor and Gordon. Slowly, he exits the town perimeter and rolls to a stop.

Looking back over his shoulder, Sam sees Michelle and Gordon climb atop the wall. Gordon motions, and the big Greyhound bus groans back into the closed position.

Sam gives them a quick nod and a salute-wave. Then he hits the gas and accelerates east, upshifting and not looking back.

3

Sam settles into the ATV's top speed, just above forty miles per hour. He knows it isn't efficient, but he can't shake the feeling he was lucky to get out of Ely at all. As the miles pass, he begins to relax and stops looking over his shoulder for pursuers.

The road is deserted, with thick tufts of weeds reaching up through the cracks and sporadic sand washes covering the lanes. Rocky hills rise and fall beside the road. Sam moves slower now, looking for an ambush, but still much faster than he could go on foot. Eventually he approaches a dusty intersection.

Bringing the ATV to a stop, Sam stands on the foot pegs and looks all around. The wind rustles through the scrub-brush. The mountains in every direction all look the same and seem equally far away. He can see a field of broken-down windmills in the distance. He suspects people are living among them, and he hopes he doesn't have to go that way.

Sam pulls out the dirty map from the clear pouch on his gas tank. Under it, he catches a glimpse of the picture of Ariel and Danny in Aspen. Sam kills the engine and sits silent for a moment. He listens, then climbs off his rig and looks in every direction, with his hand on the Walther. Satisfied he's alone, Sam spreads the map out on the pavement and begins to examine his surroundings.

Knowing he started on Route 50 out of Ely, Sam traces it southeast to a T-junction. He wants to follow 93 south, away from the windmills, but the map shows Hwy 50 continuing due east to old Interstate 15. He wants to reach Highway 70 going east through Utah before the end of the day. He wonders how long it will take, and if he'll encounter trouble at the base of the wind farm.

Sam folds up the map, leaving the current area as the top square. Stepping back to his ATV, he slides the map into the clear pocket, covering the picture as it comes to rest.

After listening to the wind in the brush and short, tough trees, Sam unfastens his pack and pulls it onto the pavement. He unclips the top and opens the drawstring. Peering inside, he wonders at the wisdom of his idea, but ultimately upends the pack, spewing the contents onto the middle of the intersection. Items bounce and roll, but all stop a few feet from where he's standing. His entire life, from one bag, now lies in the street.

His eyes fall on the remaining three-and-a-half gold bars and his dad's old titanium femur bone. The fact that he still has these items shows him just how honest the Mayor of Ely had been. He wonders if he should have stayed in Ely. Whoever else he meets, Sam knows there's little chance he'll be treated so well again. The only way to keep his money is to do a better job hiding what he has. This empty and desolate intersection might be his last chance to redistribute his handful of possessions.

Then he digs into the base of the pack. Needing more light even in the middle of this sunny day, he straps on his headlamp and stares into the darkness of the pack. The bottom has another drawstring baffle, separating the main compartment from the sleeping-bag area below. Sam carefully wraps his remaining gold bars into the folds of the baffle. Then he covers the bottom with his thick jacket, unneeded at the moment and hopefully ignored by anyone who might be digging through his pack.

Methodically, Sam fills the pack with the rest of his possessions. It calms him to see all his meager belongings and organize them again. As he pulls the drawstring closed, the pack feels smaller. He stands, pulling the pack over both shoulders and fastening all the straps. It's heavy, but not unbearable. Satisfied, he straps his pack to the ATV and climbs aboard.

When he hits the ignition, the ATV spins its starter like an industrial coffee grinder, but the motor never fires. Sam stops, fighting concern, and tries again. The engine stays silent as the starter fires. Alarmed, Sam looks for a rise or hill to use for a push-start, but the world around this intersection is mostly flat. He rocks the ATV, hearing gas slosh in the tanks and wishing he had some other way to start the vehicle. Unsure, he tries the ignition again, rocking and easing in some throttle.

After a few spins, the engine catches. A few more revolutions, and it coughs to life. Sam laughs aloud, only now allowing himself to acknowledge how panicked he'd become. As he feathers the throttle and gets the ATV running smoothly, he wonders if this is the beginning of consistent problems with his transport. A dozen possibilities battle in his mind as he drops the ATV into first gear and starts forward.

Sam rolls onward, passing the broken-down wind farm at speed. It looks deserted. He can see evidence of a makeshift shelter built from one of the huge propellers, but he doesn't stop to investigate. It's a relief to have expected a fight and not have one.

Somewhere in the distance is Interstate 15.

I never expected to be a very good father. It wasn't something that I'd really thought about, but your mom really wanted to have you so I decided to make the best of it. I was excited but clueless, and just when I thought I was getting the hang of it… I went away. Now there's no way to know what we've missed. I'm pretty out of practice and will seem like a stranger when you see me again.

Both fatherhood and prison changed me. I guess that's not too surprising. Except I imagine most people go through those things and come out more conservative. More careful. More concerned. I went the other way.

I feel like a better version of me, and it's only because I opened up more. I don't really care how other people live. I don't need anyone to adhere to my beliefs of right, wrong or whatever. The world seems a lot less black and white, and very few things seem worth fighting over.

There's a lifetime of things for you to discover, and I want you to embrace every opportunity. Whatever intrigues you – investigate. Of course I want you to be careful, but somehow it seems like most folks' idea of careful means to be timid.

Timid is useless — it doesn't make you any safer. Pick anything in the world, and there are people ready with reasons why it's bad and should be avoided. I avoided many things growing up, and I'm not better for it.

I'm sorry there's less to try now. We were all spoiled for so long that nearly every experience now carries a sense of absence. There was so much more, and it was all so easy. Now we're fighting for everything. Fighting over everything. I guess the good news is you'll be curious about things that matter. The frivolous time-wasters are gone.

And like an addict, I miss them.

Then I think of you living in a shining city, and I wonder if you have everything I dreamed for you and more. Maybe you're spoiled for choice and don't know anything else.

I'm torn. I want you to have abundance. But I want you to know sacrifice, so that the abundance has perspective.

You're seven as I write this. I can't imagine you have any perspective. I'm supposed to help you learn that…

I hope I get the chance. But I don't know if I'm up for the task.

Sam sits on the concrete barricade alongside the merging of the highway and Interstate 15. The sun sets behind distant mountains and rolling plains. It's beautiful. And deserted. From the top of this berm he can see clearly in all directions: no vehicles, no people, no movement.

This is the first interstate Sam has been on since leaving his parents' house. He's been sitting here for nearly two hours, and no one has passed by. The insanity of his journey begins to dawn on him for the first time.

Three years after the collapse, and everyone stays put. Large cities like Los Angeles look like refugee camps, with people in filthy, close quarters unable to get out. Sam traveling across the country with no money and no companion makes him seem like a modern-day explorer to the people he meets. Sitting on the side of an interstate, he thinks of how easy and common travel used to be. Now the road is an empty monument to a better time.

He hears something and looks up. A jet arrows across the clear blue sky high above him, leaving a contrail behind. People with money still travel across the country and the world. But the majority hunker down.

As the sky darkens, Sam climbs back onto his ATV and hits the ignition. For a few seconds it only spins; then the engine catches, and the vehicle rumbles to life. Sam surveys this desolate intersection once again and then turns back the way he came.

In moments, he's rolling into the long-deserted town of Holden, just off the interstate. Houses and a few businesses sit, silent and rotting. Some are already crumbling, but most of the buildings still offer a solid roof and more shelter than he'd have out in the open.

Turning off the main road, Sam goes a block deeper into the small town and picks a simple two-story home. He rolls up the weed-filled driveway and leaves the ATV idling in front of the garage. Climbing off, Sam pulls his shotgun and cocks it loudly.

"Hello?" he calls, nearly yelling.

The only sound is the ATV.

He walks up to the garage and tugs at the door. It swings up and open, revealing an empty space next to a dusty and discarded Camry. No one has touched this car for years.

Encouraged, Sam walks up the back porch and tries the door. It swings open, unlocked. Shotgun poised in front of him, Sam walks through the house with quick steps.

"Anyone here?" he hollers again. "I'm just looking for a place to stay."

He keeps moving, sweeping each room as he comes to it, and then climbs the stairs. The distant rumble of his ATV gives him a strange comfort, and if it suddenly stops or changes he'll treat it like an alarm. He reaches the upper story and walks through all three bedrooms of the small house. No one. In fact, hardly anything in the entire house. No beds in any of the rooms and only a few pieces of furniture downstairs. Sold or scavenged, whatever was once here was removed methodically.

He smiles. This house is perfect.

Stepping back outside, Sam backs his ATV into the garage, kills the engine and sits in silence for a long time. He listens for any kind of response or change in the town around him, but it really does seem completely deserted. As he grabs his pack and his weapons, Sam shakes his head at his expectation to be jumped or surprised at any moment. This trip has made him paranoid.

Then, he thinks maybe the whole world is this way now. At least the whole country must be a collection of scavengers and survivalists. Paranoia is necessary.

Closing the garage, Sam hauls his things into the house and back up the stairs. He picks a bedroom facing the backyard, where the roof of the porch could be reached from the window. Satisfied with a potential escape route, he unfurls his sleeping bag and lays out a few things for the night. The last light fades in the west and the blue twilight turns to hard darkness.

Sam finds his headlamp and slips it on his head. Before turning it on, he walks through the house again, looking at every structure he can see from the upper story. He scans for other lights. He sees only dark and deserted buildings.

Clicking on his headlamp, Sam retreats back to the bedroom. He passes the silent, dusty bathroom and is struck by the sudden urge to take a shower. Standing in the hallway, he tries to remember his last shower. It was long before he even arrived at his parents' house. Maybe he hasn't even showered since he left the prison. It seems impossible, but there's never been a good opportunity.

Now, in an empty house in an empty town, Sam misses being clean. He walks into the bathroom and turns on the shower. The pipes groan as air rattles through them. The faucet coughs violently, spitting a hunk of wet, brownish sludge into the bathtub. Disgusted, Sam turns off the faucet.

Sam turns off his headlamp as he walks to the bedroom window again. The other houses are now only sharp silhouettes against the western sky. He slips off his shoes and dirt-caked socks. His toes curl instinctively into the thin, dirty carpet. Sam smiles at himself, realizing how much he's missed just being in a house. Peeling off his shirt, Sam shakes more dirt away and ruffles his fingers through his shaggy hair. He's thin and filthy. If his wife and son could see him, he knows they wouldn't recognize him.

With a groan beyond his years, Sam slips down into his equally dirty sleeping bag. The house is silent. He looks at his Walther pistol lying on the floor only a foot away from his face. His shotgun leans against the wall. Sam feels very alone, but also safe.

When he awakens, Sam realizes he must have passed out suddenly. His joints are stiff from staying in the same position on the hard floor. He has no memory of moving or dreaming, just the awareness time has passed. When he stands up to look out the window, it's clear most of the morning is gone.

Rubbing thick crusted sleep from his eyes, Sam struggles back to consciousness. The town looks the same as it had the night before: empty, deserted, and yet strangely inviting.

Pulling on his shirt and boots, Sam wonders if every house in this neighborhood has been picked as clean as this one. As he rolls up his sleeping bag and reloads his pack, he decides to explore before moving on.

Walking back into the garage, he lashes his pack back onto the ATV and holsters the shotgun on the fender. With his Walther strapped to his hip, he leaves the garage door closed and exits through the side door. He stands outside the door, listening. Then he moves down the drive.

At the end of the driveway he stops again. Hand on his pistol, he's listening for any other movement. He expects the sound of an engine, or a person, but he only hears wind and silence.

Sadness and nostalgia strike hard as Sam looks up and down the street. The quiet houses with overgrown lawns look close enough to his old neighborhood to seem familiar. Yet he's nowhere near where he used to live, and the ghost-town feel of the street only reminds him how far away his family life has become.

Hand still on his holstered Walther, Sam starts walking down the sidewalk and deeper into the neighborhood. The lawns and sidewalks are overrun with weeds and signs of neglect. The doors and windows look covered in a fine dust blown in from the high plains and undisturbed over the years of abandonment.

The mailboxes still have numbers on them, and a few have names as well. Nothing looks out of place or threatening — just deserted, as if the whole population vanished at once. The sameness of their decay and the overwhelming silence lull Sam into a near-trance of memory.

He's watching Danny peddling his tricycle down the sidewalk. The boy's little legs pump up and down furiously, but the metal trike barely moves faster than Sam's walk. Danny bumps over sidewalk seams and drifts side to side as he goes. Then he stops suddenly, looks back to see Sam right behind him, and then he's off again.

The dusty, dirty Sam smiles at the memory of his son riding through a distant neighborhood long ago. He looks around, no longer seeing overgrown and decaying houses, but instead manicured lawns and freshly painted add-ons. In his mind there are cars in the driveways and flags hanging from the front porches.

He passes a house with an upper deck leading out from a bedroom and over the attached garage. Staring at it, he stops. His hand has fallen from his pistol, and he's remembering a night when they could see shooting stars from their deck, so close and frequent that the shower was visible in the city.

He and Ariel had gotten up in the middle of the night and dragged out seldom-used deckchairs to stare up into a moonless sky. Danny was long asleep, and they felt like they were getting away with something. It was invigorating, so much so that Ariel had smiled at him and suggested they have sex outside under the stars. Sam couldn't remember how many times they'd had sex in their marriage. Or how many times they hadn't when he hoped they would. But that night on their balcony is clear in his mind, the details and images as vibrant as if they'd happened days before. He didn't even realize how well he remembers her silhouette against the starry backdrop until looking at this abandoned balcony years later and hundreds of miles away.

Sam misses his wife. He longs for the life they had in the marginal neighborhood they so often maligned until it was gone. The weeks leading up to his incarceration dominate his memory. Ariel turned cold, while he stressed trying to think of every way of navigating the changes to come. She comforted Danny, drawing closer to him, and at the time Sam had encouraged and welcomed her response. Looking back, he wishes they'd focused on each other and how they could survive the time apart.

He's walking again, aimlessly wandering down these strange neighborhood streets but seeing his own home from years before. Amid this once unremarkable neighborhood, he begins to see the last few years in a new light. He knew how distant they were growing before the financial collapse. Once it happened, he was so embroiled in the consequences that he'd missed her. He knew her love had waned, but now he wonders if she had grown to hate him.

Sam thinks of their first night in their little house, with boxes stacked around them and Danny still a few years away. It was hot that day, but long after dark it had started to rain. The storm was so loud, it made them check the time and realize it was well after midnight — time to stop unpacking. So they opened all the windows and flopped down on the couch Ariel had owned since college. Sam propped his feet up on a box, and she had snuggled in close. The sound of the rain pounding their home on all sides made them smile. Ariel fell asleep on Sam's shoulder. He sat listening to the rain for what seemed like hours, until he awoke just before dawn with a stiff neck and Ariel still next to him.

Sam remembers when he woke her up, she'd smiled sleepily and pushed back her disheveled hair.

"Already feels like home," she had said then.

"Must be all the boxes," he'd joked.

"You know what I mean…. I never sleep well in a strange place," she said. "But that was perfect…. It must be you."

She'd smiled at him with a warmth unlike anything he'd felt up to that point. It was the moment he felt most loved by her, even more than the day they got married.

"I hope you always feel that way," he'd said.

Now Aspen seems like less of an arbitrary choice and more of a message to Sam. A strange place they had never visited before the collapse, and a city with no connection to the life they had lived. Sam can almost understand her reasons for leaving his parents' house, but her crossing the crumbling country with their son now seems as much about getting away from him as finding a respite.

Sam believes Danny still loves him. They were separated just as Sam was reaching a place of hero and playmate in the eyes of his son. Almost every night found them on the couch, with Sam's legs resting on the coffee table. Danny would sit in his lap with his little legs tracing down Sam's. They'd both cross their legs at the ankles. Hours would go by reading a book, watching a movie or playing a game on their iPad.

The idea of an iPad makes Sam shake his head, bringing him back from the memory. The overgrown lawns around him are now all he can see. A crow breaks out of the rafters of a nearby house and circles him, squawking loudly. It banks back over the house again and returns just as emphatic. Sam turns the corner and moves down the next block, letting it protect the nest that must be hidden somewhere in the abandoned house.

Up ahead, Sam sees a simple brick church, a long rectangle with columns and a steeple like churches all over the country. The signboard out front has no message for the neighborhood, and it looks as empty and abandoned as the buildings around it. Sam wonders about the correct definition of "godforsaken" as he climbs the stairs of the church, but figures this town is probably close enough. He tries the door. It opens.

4

Inside the entryway, Sam shoves his dark goggles up into his hair as his eyes adjust to the dim light. The marbled floor is clean, and the walls are bare. Any decorations or iconography were either stolen or sold long ago. Stepping to the next set of doors, he pulls and finds they swing open easily. Now he's walking down the center aisle and noticing that even though the sanctuary is stark, it isn't dusty or unkempt. He reaches the front and climbs the stairs to the pulpit before it dawns on him he isn't alone.

"Can I help you?" comes a voice from behind him. Sam whirls around as his hand finds the Walther.

"Not in here!" says the voice, and Sam sees a woman standing at the base of the stairs. She's middle-aged and thick, with close-cropped hair peppered gray with age. She holds her hands to her sides, palms up in a mixture of holy gesture and surrender. "This is a house of God. I don't want gunfire or bloodshed in here."

Sam leaves his pistol holstered, but keeps his hand on the stock. He stares at the woman, looking for a trap.

"Is this your place?" he asks.

"This is God's place," she answers with a smile. "I just look after it while He's gone."

"Turn around," Sam orders, still thinking this is a set-up. "I need to know you aren't packing."

She complies, turning slowly and showing him the back of her beltline. Her Southwestern print shirt and high-waisted jeans look clean and well kept, and her leather-worked belt only holds a multitool in a custom case.

"How can I help you?" she asks in a kind tone.

"I thought this town was deserted," Sam says.

"It is," she says as she turns back to face him. "It's just me now."

"Are you the caretaker?"

"I'm the pastor," she smiles. "You can call me Eleanor, but don't call me Father."

"You're here by yourself?"

"This is the home the Lord made for me, and I have no family but Him."

Sam drops his hand from his pistol, shakes his head at her and sighs.

"What?" Eleanor asks.

"I've heard this story before," Sam grumbles.

Eleanor sits in the first pew and looks up at him.

"Well, you have the pulpit…. Enlighten me."

Sam looks over at the lectern, then walks down the stairs to face her.

"God is punishing us, right?" Sam starts. "He's giving us what we deserve, and the righteous will hide out during His judgment and prevail in the end."

She smiles. Then she nods at Sam as if he's made a decent point.

"I've heard that story too," Eleanor replies, and then stares at him for a long time, still and silent. Then she says, "This isn't God's punishment. We did this to ourselves. When anyone spends money they don't have, it'll get uncomfortable when the reckoning comes."

"So why'd you stay here if your flock's gone?" Sam asks.

"My flock?" she snorts.

"Your congregation, whatever."

"They left to try and survive. As they should. I couldn't care for them. And I hope the Lord blesses each and every one of them." She looks around the church. "This was my first church and I fought hard to get it, so I don't intend to leave it to the desert."

"But there's no one here."

"You're here."

"I'm not coming on Sunday," Sam smiles.

"That's fine. We're doing church right now."

"Right," Sam scoffs.

"Do you think there's only one way this gets done? Is God rigid and unable to find us where we are?"

Sam shakes his head and begins to walk away.

"What brought you in here today?" Eleanor asks.

"I thought it was empty," Sam says, but keeps moving.

"You want to meet God on your own terms," she says after him. "I can respect that. I'll give you the room."

She starts walking out. Sam hears her footfalls, stops and turns. She really is leaving.

"Wait," Sam says, apologetic. "I'm not trying to get you to leave. This is your place."

"No," Eleanor smiles. "It's God's, remember? I'm just the caretaker."

Touché. Sam smiles at that. "How are you surviving?"

"Providence. Blessing. Blind luck. Whatever you prefer." She points to a side door of the sanctuary. "Five years ago, we retrofitted the electrical system with solar to keep our costs down. Even connected an electric pump to an underground well on the property. It cut our costs as we'd hoped, but I also wound up as the only self-sufficient place in town when the systems collapsed. I took that pretty seriously, so I stayed."

Eleanor just looks at him. Patient and waiting.

"How long has it been since someone came by?" Sam asks.

"A while. Most people just go straight through. Folks used to come down I-15 a lot, but it's tapered off in the last year. They might check the main street for supplies, but they move on pretty quick." She watches him closely as she says, "I heard you pull into the neighborhood. And I saw your flashlight in the old Corwin place."

"I didn't know," Sam says, apologetic again.

"It's fine. They won't be back," she smiles. "They were generous people and would be glad to know it served a purpose. You plan to stay?"

"No!" Sam says, harsher than he meant. "I'm sorry. No offence. I've still got a long way to go — I just wanted to look around a bit."

"Where are you headed?"

Sam sighs, wondering if he should stop answering this question.

"That's fine," Eleanor says. "You don't have to tell me. Is there anything you need?"

"I can always use gas."

"Can't help you there, I'm afraid. Travelers scrounged our stations long ago. How 'bout food, you okay there?"

"Yeah. Some canned stuff, and I'm hunting too."

"Good for you. My cans ran out years ago…. Never thought I'd miss canned goods, but we all got spoiled, didn't we?"

"I guess so," Sam wavers, feeling awkward now. "I should go."

"God bless you on your journey," Eleanor says with genuine conviction. "Try not to shoot everyone you see," she adds with a smile.

Sam lifts a hand in a stoic wave and walks down the center aisle. He looks back only once to find Eleanor watching him leave.

Once outside, he starts for the house where he slept. He looks up to see how high the sun has climbed. It's almost midday, and far later than he intended to stay. He walks faster, past the squawking crow and the balcony house, to get back to the garage where he stored his ATV. The rest of the town remains quiet and still, but now it all feels suspect.

He throws open the big garage door and stands in silent relief to see the ATV still there and pointed down the driveway. Climbing on, he punches the start button, and it coughs and fires to life. Toeing the gearbox into first, he rolls out of the garage and to the end of the drive. He sits there for a moment as the engine idles beneath him.

Then he turns deeper into the neighborhood and follows the route he'd walked. Tearing down the block and around the corner, he roars up to the church. Bumping up onto the sidewalk, Sam steers around the back of the church and slowly rounds the building to see a small residence attached to the back of the sanctuary. The solar panels on the roof tell him he's in the right place.

Engine still running, Sam climbs off the ATV. He goes to his pack on the back bumper just as Eleanor steps out of her home.

"Everything okay?" she asks.

"Yeah," Sam says as he digs into his pack. "I just thought you might want these."

He pulls three cans of food from his pack: green beans, corn and a fruit cocktail he thought looked terrible in the picture. These three are half of his stash, but he holds them out to Eleanor and watches her stare at them.

"I can't take your food," she says, her eyes still fixed on the cans.

"I want you to have them," Sam says. "I've got more, and you said you were out."

She steps closer, like a timid animal. Sam holds the cans out farther, and she takes them.

"Thank you. But I can't bear the thought of you going hungry on my behalf. You sure you have enough?"

"I'll be in the forest by this evening, and I won't leave the Rockies for the rest of my trip. My hunting will get easier, and I'll be fine."

"You're headed for Aspen, aren't you?"

Sam just looks at her, trying to remember if he mentioned his destination.

"I'm guessing. You don't have to tell me," she smiles as she pulls the cans close.

"You're right," Sam concedes. "I guess there aren't a lot of other destinations in the Rockies these days, huh?"

"Do you have family in the city?"

"My wife and son."

Eleanor looks at him, studying his face, his clothes and his gear.

"They don't know you're coming, do they?"

"You didn't say you could read minds," Sam smirks.

"I've heard a lot of stories over the years, and walked with a lot of people. After a while, it's like they are sharing secrets even if they've got nothing to say."

Sam rounds his still-idling ATV and climbs aboard.

"God bless you. And keep your wits about you," Eleanor says.

"Thanks," Sam answers as he pulls his goggles down over his eyes.

"Wait," Eleanor says as she steps in front of the ATV. "I've heard of others who tried to get in there. Be careful, and don't use the main gate."

"Armed guards, like all the rest," Sam says flatly as he looks at her.

"Yes, but they also scan faces and files. Once they get a record of you, they've been known to shoot on sight."

"I've never heard of anyone doing that," Sam counters.

"Just Aspen," answers Eleanor. "They've made it one of the best and most exclusive shining cities by adding some extra layers."

Sam looks off into the distance, a wave of new thoughts and concerns filling his mind. Eleanor steps to the side so he can leave.

"Have you been there?" Sam asks, finally.

"No. But a family from here tried. When I saw them off, there were four of them. When they came back through bound for Tahoe, they were only three."

Sam looks at Eleanor. There are tears in her eyes from the memory. He nods slowly.

"Thank you, Eleanor."

"No need," she says, holding up the cans with a smile. "I'll pray you find your family."

"I'll take all the help I can get," Sam says as he toes the ATV into gear and pulls his feet onto the pegs.

Rolling into the throttle, Sam turns around and drives toward the street. He looks back over his shoulder, nods at Eleanor and then thunders away.

> *When you were little we used to talk to you about heaven and hell. Once you encountered death with bugs and animals, it wasn't long before you asked what happens after a person dies. Heaven and hell simplified things without overwhelming you, but it doesn't begin to answer the question.*
>
> *I'm supposed to help you learn this stuff, but the fact is I don't know either. The longer you live, the more people you'll find who believe they have the answer. The truth is, no one knows… not really.*

If someone died and came back to tell us all about it, they'd be the only person who could actually say. But short of Jesus Christ, I've never heard of anyone coming back. If he'd come back in the last fifty years or so, we'd have it all documented and categorized and people would have copies of the details. Unfortunately he was so long ago, it's hard to feel certain about it.

But there's something out there, Danny. Something or someone far bigger than us. Let's call it God, because I don't have another word for a force bigger than we are.

As bad as things are, I understand how easy it is to say there's no God, and we're all alone down here. But things do happen in life that don't make sense. You'll learn something, escape danger or find some luck so unexpected or coincidental that it'll feel impossible without someone outside of you helping you along. I think that's what people call a miracle.

It takes a lot of pride to believe there's nothing else going on. History is littered with people clinging to their answers until one day everything they held dear was shattered. You could say that applies to my believing in God. But I think it proves we don't know all the answers and never will.... Whoever does, that's God.

In the end, there's a freedom in not being the end-all-be-all of the universe. You don't have to make sense of everything that happens to you, and you don't have to commit yourself to one immovable way of thinking.

Be open. Be learning. Know what you believe

and prepare to have it challenged. If those beliefs need to change, then change them.

In my experience, people who talk like they have all the answers and never doubt their own beliefs… they can't be trusted.

The sun is low in the western sky when Sam puts down his legal pad. He's sitting just off the side of the road among the foothills and pines. Beside him, Interstate 70 stretches west and down toward the distant, high desert plains. Eleanor and her church are somewhere down there, and farther still, Gordon and the Mayor Michelle in Ely.

Sam wonders if Andy ever returned to Tonopah, and how happy his wife and son must have been to see him. He hopes they survive the winter, and this world. Sam knows he had no business telling Andy how to be a father, but he fears that's the closest thing to parenting he might ever get.

If Eleanor is right about the city of Aspen, then he has little chance of getting inside to find Ariel and Danny. Once inside, there's no telling what other rules might be in place to root out those who don't belong. Even with his remaining gold bars and the titanium bone, he can't pretend to be wealthy or establish a "shiny" lifestyle. There will be checks. There are bound to be ID cards. If he spends much time thinking about it, the odds overwhelm him.

Sam stands and returns to his ATV and gear. He zips the legal pad into his pack, climbs aboard and hits the ignition. The starter spins, but the engine doesn't catch. He rocks the ATV and feathers in gas. It spits, and spins further. Another harder shake and the ATV tries, almost catches, and then finally stumbles to life. Sam shakes his head in relief, glad to be able to coax it to run, but knowing his days of riding are numbered.

After a few more hours going east on the interstate, Sam pulls off the highway and up onto a rock outcrop among the pines. From here he can see the roadway in both directions. He sets up his camp amid a stand of trees and watches the last rays of daylight fade.

He's alone again, feeling like the only man in the country. No movement on the interstate. No sounds around him but the wind and the scuttling of unseen animals. In honor of Eleanor, he opens a can of spaghetti warmed over his small camp stove. As he closes down the stove for the night, he shakes the small amount of fuel left in the canister. He might have two more meals' worth of stove use before he'll be cooking whatever he catches on a spit above a campfire. And though he's only a few thousand feet above the valley, the night air has the first cool bite he's felt since leaving prison. Digging his jacket out of the bottom of his pack, Sam knows this trip will only get harder.

5

The next morning Sam finishes lashing his gear to the back of the ATV just as the first rays of long, yellow sunlight hit the valley floor to the east. He stands on a rise and watches the shadows shrink. Turning toward the ATV, he stops suddenly.

A few hundred feet away stands a large wolf. It looks at him, stone still and just as surprised as Sam to discover someone else on this cold, still morning. Sam moves slowly, keeping his eyes on the animal as he wraps his fingers around the Walther hanging against his leg. The big wolf sniffs the air, turning his head toward the ATV. Something in Sam's stuff must have lured it here.

Sam walks toward the ATV. The wolf watches him, his large head tracking the movement. It continues watching, ears perked, as Sam climbs aboard and hits the starter. When the engine coughs to life, the wolf turns and runs out of sight. Some distant part of Sam's brain wonders if he should have shot the animal for food, but most of him feels they are kindred spirits. They are both alone in this strange, brutal world.

He rolls back onto I-70, snapping up through the gears and blasting eastward into the rising sun. Miles pass as he rattles along. The pines change to scrub-brush as he descends again. Then a seemingly endless high desert with red rock mesas rolls past. No sign of civilization here. This area probably looks the same as when the country was thriving. An occasional sun-baked and peeling billboard is the only reminder the world has moved on.

Settling into a numb rhythm, Sam stays on the throttle and watches mile markers tick by. The road drifts and sweeps, following the contours of stark beauty. He loses track of his mile-marker count somewhere in the mid-seventies, so he pulls over. When he kills the engine, the silence accentuates the desolate and distant feel of this road.

Sam climbs off the ATV, feeling blood rush to tingling muscles as he walks the stiffness out of his knees and back. The rattle of the ATV lingers in his hands and wrists even though he's off the quad. For a moment, Sam feels bored and annoyed by the monotony of this morning's journey. But then he catches himself, thankful this stretch has allowed him the chance to focus on covering ground.

Returning to the ATV, Sam checks his gas cans and fills the tank. He suspects this stretch of I-70 tested people's resolve and gas supplies even before the crash. Now it seems like he's the only man alive. Sam looks in both directions to see the empty vanishing point of the road. He knows he should slow down and travel as slow as possible in top gear to preserve his fuel. He doesn't want to walk.

Today's the first day in a long time I haven't feared for my life. I haven't been shot at or even seen signs of anyone since yesterday. This trip to find you has been long, and for the first time it's been monotonous enough to let me think about our future.

I don't know if I'll find you in Aspen. And if I do, I don't know if that's a good thing for either one of us. You're a boy now, and not so little. I may be your father, but you've probably been fine without me. As much as I don't like it, the truth is I was a pretty marginal dad.

Before I went to prison, you were always the interruption I didn't want. Nothing seemed to get done fast enough with you around. You were always too loud. Too unpredictable. Your mom and I fought all the time about how to deal with you. I used to think you were easier to deal with when we were alone, but then I'd see your mom and what she could give you that I never could. I don't know if you felt much love from me. I feel like I only gave you frustration.

Since you hugged me that last time, years ago, I've had a lot of time to myself. I think I've replayed almost every moment we ever had. Sometimes I did it just to stay sane. I don't have a lot to be proud of, but I hope to have the chance to do better this time.

I don't know what I'm doing. This trip to find you might be proof. I've met people who seemed like bad fathers or weak leaders, and I've told myself I would know what to do in those situations.

The truth is I'm figuring this out every single day. I'd just like the chance to take some of your screw-ups away and pass on a few of the hard lessons I've learned, so you don't have to live them. Maybe that's wrong too. Maybe you can only learn by feeling the pain for yourself, and I'll always be the old guy standing in your way. That's how I felt about my father. I discounted him until after he died. Then I realized the things he'd done continued looking out for me after he was gone.

What if I can't find you? I'm chasing a note on a photograph and pretending I'm still your dad. You could take one look at me and decide I'm irrelevant. I'm not sure what I'd do then, cause I've put all I've got in this cross-country chase.

You've been my finish line. But the more I think about it, the more I realize that if I find you it will only be the very beginning of a really difficult march.

If I find you, I hope there's something beneficial in it. I hope I can be part of making you a better man.

***

Miles away in Aspen, a large brick house with lots of windows and a wrap-around porch sits, silent and perfect, in the sunlight. The manicured lawn matches the pristine feel of the homes on either side. In fact, this whole street is modern and well cared for. The absence of cars and the business signs in the yards are the only suggestions this isn't a normal neighborhood.

A few golf carts roll through the neighborhood, their electric motors whirring as they close in on the house. The women and men behind the wheels are all well kempt in a clean mix of suits, casual clothes and workout attire. If they were driving cars instead of carts, this would look like any afternoon before the collapse.

As the carts converge in front of the brick house, the front door opens and a tide of elementary school children streams out across the porch. They range in age, but all give off the same relief and excitement at school's end. Some of the kids start walking through the neighborhood, unaccompanied and content. Other children scan the carts and then hurry to their parents.

Ariel sits in a large three-bench cart among the crowd. She waves as Danny sees her, and then looks over her shoulder for traffic as he runs up and climbs in beside her.

"How was your day?" she asks, already pulling away.

"Fine," Danny says.

He looks taller and leaner than the photo Sam carries, and he waves at a few friends walking home as his mom wheels the cart through the streets. They both glance up as the sound of an aircraft rumbles overhead. Danny cranes his neck to watch it descending over the neighborhood, landing gear extended and flaps dropping.

"What is it?" Ariel asks with a smile.

"I think that's the new Gulfstream," Danny says with wonder. "Max said his Dad got one."

"I heard it's the biggest plane they can have at our airport," Ariel says.

"I bet a great pilot could land one even bigger!"

"You think so?"

"What about Mark's pilot?"

"You'll have to ask him," Ariel says as they pull up to a stoplight. The sun turns her chestnut hair into a golden cascade. Danny looks up at her with his big blue eyes, and his forehead crinkles in hard thought.

"I thought he was gone already," Danny says in a tone Ariel can't identify. She wonders if Danny wants Mark to be gone, or if he's sad Mark isn't around.

"Not until later, Danny," she says as flat as she can and watches Danny's response for a clue to how he feels. It seems like her son's feelings about Mark are the only thing she worries about anymore.

"We going to your office?" Danny asks as their light goes green and a group of golf carts and one large diesel truck take their turn through the intersection.

"Just for a little while."

"Oh-kay," Danny says, a bit deflated but close to fine with this idea.

***

In central Utah, a cold, sharp wind rushes through the high plains as the sun sets. Sam sits huddled against his ATV, using it as a wind block. He has his pack shoved under the ATV and balls himself up in every piece of clothing he owns. The wind shrieks around the panels of the ATV, coming in surges of cold.

Sam holds his legal pad and peels off one glove to better handle the pen. Keeping himself as shielded as possible, he scribbles quickly, trying to squeeze out the last available daylight and take his mind off the bitter wind.

> *I think a lot about your impression of me. Do you think of me at all, and if you do, are they good memories? When I left you were just getting to that place where boys think their dads are amazing. And then I went away. Did you fill*

that with someone else? Did your mom find someone else? Or do you look back on the guy you called Dada and wonder where he went?

If I get to see you again, I won't be able to completely relax. I'll be thrilled, I'm certain, but I'll start to really wonder about the years to come. Of course we'll go through some rough years, but I'd like to be a dad you can remember warmly. In spite of all the terrible things this world has become. And even with the hardships. I hope your childhood memories are good ones.

I look back on my early memories, and I can't describe my father as loving. I know he loved me. I know he was very concerned about my safety and growing me into a man. But I mainly remember him as a disciplinarian. He was a man of rules and planning, who had little patience for childish wanderings or going against the plan.

Once we were at a carnival…

Well, now I wonder if you know what a carnival is? In case you don't… There used to be fairs and carnivals that would travel the country. They'd bring rides in on big trucks and set them up on the edge of town. For a few nights a year you could pay a few dollars to ride the rides. Some of them were lame. Some of them I would do over and over until my money ran out.

But one ride they always had was bumper cars. And it's exactly what the name suggests – little electric cars you drive around and bump into other cars. I wanted to drive one, but I was too little to go by myself. I had to ride with my dad, and I remember being very excited by all the people I saw laughing and crashing into each other.

Yet when we boarded the ride my father told me, in clear unwavering terms, that we were not going to drive into anyone. And we were going to avoid the tangle of people in the middle. To make the most of the ride, we would drive along the outer edge and try not to hit anyone.

The problem was, I really wanted to crash into things. I wanted to be in the middle of the crowd, laughing and bumping along. Yet the whole ride we drove in circles.

My father was looking out for me on that ride, and he continued doing that for the rest of his life. He would always tell me the best strategy for every situation based on the information he had and his own experience and logic. And while he was right more often than I care to admit, he left little room for me to explore on my own.

I'd like to inspire you, and give you a sense of adventure. But I don't want to give you all the answers either. I don't know much. In many ways, I've lived a life of safe decisions, and it still didn't work out well for me. You'll need answers, and I'd like to help you find ones that work for you. My answers aren't worth much, but my screw-ups and failures might help you recognize a few pitfalls and give you a better life than I've had.

That's what I want… for you to have a better life than I have. I wonder if that's still possible in this country? For your sake, I hope so. And if you do... when you do... I hope you can look back and say I helped you get there.

I fear you'll hate me. Maybe you already do.

Sam stops writing. It's grown too dark to see the pages clearly. He shoves his pad back into his backpack and pulls out his sleeping bag. The wind tugs at it as he pulls it from the stuff sack. He can feel sand and dirt getting ripped free from the bag's crevices as he unzips it to the bottom and pulls it over himself.

The wind continues raging, wiping all clouds from the sky. Sam looks up and sees more stars than he's ever remembered. From horizon to horizon the stars salt the blackness above him in all directions. If he wasn't so miserable, he'd be in awe.

With his sleeping bag pulled high and tight, Sam tries to sleep.

6

The next morning Sam squints against the sunlight as it works its way down the ATV and into his eyes. He blocks it with a hand and sits up, just now realizing he slumped to the ground in the night. The ATV has little windblown piles of dirt by every tire, and Sam's sleeping bag sheds a fine film of silt when he moves. He can feel grit in his mouth, but the morning is warm and still.

He stands slowly, grabbing one of the ATV's grips and easing himself up. Pulling the deer rifle from its fender scabbard, Sam blows and wipes dust off the weapon and then uncaps the scope. In brisk sweeps, Sam stares back down the road behind him, looking for movement. Then he turns and looks eastbound, inspecting the red mounds and small mesas that frame the road. He almost misses the person watching him from a high roadside perch. Then he double-takes.

Through the scope, Sam spies a young man staring at him through one-sided binoculars. There's a worn shotgun on the rock beside him and a large threadbare pack lying haphazardly on the ground. He's too far away to damage Sam, and now he's been seen. So the boy lifts his hand, a half-wave and half-salute, in Sam's direction.

Sam lifts a hand in response. He knows he'll pass right by the young man when he starts east this morning. At the moment, being friendly doesn't do any harm, but Sam will feel a lot more comfortable once he's been passed.

Sam wastes no time, packing immediately and feeling the blown dirt getting bundled in with his gear as he lashes everything to the back of the ATV. He's unnerved by being watched, and the chance of getting away helps him pack in record time. Normally Sam would suck down a water bottle and drain his bladder in a slow wake-up routine. Right now he refuses to take the time for either.

Sam fights with the ATV and, after a few half-spins and coughs, the engine rumbles into a steady rhythm. He glances toward the young man constantly, and the boy stares back through his broken binoculars. Sam slams the ATV into gear and turns back toward the freeway. He pulls his deer rifle out of the holster, loads a round, and keeps it in one hand as he drives with the other.

The young man's lookout is across the freeway and up a slight red-dirt rise, with perfect views along the interstate. While the place doesn't look lived-in, the young man hunkers down in a way that tells Sam he's used this lookout before.

As the front tires of the ATV touch the concrete, Sam stops, braces himself and aims carefully.

"I don't know what you're hoping for!" Sam yells at the young man. "But I'm headed east, I'm alone, and I've got nothing for you."

"Bullshit!" the young man hollers back. "You've got a better rig than I've seen in months. Maybe years. Those gas cans alone are worth a fortune."

"They're almost empty."

"Still worth a lot."

"Throw down your shotgun," Sam commands.

"No way in hell," the young man sneers back.

Sam leans into his scope, staring down it and resting the cross hairs on the young man's chest. "I don't want your shotgun, I have my own."

"You're a greedy bastard," the young man smirks.

"I don't want to get shot in the back."

"I don't want to get shot at all, old timer."

"Old timer?" asks Sam, incredulous.

"I'm guessing you're about 50? No chance you're as fast as me."

Sam forces himself to not be offended. He knows he looks atrocious and his gaunt face and dense beard make him hard to identify, let alone to age. On the other hand, this kid may have just said it to get a rise of anger out of Sam, because with anger comes mistakes.

"You might be right. I'm probably too slow for you," Sam admits as he sees the young man smile. "But I don't need to be fast."

He shifts his aim to the young man's shotgun. It leans against the lookout rock, useless until Sam gets closer.

The stock of the shotgun explodes as Sam's bullet smashes the wood and knocks the weapon off its perch. The young man yelps in surprise and anger. Sam sees the gun fall out of sight and hopes he's done enough for a clean getaway.

Sam floors the throttle and turns eastbound on the freeway. He sees the young man scrambling down the outcropping with a pistol in his hand and a look of pure rage. The kid is quick, knowing exactly where to put his feet and hands for a quick descent. He's getting to the freeway just as Sam passes. Hunkering over the handle bars, Sam slams the ATV into a higher gear and keeps the throttle pegged.

The boy fires his clip dry, sending eight rounds in Sam's direction. Five miss completely. One imbeds itself in one of the reserve tanks, creating a slow leak. Another shatters the only remaining tail light on the back of the beat-up vehicle. The last of the young man's shots hits Sam in the back of his right shoulder, almost missing him completely, but skimming across his deltoid and blasting a puff of blood spray.

The young man yells in triumph, seeing Sam recoil from the bullet strike. But his excitement fades as the ATV continues racing down the road, picking up speed and getting away.

Sam keeps the ATV at full throttle for a long time. The red mesas and rock outcrops change to long stretches of desert with low scrub and peaks in the distance. He feels the blood from his shoulder draining down his back and staining his shirt. The aching pain from the bullet keeps him angry and alert. Nearly two hours later, he finally pulls over and almost collapses from exhaustion. He sits at the base of a faded road sign showing less than sixty miles to Grand Junction, Colorado. The day is hot and the land offers no trees or cover. Sam knows he'll have to push on to Grand Junction today, and the thought of actually reaching Colorado feels surreal.

The pain and tension from the morning nearly overwhelm him, but

Sam's long-forgotten bladder will no longer be ignored. After what seems like the longest piss of his life, he rummages in his backpack for the breakfast he wanted to have when he awoke covered in dust. As he chews some jerky, he wonders if the young man's shotgun still works and if the kid used up all his bullets firing at Sam. He pulls broken shards of plastic from the shattered tail lamp and tosses them into the dirt. Then he notices the thin line of leaking gasoline down the back fender.

Lifting the bullet-scarred can, Sam empties what's left into the ATV's tank and then straps the empty can to the fender again. He rolls his shoulder, feeling soreness set in and looking around for a stream or pond to clean the wound. There's no water in sight, and he only has one full bottle. Normally Sam would have filled his bottles first thing in the morning, but this morning's encounter disrupted everything he now calls normal.

He pulls his last reserve can off the ATV's fender and uses half of it to fill the tank. While he should have plenty to get to Grand Junction, there's no way of knowing what he'll find there. Climbing aboard the ATV again, Sam hits the starter.

Nothing.

Panic begins to creep into Sam. He hits the starter again, and it stays silent. Climbing off the seat, Sam peels it back to reveal the battery. Powdery green corrosion flecks both terminals, but they look mostly metallic and clean. Sam wiggles both cables. He's not a mechanic. Setting the seat on the ground, he has the idea to trace the positive terminal deeper into the ATV. Walking his fingers down the cables, he finds a worn chunk missing from the positive wire. He doesn't know if this is the result of the gunfight or something else, but he wonders how he got this far. Using the only idea he has, Sam tugs and adjusts the battery wires as he hits the starter.

The starter tries, but can't move fast enough — the current is still too low. Sam kicks the ATV but only succeeds in hurting his foot. Breathing heavily and fighting off tears of frustration, Sam doubles over on the side of the road. He tries to calm himself and find a solution. All he hears is the sloshing of gas in the ATV's tank.

Standing suddenly, Sam stares back down the freeway to a distant overpass. He'd gone under it just before stopping, but now it seems very far away. With a sigh, Sam clunks the ATV into neutral and begins pushing it back toward the overpass. The process is slow, with the ATV too heavy to easily push from the side, but too prone to drift off the concrete when pushed from behind. With a painful patience, Sam slowly reaches the deserted on-ramp of the freeway and stares up the hill to the overpass.

Aiming the ATV's steering uphill, Sam goes to the back of the vehicle and squats down. He settles his back into the rear bumper of the ATV and feels his shoulder explode with fresh blood and pain. Gritting his teeth, Sam shoves the ATV and keeps pushing his legs away as he tries to force the heavy ATV up the on-ramp.

The movement is so slow that Sam thinks of Sisyphus from Greek mythology, eternally pushing a rock uphill. Sam can't decide if it's stranger to relate to the story or to have remembered Sisyphus in the first place. For a few moments, this personal question keeps Sam from noticing the long, painful push uphill.

Sweating through his clothes, Sam stops. He's halfway up the long and sloping rise and decides this is as high as he'll go. With careful movements, he rounds the ATV and squeezes the brake. Then, with a strain, he forces the ATV into a multi-point turn until the vehicle faces downhill.

Climbing aboard, Sam holds the brake and the clutch and clicks the transmission into second gear. With one last look around, Sam releases the brake and feels the ATV ease into a slow roll. The knobby tires rattle as they pick up speed. Sam tries to be patient, reminding himself how much he doesn't want to try this again. When he is nearly to the flat expanse of the freeway, Sam releases the clutch and hangs on tight.

The ATV bucks and kicks as the transmission crashes together. The force nearly tosses Sam off, but the engine spits with the sudden turn and Sam pushes the throttle to help it along. With a cough and a backfire, the engine comes to life and settles into an off-kilter hum. Sam grins, having somehow remembered how to try this without ever doing it before. He wonders where he learned the idea to kick-start an engine. Part of him wants to believe he learned it on his own, but he suspects it's just another life skill taught by his father while Sam was trying to ignore him.

I don't know when I stopped listening to my father. I'm sure it was a gradual process, but I don't remember if there was a reason or catalyst that began our separation.

I don't remember playing with my father either. I have memories of us shooting hoops or sharing a hobby, but those times feel more like teamwork than real friendship. I know most little boys idolize their father, so I guess I must have, though I can't imagine or remember doing it.

What do you remember?

Sometimes I wonder what I would've done if I'd found you and your mom with my parents. What if I had to bury all of you? There wouldn't have been much point in going on, and I doubt I would have lived long anyway. This trip has focused me in a way I needed, and taught me some hard lessons along the way.

I'd like to think chasing you has helped me acclimate to what this world is now. And it's given me a lot of time to think about you. And your mom. I'm afraid I'm dreaming of too many wonderful things. My brain imagines sunny reunions with hugs and laughter, but a growing part of me knows it'll be a miracle if I even see you from across the street.

Looking for you has given me purpose, and hope. If you're ever looking for me, I pray something or someone comes along to give you what you need to survive.

I miss you.

Sam sits on the side of the road, letting his pen hover over the page. He looks up to see the cluster of buildings in the distance standing sentinel on either side of the highway. His deer rifle lies across his lap, and Sam raises it again to peer through the scope.

The closest houses look forgotten and run-down, but farther in Sam can see people moving. To his surprise there aren't any visible walls. After a time of staring, Sam notices the whole city is ringed by a chain-link fence topped with razor wire.

From this distance, Grand Junction reminds him of prison.

Sam holsters the rifle on the fender and takes one last look at the page. Closing the notepad, he shoves it into the top of his pack.

He climbs on and releases the brake, letting the slight hill roll him forward. With a jolt, he kick-starts the ATV for the second time. Sam wonders how long the internal structures will survive his new ignition procedure.

With a burbling pop from the engine, Sam speeds toward Grand Junction.

He approaches the edge of town, backlit by the late-day sun and moving fast. He watches closely, looking for guards and expecting the escort he received in Ely. The distant gate never opens, and the edge of town doesn't seem to respond to his approach.

Sam passes the first few houses and run-down businesses on the edge of town. They are crumbling as the weather and plant life steadily reclaim them. He continues on, leaving his weapons holstered and marveling at how much of the town seems abandoned and left to the elements.

Up ahead the freeway splits to allow a business route through town or an express route for interstate travel around the city. Sam can see the only option is the business route, as the express route has been blocked with shattered concrete and spikes made from signposts and metal shards. He barely slows down as he passes, staring in wary confusion at the blocked freeway, but continuing on to town. He needs supplies no matter what.

As the abandoned buildings grow more dense around him, Sam realizes this is the largest city he's been through on his journey. Suddenly he knows the multistory buildings he's passing could easily be used as lookouts. While he doesn't have the escort of Ely, there's no question he's being watched. Undaunted, he continues on, moving fast and fighting his desire to draw a weapon. Anyone watching would have the advantage, so he decides to not look like a threat.

The fence comes into clear view now, with a tall well-made double gate built across the road. Both gates are at least twelve feet high, with razor-wire tops, and wheel-mounted for easy movement. A guard station stands between the two entrance gates. The fencing on either side is two stories tall and still razor-wired. It's an elaborate set-up.

Letting the ATV slow, Sam rolls up to the first closed gate and stops. He sits looking at the guard station as the engine idles. He stares for nearly a minute before a man steps out of the guard station with AR15 rifle over his shoulder and black nondescript fatigues. The man walks straight up to the gate as if he's seen a dozen people like Sam today and has become bored.

"Here to see Curtis?" the guard asks.

"No. Who's Curtis?" Sam answers.

This changes the look in the guard's eyes.

"You can't trade without a license."

Sam sits back on the ATV, letting it idle. He looks at the guard and then his gear.

"I'm sorry," Sam begins slowly. "I don't know who you think I am, but I have no idea what you're talking about."

The guard sighs. He looks annoyed and bored again.

"You need supplies. Probably gas. And you're willing to pay with something you found or killed for." Then he looks at the rest of Sam's rig with a palpable disdain. "But you can't trade here without a license, and the licenses come from Curtis."

"Ah," Sam says, acting like he understands but sensing he's barely scratched the surface of this place. "So I guess I do need to see Curtis."

"Well, you'll have to wait 'til business hours tomorrow."

"You're kidding."

"No, sir."

"Can I come in and spend the night?"

"You'd have to pay for it."

The guard looks at him and slowly crosses his arms.

"Let me guess… I can't pay for it unless I have a trade license."

The guard almost smiles. Then he gives a curt nod.

"Look," Sam says, trying to be disarming. "If I shut this thing off, I don't think I'll get it started again."

"Don't care."

"Can I come inside this first gate and shut it down?"

The guard gives one minimal head-shake.

"So where do you recommend?"

"Until you pass this gate, you're not my problem. And you're not coming in."

The guard turns and wanders back toward his station. Sam sits for another long moment with the engine idling. He thinks about the alternate route he saw blocked, forcing everyone to this gate and some variation of this conversation. He knows turning off the ATV means it won't start again, and there aren't any hills nearby. Even if it started, he doesn't have enough fuel to get to Aspen.

Tired and frustrated by his lack of options, he decides to make himself hard to ignore. Sam kills the engine, letting the ATV fall silent there in the middle of the road in front of the outer gate. He climbs off, letting his hand rest comfortably on the Walther as he rounds the ATV to pull off his backpack. Then stepping to the front of the vehicle, Sam looks at the guardhouse, pulls out his sleeping bag and builds his makeshift camp right there on the concrete.

The guard never emerges as Sam uses the last of his water and cooking fuel. The night spotlights turn on around the entrance, shining into the area between the two gates and right outside the guardhouse, reminding Sam he's just outside. As he finishes his meager meal, Sam pulls his sleeping bag up around him and leans against the front brush bar of the ATV. He never pulls out his pad to write. He watches the guardhouse. He suspects he's being watched, and he wonders about the procedures and technology inside.

After so many miles of lawlessness, Sam is encouraged by the idea of order and rules. And yet, something about this place gives off a military coldness. He wonders if coming here will be a mistake.

Part 4

Grand Junction

1

A horn blast shocks Sam awake. He looks up, groggy, to see a huge truck towering over him. The diesel engine clatters as the truck pulls halfway through the outer gate of the city. Sam's little camp and ATV block the way, and for a second he feels intimidated.

Sam recovers as he stares up at the truck. He stands and lets his sleeping bag fall away while he drops his hand to the holstered Walther on his hip. Then he rounds the front of the truck and comes face to face with another guard.

"What the hell are you doing?" the guard barks. He's older and more seasoned than the one the night before.

"I'm waiting to see Curtis," Sam says without apology.

"You're in the middle of the road!"

"Yes. I asked to move inside and out of the way last night, but was told I wasn't anyone's problem."

"This morning you're a problem."

"Can I come in now?"

"Move your rig."

"I can't. It won't restart."

"Don't give me that bullshit."

"No bullshit. As I explained last night, once I turned it off it was done. That's why I tried to get inside." Sam works to hold in a smile. He's actually enjoying this: holding others hostage by their own procedures.

"Push it out of the way," the guard growls. It's clear he is clinging to his professionalism.

"Where can I find Curtis?"

"It's too early for Curtis."

"Then I'll just wait with my gear until he's up and available."

"Move. Your. Shit!" the guard snarls, spitting out each word.

Sam looks around. There are two guys in the cab watching him. Another guard leans out of the guardhouse. Curtains are pulled back on a few buildings on the street beyond. Lots of witnesses to this exchange, and Sam knows he's reached a breaking point.

Walking slowly, Sam goes back to his ATV. He gathers up his sleeping bag, taking his time, and stuffs it into the stuff sack. After refilling his pack, he walks it back to the rear frame and lashes it on. Then he kicks the ATV into neutral and pushes it away from the truck and toward the open gate.

"That's enough," the guard warns as he raises a hand.

Sam waits. The truck pulls away and the large outer gate is pulled closed again. Once the chains are relocked, Sam pushes his ATV back into the middle of the road.

The guard glares at him. Sam offers him the nicest smile he can muster and says, "Let me know when I can come in and get out of your way."

The guard shakes his head and goes back to the guard station. In the harsh morning light Sam can see him talking on a radio. He hopes the man isn't getting orders to shoot him and call it a morning.

The truck lumbers away, then turns down a side street headed north. He hears something that sounds like a muffled scream from far away. He watches the truck go, trying to hear the sound again and unable to see inside. Now there's just the sound of the diesel engine. He wonders where the truck is going.

About an hour later, Sam sees the inner gate slide open. A handful of men walk straight toward him without looking at the guardhouse. The outer gate stays closed as the lead man, sharp-featured and gaunt, steps close to the chain link.

"Morning," Sam says, sitting on his ATV.

"It is morning," the man responds as he stares at Sam, scanning him slowly and taking in details with his dark green eyes. Sam feels as if this man's gaze has actual weight, and it makes him uneasy.

"Here I am," the man says with no emotion. "You wanted to see me."

This is Curtis. Sam jumps off the ATV and his hand goes to the Walther on instinct. The men around him all bristle and raise weapons at Sam's movement. Curtis doesn't even look at them; he just raises a hand, and they all pause.

Sam and Curtis look at each other in silence. Sam wills his hand away from his pistol and takes a step toward the fence.

"You're Curtis," Sam says, knowing the answer already. Curtis gives a nod so small it's barely perceptible.

"And you're Samuel Kerr. A few months out of prison with your debt behind you."

"You scanned me," Sam breathes. He feels violated but also idiotic for not realizing this before.

"What can I do for you, Mr. Kerr?"

"I need gas. Some supplies. And I can pay."

"Common requests. But rare commodities."

"You're not going to let me in, are you? Cause I'm a debtor."

Curtis takes off his thin outer coat, handing it back to one of his men. He keeps his eyes locked on Sam. Then he smirks and slides his left sleeve up to his deltoid. Sam sees the messy bulbous scar that shows Curtis once dug a chip out of his shoulder. He was either a prisoner or in the military.

"We all have a past," Curtis says, giving away nothing. "Our concern is that travelers like yourself are often… reluctant… to integrate into our city."

"Reminds me of prison," Sam says as he looks back and forth down the high fencing.

"If you don't like this, you should see the Shining Cities."

"I have."

This response seems to strike Curtis, and he tilts his head as if letting the words drip their way into his brain.

"Have you?"

"If you read my file, then you know I'm telling the truth. So, I still need fuel, supplies and probably a mechanic to get this thing running again."

Sam turns to look at his ATV. When he turns back, two of Curtis's men are aiming guns at Sam.

"You were asked to leave," one of the men rumbles.

"I was told there are procedures to follow. I'm fine with that. But if you've closed the gates to anyone new, then no one bothered to tell me."

The bodyguard goes silent and looks to Curtis.

"You're an intriguing one," Curtis says as he looks Sam up and down, studying the caked dirt and disheveled gear. He leans toward the fence and sniffs the air. "But you're not coming in here like that."

Sam looks down at himself. He's never been this dirty in his life.

"I'd welcome a shower," Sam admits. "Tell me what I need to do to get some help."

They look at each other. Sam doesn't back down. Curtis' smile grows.

"You do exactly what these gentlemen say. Follow our entry procedures. Then you and I can have a conversation. Those are the rules." Curtis almost whispers, "Yes. Just like prison."

Sam looks back at his gear. He really has no choice. Grabbing his backpack, Sam stands at near-attention and looks at Curtis. With no idea what to expect, he's as ready as possible.

He nods at Curtis. A moment passes. Sam begins to wonder if the nod was noticed.

"Prep him. One hour," Curtis finally says, and in an instant everyone is in motion.

Curtis turns from the gate, takes back his long coat and pulls it on as he walks away. Sam keeps his eyes on the man, but he never looks back. The chain-link outer gate opens, and two of the bodyguards step out. They dwarf Sam: one a blond farm-boy bouncer and the other a bald, muscular Black athlete, both tense.

"We will do an inventory of all your belongings," Blondie states with no inflection. "Once every item is cataloged, you will be allowed to keep anything that isn't deemed a threat to the public welfare."

"What?" Sam begins, but Blondie continues.

"Any disputed items will be held until approval by authorized personnel."

"Who's authorized?" Sam asks.

"Do you understand these regulations."

"What. Yes. No… I have questions."

"Exemptions to the standard entry procedure require official declaration and private approval," Baldy states with a monotone, robotic precision. "Do you wish to file an exemption and await the result?"

Sam looks between the two towering men. Then he looks past the inner gate.

"I get everything back?"

"Anything that isn't a public threat," Blondie responds.

"So, no guns?"

"Each citizen is allowed one firearm at all times," Baldy chimes in. "No citizen is allowed more than two without special authorization."

"Yeah. Okay. I get it," Sam resigns himself.

Baldy grabs Sam's arm. His fingers find nerve endings in the soft flesh of his armpit. Pain explodes in Sam's side. He tries to protest but only hollers a string of screeching noises.

With the pain distracting Sam, Baldy easily guides him where he needs to go. They push forward as the inner gate opens. Walking through, they turn to a nearby run-down building, fronted with a blank brick wall set between two fire hydrants. They shove Sam toward the wall, and the pain briefly subsides. Sam turns to see Baldy staring back at him.

"Strip down," Baldy barks. "Put each piece of clothing on a separate hook."

Sam looks back, blank.

"Where did I lose you?" Baldy almost smiles. "Take off your clothes and put them on the hooks to be hosed and screened."

Sam looks at his Walther pistol, still strapped to his hip. He stares at Baldy.

"Take that off and hook it by the belt. I'll keep it dry."

Sam sees the large hose lying near Baldy's feet, growing tight with water.

Wondering if he should have avoided Grand Junction all together, Sam removes the gun belt. He sees the line of spring-loaded clips fastened to the brick wall. Tentatively, he hangs the gun belt. Then he clips his shirt and, with a shower of dust and rocks, peels off his worn-out boots. His tattered socks are clipped beside his shirt, and another for his pants.

In the corner of his eye, Sam can see the blond guard pushing Sam's ATV inside the gates and along a nearby wall. Two people with clipboards step out of the guardhouse and move toward Sam's gear. The tiny hut seems to always have an abundance of people inside. It strikes Sam that the guardhouse must have a tunnel leading deeper into the city. Anyone watching would have trouble identifying this town's actions or the scale of its security forces. And anyone who's needed seems to suddenly appear from the guardhouse.

A blast of water brings Sam back to focus on Baldy. The big guy wields the firehose as the high-pressure water tries to push Sam into the wall and tear off his tattered boxers. He braces himself, the pressure and cold turning his breathing into desperate gasps.

Then Sam gets a sudden respite as the stream leaves him, and Baldy blasts his way down the line of hanging clothes. Sam tenses, watching new tears form in his clothes as the water forces out the weeks of dirt and wear. To his surprise, Baldy avoids the hanging Walther altogether and turns the hose back down the line toward Sam.

Another cold shaft of water pushes Sam like a hand against his chest. Baldy takes one hand off the hose as if it were a thimble stream and motions for Sam to turn around. He does, and the water slams his back and legs. Rivulets of red-brown water drain to the ground around him, and it feels like he's losing a whole layer of skin.

The water stops as abruptly as it began, and Sam braces himself against the wall, weakened. He watches the clipboard-bearers peeling everything off the ATV and lining it up in a long string of individual items. Every pocket and fold of his pack gets disgorged. One person sets his things out, while the other scribbles on the clipboard.

With his boxers still dripping and his whole world now lying on the street, Sam watches one of the clipboard-bearers heading his way. A thick sturdy woman, she pokes at each of Sam's scraps of clothing and writes fast. She never looks at him until she gets to the Walther. Tucking the clipboard under her arm, she draws the weapon, expels the magazine, checks the action and reassembles it with a quick assessing glance. Her eyes then drift to Sam, seeming to quantify him based on his belongings and his weapon.

Sam sees the other assessor reach his legal pad. The slight man picks it up and begins flipping through the pages.

"Please don't," Sam starts, before Baldy and both assessors snap their heads in his direction. He goes silent as Baldy steps close.

"You agreed to this assessment as a part of our entry procedure."

"I know, but that's a very important—"

"Doesn't matter," Baldy interrupts. "Keep your mouth shut unless they have a question. It'll go faster that way."

Sam sees the assessor put the legal pad back down on the ground among his line of things. As he moves to the next item, Sam relaxes.

Sam looks at his clothes, pulling them from the hooks to find them in damp shreds. A fleece shirt and a pair of nylon pants lie in the distant row of his belongings, but look almost as bad as the ones in his hands.

Just as Sam starts to put his tattered pants back on, Baldy steps up next to him.

"Here," he says, almost kind. Baldy thrusts a folded set of blue coveralls and a pair of socks toward Sam. "Standard temps. You will have to buy them or return them after your meeting."

Surprised and suspicious, Sam takes them. For a moment he considers taking off his damp and worn boxers, but he can't bear the extra level of exposure. He steps into the coveralls and zips up the front. They fit terribly and bring back memories of prison.

"This way," Baldy motions.

Sam turns to get his Walther down from the hook.

"No weapons with Curtis," Baldy barks.

Sam pulls the holster close and looks hard at the bald man. "You said every resident could carry one."

Baldy looks back, blank at first and then with the flicker of a smile: "You were listening."

"You can wear it to the office," Baldy says as he starts walking off. "But you'll have to give it up when you're inside."

Sam doesn't speak, but pulls the holster around his waist and fastens it quickly. He can feel his damp boxers being squished into his coveralls. With a final glance at the people cataloging his gear, Sam grabs the fresh socks and his hosed-off boots. Baldy continues to walk away, and Sam runs after him barefoot.

2

The bald guard walks fast, making no attempt to slow down for Sam. With his boots in one hand and socks in the other, Sam grits his teeth and keeps moving along the concrete. At one point he steps on a pebble, and pain shoots up from the arch of his foot. He hops for two excruciating steps before dropping back into cadence. They've gone a few blocks already, and the city begins to look alive.

As Sam shuffles past a few residents, they glance up with a knowing look. He realizes this trial is somehow a common thing and wonders how many people have done this same barefooted chase behind a guard. They walk right down the middle of a main street, with pedestrians making up the only traffic.

Sam has almost caught up to Baldy as the man steps into the run-down remains of an old car lot. The used offerings still sit as if ready to be sold, but most wear a thick layer of dirt. In front of the empty office building, Baldy walks up to a waiting Prius.

"In the back," Baldy barks as he drops into the driver's seat.

Sam hurries to climb in, dropping his stuff on the seat beside him and glad to be off his aching feet. The Prius is already moving, rolling under electric power and giving off a slight whine. Looking around, Sam realizes this is the first car he's been in since getting out of prison. For years, he'd only been in CNG buses moving debtors between worksites and prison camps. He tries to remember the last private car he was in and concludes it was probably the run-down Honda he had before the collapse. The memory feels decades old.

As they drive down the main road, pedestrians slip out of the way as if on instinct. A few people look at the car, but most ignore its passing as mundane. Sam wonders how much gasoline this town has stockpiled and if they have a solar plant to keep things running. Pulling on his socks, he sees Baldy turn off the main road and into a college campus. Though a small school, it still has unmistakable matching brick buildings and lawns neatly manicured around well spaced trees. Sam ties his boots as he watches people walking the clean sidewalks with no sense of how out of place this campus is in this broken world.

Baldy turns into a small parking lot and pulls into a space beside a golf cart and a large swooping Tesla Model S sedan. Sam climbs out, following Baldy's lead, and looks at the Tesla in amazement. Who in this town could drive a car like that, and how would they keep it charged and running well?

"Don't touch the car," Baldy says, and Sam realizes he's standing there staring.

"Does it work?" he asks, marveling.

"Of course it works. No point in having it otherwise."

The big guard turns and starts along a sidewalk. Sam follows as they move among the other people criss-crossing the campus. He looks around for any indicators of what buildings were called or the name of this school, but notices all the signage has been removed or changed. Up ahead stands an imposing building with a large glass corner entrance. It reads "City Hall" above the doors, but Sam is certain it used to be something else.

Once inside, they stand in a large lobby with worn couches in clean surroundings. People of all ages and types wander around, talking quietly, while others slump in boredom. It seems like the worst waiting room in the world.

"Have a seat," Baldy says.

"Where's Curtis?" Sam asks.

"Everyone here's waiting to see Curtis."

Sam looks around the room. He's horrified.

"Most of them won't get to," Baldy says with a whispered smirk. He watches Sam to make sure he sits, and then turns and climbs a large central staircase.

Sam thinks of all his personal belongings laid out inside the fence a mile away. He can feel his damp boxers seeping through the borrowed coveralls. He has his Walther, but everything else may be gone forever.

This feels like a huge mistake.

People glance at him, trying to not be noticed, but Sam sees them. He realizes he's the only person in the room with a weapon. Shifting the Walther more into his lap, he keeps his hand on the pistol and watches people struggle to not look at him. The awkwardness makes Sam smile. It feels timeless.

Then the thought of his situation returns, and he stands. All the other strolling people suddenly make sense as Sam begins walking around the lobby in an anxious amble. He forces himself to make note of each person, remembering traits and even thinking up names for them.

"Mr. Flytrap" leans against a pole, his eyes unfocused, and then springs into action with arms waving at some unseen swarm of insects.

"The Call Girl" sits near a window, folded over a chair with limbs sprawled wide. She's gangly but athletically built, and locks eyes with every person that comes near. Each time Sam circles the room, she stares at him and smirks. There's an untamed sexuality to her, and the sense she'll use it as a weapon.

Sam decides the only person in the room that truly disturbs him is the man sitting completely still and alone in a dark corner formed by the upper landing. Only his eyes move, and he seems to be assessing everything with a near-robotic precision. On his third circuit of the waiting room, Sam names him "the Assassin," and hopes he'll never see him again.

"Thank you for coming," a curt female voice says from the top of the stairs. Sam rounds the room and looks up to see a well dressed brunette turn away from a man in his sixties as he slowly descends.

No one approaches the man or even acknowledges him as he reaches the lobby. Sam walks over anyway.

"Did you meet with Curtis?" Sam asks.

The old man looks startled that anyone is speaking to him.

"I. Uh. Only at the end. He's very busy." The man starts to move past

Sam.

"How long did you wait?"

The man stops and looks at Sam. Other people are watching and listening now.

"Dunno. Few hours, I guess." He looks around the room, almost apologetic at those still waiting. "There was some sort of ruckus at the main gate."

Sam knows his arrival and insistence to see Curtis at the gate was the "ruckus" that pulled the leader away, but he sees no sign the old guy puts this together. Sam looks up at the stairs to see no one on the landing. The old guy shuffles out the door. Sam feels eyes on him and looks around to see both the Call Girl and the Assassin staring back at him. Others look away, but their eyes remain.

"Samuel Kerr," says the curt woman. She's appeared at the top of the stairs without Sam noticing.

He looks up at her. She looks as impatient as any overworked secretary he's ever seen. With a tentative glance toward all the others waiting, Sam steps over to the stairs.

"Yes. You are keeping everyone else waiting," she says, reading his mind.

He climbs the stairs sheepishly. The curt woman waits at the top. Once he reaches her, Sam can see she's in her early fifties and thick from early menopause. Her business suit is so nondescript it succeeds at being timeless. She begins walking away the second Sam steps onto the landing, and he falls in behind her.

They walk down a long corridor with rooms on both sides. The whole floor is very clean and well lit by high skylights. Sam can't help but look through the open doorways as they pass.

A quick glance through the first door shows three people debating while surrounded by walls of whiteboards covered in lists and calendars. They are animated, with their voices hushed in conspiracy.

It suggests planning at a level Sam didn't know still existed.

The next open room has a series of couches and a small kitchenette, suggesting a break room or green room. As he passes, Sam can see a lot of young women inside, sharing stories and mugs of something. He can't tell how many there are, but they watch him pass with the same look the Call Girl gave him downstairs.

The short hallway ends at a large desk that intrudes into the T-junction of the hallway.

"Samuel Kerr," the curt woman announces to the guy behind the desk. The desk guard reaches under the desk and looks back blankly.

Just as Sam approaches the desk, two large men appear on his left. One of them is Baldy from the gate. Sam smiles at him, then takes it back.

"Your Walther goes there," Baldy says, pointing to a large gray plastic tub sitting in the left hallway. "We proceed when that's been done."

Sam steps toward them and they part to let him approach the tub. Both men tense and fall in behind, ready to tackle him if he makes a wrong move. Sam doesn't notice because the contents of the tub then come into view. His belongings are at the bottom.

Some things in the tub are still dripping wet, but he recognizes his pack, sleeping bag and clothes. He unfastens his Walther slowly, drawing out the movement so he can keep looking into the tub and do a quick inventory. There's no sign of his notepad, the rifle or the shotgun. The gold is nowhere in sight. Sam wants to dig through everything in the tub but can feel the guards' eyes on him.

"Nice and slow," Baldy says over Sam's shoulder. Sam lowers the Walther, still in its holster, and places it on top of the pile.

"Where's the rest of my stuff?" Sam asks as he turns back to the men.

"Any questions will have to wait for Curtis," the other guard says before Baldy can respond.

Frustrated now, Sam motions for them to get on with whatever is next. Baldy smirks and starts down the hallway. Sam follows close, with the other guard walking behind him. Baldy stops at the large double doors near the end. He knocks twice in quick succession and then motions for Sam to enter.

Sam looks at Baldy and the open door. He inhales slowly, then sighs it out and steps inside.

The office is large, and Sam guesses it was once a conference room. Built in shelves along one wall probably once housed a boxed set of something, but are now crammed and double-stacked with every kind of book imaginable. Tall free standing bookcases have been brought in to line the other walls and stand in the open space. Sam can't help but marvel at the range of titles catching his eye.

"See something you like?" Curtis calls from across the room.

Sam looks down the central aisle between the rows of bookcases and sees Curtis sitting behind an enormous desk. He's very upright, with his arms extended and hands gripping the edge of the wooden surface. There's a stack of things on the blotter in front of Curtis: Sam's gold bricks and his legal pad.

Curtis' eyes never leave Sam. He's watching for a reaction.

Sam peels his eyes from the desk and looks at the bookshelves again.

"I didn't know anyone had this many books anymore," Sam says.

"We keep every one we find," Curtis says. "There's a Julia Child cookbook somewhere, in case we stumble upon some lobster."

"It's a library?" Sam asks.

"You can't check anything out. It all stays here. Have a question, and we probably have the answer. It's our version of the internet."

Sam smiles and shakes his head, remembering the power of looking up any inane question on his phone. This room seems archaic by comparison, but he recognizes the power here.

"So all the people downstairs really are here with questions." Sam turns to Curtis, "And you literally have all the answers."

Curtis continues to stare as Sam steps toward the desk. Two chairs face the leader, and Sam stops between them.

"I'm more interested in people's questions," Curtis says as he drops his eyes from Sam to look at the items on his desk. Slowly, he brings his eyes back up to Sam. "And their stories."

Curtis motions toward a chair. Sam sits.

"You wanted to see me," Curtis says.

"I was told I had to," Sam replies.

"I make the point to meet every newcomer. You're the first one in more than six months."

"I've seen people in the last few days."

"Oh, I know they're out there. They just don't want to come in here."

"If I knew you were going to take all my things I would have thought twice."

"You said your ATV was broken and out of fuel."

"It is. And I can pay to get it rolling again."

Curtis leans back for the first time since Sam arrived. He rocks back in his chair, looking at the gold bars and then at Sam.

"Let's talk about that."

Curtis looks him over. Sam is very thin, with a scruffy unkempt beard and dirt still lingering in the creases around his eyes. There's a tension to Sam, like his body is wound tight and ready to retaliate.

"Where'd you steal the gold?" he asks.

"I didn't steal it," Sam replies.

"Nobody's got gold anymore. There haven't even been stories of it in…" Curtis scratches the side of his face, thinking and watching Sam. "Well, I haven't heard of any gold outside the Shinys in two years."

"It was my father's."

"Did he live in one of the Shining Cities?"

"He's dead."

A long silence passes as Curtis squints at Sam. He then looks at the three-and-a-half dented gold blocks on the desk in front of him. He picks one up, feeling the weight of it and turning the bar slowly.

"And what was your father doing with bars of gold? Did he know something the rest of us didn't?"

Sam takes a deep breath, looking away from the gold and down at the filthy rug in this showy office. "Yes, he did."

***

In Sam's memory, the sun still shines on the umbrellas shading the patio. Couples and families enjoy the breeze and decadent plates of food. Some laugh and tell stories. Others comment on the pine-tree scenery or the perfect weather.

In the corner of the patio sits the fatter, younger version of Sam, flanked by Ariel and young Danny. The boy looks about two, still a long time before the world changes. Sam's mother and father sit across the table. His dad has barely touched his food.

"Once we left the gold standard, there was no chance of recovery. When every dollar is backed by something of real value, then you're safe. But we've got every country in the world printing up new money when they run into debt. The whole system is on credit and headed for default."

Sam half-listens. He's heard some variation of this speech many times before and knows enough to respond as needed and act like he's engaged. He puts his credit card into the sleeve for the bill, and sets it on the end of the table for the server.

"How much do you have on that card now?" Sam's father asks.

"I don't know, Dad," Sam responds, wanting to change the subject.

"Plastic money is the end of the whole thing, Sam. Gold. Precious metals. That's all that's going to matter eventually. Those that have it will survive. Those cards you carry may as well be Monopoly money."

The waiter snatches up the sleeve, and Sam's father lowers his voice.

"How much could you liquidate, if you had to?" he asks Sam.

"I don't know, Dad, okay? I'm not going to break down our finances with you." Sam looks at Ariel and can tell she can't wait to leave this lunch. Danny makes gurgling words as he plays with her smartphone, swiping through pictures and a children's game with ease.

"Samuel," Sam's mother interjects, using his full name for emphasis. "We're just worried…. If anything were to happen, we want to know you've got options."

"It's going to happen," Sam's Dad interrupts her, and she goes silent again. "Any debt you have is going to be levied against your assets, which are what… your cars, maybe your furniture and electronics?"

"If it's all going to collapse, Dad, then what the hell's gold going to matter? There'll be nothing to buy, and we'll all be living in lean-tos."

"Not if you own your home."

"Easy for you to say."

"This credit system is a disease. It's like a drug to people, to whole governments. I can't believe it's gone on this long!"

"So I should sell all I own and buy gold, huh?"

"Sam. It's the debt I'm talking about. Get out of debt. Get into something with real value."

The waiter returns the sleeve with Sam's card and a receipt to sign. He signs, adding a generous tip, and closes the sleeve.

"We have so few assets, Dad. I don't think it's worth the trouble."

They look at each other. Danny makes an excited shriek at his current game of choice. Ariel rubs his head lovingly, and the boy smiles at her.

"When it happens," Sam's dad begins again, "I want you to have a plan."

"You can stay with us if you need to," his mother interjects. "We have the space."

"Absolutely," his dad agrees. "At least get enough hard currency to make the trip."

"I'll look into it, okay." Sam stands. Ariel shoots up with him, and she grabs Danny from the high chair. They are beyond ready to leave.

Sam slides his hand behind Ariel's back and leans into her ear.

"I'm sorry," he whispers.

"I know," she whispers back as they head for the door. Sam's parents follow at half-pace.

***

As his mind returns to Curtis' office years later, Sam can almost feel the perfect temperature of that patio and the clean, seductive smell of his wife's hair as he'd leaned in close.

Curtis stares at him, trying to gauge if Sam's reflection is over.

"That was less than two years from the reconciling," Sam finally says.

"Your father was a smart man," the leader says.

Sam looks off into the distance; his focus slowly returns.

"Yeah. He was." It hurts Sam to say this. He wonders if he ever complimented his father. Over the years, he'd grown to hate most everything the man had said and discounted each speech as the ramblings of a crackpot. Now though, Sam wishes he could at least tell his father he was right.

"How'd he die?" the leader asks.

Sam grows hard again. The stupidity of his parents' death overshadows their wisdom and preparation.

"He was killed in his debt-free home. A shotgun to the chest. My mom —" The thought catches in his throat in a sudden rise of emotion. He pushes it back down and refuses to acknowledge what he suspects happened that day. "My mother was shot in the kitchen. She was unarmed and wearing house slippers. Whoever did it didn't even find their valuables. Lucky for me, I guess."

Curtis sets the gold bar down. It thuds with weight.

"Okay. What do you need?"

"About 10 gallons of fuel and some help fixing the ignition on my ATV."

"Just 10 gallons?"

"I don't have very far to go."

The two men look at each other. Curtis lets this go on a long time.

"They'll shoot you on sight at Aspen," Curtis says.

"I heard," Sam replies.

Curtis ruffles the pages on Sam's legal pad. He scoops up all the gold bars and pulls them close. Sam tenses.

"You don't have anything to buy your way into a Shiny. This is nothing to them."

"Will you accept it?" Sam asks. His eyes drift to the corner of the room where there are cameras capturing this whole discussion. "Can I have your permission to trade? Is there something else I need to do?"

Curtis drops the gold bars out of sight. They thud to the floor.

"Explain this to me," says Curtis as he looks down at something behind the desk.

In a blur, he pulls a metal object into view and smacks it down on the desk blotter. It rings upon impact. Sam looks at his father's titanium femur.

Sam swallows back his emotion. He stares at the bone. "That was also my father's," he says.

Curtis recoils, making a show of it. A creepy smile crosses his face as if he's entertained by something taboo.

"You cut a titanium bone out of your father's corpse!" he says, close to laughing.

"Yes."

"That's it?" Curtis asks, almost disappointed. "Just… 'yes'? You're one warped individual."

Sam keeps looking at the bone. He can feel his eyes tearing, and he wills them to stop.

"How do I know you didn't kill your parents?" Curtis asks, leaning forward. "You got out of prison with nowhere else to go. No money. No prospects. The world gone to shit, and there they are with a small fortune. What's murder and stealing to a man willing to mutilate the dead?"

Sam snatches the femur off the table and leaps to his feet. He's got it by his side in a white-knuckle grip, holding it like a club. Curtis shoves himself back in his chair, his hand instinctively retrieving a hidden pistol as he pulls away.

Sam hears the running footsteps behind him. He stands very still, but there's no fear in his eyes. He keeps gripping the femur and staring at Curtis. He watches Curtis motion to the men to stop just out of reach. Curtis watches Sam with curiosity, with the pistol pointed right at his chest.

"I expected my dad to be waiting at the curb when I got out of prison. When he wasn't there, I had no choice but to start walking. Days later, I arrived to find my parents murdered and my wife and son long gone."

Sam lifts the bone up into view, stretching it out with an open palm like he's presenting a trophy.

"This… is all I have left of the family I knew."

Sam lets the rod fall to the desk, and the titanium clangs with a lingering ring. Sam seems immune as he stares at Curtis.

"I've done everything you've asked. I've subjected myself to your bullshit. I've answered every question you have. And all you've done is accuse me of stealing and killing to get the only things that are actually mine."

He raises his hands, palms up, like a man on a cross. Curtis lifts his pistol with the movement. Sam can feel the two thugs behind him tense.

"Either let me buy what I need. Or shoot me." Sam stands there, unblinking. Curtis stares back. The hint of a smile flickers on his face.

Suddenly, he tosses his pistol onto the desk blotter and breaks into a grin.

"Goddammit. I like you. You're ballsy with a big dose of don't-give-a-fuck."

"Does that mean I get what I need?"

"How long you been traveling?"

"That's not an answer," Sam presses.

"How long?"

"Weeks. Months. Since California. What's it matter?"

"When's the last time you got laid?"

Sam boggles at the question. "What?"

"You're wound up pretty damn tight, I'm thinking you need the release."

"I need the gas. And some supplies. I'm not here for company."

"Look, Sam. I don't care what it is you're into. Don't like women, let's talk about it."

"I have a wife. In Aspen. What I'm into is finishing my trip to see my family."

Curtis turns again, darker and taunting. He fans the pages of the legal pad. "Is that what this is all about?" Curtis asks, as Sam fights the urge to lunge for the pad.

"That's for my son."

"I know. I read it."

Sam goes rigid, feeling violated. He glances over his shoulder now, seeing the two big men still watching him. The sense he'll never leave this town creeps in from the edge of his mind, but he pushes it away.

"My son was three when I went in," Sam begins. "He's seven now. And I have no idea what to say to him or how to be his father. Writing him feels like practice."

"So what happens when you're dead?"

Sam glances at the big guys again, feeling threatened now. Curtis looks at him, slow and thoughtful.

"You're writing things down in case you don't get to tell him," Curtis says. "But if you died on your trip, how does this get into Aspen?"

Sam looks at the floor. "I don't know. I figured I'd make it and then destroy what I'd written."

"Destroy it?" Curtis asks. "Seems like you're better off on these pages. Once your boy's in front of you, my guess is you'll just fuck him up."

Sam lifts his head again, looking between Curtis and the pad.

"Stay here. Keep writing." Curtis slides the pad toward Sam. "This'll be the most satisfying parenting you'll ever do. We can find a good use for you."

"You're forcing me to stay?"

"No. You can go in a few days. If you still really want to."

"A few days?"

"I want you to see what we have to offer." Curtis pulls a stack of poker chips from a desk drawer and nods at one of the guys behind Sam. Baldy steps past Sam and takes the stack of chips. He looks at Curtis, a bit surprised.

"Take him by the campus store," Curtis says to Baldy as he looks at Sam. "Get him some clothes and a place in the dorm."

Sam eyes the fistful of cheap plastic poker chips in Baldy's big hand.

"Why can't I just trade gold for what I need, and then go?"

Curtis leans on his desk now, his patience waning.

"You're not the only one in this equation. There are things that happen on our schedule, and you don't get to disrupt that. Maybe there's a part in our city for you. Maybe you'll still want to leave. But until I say so, you're here."

He nods, and Baldy and his partner each grab one of Sam's arms. They turn for the door, walking him past the columns of shelves.

"What about my things?" Sam hollers over his shoulder.

"I'll see you tomorrow," Curtis says as Sam is pushed from the room.

3

The morning sun floods the pristine, modern kitchen with light. A new thin laptop sits open on the spotless counter. Mark, a trim, well-groomed man with a shaved head, sits looking at a web browser. He sets down his coffee mug and scrolls lower, reading.

"Fucking Californians," he says.

"What is it?" Ariel answers as she steps around the corner and up behind him. She puts a hand on his shoulder and reads the screen.

A news website fills the browser, crisp and dense with information. The headline on the screen reads: "Tahoe to Institute Merit Hearings." Ariel scans the article as Mark takes another sip of his coffee and shakes his head.

"It's not that bad," Ariel says. "Maybe it will work for them."

"There's no way to control a merit system!" Mark says. "The cities barely survive because they're a closed economy. The minute you open it up to anyone with a sob story, the exclusivity and financial standards are lost."

Ariel steps away and begins making herself a cup of coffee.

"It's not like they're going to throw the gates open and let anyone in," she says. "You'll have to prove family ties and how you can be an asset. And you know the city and its resources will be taken into account."

"Once we start letting those people in, the whole thing's going to collapse again."

"Those people?" Ariel says as she turns to look at Mark.

"You know what I mean."

"Babe, Danny and I were those people. I had to prove myself to you to stay here."

Mark reaches over and squeezes her hand. "You are the exception. You were here at the beginning, and you had something we needed."

She smiles at him, sly and sexual. "I had something you wanted."

He shakes his head. "That had nothing to do with it." She raises an eyebrow at him, and he grins at her. "Okay… it had a little to do with it."

"So a bunch of dirty Californians try to talk their way into Tahoe. So what. It gives them hope."

"It's not hope. It's credit, all over again. Giving people things they can't afford and haven't earned."

Danny steps into the room; he's dressed for school and dragging his backpack behind him.

"You ready, honey?" Ariel asks.

Danny nods, looks at the floor and then up at his mother. "Are more people going to jail?"

Ariel shoots a look at Mark. "No, Danny. Rules are changing in a different city."

"Are we going to have to let everyone in?"

"Don't worry, D, no strangers are coming in here," Mark says as he smiles. "We're still the best place to be."

Ariel steps by Mark and gives him a quick kiss on her way to the door.

"Come on, Danny. Let's go."

Danny shuffles behind her, backpack dragging.

"Pick up your pack, son."

They step out the back door, and Mark turns back to his coffee.

4

The door of a small, empty dorm room swings open, and Sam gets pushed inside. He's holding a stack of folded clothes, sheets, towels and a few toiletries. The stack is high enough to be unwieldy and difficult to see around. He bumps into the foot of a bed and turns back toward the door. Before he can say anything, the door is pulled closed behind him and he's alone.

Dropping the stack on the thin bed, Sam looks around the room. There's a layer of dust on top of a general sterile feel. There's another bed and cramped desk on the other side of the room. Matching halves, both empty. It reminds him of his cell.

On the floor lies his backpack and most of the stuff he brought to town. It's disheveled, with items shoved halfway into pockets and tossed around, but seeing it brings relief. He sits on the side of the bed and pulls the pack closer. With slow, methodical moves he pulls everything out and lays it on the opposite bed. Each piece has its place, and as the inventory spreads before him, he can instantly tell what's missing.

The clothes he wore since California are gone. He wonders if they are still hanging on the wall where he saw them hosed down. His good jacket and warm layers remain in wadded dirty balls. The titanium femur bone is nowhere to be seen. The gold bricks haven't been returned. All his weapons and ammo are missing.

In the top pouch of the pack he finds the only real surprise. His used legal pad, the spare pad and his ratty collection of pens are all right where he always put them. He knows they are of no real use to him and won't get him any closer to the gates, but he fans the pages and lets a warming relief flow over him. It's the first time he hasn't felt dread since entering this city.

Leaning back against the wall, Sam closes his eyes and listens to the sounds of the building. He can hear others through the walls and in the hallway. The voices don't sound strained or hushed. It reminds him of his own college dorm decades prior, and seems much more relaxed than his time in the Rec prisons.

Opening his eyes kills the illusion. This is a prison. He's walked halfway across the country to wind up in a room no bigger than his debtor cell. Pulling to his feet, Sam tries the door and is surprised to find it unlocked. He steps cautiously into the hallway.

Two older men stand in a doorway a few rooms to the right. One of them looks over his shoulder at Sam but then returns to his conversation. To the left, the hallway leads back toward the main doors, and he notices men and women coming and going freely. If it weren't for the simple clothes and range of ages, it could almost pass for a college.

He turns left and starts down the hall.

"Can I help you?" one of the older men calls from behind him.

"Nope," Sam says, turning. "Just going exploring."

"I'll show you around."

"That's okay."

The man closes in behind him, moving much faster than expected. Sam speeds up, but the old guy matches his pace.

"Slow down a bit, there's no reason to run," the old man says, even though he seems more than capable.

Sam stops suddenly. The man shuffles to a stop as well, surprised.

"Tell me something," Sam says. "Where do you live?"

The man stammers for a moment, caught off guard by the question.

"Is it on this hallway?" Sam pushes.

"No… I'm in the bigger dorm across from the main building…."

"The one with Curtis in it."

"Yeah."

"So you're not just being friendly. You're supposed to be my shadow." Sam lets the blood rush to his face but keeps his voice calm. "And you or your buddy down there are going to stay outside my door and report every time I leave my room until I see Curtis again tomorrow. Right?"

The old guy nods. "Sorry."

Sam scoffs. "Okay, I'll make this easy. Where's the bathroom?"

"Two doors down from your room. The other direction."

Sam begins walking toward his room again. The old guy follows.

"Is there anyone on this end of the hallway?"

The old guy says nothing and just keeps pace. Sam reaches his room and grabs the handle.

"Then I'll either be in here or the shitter. You can tell Curtis."

Sam steps inside and slams the door behind him. For a second, he's surprised to find a lock on the doorknob, and even a deadbolt. But as he turns them he realizes they are remnants of privacy from when this was an actual college. Now, the locks may keep others out, but they do an even better job of keeping Sam in.

He sits on his bed again, head in his hands. After a long silence, he pulls the legal pad over and grabs one of his tattered pens.

> *Life is shit. There will always be people over you who believe they're doing the right thing, even though they have no idea what they're talking about. They'll force you into their system and tell you how to be.*
>
> *Unless you're rich or mean, you won't get ahead. Ideally you'll be both rich and mean. A real wealthy asshole with a Napoleon complex and a skanky bitch half your age hanging on your arm.*

Then he stops. Sam glares at the words scrawled on the page. They're dented into the paper as if he tried to carve them with his pen tip. Even the handwriting is clipped and messier than normal.

For the first time since starting to write, Sam rips out the page. The two pages underneath still bear an imprint of his scratchings. He rips them out as well.

Then he just sits. Heartbroken. Completely convinced he won't make it to Aspen. Tears well up in his closed eyes, and he wipes them away like an annoyance. He's exhausted. He's angry. And he's trapped. Of all the ways he imagined failing in this journey, he always thought it would end on the road. Now he's caged again and — while safe in the best accommodation he's had since prison — it feels like a death. This may be the closest he'll get to his goal.

He grabs the pad again. He sits with the pen ready, trying to think of something worthwhile to tell his son. He sits for a long time.

> *I always struggled with being your father. I hated myself every time I had to discipline you, even though I knew I had to do it. The thought of you being a brat,... I couldn't take it, and I had to do something. Every day I wished I didn't have this role in your life. And every day I knew I must stay and do right by you. My own shit was just that... my own. You didn't deserve it. You deserved a guide. A leader to help you figure out the world. As much as I struggled with it, I had to stay.*

> *The strangest thing. The real surprise. Was anytime I'd leave. It would break your little heart. We'd do our little routine of hugs and fist bumps... and squeezes. I wonder if you remember that. Three squeezes of your little hand to say "I love you." And you'd squeeze back, four times, "I love you... too." You were doing it from the time you were two, and your mom and I had done it since we were dating. It was our little thing, and you and I would do it every time we'd part.*

Leaving for work or an obligation was never a big problem for me, as it just felt like life. The "have tos" felt immovable, and teaching you that I had to leave for those things felt like an important lesson.

The hard part was leaving when it wasn't required. The times when I'd just need to go away on my own. We'd go to a movie, or out with friends, and I'd watch it snap you in half. You'd want to come with us, and the lack of obligation would overwhelm me and I'd suddenly want to stay. I'd still go, knowing it was important for all of us. And any time I did, it would recharge me to be a better father. But the whole time I'd be haunted by my leaving. Not the going part, but the terrible thought in the back of my mind that something was going to happen. I'd be maimed, or killed, and you'd never get me back.

I'm not easily frightened. I'm too logical and matter of fact for most normal fears. But the idea that something beyond my control could leave you without a father... that thought haunted me. And in those moments where I went away voluntarily it felt the worst. I'm grown. And for better or worse I had a father that walked me through the world before I could do it on my own.

I never wanted you to have to cope without me. I dreaded the idea of you trying to figure out why I'd gone away, and never knowing what I would answer when you had questions.

But I'm long gone. And when they took me to prison it was an obligation, so I didn't feel the

> *full force of my leaving. Now I'm close enough to think I might actually see you, and all I feel is that familiar pit in my stomach and fear in the back of my mind. What if I don't make it home? What if you never see me again? Will you even know I wanted to be with you? Will anything I said ever matter?*
>
> *I wanted you to be able to count on me. And I left. I'm sorry Danny. Somehow I hope you know.*

Sam sets the pad aside, suddenly aware of his own exhaustion. He lies down on his side and stares at his things still laid out on the opposite bed. His eyes scan over them, thinking of the days of use in each item. He stares at the pen still in his hand as his eyes grow heavier. The emotional drain of the past few days weighs more than the physical strain. Sleep takes him.

When he awakes, it's daylight. He slept all night and into the next day. Picking up his watch, he confirms it's been more than twelve hours since he collapsed. It seems impossible he would have slept that long, and it makes him uneasy.

His eyes fall on the little stack of new clothes, towels and sundries he bought at the campus store. All of it was paid for with the chips Curtis gave him. Everyone at the store had seemed very helpful and understanding of his overwhelmed and distrustful demeanor. At the time, he'd written it off as a common thing for every new resident. Now he wonders if it was all a ruse. He'd been handed a pocket sandwich of some kind. Hot and freshly made, free of charge. Had that been specially made to drug him?

Sam realizes he has no idea how to trust anyone. His many years of prison primed him to live in doubt. Then he was released into a world where nearly everyone is trying to kill him. Now he only assumes the worst. While he knows this has kept him alive, Sam hates that it's who he has become.

He sits on the bed and looks at the stack of clothes and sundries. Then he picks up a towel and the soap and spends a long time just scrubbing his face and hands in the room's tiny sink. He takes his time, rubbing sleep from his eyes and really staring at himself in the mirror. The man looking back is thinner, older and harder than his own image of himself. But he studies the face as he revels in the clean.

Time to face facts, he decides. His raging against Curtis the day before won't get him out of Grand Junction. Drugged or not, he's had much needed sleep and is in the last outpost he'll find before the walls of Aspen. He needs to find out what Curtis wants and what he can offer. And he needs to remember anything could be a trap.

He slides the towel over the dusty ring by the sink and looks at the collection of things on the spare bed. Then he sits on his bed again and picks up his notepad.

> *When you figure out what you want to do. If it's big or small. You're gonna find people who'll tell you no.*
>
> *Of course you can't get everything you'll ever want. And you can't decide that every little thing is worth fighting for. You may have heard people say "pick your battles." That's about choosing what's worth the fight.*
>
> *So you've got to pick. You've got to decide what's important enough.*
>
> *I can't begin to guess what it will be for you, but there will be things you can't get away from. The things that really matter to you. The stuff that you'll stay up all night to do.*
>
> *When you find that passion. Never accept "no".*
>
> *There's always another way. Someone else you can ask, or another way to approach the problem.*

> *Listen. Try and understand why you're being told no. Then work for a way around the issues. Fight and claw and redirect your efforts until you find the way through.*
>
> *If you need a "yes" and you haven't fought long enough to get one, then you didn't want that thing as bad as you thought.*
>
> *The vital stuff. Find it. Get your yes. No matter what.*

He looks at this entry for a moment, remembering the one he threw away. Then he puts the pad down.

Standing, Sam dumps his jumpsuit from the day before and dresses in his new clothing. The thick cargo pants feel stiff and clean. He runs his hands over the perfect pockets and solid seams. The new socks, a low-grade gym sock, feel luxurious compared to what he'd worn out over the past weeks. The shirt he pulls down over his thin chest is a quick-dry nylon, an unexpected find in the campus shop. The shoes are his only real disappointment: an athletic running shoe better suited for a stroll around campus than a hundred-mile trek. Sam suspects Curtis doesn't want the local shop providing shoes good enough for walking away.

Looking at the stuff on his bed, Sam wonders if any of it could be a viable weapon. He quickly realizes there's nothing here. Curtis has all the weapons. Sam needs his guns back before he leaves. As much as he doesn't want to meet with Curtis again, there's no other way out of town with all of his things.

In two quick steps, he reaches the door.

A young guard springs to his feet as Sam steps out into the hallway. He's mid-twenties and larger than Sam but trying to not look skittish. Sam looks at him, and the kid attempts a menacing demeanor. It isn't fitting.

"I'm ready to go see Curtis," Sam says.

"Uh...," the guy says before pulling himself together, "I don't think he's ready for you yet. I think he'll send for you when he is."

"You sound really certain. How 'bout this? I'm gonna go take a piss, and when I come out we'll go over to his office, and you can tell him I'm ready."

The kid opens his mouth to say something else, but Sam steps into the bathroom.

A few minutes later, Sam flings open the door of Curtis' building. Everyone in the room looks up at the aggressive move and watches Sam enter. The guy behind the desk eyes Sam and then the young guard a few steps behind. The guard shrugs his shoulders as Sam steps up to the counter.

"I'm here to see Curtis," Sam demands.

"You and everyone here," the guy behind the counter scoffs.

Sam looks around. There are less than ten people in the large waiting area. Some look like they may be sleeping here.

"Just let him know, please."

The guy shakes his head at the young guard standing right behind Sam. Then he types a few lines into the ancient-looking computer in front of him.

Sam continues standing at the counter.

"Have a seat," the guy says. Sam looks back at the man, unblinking. He stops typing. "I've put you on the list. Have. A. Seat."

Sam stares for another beat and then offers the kindest smile he can gather. He nods his head and turns for the chairs. As he moves through the room, the young guard stays with him.

"What exactly do you think I'm going to do?" Sam asks him.

"I was told to stay and watch any move you made outside your room."

"Well, we're not outside my room anymore, we're in a whole other building. Go get a coffee or something."

The kid looks at him. Sam sighs, sits, and the kid sits beside him.

"I'm Sam," he says, extending his hand.

"I know," the young man says.

Sam leaves his hand out. The young man looks at it for a moment, then shakes.

"I'm Jesse."

"If we're gonna be spending so much time together, I may as well know you a little bit."

"Yeah. I guess so."

"How long have you been here?"

Jesse looks stumped for a second. "You mean here in town, or working guard duty?"

Clearly Jesse is a big kid, but not a sharp one. Sam changes his approach.

"Where did you grow up?"

"Here in the Junction. I played football at the high school about a mile from here."

"Were you the center?"

"How'd you know?"

"Lucky guess."

They sit for a moment. Jesse seems to need another prompt to go on.

"So you were here through the crash?" Sam asks.

"Yeah. I wanted to go to Denver, but—"

"It went to shit. Like everywhere else," Sam says, and Jesse nods.

"They ended up with refugee camps and tent cities like L.A., right?"

Jesse nods again. "Yeah. First winter they had a bunch of people die from exposure. They couldn't keep the power on…. It was bad."

"I heard."

"I stopped looking around. This was the best place to stay."

"So Curtis set things up right away?"

Jesse doesn't answer.

"Did people like him before?"

Jesse sits quietly. His eyes drift to the reception desk, searching it to see if anyone's watching. Sam waits, letting the questions linger.

"I. He. He wasn't around before. I didn't know him."

"Really?" Sam looks around the room, making a show of the gesture. "How did an out-of-towner wind up running the place?"

"The mayor was here for a while. Curtis started helping him, I think. It was before I was working with any of them…. We were just fighting for food, ya know?"

Sam nods, letting him talk.

"Then the mayor died. It was weird. No one really knows what happened — it was all just rumors. But, Curtis was here to start building the fences and keep scavengers from taking over the place. No one else seemed to know what to do."

"What did he do before?"

"Military, I think. Some sort of special forces… like a SEAL, or those Army—"

"Jesse!" a woman's sharp voice interrupts him. They look up to see the squat, middle-aged woman from the front desk standing nearby. "Quiet. Stop talking to him!"

Sam looks at Jesse and then the woman.

"What's the problem? I asked him a question…."

"There's no talking in here."

"I was here yesterday. There was plenty of talking." Sam says.

The woman glares at him. The other people waiting all look their way.

The man from the front desk walks over.

"Curtis will see you now."

Sam looks around the room at the handful of others waiting for their time. They were all here before him. He expects some of them will never see Curtis face to face. He thinks about his dad's old saying, "The squeaky wheel gets the oil."

Sam has certainly disrupted enough of the morning to be sent to the front of the line, but he isn't sure he'll like what awaits.

"Thank you," Sam says. He gets to his feet and follows.

5

Sam climbs the stairs the same as the day before. The man from the front desk hands him off to the same middle-aged woman. Jesse no longer follows.

They walk down the hallway, toward the additional reception desk. It feels like a time warp, everything the same as the last time. In the whiteboard room, the same guys debate a strategy so convoluted it looks like a child's scribbling on the walls. As he glances in, he notices a bit of simple computer code on one of the whiteboards, and the men go silent until he passes.

The green room houses the same cluster of women with smoky eyes and knowing glances. They eye him again, but Sam can't tell if they're seeing him as a predator or prey.

Sam and his escort stop at the reception desk, and he expects guards to appear and walk him into Curtis' office. Instead, a tiny girl behind the desk points silently at the two chairs along the wall. Sam looks at her, confused. She appears both underage and undernourished, and her stoic silence seems more like fear than confidence.

Sam sits. He watches her. She catches him staring and glares back. He lets his eyes wander. No one else enters the hallway, and he starts to debate if he could just walk down to Curtis' office.

"Sam, thanks for joining us!" Curtis says from behind him.

Sam turns toward the voice, looking the opposite way from before, and sees Curtis approaching with his hand outstretched. Sam stands, shakes and opens his mouth to speak, but Curtis starts again.

"You're earlier than I hoped, but I know you're anxious. Frankly, I am too."

Curtis' hand is on Sam's shoulder, a friendly gesture with a subtle leading push. They turn down the hall and head away from the reception desk.

"There's a lot of things to still work out, but I'm hoping we're far enough along for you to really shed some light."

Sam boggles as they step into a wood-paneled classroom with a central conference table, a projector and a screen. Two other men watch him enter — one is Baldy, the guard from the day before and the other is thin with glasses and sharp hawk eyes. Sam can almost feel the man's stare, and it makes him uneasy.

"You've met Dixon, my head of security," Curtis says as he motions to Baldy. Sam nods, glad to have the man's name and role.

"Good to see you," Sam says. Dixon nods.

"And this is Lawrence," Curtis says toward the other man.

"Hello," Sam offers. Lawrence only raises his eyebrows and continues staring.

An awkward silence ensues, with Curtis looking at the three men. Then he smiles and points Sam to a chair. Lawrence sits at the head, under the ceiling projector and four chairs away. Sam still feels too close.

"Show him," Curtis orders as he dims the lights.

The projector comes to life and shows a picture of a huge metal gate. The photo has pine branches in the edges and looks like it was taken with a long surveillance lens.

"Do you know what that is?" Curtis asks as he sits beside Sam.

"It's the gate of a shining city."

"Yes. But more specifically, it's the Aspen gate."

Sam eyes it, trying to hide the instant surge of adrenaline at the sight of it.

"How would you open it?" Curtis asks.

Sam looks at the photo for a long time. A windowless titanium gate, twenty-feet square with a seam down the middle. The gate is the only opening in a blank titanium wall. It looks impenetrable.

"He doesn't know," says Lawrence, his voice a whisper of disgust.

Curtis' eyes dart to Lawrence and then back to Sam. He waits, watching Sam search the photo.

"I can't tell if it's like all the rest," Sam starts. "Does it have any changes or customization?"

"No," Lawrence breathes.

"How close have you gotten?"

No one answers.

"I heard they shoot on sight. Is that true?" Sam asks.

"Don't believe everything you hear," Lawrence says.

"They don't particularly like people strolling up to the gate," Curtis answers. "But it's not like they have a firing squad. This is the main gate, and it gets a good amount of use. We've seen it open."

"But this is also where they focus their security," Dixon says, his voice a cold statement of fact. "We need a way around it."

"Then you'll need to find the terminal," Sam says as he stands. Dixon and Lawrence tense, but Curtis leans back, unconcerned. They watch Sam walk up to the picture, his shadow casting on the image.

"Most of the time, they put them here," he points to the frame of the door. "About chest-high and inside a locked access hatch. The locks are shitty. Only enough to slow you down a bit. That's your biggest problem."

Sam steps out of the projection and looks at the three men.

"Go on," Curtis says, rolling his hand as if to pull it out of Sam. "Why's the hatch a problem?"

"I don't mean the hatch. I mean the time. Every second you spend at this gate is time for them to create ways to chase you off. I suspect the right person could hack the terminal and get in, but having enough time to try it...."

"Could you hack it?" Curtis asks Sam. Lawrence scoffs but says nothing.

"I didn't work on the doors."

"You picked up trash," Lawrence interjects, clearly unable to contain himself any longer.

The four men glance back and forth at each other. Sam settles his eyes on the floor.

"Yeah. I worked with the trash system. The incinerators. Dumpster hatches. I wasn't on the entrance door."

"So why is he here?" Lawrence glares at Curtis.

Curtis looks back at Lawrence. The light demeanor he's been showing now melts away.

"How many people even know there's a hatch on one of those doors? Us. Five or six others. No one else has even been close enough to see one," Curtis says.

"No one else that lived," Lawrence says.

"And yet... Sam here can tell us about the access hatch from a photograph that doesn't even show it clearly."

Lawrence blinks. Curtis turns to Sam.

"We've all read your file. We know you were trash crew. But we also know you were a programmer before your Rec assignment." Curtis pauses, staring deeply into Sam. "So while I'm impressed that you know about the access panel, I want to know if you can hack it."

"With a lot of time... maybe."

"How did you plan to get in?"

"I don't know."

"Bullshit. You didn't walk halfway across the country and not come up with a plan."

"I wasn't sure until right now what the Aspen gate would look like. I worked on the Tahoe Shiny. Even got shipped up to Carmel for a bit. Both of them were different because of the terrain."

He steps up to the projection again. He scans the edges of the photo, looking at the top of the wall.

"They probably have sentry positions on the top."

"And cameras," adds Dixon.

"So you'd have to do it at night," Sam suggests.

"Can't be done," Dixon says.

"They've got an extra layer, Sam," Curtis explains. "They close down at dark, with an additional blast door that slides into place."

The projection changes as Lawrence advances to the next slide. The image is cast in the dull-green glow of a night vision photo. It shows the gateway completely sealed by a well-fitted metal sheet. Sam stares at it.

"Never seen that before," Sam says.

"It's not titanium," Lawrence says. "So we're pretty sure it was done after the wall was built."

"But you said it hadn't been customized?"

"I didn't think…" he trails off. Then he straightens and finds his backbone again. "This is the only city I've seen."

"So you don't know shit," Sam says before thinking. He instantly regrets it, now fearing a retaliation.

Curtis looks over at Dixon. Grins. And then laughs. Lawrence fumes, his eyes boring into Sam.

"Lawrence," Curtis says, "show him what you've made."

Lawrence stands, straightens his clothes and goes to the large, double closet doors behind him. Sam watches him grab both handles, pause and then open them with a revelatory flourish. Internal lights flicker on, illuminating a full-size mock-up of the gate's bottom seven feet.

The model is crude, with mismatched materials representing the gate. But as Sam looks back and forth between the projected image and the mock-up, he's amazed at the meticulous detail. Lawrence reaches behind his creation and flips an unseen switch.

The gate hums, locks clunking.

"We got a copy of the build specs," Lawrence explains. "Incomplete. But there was enough to work from."

Sam just stares.

"So," Curtis smiles at all of them in turn, "now you know why we're all here. How would you do it?"

Sam steps toward the model, tentative and almost reverent. Then he moves in close to the side panel, tucking inside the gate frame and looking at the small covering at chest height.

Looking up, he imagines the other half of the gate and the top of the wall beyond. He stares past the men in the room as if looking up the entrance road.

"You've seen it opened," he says, still distant in thought.

"Deliveries mainly," Dixon responds.

"How often?"

"About every two weeks. But it's an armed convoy."

"How long does it take them to open the gate?"

"A few seconds. We've never been close enough to see the code."

Sam looks at the panel, leaving it closed and stepping back. He reaches toward it.

"It's not a code," Sam says as he thinks. "It's a card reader."

"Why?" Curtis asks.

"It's this panel," Sam says, pointing. "I never thought about it until now, but even when they bussed us in to work, no one stopped long enough to open a locked panel and input a code. The only way to interact that fast would be a keycard slot or reader on here somewhere."

There's no such thing on Lawrence's model. The panel is a solid sheet screwed down on the corners.

"Do you have any closer pictures of the panel?"

Sam watches the men trade glances. They don't.

"What about other entrances?"

"They're smaller," Dixon says. "And they're in areas that are harder to reach. More like one-man doorways."

"Do they have the same kind of access panels?"

"No. They are more like emergency exits," Lawrence adds. "No handles on the outside, so they probably have an alarmed electronic lock and some kind of crash bar."

"Could you disarm one of those?" Sam asks, but Curtis interrupts.

"That's a choke point. We could only go in one at a time," Curtis says with an edge. "We've got equipment and a lot of people to move through. It has to be the main gate."

Sam watches Dixon and Lawrence look away. They've fought over this plan.

"Okay," Sam starts cautiously, "what about using those as for a small group, like a Trojan horse?"

Lawrence brightens. Dixon looks at Curtis.

"Go on."

Sam looks at the main gate model again, then the access port without a card reader.

"If you could get in the side doors, you could send someone in to open up the main gate."

"Just walk right in there, huh?" Dixon laughs. "They'd be shot on sight."

Sam looks up, as though the model continued to the top of the wall. "They're going to shoot you from up there. Especially if you've stopped a convoy of people while someone digs around in the access panel."

"Do you think you can hack it?" Curtis asks.

"No way. It's suicide. Whoever stands here with a screwdriver will get a bullet in the brain. You need a keycard. What do you know about the supply runs?"

"We could probably overrun it," Dixon says.

"We'd lose a lot of people," Curtis answers.

"Wouldn't it be less than walking up without a way in?" asks Sam.

They look back and forth between each other and Sam.

"You still haven't answered my question," Curtis smiles, but his tone isn't friendly.

"I'm telling you everything I know," Sam answers.

"No. How are you getting in?"

Sam backs away from the gate mock-up and the other men.

"Gold. Guns. Begging. I don't know what it will be, but I'll do whatever I need to."

"And you'll get shot. Robbed. And left to rot outside the walls."

"Maybe. But I have to try. If my wife and son are in there—"

"That won't matter for shit!" Curtis roars. "If they're in there, the last thing they'll do is stick their necks out to get you in the door. They'll want you to go away."

Sam looks at the projection of the gate photo. It invigorates him. It reminds him that he is only one day's ride from finishing this journey.

"I have nowhere else to go."

"We can find you a place here," Curtis says, returning to his friendly tone. "Your experience inside the Shinys can help us claim them for regular people. We all deserve what they have in there. You do too!"

"No. I got what I deserved."

"That's the Rec program talking," snaps Curtis. "They filled your head full of bullshit so you'd keep building for all the rich folks."

"They're perpetuating a class system," Lawerence says. "And that's never worked. It's always overthrown."

"It's worked in every culture in the world," Sam sighs. "We never officially had one here, but it's always existed. There's a ruling class, served by those below them. We want to believe we can all get to the top, but it's a lie. Maybe it was true once, but now the rich are untouchable. We all have our place."

Curtis sighs and shakes his head dramatically. "I thought you'd get it. I thought you could see what we're doing here!"

"I get it," Sam smirks. "I understand that you think you'll overthrow the city... turn it into some utopia where everyone gets an equal portion, flowers bloom in the winter, and everyone sings 'Kumbaya' until they pass out."

Dixon bites a smile and turns away.

Sam points at the gate, "But you go in there, and you'll just destroy it."

"Then why even try to get there?" Curtis asks.

Sam looks at him. Then he looks at the mock-up of the gate.

"I did three years to protect my family. I kept my head down and did my job. I worked off my debt. Our debt. I counted days. Just for the chance to be with them again. That's what I deserve. It's what I've earned. I don't want a seat at their table. I don't need their linen and champagne. My family got in there. And I belong with them."

"You'll wind up dead in their trash," says Curtis. "Fitting."

He stares at Sam. Sam looks back. A long moment of silence passes between them.

"Can I go now?" Sam asks.

"Gents, leave us," Curtis says, nodding Lawrence and Dixon toward the door.

The men exit, and Curtis waits, silent and unmoving until the latch clicks closed behind them. Then he motions to a chair across the conference table, the one farthest from the door.

Curtis sits in the chair across the table, his back to the only way out.

"You deserve a lot more than you think, Sam. Probably more than most."

"I thought you wanted to make everyone equal?" Sam asks.

"No," Curtis smirks. "Everyone isn't equal. Some people are better than others, and always have been. I haven't promised folks here that they'll all be the same. No one expects that. We're not communists. There's no welfare."

He leans forward, studying Sam and smiling as Sam tries to put the pieces together.

"What I want. What we want. Is for everyone to have a chance. What you do with opportunity, that's what makes the difference. When you aren't allowed opportunity. When hard work and effort aren't rewarded. Well… that's when the system is broken. It needs to be fixed.

"What makes us different from the folks in Aspen isn't that wall. It's the information. The opportunities. The internet. The news feeds. The connection to the larger world. Without that, we'll always be living in shit."

"Nice idea," Sam nods. "But you'll still get in there and ruin it for everyone. People aren't nice. Or fair. Or willing to give up on revenge. You'll just replace their bubble for your own."

"You are quite a cynic," Curtis grins. "It's a good act. Probably honed while you were inside. Except I see your desperation. Some part of you still believes in fairness and taking what's yours. You wouldn't have fought your way here otherwise."

"What are you offering me?" Sam asks. "I was headed there all by myself. I don't need you."

"You came to me, Sam. Refusing to leave and insisting on gas and supplies."

"You have things I need. And I offered to pay."

"We scanned your chip," Curtis says, pointing at Sam's shoulder. "I plugged the number into a broken-down sat phone station we stole a year ago. And your record showed me just the man I needed to help us. You've probably been in more of the Shining Cities than anyone I've ever met," Curtis says. "We need you."

Sam sighs, the oppression of prison settling on him. "Even if I can get you in. And I do mean... if... Getting in the door isn't going to change a thing."

"They're holed up in there. Living the life we all remember. What they have isn't fair," Curtis says.

"Life was never fair. Even before the system went to shit. There are always those with more. And you don't want equality any more than they do."

Curtis bristles. "I've got thousands of people looking to me. And I want every single one of them to have every luxury and opportunity that's out there."

"As long as they keep looking to you," Sam smirks. "You want to keep your ruling status, but with better chairs and some decent internet."

They stare at each other. Curtis fumes but tries to hide it. Sam sits looking back at him, knowing he has nothing else to lose.

"What is it you want?" Curtis asks, trying a new tactic.

"I want to see my family. And start again."

"That's naively optimistic of you. How do you think that's going to happen if you don't have an army behind you?"

"I don't know. I figured I'd buy my way in, and see what I need to do to stay."

"You don't have that much gold."

"Not after you took it from me."

Curtis is silent. He looks at the projection of the gate, and then at the model behind Sam.

"So, I let you go. But you don't get in. Then what?"

"I'll figure it out."

"I'll tell you what happens," Curtis leans forward, a sharp look in his eyes. "You'll wind up back at my gate like everyone else who thought they could find something better. And I won't let you in the next time."

"I won't come back."

They stare at each other in silence. Sam is resolute. Curtis finds a smile.

"You know our plans," Curtis says. "If I let you go, it puts me and my people in danger."

"I know you want to break into Aspen. Same as me. With no idea how to do it."

"You could warn them."

"If the stories are true, they'll kill me before I'd get the chance."

"Probably. And if I see you again, I'll kill you."

Sam nods. "Does that mean I can go?"

Curtis almost laughs. "Tomorrow morning. East gate."

"Why not now?" Sam asks.

"Because we have to decide what you can take. And I have other things to do today."

6

In his Aspen office, Mark sits behind a large, clean metal desk. Windows on three sides display the manicured city and the peaks rising close in the morning sun. Dense green grass covers the ski runs, their contrast against the pine forest as clear as in the winter snow. He looks out at the runs, and watches a mountain biker blur down a pathway cut through the grass.

Itching at his button-down shirt, Mark wishes he was on a bike. He turns to look at the weathered man across the desk. Jackson is barely older than Mark, but his outdoor lifestyle and cowboy clothing make him look older.

"Twenty percent less?" Mark asks.

"I didn't believe it either," Jackson says. "Plus, we're having to go farther for the hunts."

"So how do we get your numbers back up?"

Jackson leans forward. "It's not just the hunts, Mark. We had a low ski year too. I don't know the numbers, but bet you it was less. The tourists see what's going on over here, and they're staying away."

"We're the safest place in America," Mark says.

"Yeah. And we'll always have some folks that want to come play cowboy and go on a hunt. But if we're down this much again next year…" Jackson trails off and looks over his shoulder out the window.

"Alright, Jackson," Mark sighs. "I'll see if we can move some ad dollars around. Lean on our safety record."

"You get 'em here, and I'll take them out on an adventure," Jackson grins.

"Thanks, man," Mark says, and Jackson stands and leaves.

Mark knows how vital European tourists are to Aspen's survival. The burden of keeping this place safe and intriguing to overseas visitors seems to grow with time. His laptop still shows a full roster of incoming planes from all over the world. But there have been fewer requests.

The full-time population has a low birth rate, but it has grown every year as citizens of other shining cities try to transfer. Aspen has become one of the best places in America, but income is still sliding. When the National Guard served as the security force, no one with means stayed away. But since the troops were re-tasked to keep the peace in large cities like Denver, all the shining cities have been strained.

Mark knows Aspen's growth and improvement require more of him. His entire staff will have more work ahead of them. Distractions will cause problems. He'll need Ariel more than ever, and wants her with him. That means he has to talk to her about the boy.

"Mark," chirps the voice of his assistant from his laptop speakers. "Eli's back with a report."

"Send him in," Mark answers.

Normally, Mark leaves his laptop open for a channel connected to his assistant, Brooke. She listens in on his calls and meetings, helping him keep to a schedule and see problems before they develop. He's learned that the more she knows, the more things run smoothly. With a few exceptions.

"You're a bit late, aren't you?" Mark asks as Eli steps into the room.

"Yes," snips Eli. He's a tall, thin Asian man with huge shoulders and spindly limbs. He doesn't say much.

"Full tanks?"

"Yes. One last time."

Mark looks at Eli. Then he closes his laptop, blocking Brooke from the conversation.

"What's the problem?" Mark asks, leaning forward.

"The depot will be dry in days."

"When will they get a resupply?"

"No idea. They've been told they're too far from the chain."

Mark looks past Eli, out the window to the distant grassy ski runs. He knows this is either extortion or the work of another mayor. With only twenty shining cities still operating as intended, the competition for supplies and tax-paying citizens is growing.

With his immigrant file full of applicants from cities in California and Texas, Mark can narrow down the places and people who would most like to see Aspen fall.

"Anything we can do?" he asks, knowing the answer.

"Longer fuel runs. Week or so driving to California."

"You'd be ambushed."

"Probably."

Eli says this with no humor and no fear. He stands looking at Mark for his next assignment.

Mark pulls open his computer again.

"Hey, Brooke," he says casually. "Find Thomas for me."

There's a flurry of key strokes and mouse clicks. "He's at the arrivals hangar," she announces. "You want me to get your cart?"

"No. Have him come here."

"Will do."

Mark looks out the windows again as Eli leaves.

***

Miles away, Sam stands at the east gate of Grand Junction, the other side of the city from where he entered. Here there's just an oversized door in the city barricade. Houses stand closer, and the men on the walls have guns visible.

The pack on Sam's back looks tattered in contrast to his clean clothes and shoes. He is clean-shaven and freshly showered. Only the bulging pack reveals his journey. He has no weapons, and his ATV is nowhere in sight.

Guards stand on either side of the gate, watching him. He waits. No one speaks to him, but many glare. Turning back toward the city, he can see a few people peering out of windows. It seems no one is happy to see him leave.

The whine of a golf cart grows louder and comes into view with Dixon riding on the back bench. It stops just in front of Sam, and he recognizes Jesse behind the wheel. The big kid won't look at Sam, still sheepish from his failure to keep him contained in the dorm.

Dixon climbs off the back bench with Sam's shotgun in one hand and deer rifle in the other. As he straightens up, Sam can see the Walther shoved in the big man's belt. There are boxes of shells stacked on the floor of the golf cart.

"Pick two," Dixon says.

"Two?" Sam replies. "They're my guns!"

"That's the deal."

"Where's Curtis?" Sam asks.

"He's busy. I'm giving you your options."

Sam glares at Dixon. Both men know this was never discussed. Jesse continues to look everywhere but at Sam. Dozens of others gawk at this exchange, all tense.

"I still get the ammo."

"I brought plenty for each. Whatever you pick, I got you covered."

Sam's stalling. He thinks about the way he uses these three weapons. The weight and size of the ammo also crosses his mind as he looks at Dixon. The shotgun has proven itself for close-range damage, but he doesn't want anyone getting close to him.

"The Walther and the rifle," Sam says.

"You sure?" Dixon asks, cocking an eyebrow.

Sam knows how rare it is to have an accurate rifle. And the Walther can't be left behind.

He nods at Dixon. The big man hands the shotgun to Jesse and the other two weapons to Sam.

"Where's my ATV?" Sam asks.

Dixon turns back to him with boxes of ammo. "You're walking."

"What?"

"But not in those clothes," Dixon says as he sets the ammo down.

Sam blinks at him, not following.

Dixon lifts Sam's old, worn-out clothes from a bin in the cart and drops them on the ground. Then he drops Sam's tattered boots.

"I paid for these," Sams says as he tugs on his new clothes.

"You paid the store for supplies. And you've got a pack full of food. The clothes stay here."

Sam slides his pack to the ground and picks up the disheveled clothes. He looks around for some place to change.

"Right here," Dixon says. He's enjoying this.

"Then you'll let me out?" Sam asks as he glances at the gate.

"That's the deal."

Sam sighs and begins stripping down. He knows everyone is watching and humiliation is intended. The old shirt and shorts feel familiar but threadbare. His boots are unevenly worn, but might prove more sturdy than his sneakers.

"Where's my ATV?"

"What you see is what you get," Dixon says.

Sam suddenly realizes he's facing a hike of more than a hundred miles to Aspen. He suspects Curtis will try to take the city before he even arrives. Someone in this town will be riding his ATV.

"What else is there?" Sam asks, concerned.

Dixon reaches back into the bin and comes up with the titanium femur.

"And my gold?" Sam asks as he takes the femur.

"You knew this was going to cost you."

"Three-and-a-half bars. And my ATV?"

"Do you still want to go?"

Sam opens his pack and shoves the femur down the back. Then he picks up the ammo and crams the boxes into gaps and pockets.

His pack is much heavier when he lifts it again. The sheer weight of water and ammunition makes him miss the ATV.

"Good luck," Dixon says. He almost means it.

"Thanks," Sam answers flatly.

The big man waves at the guards over Sam's shoulder. Sam turns to see the gate open with a shriek of rusted hinges. He steps to the opening, seeing an empty and dilapidated neighborhood beyond.

The heat is already rising, and there won't be much shade until he gets out of the city. He steps past the walls and heads for the distant forest beyond the houses.

***

In Mark's office, Thomas finds Mark still standing at the huge windows.

"You okay?" Thomas asks.

"When's the last time you were on a bike?" Mark asks.

"Long time."

Thomas steps up beside Mark, and they both look out the massive windows. A biker makes his way down the switchbacks, quick and agile. The two old friends watch for a moment. A whole conversation passes between them in the silence.

Thomas is small and wiry, with sinewed arms and a thin and chiseled face. His shaved head has enough stubble to reveal his bald spot. He looks older and angrier than Mark, but in fact he's neither.

"Did you talk to Eli?" Mark asks.

"Yeah," Thomas answers.

"So?"

"We're pretty much fucked."

"What about a convoy?"

"I could paint big targets on the side, just to make it easier."

Mark smiles at that, in spite of himself.

"So we'll fly it in."

"We're already flying in the jet fuel. You add the gasoline, kerosene and natural gas stores we're using, and you'll have your own damn air force," Thomas says.

"I need some options," Mark says.

"Someone's looking to get paid. So pay them."

"This is bigger than that. They're trying to run us dry."

"Who?"

"Tahoe. Maybe Carmel," Mark says.

"Carmel doesn't give a shit about what we do. They'll always be the top spot. Tahoe is watching — we know that."

"Tahoe's taking in refugees. And they know we aren't."

"They need all the resources they can get. And they're closer to the refineries."

"I know," Mark sighs.

"You want me to hit them?" Thomas asks, serious.

Mark looks up, surprised. "No. I...." But Thomas can see in his eyes that he likes the idea. Removing another shining city, especially one as large and inclusive as Tahoe, would ease supply issues.

Mark smiles at Thomas in a moment of menace few have seen and Thomas would never betray. Then Mark recovers his professionalism. "I want you to go back to the depot."

Thomas starts to protest.

"I know Eli was just there," Mark admits. "But figure out what you'll need to protect all our fuel trucks. Go and drain our suppliers. No one will suspect us back so soon, and we've got to buy some time."

"I'll need a couple days to prep it. And then a few to make it happen."

"Take what you need to do it right."

"You're the boss," Thomas smirks.

"No. I'm just the face," Mark replies, an old mantra between them.

Thomas reaches for the door and then stops. "Before I roll out, let's find some time on our bikes."

Mark smiles, and Thomas leaves. They both know they won't find the time.

***

Curtis walks down the hallway from his office, Dixon on one side of him and Lawrence on the other. They approach the stairs to the lobby, as the sound of voices rises from below. Curtis stops on the landing and looks down at the staff members and security force he built from nothing. They murmur back and forth, expectant. Some look confused. Others look enraged.

He raises his hands over his head and whistles. It's a sharp, clear break in the chatter, cutting everyone short. They all look up.

"Thank you," he says. He lets silence hang in the air. He scans over them slowly, making eye contact, smiling at some and nodding solidarity at others.

"I know this was a last-minute gathering," he begins. "I'm glad to see all of you. And I owe you an explanation.

"Yes. I let a man go this morning. I didn't want to. I asked him to stay. We told him of our plans in hopes he would want to help us. I believe we had a place for him. He still wanted to leave.

"Many of you have asked why I did this. Why tell a stranger our plans and then let him go?

"Because we are not a prison. We are what this country should be. So a man can choose the wrong path just as freely as the right one.

"And I did this because the time has come. A time for change. The time I've promised you. The time we've talked about and planned for. The time to take back what's ours. The time to stand up, and tell the one percent behind those walls that we will not be silenced.

"This country used to be about dreams. About fighting and working hard to achieve everything you could imagine. Anything was possible.

"Now, a hundred miles from here, there's a city that says that's not what America is anymore. We have to stay here and stay silent. To settle for less. To let them have things the way they used to be, while we fight for the scraps.

"I will do anything to get us inside those walls. I will enlist any man. I will pull any information...."

* * *

***

East of Grand Junction, the late-afternoon light flickers through the trees. Sam knows it will be dark soon. He takes another bite of the tough jerky in his hand and waits for the water to boil on his tiny camp stove. His resupply should give him enough food for two weeks, but he hopes to reach Aspen in less than one.

He looks back in the direction of Grand Junction. His feeling of subtle oppression is lifting.

***

Curtis pans over his audience, letting his words sink into them. Then he continues: "No one will stand in our way. The people hiding within those walls will soon learn that real people of this country will still stand against those who oppress them. We will be free. We will thrive. We will take back the world we deserve. The world we remember. Together."

His staff members applaud. A few cheer. Others share a nod of agreement.

***

The quiet howl of a light wind and the gas whoosh of the stove are the only sounds in Sam's camp. Without the constant noise and vibration of the ATV, he finds his mind wandering deeper into buried memories. Fragments of music play in his head, sometimes entire lyrics of songs he never remembered liking. Scenes from movies rise to the surface of his mind as if he'd seen the film the day before. It's as though the lack of stimulation has led his brain to do a self-cleaning purge. He wonders what buried memory might be next.

Among these divergent thoughts come memories of his time with Ariel and Danny. Unlike past recollections of milestones or grand moments, the ones surfacing now are darker. With no one to talk to and no escape from these thoughts, Sam pulls out his legal pad.

I always thought I was patient. There was a

time your mom even told me I was. She even said she liked it. My calmness kept her sane.

I think I even took some pride in it. Believed I was able to handle anything without getting out of control.

But you changed all that. I found the end of myself more times than I could count. So easily. A whine from you. A needy moment when I had no more to give… and I would lose it. An irrational violent anger from somewhere I didn't recognize.

I'd always hate myself afterward. Try to apologize to you. But I fear you held on to those moments. Sometimes I wonder if you remember my anger more than my happiness.

I hear my own father in my memories. It seemed like he was always correcting something and very rarely enjoying anything. Every situation needed to be better. And I'd hear that when I spoke to you. Disdain. Disappointment.

But I think the real disappointment was the fact I couldn't be better than the dad I had. My patience was thin.

I so want to see you. And do better. I'd love to think you'll be thrilled to see me. But I wonder if you'll just be waiting for me to lose my patience. To give up and yell at you because… Because you were three. Or now that you're seven, because you're seven.

You're seven. I've missed half your life.

He looks up to see the water boiling on his single-burner stove. The sky overhead is frosted with stars. The small trees and dusty scrub-brush around him block the wind but not the view above. Looking at the page again, Sam realizes he can barely see the words. He shoves the pad back into his pack. Then he opens his dehydrated camp dinner and pours it into the boiling water.

After the time in Grand Junction, his loneliness feels familiar. And in spite of the snippets of another life rolling through his head, he feels at home.

When the morning light begins filtering sideways through the scrub-brush and trees, Sam finishes loading his pack and looks around his campsite. Other than the dent in the earth, there's no evidence he was here. He starts moving, happy and quick, on the well-marked trail, going east into the dense pine forest and over the mountains. He expects to cover a lot of ground. He expects to be alone.

He is wrong.

7

Danny sits in the golf cart, unmoving. Ariel waits behind the wheel, thinking of the day ahead. Kids walk past their cart and into the small school house. Danny continues to sit.

"Have a good day," Ariel says.

Danny continues to sit. Ariel shifts the cart into reverse, and the backup chirp begins repeating.

"Love you…" she says, without looking at him.

The boy leans forward, slow and catatonic. He steps out of the cart, shoulders slumped, and moves toward the school.

She puts the cart in park and watches him. He doesn't look back.

"Danny."

Danny continues his slow trudge.

"Daniel William Kerr."

His full name in a perfect motherly tone brings him to a halt. He half turns, expecting trouble. Ariel walks up to him and leans down to his face. She's soft now and concerned.

"I don't like it either," she says as she lifts his face to look at her.

"So why?" he asks. It's not the first time.

"There's. It's…."

They look at each other. The rest of the kids have already gone into school. The golf carts that were here have now left. They are alone.

Ariel looks at the school. Then she looks at Danny.

"Come on," she says, smiling at him.

She extends her hand. He's trying hard to outgrow this gesture, but she hopes he'll take it this time. He just looks at her. She turns from the school toward her waiting cart.

Danny smirks and takes her hand. They climb into the cart, and Ariel drives them away from school. The streets are quiet. Ariel pushes the cart as fast as it will go, reveling in the open space.

She blasts through a four-way stop and onto Main Street. They dart past landscapers manicuring the common areas. One recoils as they blur by.

"You nearly hit him!" Danny laughs. It's the biggest smile Ariel has seen in days.

"Not even close!" Ariel says.

"Where are we going?"

"You'll see."

They wind up off of Main Street, past many houses and deeper into a neighborhood. The homes begin to look less cared for, with overgrown yards and dense brush.

Ariel wheels the cart into a cul-de-sac and up to its edge. Before them is an empty lot, cleared for building. A foundation was poured years ago, but now it sits abandoned, with weeds invading. The view beyond shows the whole Aspen Valley, including the runway and distant walls of the city.

Ariel turns off the golf cart, and they both look out over the town below.

"This is still my favorite view of the city," Ariel says.

"Me too," Danny says.

They sit in silence, watching a plane lift off the runway, seemingly headed right for them. Then it banks hard, climbing out and streaking east. No doubt headed for Europe.

"I love you," Ariel says.

"I love you too," Danny responds.

They watch the plane as it leaves contrails in its path.

"I know you don't want to go. The truth is, I don't want you to go either."

"So why do I have to?" Danny asks. His voice cracks, and he catches himself to keep from crying.

"It will be better for you. Safer. Better schools. Lots of things I can't get you here in Aspen."

"But you're not coming with me."

"No," she says. It's her voice that catches now, and she takes a moment to recover. "They don't allow moms at this school."

"What's wrong with my school?"

"Your friends keep leaving. Every year the school is smaller. And with all the elementary grades together now, it's a hard way to learn. Plus, you're almost the oldest kid in class. You need new friends, and challenges. There'll be sports and the chance to travel to other places!"

"Can't you talk to Mark?" Danny asks, almost pleading.

"I already have," Ariel sighs. "We've talked about it a lot. When he brought it up, I didn't like it. It was hard. But then I thought about all the great things that can happen for you. All the things you'll learn. I had to think about what's best for my boy. And the man you'll grow into because of this. Mark found this school. He researched them all, and this is by far the coolest one. I know it doesn't feel like it, but he wants what's best for you too!"

Danny starts to cry now. He's trying to hold it in, but tears break free and roll down his cheeks. His lip quivers, but he pulls it straight.

Ariel takes his hand in hers, and they look out across the city again.

"I always want the best for you. Even if it hurts me sometimes."

"I'll hate it there."

"No, you won't. The things you like here — skiing, biking, being outdoors — you can do all those in Switzerland. In fact, I bet you might like them more there! You'll miss Aspen sometimes. We'll miss each other. But I'm a bit jealous. You're gonna do great."

He squeezes her hand, three times. Each squeeze represents a word: I. Love. You. A silent code between them since he was born.

Ariel squeezes back, four times: I. Love. You. Too.

Tears roll down Ariel's cheeks, but she's smiling.

Danny's crying now, his lip curled under and from his eyes a constant stream. He's quiet and broken. Ariel wraps him in a hug, and the sounds come. A soft weeping.

***

Sam slows on the trail, listening. A sound like a giant broom filters through the forest and then stops. It comes again, a great shaking of limbs and pine needles all rubbing together.

He knows this isn't the wind. The sound is specific and directional, as if from a single tree. Sam wonders if a bear is rubbing against the bark like something from a nature film. Then he wonders if there are any bears in this forest at all.

Moving off the trail and toward the sound, he's cautious and focused.

A voice stops him cold.

"Get away!" a woman screams in a primal yell. "Get the fuck away from me, you filthy piece of shit!"

Sam grabs at the closest trunk, an unthinking gesture. He cocks his head toward the sound, catching heavy breathing and something else he can't decipher.

"Stop it! Get away!" she screams.

Then the voice fades at an exhale of pain and pure frustration.

Sam's hand is on his holster, the Walther ready. He's staring in the direction of the sound now, waiting for what's next.

"Come on then, motherfucker!" the woman yells. "You really want me? Give it your best shot!"

Sam breaks into a sprint, drawing his pistol as he goes. He vaults a log and never breaks stride. The Walther blurs up and down in his hand as he pumps hard through the trees.

The sound of growls can be heard as he closes in. The woman hollers something unintelligible.

Then he sees a clearing up ahead, with a tiny two-track road cutting toward it through the pines. Darting onto the road, Sam sprints toward the clearing.

Pistol raised, he comes to a stop at the edge of the clearing. Across the space sits a woman at the base of a large pine with her hands tied around the trunk behind her. Three coyotes, the size of malamutes, bare their teeth and growl at Sam. Two of them look back at the woman and take another slinking step forward. She kicks one in the snout. It recoils, but Sam can see her other shoe is already torn and bloody.

The closest coyote bristles at Sam. He stares down the pistol sight, wanting to shoot but not daring to miss.

"Shoot them!" the woman demands as she kicks again toward the others.

The coyote hunkers, eyes on Sam. It's a loaded spring, and he can't take the chance.

The Walther kicks when he pulls the trigger. The coyote's head caves in a red mist as if hit with an invisible pickaxe. The body drops lifeless with a half-whimper.

As the sound bounces off the tree trunks, the other two coyotes tuck their tails in submission. They watch Sam closely. One sniffs the air in the direction of their fallen friend.

Sam takes one step into the clearing, and the two coyotes run. They bound, leaping and carving through tight trunks, as gray blurs that are soon out of sight.

The woman is panting now. Hyperventilating in a combination of relief and terror.

Sam exhales, unaware he was holding his breath.

"OhMyGodOhMyGodOhMyGod!" the woman repeats like a mantra.

Sam steps close to her. She continues chanting while staring at his pistol. He holsters the Walther and kneels to look her in the face.

"Are you okay?" he asks, and instantly feels stupid. His eyes register the bloody tip of one foot and the raw rub marks where her arms are lashed around the tree.

Stepping behind the trunk, he grabs the bloody ropes binding her wrists. She tugs away, untrusting, but he pulls his multitool from a pocket and begins sawing one of the coils.

She goes silent now, watching him awkwardly over her shoulder. He snaps two of the cords and unwraps the rest. The woman pulls free when he's half done and backs into the center of the clearing in terror.

Sam stays kneeling behind the tree. He looks at her and closes the blade on his multitool. She stares back, her brown eyes wet and her face streaked with tears. Her shirt is torn above one breast, exposing bare skin beneath. Her arms are covered in scrapes and abrasions. Sam can't tell if they are from the tree or forest predators.

But the bruise on her cheek is clear. She was hit in the face before she wound up tied to this tree. And whoever put her here expected her to die.

"Who the fuck are you?" she yells at him.

"I'm not going to hurt you," Sam says in the calmest tone he can find as his adrenaline rages.

Her eyes move from the big pack on his back to the pistol, and then to the knife now closed in his hands.

She struggles to stand. As she straightens, it's clear her torn foot is excruciating.

Sam rises slowly, keeping the tree between them. She tenses and nearly loses her balance.

"How long have you been out here?"

No answer, her eyes darting as she continues sizing him up.

"Who did this to you?"

Still nothing. She takes one limping step backwards, away from Sam.

"When's the last time you ate?"

"Couple days," she says. Her answer seems to surprise them both.

"I've got plenty of food. Jerky. Some dried pasta."

"You're not with them, are you?" she asks.

"I'm all by myself."

"Curtis didn't send you out here?"

Sam recoils as if this question had literally struck him. He looks at the bruise on her face again.

"No..." he says, slow and quiet.

The woman loses her balance now, giving up and falling back to the earth.

"Thank you," she breathes. It's almost a whisper.

"You're welcome," he says. Then he sits down next to her.

They sit together in the clearing, silent for a moment.

"I'm Laura," she offers.

"Sam," he smiles back. "Good to meet you, Laura."

8

Ariel lies under a high thread-count cotton sheet, one leg curled and the other foot protruding. Mark stands in the door of the bathroom, looking at her. He steps closer, his hand gliding up the exposed leg as he kisses her on the temple.

She makes a humming sound, happy and sleepy all at once. His hand keeps climbing. Ariel grins at him, eyes still closed.

"He's in the next room," she murmurs.

"Our door does lock," Mark smiles back.

She rolls on her back and looks up at him. A soft morning light seeps in at the edges of the thick curtains, and she can see he's freshly shaved. He's still as handsome and chiseled as when she first met him here almost three years ago. There's more stress in his face most of the time, but in this moment it's gone.

"You know he'll come through the door any minute," she says.

"He's gotta learn sometime," Mark jokes back.

"No one should have to see that!"

"I know," he says. His hand comes to rest high enough to make her flinch. He kisses her forehead and then backs away slowly. "Good morning, my love."

She smiles at him and watches him return to the bathroom.

"That's one thing about next year," she says. "No need for the door lock."

He looks at her in the reflection of the mirror. "That's true."

Her smile fades, and she goes somber. "I'm going to miss him."

He turns and comes back to sit on the end of the bed.

"It'll be good for him," Mark says.

"I know, I know," Ariel says. "He's outgrown what we can do for him here." She sits up and looks at Mark. "It's just made him so sad. I hated it."

"I'm sorry," he says as he hugs her.

"Am I a terrible mother?" she asks.

"What?" Mark replies, pulling back and looking at her. "No. Absolutely not."

"I'm sending my child away!"

"You're sending him somewhere that will make him better. You're self-aware enough to know that the best thing for him is something you can't provide. Most mothers would homeschool in some hovel somewhere and believe they've done their kids a favor."

She thinks about that for a moment. Her eyes grow distant.

"Look," Mark continues, "you can go visit him for every holiday if you want. I guarantee you he'll be saying, 'Mom, you don't have to come for this one' in half a year. He's going to thrive there."

She nods, trying to convince herself.

Mark pulls on a pair of well-tailored khakis and starts buttoning his shirt.

"Do you want me to talk to him?" he asks.

Ariel shakes her head. "No, we've talked it through. He knows his time here is ending. It's just hard."

"You're doing the right thing," he says. He steps to the bed, grabs her arm and kisses the top of her head.

"I love you," she says.

"Me too," he answers.

***

Curtis sits in the paneled conference room with Dixon and Lawrence. He stares at the mock-up of the Aspen door. Lawrence eyes him, unsure. Dixon waits patiently.

"Can we do this?" Curtis asks.

"There will be casualties," Dixon answers. "But fewer than walking up to the main gate."

"If we find the convoy," Lawrence says.

"We know where they go for fuel," Dixon says. "We can wait them out."

"That could be weeks," says Curtis. "We can't be exposed with our whole force waiting on them to go to the gas station. Put someone on it. Give them Sam's ATV and one of the working satellite phones."

"We only have the base station and two portables left," Lawrence cautions.

"That's all we need," Curtis says. "I want everyone prepped to leave with a 15-minute warning. Drill them, Dixon…. They need to be ready to go when we get the call."

"Will do, Boss," Dixon says as he stands to leave.

***

Sam finishes bandaging Laura's torn foot as she sits against a tree. He eyes the dirt road that continues eastbound through the pine trees. As strange as this encounter has been, it has revealed a faster route.

"Okay, try that," Sam says. "Go slow."

Laura cautiously rises to her feet, bracing against the tree and putting weight on her bandaged foot. She winces, but stands.

"It's okay," she says. "Hurts, but I can walk on it."

She demonstrates, starting in a slow circle around the clearing. She limps far less than Sam expected, and as she walks Sam can see her trying to banish it completely. This woman is tougher than he realized.

"Don't overdo it," Sam says. "Take it slow."

She's turning back to him now, still working the limp out of her step.

"We can't stay here," she says.

She comes to a stop in front of him. Sam sees intensity and fear in her light-brown eyes. It strikes him that her eyes are almost hazel, a color he's rarely seen. She's close now, staring up at him. He looks down, breaking her stare. His glance drifts past the deep plunge of her cleavage exposed by her torn shirt.

"You're right," Sam says. "But we can stay on the road and make things easier for you."

"I'll be fine," Laura says. "We can't stay on this road. They'll find me."

Sam pulls an extra shirt out of his pack.

"If anyone comes down this road, they'll be driving and we'll hear them."

He hands her the shirt. She glances down at her own cleavage, smirks and takes it.

Sam grabs his pack now. Laura can tell it's heavy. He takes a few steps down the road, deeper into the forest and away from Grand Junction.

Laura looks back the way she came, then turns to Sam. She relaxes a bit and starts toward him.

"Where are we going?" she asks.

"Aspen," he answers.

Part 5

The Lookout

1

Hours later, the thin road cuts through another open spot in the pines. A deer turns to look at Sam as he enters the far side. He stops and lets Laura step up beside him. They both watch the deer, still chewing as it slowly starts to walk into the trees.

"How's your foot?"

"Am I slowing you down?"

"It's not you," Sam smiles at Laura and takes off his pack. "Before Grand Junction I had an ATV and was making great time."

"What happened to it?"

"I had to trade it to get out of town."

"Curtis," Laura says, spitting out the name.

Sam sits in the shade of the trees behind them. He pulls water and jerky from his pack, sharing them with Laura.

"Where'd you come from?" she asks.

"California," Sam says.

She sits beside him, ripping off a piece of the jerky.

"Why'd you come to the Junction?"

"I just needed supplies," Sam says. "What about you?"

"It was the closest place," Laura says. "I was taking classes in Boulder when Denver went to shit. A group of friends and I started west in our car. Of course, so did everybody else."

"Where were you headed?"

"Don't know. My friend's parents had a house in Salt Lake. My parents are in Idaho."

"What happened?"

"Well, you know how no one's cards worked, right?"

Sam nods, and she continues.

"We didn't have a full tank of gas. We hadn't even packed, really. It was just last-minute panic with everyone else. Cars all around us started dying on the side of the road. People were walking with stuff pulled from their cars. I-70 became just as many people walking as driving. Our car lasted 'til almost Glenwood Springs, and then we were walking too."

Sam picks up his pack again. They continue down the dirt road.

"Did you try to go to Aspen?" he asks.

"They were already blocking the road," Laura says. "Aspen went on lockdown pretty quick, like someone knew this was coming and had picked it already."

Sam has never thought of this. When the crash happened, he hadn't tried to go anywhere and believed the system would be restarted. In the days to follow, as news became hard to come by, he never imagined locations had been preselected for Shining City defenses. The idea now seems so obvious he can't believe he missed it.

"How'd you find this out?" he asks.

"News spread pretty quick. People were headed to Aspen and weren't coming back. Folks were getting shot for jumping barricades. That's what I heard. I didn't want to get close."

"So you went to Grand Junction?"

"Not right away. You remember when we weren't allowed to go out at night?"

"Yeah. Martial law helped for a bit."

"We were all scared to travel anywhere if we couldn't get there before dark. So, Glenwood was home for a while, but all the small places ran out of stuff first. It turned into a dangerous place."

"Why didn't you go back to Denver?"

"My friends did. It was the closest big city. But I was too scared. Of course no one had the internet anymore, so we had no idea what the fuck was going on. Amazing how lost we were without it. I just had a terrible feeling about going back to Denver. If we'd had five minutes of internet we'd have known how bad it was."

"It was one of the worst," Sam remembers. "Except for maybe L.A."

"I'm pretty sure my friends died in the riots. Or starved. I don't know."

They start walking down the dirt road in silence. It's barely more than a two-track through the pines now, overgrown but still faster than walking through the wild undergrowth. Laura's limp is almost gone, but Sam suspects it will feel worse when they stop for the night.

"No one travels anymore," Laura says. "What are you doing?"

Sam pushes up his sleeve and shows her the scar on his shoulder. She nods.

"Debt Rec or military?"

"Rec," Sam says. "And when I got out, I went looking for my family. Most of them are dead. But my wife and son are in Aspen. Or were."

"That's a long way to go if you're not sure."

"I don't have anything else."

Laura nods at this.

The dirt road broadens and connects to a turnout on the side of a paved road. They stop just inside the forest. Sam listens as he unfastens his rifle from his pack. Cautious, he steps through the turnout and up to the road.

They look both ways in silence.

Weeds punch up through the concrete. The road edge is crumbling back to dirt. The lonely, forgotten mountain road stretches north and south, with bends in the distance. No cars parked or abandoned in either direction for as far as they can see. It would be even easier to walk it, but would leave them exposed and going in the wrong direction.

They cross. Sam moves quickly, expecting an ambush. He pauses at the far side and steps to a nearby mile marker. He notes the road number on the bottom and then walks into the dense, uncut forest on the other side. Laura follows.

"Can't we just stay on it a while?" Laura asks.

"No. Wrong direction. But it helps us."

Sam drops his pack and digs out a well-worn paper map. He finds the road on the map.

"You know where we are?" she asks.

"Kinda," he says, "but it's not like seeing an exact pinpoint on a phone."

"Yeah. Can't believe you made it this far without that!"

"I was on roads. No one uses them, but they still go where they used to, and they have signs."

He gauges where they are in relation to Aspen. Laura has slowed him down, but the dirt road helped. Three more days, he thinks, maybe four.

"It'll be dark in two or three hours. Can you do a bit more before we stop for the night?"

Laura flexes her foot. "It hurts, but let's keep going."

Sam nods. He starts through the forest, blazing a path eastward. This will be much slower.

"How are you getting into Aspen?" Laura asks as they crunch through the undergrowth.

"I don't know how my family got in. Hopefully they'll accept me the same way."

"Do they even know you're coming?" she asks.

He glances back over his shoulder at her and smiles. "My smartphone's out of juice."

"They'll shoot you," she says.

"Maybe."

"There's a lot of other places we could go."

"Where would you go?" Sam asks, wanting to change the subject.

"Denver, I guess. Curtis said it got better after the National Guard took over." She sighs. "But he was probably full of shit on that too. So. Anywhere but where he is."

"I agree with you there," Sam says.

They trudge on in silence as the late-day sun casts amber columns through the pines.

***

Hours later, the sky has turned a deep blue, and the first stars are visible overhead. Sam starts his gas stove as Laura lies on his unfolded sleeping bag.

"Were you close to Curtis?" Sam asks.

"Close enough to get this," she answers, touching the fading bruise on her cheek.

Sam nods, his gaze lingering on her.

"Stop it," Laura says.

"What?"

"Feeling sorry for me. I don't need that shit."

"I didn't… I wasn't… I just…." But Sam can't find what he wants to say and looks back at the stove. He starts heating their dinner.

Laura watches him for a moment. He's in his element, and she knows she has disrupted it.

"How long have you been on the road?" she asks.

"I don't know. I didn't bother to count."

"How long were you in the Junction?"

"Couple days."

"So you only saw what he wanted you to."

"I saw enough."

"Did you see the green room full of girls?"

"Yeah. What's that about?"

"That's the realest place in the Junction. Everyone in there is on call. For Curtis. Or others."

"Like Dixon and Lawrence?" Sam asks.

"Lawrence. That creepy son of a bitch is the last person you want to get called for. I never did, but I heard the stories."

"So you knew those girls?"

"Hello?" Laura looks at him. "I was one of them. Damn good place to be. We ate well and knew every secret in town."

"How?"

She smiles. It's the look of a predator. "Men are easy. Work them up right, and they'll tell you their darkest secret for a chance to cum."

Sam thinks of the times he was enraged at Ariel, and she'd defuse him with a night of great sex. Now it makes him feel weak and ashamed.

"I bet Curtis loved talking to you about the Debt Rec program," Laura says.

"He had a lot of questions about it."

"Didn't tell you why, though, did he?"

"It was all about the Shining Cities. I was on work crew, so he—"

"Bullshit," she interrupts him. "He probably hasn't met another Debt Rec since he left the program."

"I thought he was in the military," Sam says.

"That's what everyone thinks. And he took out his chip so no one knew the truth anyway. But I met him when I first got to the Junction. He had nothing, but he told a good story about coming back from overseas right as the crash happened. My favorite was when he talked about landing in Dallas to discover he'd been decommissioned into a crumbling world."

Sam splits the small dinner into two portions and goes to sit beside Laura. They begin to eat, but Sam's confused.

"You think he made up that story?" Sam asks.

"I know he did," Laura says between bites. "He was a janitor at the stadium in Dallas, and ended up owing around three thousand dollars when the debts were called. It was so insignificant compared to most cases that they assigned him to keep the debt‑processing building clean. They cut him loose in two months."

"How do you know that?"

"I'm telling you," she says with a matter of fact certainty. "We met when he was first telling stories to anyone who would listen in Grand Junction. And there weren't any military guys around to call bullshit. Everyone knew him as the guy from the front lines. So when it was clear they needed their own leaders, he was launched to the top."

"Who put him in charge?"

"No one. We had a vote, and the former mayor of the Junction won." She stops, takes another bite and thinks for a moment. "Can't remember the poor bastard's name. He made Curtis the head of town security. Trusted his judgment completely. And it got him killed."

"Curtis killed him."

"I think so. No one will ever know, and it's one of the few things he never said to me. But…"

"Did all the girls know this?"

"No. Some had heard parts of the real story when he was drunk or begging for it. Most of them thought it was made up, like some role-playing thing. But I think those were the only times he told the truth."

"There's no way to know what's true then."

"You think I'm full of shit, I know. But think about Dixon. That guy was some bad-ass cop before everything went down. And the only security Curtis ever set up was telling Dixon to go do it. I think Curtis had played every military strategy game known to man, but had no idea how to set up order in a small town. Smartest cover he ever did was handing it all to Dixon."

"Curtis was in charge of everything when I was there," Sam says.

"Did you ever hear him dictate strategy? Or establish a plan? I'm betting he gave a lot of speeches but didn't actually plan or do a damn thing."

Sam thinks back over his time with Curtis. All their talks were long, and Curtis had been persuasive and charismatic. But even when talking about the Aspen door, Curtis seemed unable to pick a strategy.

Laura's story seems absurd at first. But the more Sam thinks about his brief time with Curtis, the more he wonders if she might be right.

"How could he fool the entire town?" Sam asks.

"He gives a great speech," Laura answers. "He speaks to people's fears and dreams like some mind reader, and by the time it's over they'll follow him anywhere."

2

Curtis lies in the middle of a king-sized bed, leaning against the headboard. He watches the tall, thin blonde pull on her panties and stand.

"What got into you tonight?" Curtis asks.

She smirks at him, hands on her hips.

"No pun intended. You were a woman on a mission."

She crawls across the bed, breasts dangling, and kisses him.

"I want you happy," she says.

He's looking at her. Studying her. His eyes turn darker.

"You're scared of me."

She pulls on her shirt over bare breasts. "No, I'm not."

"Look at me."

She turns, but he notices a tiny hesitation in her movement.

"Come here," he says as he hooks a finger toward her.

She rounds the bed dutifully, her eyes on the ground. Curtis watches her approach and stand at the bedside. He waits for her eyes to come up.

"I know you and Laura were friends," he says. "And I'm guessing she told you how much she wanted to marry me."

The woman nods, her eyes back on the floor.

"But you understand I can't play favorites. What do you think would happen to all you girls if I wound up with a wife?"

He reaches out and grabs the woman's thin wrist.

"Well?"

"You wouldn't need us anymore," she says.

"I couldn't take care of you. You couldn't take care of me. We're all in this together."

He sighs, like a disappointed parent. "Laura didn't understand that like you do. She got angry."

"Did you kill her?"

Curtis lets go of her wrist and recoils.

"God, no! I could never do that. I couldn't lay a finger on her."

The woman knows this isn't true. She's seen the bruises and had some herself. But she won't dare say this.

"We agreed that she should go," Curtis shakes his head. "I think we'll all miss her."

The woman nods and tries to keep the tears in her lashes from falling.

"But, life is full of changes. And if she'd been here tonight instead of you, it wouldn't have been nearly as much fun. So we might be better off…. How else would we have ever known!"

She looks at Curtis, tentative.

"You can always ask me anything. And I'll always tell you the truth." He looks her up and down. "You're my new favorite."

She digs deep and finds a smile.

"Now go…. I have to sleep."

He turns off the light before she's even gathered all her clothes.

***

Early the next morning, Sam awakens with the first blue light of dawn. He sits up and looks at Laura. She's still asleep in his sleeping bag on top of the foam pad. He's wearing most of his warmest clothing, and slept right on the ground. He envies her in this moment.

He gets up and wanders into the woods, letting his limbs loosen with the blood flow. The forest is quiet and still dark. He leans against a tree and relieves himself, keeping his back to their little camp. He knows Laura is slowing him down, but he can't leave her. The two of them combined will consume all his food and supplies far faster than he would alone. There should be enough to make it to Aspen, but if they don't let him in right away, he could be in real trouble.

He finishes and zips up, now wondering where Laura fits in his plans. He can't imagine he'll be able to talk them both into Aspen, and Ariel will be far less likely to speak up for him if he's traveling with a woman. Laura complicates everything about his trip. The best thing would be to separate from her and go back to traveling alone. But the truth is, it's been so long since he spent any time with a woman that he's drawn to her. He knows it's a natural response; she's attractive, easy to talk to and interested in him. He still hates himself for it.

Returning to camp, he sees Laura is still asleep. He takes the camp stove and lights it, the flame jumping to life with a hiss.

"Hey…" Laura says.

He glances up to see her looking at him with a sleepy smile.

"Sorry to wake you," Sam says. "Did you sleep well?"

"I still can't believe you gave me all your stuff."

"Anyone would've done it."

"No. Most wouldn't have."

He looks at her again, and she's smiling at him. It's a warm, inviting look, and it turns him on. He tries to focus on the little stove again.

***

A few hours later, Dixon stands outside the Grand Junction fire station. A group of ten are gathered in front of him. These are his best people, including Jesse, the big kid that tried to watch over Sam. Both men and women make up the team, and they range in age from Jesse to

Paper Father

Leonard, a long-retired fireman who's pushing eighty.

All around them sit an assortment of vehicles. The panel-truck Sam saw when he first arrived is here. Three long-travel suspension motocross bikes lean together. Sam's road-worn ATV is parked next to an even larger model. Two four-seat UTVs sit next to the fire-station door, and a blacked-out two seater with a makeshift mount on the roll cage sits by itself. A .50-caliber machine gun sags in the mount.

"We'll know more once Aaron gets to the lookout," Dixon says. "When he sees they're on the move, we'll have just enough time."

Aaron, a small, rail-thin guy in his late twenties, stands next to Sam's ATV. He's wearing a small backpack and a pistol holster on his thigh. Dixon hands him one of the two satellite phones, and Aaron shoves it into one of the large pockets of his cargo pants.

"How long do I wait them out?" Aaron asks.

"Stay until you see them," Dixon orders. "This is our big push."

"We can't take a convoy," Leonard says.

Dixon looks at him, and the old guy doesn't blink.

"When Aaron goes, we start training," Dixon says. "We'll have strategy, not numbers. Then once we have the convoy, the numbers will follow."

"Everyone?" asks Jesse.

"We're going to lose a lot of people," Dixon admits. "But there's enough of us to take it."

Leonard laughs, a short sound somewhere between a honk and a cough.

"What?" asks Dixon.

"I been here my whole life," Leonard smiles. "Glad to stay far away from those pricks in Aspen. Now I'm risking my life to get in."

"We thank you."

"Shut it," snaps Leonard. "I'm not looking for your thanks. I've had a good run. Let's go knock 'em down a peg. Or seven."

Dixon smiles at that, and turns back to Aaron.

"Take the ATV," he says, pointing at Sam's.

"I'll be faster on the bike," Aaron answers as he moves toward the cluster of three.

"Suit yourself," says Dixon.

Aaron pulls the tallest motocross bike from the collection. The suspension is so high he can barely get his leg over the seat. He settles on to it, rocking the soft suspension.

"I'll be there in a few hours," he says. "I'll check in when I arrive."

"No," Dixon says. "Save the battery on that phone. I'll have the other one with me all the time. Call when we have to move… or if something goes to hell. Otherwise, wait."

Aaron kicks the bike to life. It screams as he twists the throttle. A flick of his foot puts it in gear.

Dixon nods, and Aaron takes off with the bike still screaming. They listen to the sound as it fades toward the eastern gate.

***

Deep in the forest, Sam walks behind Laura and watches her limp. As they move, it seems to lessen. The day grows warmer, and the thin game trail beneath them leads almost due east. They walk on in silence, both struggling against the altitude. Sam pulls in big heaving breaths, his chest straining against the straps of his loaded pack. Laura gasps as well. She's wearing the top of his pack, which doubles as a small daypack. He appreciates her carrying their extra water. He still has a lot of weight.

Cresting a rise on the shoulder of a mountain, they stop and look farther east. Another valley and peak greet them, with more in the distance. Three days together, and Sam hopes no more than three to go.

Looking at his compass, Sam nods. The game trail winds down from the ridge, continuing the way they need. Sam steps in front of Laura; they don't speak but continue sucking in each breath. Laura does smile at Sam, and he winks back as he starts down the mountain.

By midday, they are resting on the bank of a river on the valley floor. The next range of peaks looks immense, but knowing what they've come through brings a sense of deja vu.

As they finish pieces of jerky and camp food masquerading as lasagna, Sam thinks of his legal pads. He hasn't written a word since connecting with Laura. He feels the need to make an entry.

"What's wrong?" Laura asks.

"What?"

"What's bothering you?"

"Oh. Sorry. Nothing," Sam lies.

"You went away for a while," she says. "Where'd you go?"

"It's nothing."

"Family?"

Sam nods, hoping for any way to end this line of questioning. He looks over at the lid of his pack, now converted into her small daypack. Even though he remembers taking the pages out to hide in his main pack, he still fears she'll find them.

He stands and begins to repack. Laura watches him.

"Anything I can do?" she asks.

"Yeah, if you'll put the water back in your pack and maybe the stove as well…."

She stands, walks away from the gear and close to Sam. He lifts his eyes to meet hers.

"I'm sorry," she says.

She hugs him. Sam is initially so surprised that he stands rock-still. Then, as the hug continues, he wraps his arms around Laura. He softens. His apprehension fades. For a few moments in the forest they just stand and embrace.

"Better?" Laura asks as she pulls back enough to look at him. Sam nods.

"Family shit's the worst," she continues. "There's no way around it, you just gotta keep walking through."

"You're right," Sam says. "Like these mountains."

She smiles and closes her small backpack.

Sam looks around, wishing he could write about this stream and view. He can't bring himself to stop and pull the pages out in front of Laura. Then it dawns on him that she might already know about his writings. Curtis could have told her.

Then a more disturbing idea blooms. He wonders for the first time if Laura was planted in his path. He dismisses the thought as absurd. He looks at her lingering limp on wounded toes and knows she was left to die. But the thought remains.

3

Mark turns his golf cart into a hard turn between two Gulfstream jets. Beside him, Danny smiles at the sudden jerk. He laughs, both amused and nervous.

They squeal to a stop behind a white and blue G6, its stairs extended to the tarmac. Mark steps out of the cart and up to the stairs. Danny slides across the cart bench and steps up beside him.

"This is called a Gulfstream," Mark says.

"It's a G6," Danny says.

Mark smiles, surprised. "Oh. You know about these."

"They're awesome."

"Have you been here before?"

Danny looks at his feet. Mark lowers himself down to look Danny in the face. "You're not in trouble. I'm impressed. I didn't know you knew anything about airplanes."

"I've come here a few times."

"But you've never been in one, right?"

Danny shakes his head.

"Well," Mark smiles and stands. "Let's go."

He walks up the stairs and ducks into the cabin. Danny is shocked.

"Come on," Mark says from just inside the doorway.

Danny sprints up the stairs. He stands wide-eyed. His head darts back and forth as he looks between the cockpit and the luxurious cabin.

"You can come look," says the pilot. Danny jerks in surprise. Then he smiles and stares into the cockpit. It seems like a spaceship. There's a noise behind him, and he glances back to see the door closing and

Mark buckling into a seat.

"What are we doing?" Danny gasps.

"You've never flown before, right?" asks the captain.

Danny shakes his head. He looks between the pilot and Mark, who smiles at him from the front row of the cabin.

"Well, it's just a short flight today," the pilot says. "Why don't you be my co-pilot?" He points at the right-hand seat and then starts the engines.

Danny clambers into the seat to find a booster cushion already waiting for him. He can barely see over the gauges, but it's enough. The pilot helps him buckle in and then puts his hands on the throttles.

"You ready?"

Danny nods in a blur. Mark laughs from behind him.

The plane throttles up and begins to taxi toward the runway.

***

Later that night, Mark steps out of the dark streets and into the house he shares with Danny and Ariel. She's in the kitchen, working on a laptop. She glances at the time. It's after ten.

Getting up, she walks to greet him in the entryway. She wraps her arms around his neck.

"I'm sorry you're home so late," she says. "I know the thing with Danny really took up time."

"It's alright," he says. He gives her a quick kiss and then steps out of her arms and toward the kitchen.

"How'd it go?" Ariel asks.

"Good. He seemed to love it. What did he tell you?"

"When I put him to bed, he told me you let him fly?"

Mark laughs. "The pilot had him put his hands on the stick when we were in the air. It was nothing."

"It made a big impression."

"I'm glad."

He gets himself a beer and rubs a hand across his face. Ariel has seen him do this many times, and knows he's hiding something.

"What happened?"

Mark turns and tries to shake it off, but can't. He takes a sip of his beer and looks at her.

"He asked me if he had to go."

Now Ariel looks at her feet just like Danny did.

"What did you say?" she asks.

"I said he did. I told him he'd be happier. And he told me he would probably die."

Ariel smirks at that. "Bit melodramatic."

"Yeah," Mark says. "I wonder where he gets that from."

Ariel glares at him. Then she smiles.

"He asked why I was sending him away," Mark continues. "He said you told him he could stay."

"I didn't."

"I know."

"He's seven."

"He's a manipulator."

"He doesn't want to leave his mother!"

Mark raises his hands in surrender.

"I get that," he says. "He's also wanting to split us on this."

"I'll talk to him again."

"No, I handled it."

"What does that mean?" Ariel asks.

Mark takes a long sip of his beer. Then he pauses even longer before looking at her again.

"I told him that it sucks to have to be a big boy. It's not always fair. But the hard stuff helps us grow up into better people. And I want to help him be the best Danny possible."

Ariel smiles.

"He asked if I'd done something hard at his age. So, I told him about signing up for T-ball when I was six, and then realizing I hated it."

"You never told me that," Ariel says.

"I didn't? I could have sworn Thomas or I would have told you. That's how we met. My dad told me I couldn't quit. Other kids were 'counting on me,' so I stayed with the team the whole season. I sucked. I hated it. But I met Thomas, and we became best friends. I never signed up for baseball again."

"You told this to Danny?"

Mark nods. "He sat for a long time and thought about it. Then he asked me if I thought he'd meet his best friend in Switzerland. I said I think he will."

Ariel steps close to Mark and hugs him from the side. He slips an arm around her waist.

"You're a good dad," she says.

"I'm not. Not to him. That role's taken."

Ariel looks up in surprise. "He mentioned his dad?"

"He asked if I thought his dad would ever come to Switzerland and see him. I told him we don't even know where his dad is. But if we ever see him, we'd help him get there."

"That's nicer than I'd be about it."

"Doesn't matter anyway."

He squeezes her closer. She hugs him back.

4

Sam and Laura have found a road. It's an overgrown two-track through the forest, with heaves and rocks breaking the path, but it is a road. They move faster now, free of the denser trees and brush around them.

"I'd say a logging road, but we haven't seen a clearing," Sam says.

"Probably a maintenance road," Laura guesses.

"I don't see anything worth maintaining."

They continue east, catching glimpses of distant peaks through the trees. The road ambles downhill, toward another valley.

For the next few hours they settle into a mostly silent cadence. The road allows for mindless hiking, and the grade makes them go ever faster. This trance-like state is part of the reason the sound doesn't register at first.

Sam stops suddenly, and it snaps Laura from her own trance. They stare at each other, eyes growing wide as the high-pitched engine noise increases. Laura looks paralyzed, unsure what to do.

Sam glances at both sides of the road, noting dense ferns and thick trees. To their right is a huge merged trunk of two ancient pines. He snatches Laura under the arm, pulling her along as he crashes off the trail and sprints toward the pines.

"Wait, shouldn't we…" Laura says, still confused.

He pulls her on as the tire roar can now be heard along with the engine. Whatever this is, it's moving very fast. Sam turns behind the thick merged trunks and pulls Laura up beside him. Without thinking, he drops his pack and draws the Walther from its holster.

Laura looks at him, suddenly frightened.

"What is it?" she asks. He just shakes his head.

They hunker for only a few seconds before the engine source comes into view: a young guy on a huge motocross bike. The engine screams like a primal creature, and the suspension hammers away at the two-track road.

The rider streaks by them, oblivious. They rise to their feet and watch him fade into the distance, leaving a dust cloud settling behind him.

"Holy shit," breathes Laura.

"He was flying," Sam says as he holsters his pistol.

"That was Aaron," Laura says, almost to herself.

"What?"

"I know him. He's from the Junction."

"You sure?"

Laura looks at her torn shoe, feeling the damaged foot anew.

"He left me to die," she says. "Do you think he's looking for me?"

"Not at that speed," Sam says. "He's going somewhere. I'd think Aspen, but he's not going to sneak up on anyone with that thing."

"He's their scout," Laura confides. "Aaron's the kid they send out to find things."

Sam picks up his pack and starts back toward the road. He looks in the direction Aaron vanished, listening to the engine still bouncing off the forest in the distance. As he reaches the road, he can see a freshly cut trail from the bike's knobby tires. Far away, the scream of the engine subsides, then blasts again in a new octave.

"He just slowed down, or turned," Sam says to Laura as she steps up beside him.

They stand in complete silence, straining to hear the last bits of the engine. It's faint, and almost drowned out by the wind, but the sound doesn't fade completely. They strain for a long time, each hearing bits of the bike still moving. Then it cuts out, suddenly stopped.

"What do you want to do?" Laura asks.

"You're sure you know him?"

She nods, confident.

Sam looks at the track in the dirt. He begins to follow it like a trail of breadcrumbs.

"Let's see where he went," Sam says.

"He'll kill us."

"I don't think he's looking for us. And it sounds like he found something." Sam picks up his pace and alternates between checking the tire trail and scanning the forest.

Laura struggles to catch up, but she follows.

Nearly an hour later, they reach an intersection. Sam checks his compass. The road they've been on continues straight through the intersection, going northeast into the forest. But tire tread pathway arcs to the right, turning nearly due south and following a thinner two-track through the trees.

Sam and Laura stand together, looking at the clear turn in Aaron's path. If he'd come upon this intersection by himself, Sam would have chosen to continue straight. But he knows Aaron has a much better sense of where he is than Sam does. He suspects the rider is headed for Aspen. He hopes.

They turn and stay with Aaron's tire trail. The new road is more overgrown and the tracks aren't always visible, but they reappear in every sandy patch of earth. The long sidelight of afternoon gives way to a blue dusk as they move along the shadow side of the mountain. Sam hopes they'll find Aaron's stopping place before nightfall.

By the time the trail becomes too dark to follow, they discover something else.

"Is that a house?" Laura whispers.

They crouch down in the trail, straining just high enough to see through ferns and undergrowth toward the distant lights.

"Definitely windows… with lights on," Sam says, even though he can't believe it.

They move down the trail, keeping their eyes on the structure. It comes into view slowly: a forest cabin with a sleek modern style. While still deep in the forest, they can tell the main level has floor-to-ceiling windows and probably expansive views in the daytime.

Sam and Laura stop, transfixed. The sight of this hidden getaway, complete with electricity and huge windows, boggles Sam's mind.

Laura leans toward him and whispers, "I know what this is."

He turns to her; she's more visible now from the light of the distant house.

"They call it the Lookout," she says. "They spy on Aspen from here."

"We can't be that close," Sam says.

"I don't know…. It has to be. Curtis talked about a place, all windows and powered by solar. How many of those can there be?"

Sam looks at the house. For all he knows, there might be hundreds of homes fitting that description. But he doesn't believe they could see Aspen from here.

"I can't see Aaron," Laura says.

Sam takes off his pack. He pulls the rifle from the side and raises the scope to his face.

The last light of dusk is fading, and the lights in the house glare in comparison. Through the scope, Sam can see into the house. It looks lived in and well kept, as if untouched by the years of decay plaguing the rest of the country.

Looking around the building, Sam sees the motocross bike. The light from a nearby window casts across the seat and tank as it leans against the side of the house.

"He's there," Sam whispers as he lowers the rifle.

They stand together in silence for a moment, staring at the house. Laura opens her mouth to say something, but she can see the debate raging in Sam's face.

He shoulders his pack, then picks up the rifle again. With his free hand, he draws the Walther and holds it out to Laura.

"Do you know how to use this?" he asks.

Laura takes the gun and peers at it in the dim light from the house. She finds the safety with her thumb and flips it to red. Then she flips it back.

"If I have to," she says.

"We're going to surprise the hell out of him. I don't think we'll need them, but…"

He trails off as he looks at the house again. Laura smiles as he peers through the scope.

"Okay," Sam says as he slinks down the trail toward the house.

Laura stays close, moving well, her injured foot long forgotten in focus and adrenaline.

As they get close enough to be seen, Sam moves into the shadows made by the few non-windowed walls. Their approach brings them up behind the bike and near a back door.

Laura glides up silently and presses against Sam in the darkness. He points to himself and motions a half-circle around the house. Then he points to Laura and the back door.

She nods, understanding his plan. He holds up two fingers and mouths a silent "two minutes." She nods again. Sam offers her a tiny smirk and then crouches, starting around the house.

Laura grips the Walther, her hands sweating. Switching hands, she wipes her palm on her filthy shirt and then takes the pistol again. Her thumb finds the safety, and she switches it off.

Sam rounds the house, looking for a front door. He remembers stories of small-town people leaving doors unlocked in the middle of nowhere. He always thought it was impossible, and yet in this moment he's counting on unlocked doors.

When he left Laura, he began counting down from one hundred twenty in his head. When he sees the front door, flanked by two floor-to-ceiling windows, he loses count. He risks a quick step through the shaft of light from one window to put himself in the shadow of the door. He reaches the doorframe and restarts his count at sixty seconds. He hopes Laura is somewhere close to the same.

Laura forgets to count. She stares at the doorknob of the solid back door. She shuffles a step closer. She reaches for the knob. Then she curses under her breath. Horrified at making a sound, she slaps a hand to her mouth and expects the door to swing open. When it doesn't, she starts to count down from twenty, certain two minutes has almost gone.

Sam points the rifle, ready in his right hand, at the sky. He slides his left hand inside the modern door pull of the front door as he leans against it with his shoulder. The last few seconds of countdown go by silently in his head.

As Laura reaches for the back door, it opens! Her hand hangs in space as Aaron steps into the doorframe and stops short.

"Ah!" he starts, as light from the house reveals Laura.

BLAM! The Walther spits fire as Laura pulls the trigger with a frightened jerk.

The bullet catches Aaron in the left side, tearing out a chunk of his torso and spraying blood into the kitchen behind him. He wheels, turning back into the house and crashing into a counter.

"Fucking bitch!" he screams as he scrambles toward the living room.

Laura steps into the kitchen, closing fast. Her surprise has given way to cold purpose.

BLAM! She fires again, taking aim this time and thudding a shot into his upper back at close range. He falls into the refrigerator, and tries to recover.

Sam flings the front door open and lowers his rifle. The second shot rings through the house, finding every resonant thing and lingering. He runs, navigating an unknown floor plan and scanning for movement as he chases the noise.

As he rounds the couch toward the small kitchen, Sam notices a pistol and satellite phone on the coffee table. Aaron makes a gurgling sound that leads him onward.

Laura strides through the kitchen as Aaron leans on the fridge and turns to face her. Blood seeps from a huge exit wound in his chest. He holds up a hand toward Laura and struggles to stay standing. It's a miracle he isn't dead yet.

Sam turns the corner to see Laura level the pistol at Aaron's head. Aaron breathes a wet inhale and claws at the air inches from the barrel. Laura pulls the trigger, and Aaron's head rocks back and ricochets blood and gore off the fridge in all directions.

Sam recoils as spray hits him in a red mist. Aaron's dead body slides down the front of the fridge, leaving a trail of blood and a bullet imbedded in the stainless steel.

"Fuck!" Sam yells as he wipes his face and smears the blood.

Laura blinks and looks at Sam. She lowers the gun quickly, then drops it on the counter. A line of smoke belches from the barrel.

"He deserved it," she says.

Sam lowers his rifle. He sees the puddle of blood forming under Aaron. He props the rifle against the wall and steps over the body. In a quick motion, he grabs the Walther, flips the safety and holsters it. Grabbing one of Aaron's arms, he pulls the body toward the open kitchen door and glares at Laura.

"Help me," he growls.

She does, grabbing the feet as Sam hoists the gory upper half of the body by the wrists. They quickly step outside, leaving a dripping trail.

A moonless night has descended, with the only light coming from the home's many windows. Sam looks both ways and decides to round the house the opposite direction from the front door. They shuffle quickly, getting to an edge of the dirt driveway and half-tossing, half-dropping the body over the small berm and into the undergrowth. It thuds and slides to rest in the darkness.

"Son of a bitch," Sam spits.

He passes Laura and stomps back into the house.

"My god…" he says.

Laura steps into the kitchen behind him. A sticky smear of blood nearly two feet wide runs the length of the tile. The refrigerator looks like a modern art project gone wrong. Sam flips off the kitchen light and steps into the living room. Suddenly the house feels very bright, and he goes around quickly turning off almost every light.

Laura stands in the doorframe of the kitchen, watching him until he stops by a single side-table lamp, the last light in the house. He leaves it on. His shoulders slump, and he realizes for the first time since they arrived that he's still wearing his backpack. Unbuckling the straps, he drops it to the rug with a thud.

"I'm sorry," Laura breathes.

"Are you okay?" Sam asks.

She slides the daypack off her shoulders and rubs her arms. Goosebumps follow.

"I think so," she says.

They stand across the room from each other, both silent and taking long, deep breaths. Sam keeps clenching and unclenching his fists. Laura's hands begin to shake.

"He tied me, left me…" she says in a shrieking, fearful inhale.

He sees her goosebumps and shaking hands in the dim light of the single lamp. He crosses the room toward her, his hands up and arms out for an embrace. She tenses, and he stops. Then she takes a step toward him, and they meet in a desperate hug.

Two quick, clipped sobs escape her lips as she squeezes him.

"He's gone," Sam says.

5

As Sam and Laura step back from their embrace, they feel self-conscious. Sam picks up Aaron's pistol and satellite phone from the coffee table and begins to walk around the house. Laura watches him.

They have entered on the upper story, with the small kitchen on the back. The majority of the level sticks out of the pines and into space — with a glassed-in dining area and separate living area, complete with deep couches and a fireplace. The entire floor is set up perfectly for entertaining. A high-power telescope stands in a glassed-in corner, with one glass wall covered in haphazardly taped maps and lists. This isn't the work of the original homeowners; one quick glance tells Sam these are details and observations about Aspen.

He moves on, finding stairs descending to a lower floor dug into the rock of the hillside. Laura follows him, tentative, as he leads with Aaron's pistol and flips on lights with the antenna of the sat phone.

Three bedrooms and a full kitchen are hidden away downstairs. Windowless on two sides, this floor looks more lived in than the museum-like design upstairs. Only the master bedroom, with large modern furniture and an all-windowed corner, seems to bridge the gap between the two spaces.

As Sam wanders through, in a post-adrenaline trance, they step into the immense master bathroom. Warm, wet air still lingers, and drops of water cling to the glass shower walls. They see stacks of towels and a clouded mirror, realizing together that Aaron had just finished a shower as they approached.

Laura walks to the huge round bathtub. She stares at it like it's a luxury from another world.

"Can I…?" she asks, timid.

Sam stands still for a moment, seeing her blood-smeared face and clothes. Then he sees his own blood-spattered face in the mirror.

"Of course," he says. "I will too."

Laura has already taken off her shirt. Her shoes and socks follow quickly, and she reaches for her waistline as she sees Sam leaving.

"Don't go," she says, afraid.

"I'll be in the next room," he says, trying not to look back at her.

She finds him there, a half hour later. He looks exhausted, but he's sitting in a bedside chair, watching the door to the bedroom and listening for other movement in the house.

He can't believe how different she looks, wrapped in a robe and dabbing wet hair like a woman on a luxury vacation. This would have seemed normal in a world he hasn't seen for years.

"Go on," she says, sounding refreshed and relaxed. "It's your turn."

Sam stands, feeling as bad as he looks. The idea of a shower nearly brings him to tears, and he shuffles toward the bathroom.

"I'll see if there's anything normal to eat," she says as she turns for the doorway.

"No, don't!" Sam blurts out, scaring them both.

"I'm not going upstairs," she assures him. "I'll check the kitchen down here."

He looks at her, his guard coming down slowly.

"I'm okay," she reassures him. "Go take a shower."

Sam does. He can't help but stare at himself in the mirror as he peels off dirty and blood-stained clothes.

Standing under the water, he rubs his face and watches the brown- and red-tinged water fall away. He scrubs himself so hard it almost hurts. Finally, with the bathroom like a sauna, he steps out and wraps a towel around his waist. He can't bring himself to put his filthy clothes back on. Now he understands why Laura came out in a robe. He leaves the dirty clothes where he dropped them and steps into the master bedroom.

Aaron's gun and the satellite phone are right where he left them on the nightstand. Laura sits with her back to him in a chair by the window. She looks over her shoulder.

"You feel better?" she smiles. "I feel like a different person."

"Yeah," Sam marvels as he walks over.

He sees she has a bottle of wine, two glasses and a plate of sausage and cheese. He stops, struggling with the scene and half-convinced it's a dream.

"I know, right?" Laura says. "This is what they had."

Sam takes the chair across from her and looks at the things on the table between them. He's struck again by the sense they are on vacation. His whole journey so far — culminating in the blood-soaked kitchen — now collides with this civilized moment that feels almost normal.

"I shouldn't have been surprised," she begins as she pours him a glass of wine. "Curtis promised he'd bring me out here sometime… and said that whoever owned this place was a wine snob and pretentious as hell.

"I didn't believe him at first. I thought it was another bullshit story. But then a couple of the girls did actually see it — guys brought them out here to fuck like the world used to be. No one told Curtis that, of course."

The wine hits him with a fuzzy disconnection almost as soon as it enters his system. The sausage and cheese seem like the best the world has ever created. They sit and talk with a casual, relaxed candor.

When Sam tells her about his writings, Laura asks to read them. He is still clear-headed enough to refuse, but he does talk about some of the entries. After a few glasses of wine, he works his way to the downstairs kitchen with a definite buzz. He finds two tall glasses and fills them with water from the faucet. For a moment, he wonders how this house is still working as though the world was normal. He also wonders what happened to the owners.

Back in the bedroom, he finds Laura standing and looking out the window. He hands her a glass, and she turns to him with tears in her eyes.

"Thank you," she says, and hugs him.

He sets the glasses down on the table and hugs her back.

"I thought I was going to die.... And now I'm here."

She's breathing heavy, almost crying, against his chest. The smell of her damp hair and the press of her breasts stir him without a thought. He's certain she can feel him getting hard. When she turns her face to him and kisses his neck, he knows, and now he's harder still.

He doesn't know how long it's been. He can count the years in the Rec program, but the time before that had been dry as well. He and Ariel had dwindled to having sex that felt obligatory. He needed, and she relented. But he can't remember the last time they'd really craved each other. Or, at least, the last time she craved him.

Laura's mouth meets his in a hungry search. He pulls her close. Her arms drop to his waist, pulling at the towel. It comes free, and he steps out of it as he lifts her and turns for the bed. Her legs come up, wrapping around him. He can feel her bare skin beneath the robe.

Laying her on the edge of the bed, he stands and pulls her robe open. He sees the scratch above one breast where a wolf snapped at her. He drops to that nipple, caressing it with his lips and tongue and feeling it go hard in his teeth. She twists beneath his touch, her legs around his waist, pulling him.

Laura's hands find him as he brings his face to hers again. Sam tries not to go quickly as she places him against her. He cries out when he grabs her hips and thrusts himself deep inside her. She moans and grips his arms, her eyes wild.

It is forceful and deep, both of them moving with a tense, strong craving. He is above, then below, then on top again as he climaxes with a force he can't remember. Laura practically purrs, and when they part and crawl into the bed, they're asleep in moments.

***

Hours later, Sam wakes with a start. He's disoriented and spins in the bed toward a strange green light.

Beside him, Laura tenses and covers the screen of the sat phone. Sam sits up, rubbing his eyes.

"I'm sorry," she says. "I didn't want to wake you."

"What are you doing?"

She takes her hand off the screen, and her face is lit by its green glow.

"I've never used one of these," she begins. "It's like any phone, right… like a cell phone."

"I think so," Sam mumbles, still foggy. "But there can't be that many still around and working. You have someone you want to call?"

"I don't remember anyone's number."

He reaches for the phone and scrolls through the menus. He opens the list of recent calls and notices the numbers there labeled GJ01 and GJ03. He then finds the contacts page and sees those numbers listed again.

"The other Grand Junction phones?" she asks.

"That's my guess too. One of them is probably Curtis."

She grabs the phone from him. "So it's worthless."

"Unless you want to call Curtis," he smiles and lays down again.

She sets the phone on her bedside table, next to Aaron's gun. Sam looks at it, concerned.

Laura rolls back to him, sliding in close. He accepts her, enjoying her head on his shoulder and arm across his waist. He can't resist drifting his fingers down her bare spine. He glances toward the sat phone, suddenly hating the link back to Grand Junction and wishing there were some other way to use it.

Then Laura's hand drifts lower, finding him beneath the sheets. His thoughts of the sat phone drift off as he goes hard in her fingers.

"Sorry to wake you," Laura whispers.

"It's not so bad," he smiles.

She moves, sliding above him and sitting up. He gazes up at her breasts and thin waist. She continues stroking him as she moves where she wants.

"My turn," she says as she guides him in.

Sam gasps as he enters her, and she rides him to fill her needs. It's slow and rhythmic, her hips surging and grasping as she builds for a climax. He tries to concentrate, wanting to hold out long enough to let her finish.

He does, just barely. And then he sleeps more soundly than before.

6

Sam wakes at first light, as he has every morning since leaving the prison. He gets up, sees Laura still asleep and goes to the bathroom to find his clothes. The dirty pile on the floor repulses him, so he chooses the robe behind the door. The idea strikes him that if the home has power, it might also have a clothes washer. He wonders how much of the solar power would be drained by that luxury, but he gathers up his and Laura's clothes and goes in search.

In the laundry room, he smiles at how normal this feels, as if the world had never changed. The washer and dryer both show live LED numbers on the front, but he knows the dryer is bound to use too much power. He loads the washer, but doesn't find any soap. Concluding that a rinse is better than nothing, he starts the machine.

He returns to the bedroom and finds Laura still sleeping. He thinks the sat phone is in a different place on the bedside table, as if she looked at it again. Aaron's pistol still sits beside it, and for a second he thinks he should take it with him. Shaking his head, he decides he's being paranoid.

He leaves her sleeping and goes upstairs.

The morning light transforms the upper floor. The views to the east amaze him with a dense line of treetops sloping away to distant foothills and faintly visible buildings. He notices the far wall again, with its clutter of maps and documents standing in contrast to the rest of the room.

Sam steps closer, around the enormous telescope, to the map wall. He studies the most prominent map, a topographical square with a star beside one tiny forest road. He compares the map to the undulating hills out the window. He decides the star must be this house, and begins using the other maps to figure out their location.

Soon he's looking through the huge telescope, training it on the distant buildings at the base of the foothills. His excitement builds as he cross-references the maps and the view through the lens. He now understands this house's nickname as the Lookout. From here, there's a clear view to the main road running through the center of Carbondale,

Colorado. Anyone traveling north would be coming from Aspen. Sam guesses the intersection he can see is twenty miles from the Shining City gate.

Downstairs, Laura sits up in bed holding the sat phone. She listens to the house, hearing the rumble of the clothes washer somewhere on the lower floor and the creaks of Sam's footsteps overhead. She scrolls through the saved numbers on the phone, settles on GJ01, and hits the "send" button.

She breaks out in a paranoid sweat as she hears the ring. Her eyes fix on the ceiling, listening for a change in Sam's movement. The phone keeps ringing. Then it stops with a second of static before she hears:

"What's wrong?" Dixon says with a morning thickness in his voice.

Laura waits, unsure what to say, her mind racing.

"Aaron?" Dixon says and clears his throat. "You okay?"

"Aaron's dead," Laura says, almost surprising herself.

"What? Who is this?"

"Dixon. It's Laura...."

There's a long silence now.

Dixon sits on the edge of his bed in Grand Junction. There's a woman from the green room asleep next to him. He looks at her, feeling the connection to Laura.

"I want to talk to Curtis," she says.

"No way." He stands and dresses on the move.

"I've got information. But it's only for him."

"What happened to Aaron?"

"I'll tell Curtis."

Dixon sighs as he steps out of his small college-campus duplex, pulling on his shirt as he bolts toward a golf cart.

"He thinks you're dead."

"What I've got will get me back in…."

Dixon drives full speed through campus, the motor whirring.

"Killing Aaron isn't going to do it."

"You know he was a prick. But I didn't kill him."

Now Dixon's confused, but he stays silent as he wrenches the golf cart to a stop in front of a good-sized house on the edge of campus. Dixon runs past the sign in the front yard declaring this to be the home of the college president.

"How'd you survive?" Dixon asks.

"Curtis…" she whispers.

Above her, she can hear Sam walking across the upstairs room. The clothes washer is on a spin cycle, making it louder but warning of silence soon to come.

She waits, hearing Dixon's breathing on the other end. Then a muffling sound. Then nothing.

Dixon stands in the doorframe of the upstairs bedroom. He has a hand clamped over the microphone of the sat phone.

"I'm sorry, sir," he says into the shaft of light waking Curtis.

"What the fuck!" Curtis yells at Dixon's silhouette in the doorway. "Is Aaron on fire?"

"Aaron's dead, Curtis," Dixon says. He steps into the room and extends the phone. "It's Laura."

Curtis looks at him, stunned. Dixon doesn't waver. Curtis snatches the phone out of his hand.

"Who is this?"

Sitting on the bed, listening to Sam walk from the kitchen to the telescope, Laura can't help but smile at the sound of Curtis' voice.

"It's me...."

Curtis goes wide-eyed, his mind racing. He recognizes her voice.

"I don't know how it's you," he says. "But you listen to me very carefully—"

"No, fuck that," Laura spits in a sharp whisper. "I'm at the Lookout. That guy Sam found me, and he doesn't know I'm calling."

"Sam...?"

"He shot Aaron. Killed him on the spot. And I don't know what he'll do to me. You have to come get me."

"That's not going to happen."

"I can keep him here. Let me earn my way back in...."

Curtis thinks about this, trying to put the pieces together. It makes his head hurt.

"You're at the Lookout? How did Sam find you?"

"I don't have much time. I'll call you back, but you have to come here. I'll give you him for me."

"I don't want him."

"You want me," she says, turning the words into a seduction.

Curtis feels a blush. Dixon sees it. She really is someone special to him.

"I miss you," she says. "And I know you don't want him ruining your plans."

"So you kill him," Curtis says. "Then you can come back in."

"You know I can't do that. But you know I can keep him here."

Curtis knows her skills. She knows he does. It makes him angry and excited all at once.

"Dixon will do it," he says as he stares at Dixon. "And when it's done, we'll talk about the rest."

"I gotta go," she says and hangs up. The washer spins wildly in the background. She sets the sat phone down and tries to stop sweating. She gets up, goes to the bathroom and splashes water on her face. As she dabs herself dry, she smiles in the mirror.

In Grand Junction, Curtis stares at the sat phone. Then he looks at Dixon.

"Go to the Lookout," he growls. "Kill that pretentious difficult asshole, and call when Aspen is on the move."

"And Laura?"

"Bring her to the rendezvous. I want the story straight from her."

"Will do," Dixon says as he grabs the sat phone and heads for the door.

"Dixon," Curtis calls after him. The big man turns back.

"Don't fuck her. Don't injure her. She's mine."

Dixon nods; he truly can't guess what Curtis has planned. The thought frightens him.

Phone in hand, Dixon exits the house and jumps back into his golf cart.

7

Sam hears the clothes washer wind down from its spin and turns toward the stairs. Laura rises into view, coming up in her robe. She smiles at him, sleepy but happy.

"Good morning," Sam smiles.

"Hi," she grins as she crosses to him and wraps her arms around his waist. "Did you do the laundry?"

Sam laughs. "Yeah, almost feels normal."

"Let's just stay."

Sam darkens and looks out the window.

"I don't mean forever," Laura says. "Just a few more days."

"We're close now," Sam says.

"Can you see Aspen from here?" she asks as she eyes the maps and telescope.

"No. But that's Carbondale, about 20 miles north. With the bike, we'll be there in a day or so."

"I can't go," she says.

"Why not?"

"What would your wife say?"

"We're not…" Sam stumbles. "I figured you'd want to come. I don't want to leave you here."

"Then don't go," she says.

Sam sighs and steps away from her. He looks at the floor and then out the windows at the distant intersection.

"I have to," he says, almost in a whisper.

"So what am I?" she asks.

He doesn't answer. A long silence of nothing hangs between them. Sam starts toward the stairs.

"I'm going," he says as he steps down toward the laundry room.

Once he drops out of sight, Laura throws her arms up in frustration. She looks around the room. His pack leans up against the wall. She smiles.

Downstairs, Sam pulls the damp laundry from the washer. He moves around the lower level, hanging clothes on chair backs or doorknobs to dry. When he enters the bedroom, he sees the sat phone facing the other way on the side table.

He picks up the phone and checks the recent calls. He sees the call made moments earlier. He sets the phone down again, just as he found it. In disbelief, he sits heavily on the bed as a wave of horror passes over him. He has to get out of here.

"Hey," Laura calls from behind him.

He turns to see her standing in the doorway, her robe loose.

"I'm sorry," she says as she approaches.

Sam finds a smile for her and stands.

"Me too."

She hugs his waist, her head on his chest. "I'm scared to be left again."

He feels sorry for her. He also feels stupid for trusting her.

"You can still come with me."

"I'd rather you stayed."

They break apart. An uneasy truce between people with secrets.

"I will for a while," he says.

She smiles. Her eyes flick to the bedside table and back up to Sam.

"Our clothes are still wet," Sam says, changing the subject.

"Put them in the dryer."

"It'll use a lot of power."

"That doesn't matter if we're leaving," she lies.

Sam nods. She has a point. Laura begins to gather the clothes back up.

"You go figure out where we're going. I'll get this," she says.

"Okay," Sam says as he climbs the stairs again.

Laura stops and listens to him moving across the upper floor. She pulls Sam's legal pads from behind her back, hidden inside her robe. She opens the drawer of the bedside table and slides the writings inside, just below the sat phone and Aaron's pistol.

Sam stands over his backpack, his mind racing. He knows Laura called the other sat phone, which means someone in Grand Junction knows they're here. He wonders again if she was a plant all along, left to pull him back. The idea is absurd, but he can't shake it.

There's a pit in his stomach. It grows like a ball of acid, fueled by distrust and fear. Questions race through his head. Who did Laura speak to? How long before someone will come here looking for them? Did she sleep with him just to keep him here this long? And why did he sleep with her?

He wants to sit and think this through. He wants to write down his thoughts and process this as some sort of helpful lesson for his son. But he has to get out of here. And in this moment, he can see no lesson in this — only a cautionary tale.

Nervously, he eyes his pack. The small daypack sits beside it, and the rifle leans next to them. He walks over to the corner with the maps and looks through the telescope again. No movement in the center of Carbondale. But if anyone stands here to watch, they will see him go right through the intersection. The sooner he gets there, the better.

He turns and walks through the kitchen, his eyes glancing at the bullet in the fridge door. Stepping around the line of blood on the floor, he opens the back door and steps out to the motorcycle. It's higher than his waist on long-travel suspension, but he throws a leg over it anyway. He's feels very naked sitting on this bike in just a robe. Setting the weight beneath him, he wonders how well he can handle it on a rough trail. Thankful to see the key in the ignition, he turns it enough for the fuel gauge to register. Three-quarters of a tank should get him most of the way to Aspen.

Then he wonders again if Laura will go with him.

Stepping back off the bike, he eyes the tiny fender over the rear wheel. There's nowhere to put their supplies. They'll have to be worn.

Back inside, he goes to their packs. Pulling the water and supplies out of the pack Laura used, he consolidates by refastening it to the top of his pack. He opens the main compartment of this pack and pulls out some food. He realizes they haven't eaten since the wine and cheese the night before. He thinks about being with Laura. The feel of her is fresh in his mind, and he hates himself for wanting it again.

He hopes, against his own suspicions, that she didn't call Grand Junction to betray them. Meanwhile, his hands do a quick, practiced inventory of the pieces inside his pack. Everything has a specific place, and a quick touch confirms them in a compulsive check that's become part of his daily routine.

He stops. His hands rustle the pack open, and he looks inside. His writings are gone. The pads had been in the top of his pack before he loaned that to Laura. Then he'd hidden them at the back of the main pack, under almost everything else. He looks inside, peering down, desperate.

Sam's anger rises. He stands and grabs his Walther from a nearby shelf. Gripping it, he marches downstairs.

He finds Laura in the bedroom, standing next to a pile of clothes from the dryer. She's wearing panties and fastens her bra as he enters the room. The sight of her stops him, unsettling his anger for a moment. She smiles at him: a barefoot man in a robe with a pistol in his hand.

"Cute look for you," she says.

"Where's my writing?" he says.

"What?"

"The legal pads from my pack. What I'm writing for my son."

"Where'd you last see it?" she asks as she pulls on her mostly dry shirt.

"I didn't misplace it. You took it," Sam growls.

"I've never even seen it," she says, pulling on her jeans now.

Sam pulses his grip on the pistol. For a moment he wonders if he missed something.

"Get dressed, and I'll help you find it," Laura says with breezy calm.

He steps toward the bed, eyeing his clothes.

"Were you going to shoot me?" she asks, smiling.

"I have to find it. I can't leave without it," Sam says.

He notices a knowing smirk in her eyes when he says that. He raises the pistol.

"Where is it?" he asks, cold.

"What's wrong with you?"

"You called someone in Grand Junction this morning."

Her eyes flick toward the sat phone and come back to him. She shrugs.

"What did you tell them?"

"Nothing."

Her eyes drop to it again. Sam aims and fires. He shoots the sat phone off the side table, sending shrapnel in all directions and knocking Aarons's pistol to the floor. Laura recoils, stumbling back and falling over.

With the gunshot still ringing in the room, Laura grabs Aaron's pistol and jumps to her feet. She aims at Sam, enraged.

"Yes. I took your fucking journal," she says as she stares down the barrel.

"Where is it?" Sam says from behind the Walther. He's almost hysterical.

"I'm sorry. You're my ticket back in."

Sam boggles for a moment, his pistol wavering as he tries to make sense of this.

"Back with Curtis?" he asks. "He tried to kill you!"

"No. I questioned him. He had to punish me. I deserved it."

"He's no one. You said it yourself."

"If I give you to him, he'll take me back. It's the best life I can have."

"That's insane. I'm going. You can come too. Where's the journal?"

"I hid it. I can't let you go."

Sam takes a step toward her, gun still raised. "Where is it!"

Her eyes betray her again, flicking toward the side table. Sam sees it and darts for the drawer.

Laura fires! But she's unable to match Sam's movement. The bullet graces his back as he ducks for the drawer. White terry cloth explodes off of him in a red mist.

Sam stumbles against the bed, bringing up the Walther. He aims for Laura's chest. One shot. Then another. The first catches her in the collarbone. The second blasts her in the sternum.

Sam rolls off the bed, hitting his head on the side table as he goes down. Laura falls back and hits the floor hard.

Sam tries to get up, his head reeling from the blow. He pushes up off the carpet, and his back explodes with pain. He sits against the bed, finding his Walther and looking to Laura across the room.

Laura lies on her back, with Aaron's pistol just out of reach. She stares at it, reaching and wriggling for it, but feels like she's staked to the ground. Her breathing comes in wet gurgles. She sees Sam step into view above her. He looks down, his eyes blinking to focus.

Sam can see Laura fading. Tears stream from her eyes. Blood spittles on her lips with each exhale. She tries for the gun again, so Sam puts his down and kneels beside her. At first she tries to move away, but can't. Tears well in his eyes — hating this, but knowing there's nothing he can do. He takes her hand in his, and she stares at him. Her eyes are frantic. She tries to speak, but can't.

Sam shakes his head and tries to smile. The tears muddle everything. He looks at the bloody hole in her chest, blood leaking and pooling. He puts a hand on the side of her face. Her eyes are heavy now. He tries his smile again. Laura gives a long, wet exhale.

She's gone.

Sam drops his head and squeezes tears from his eyes. He stands, taking his Walther with him. Stepping to the side table, he opens the drawer to see the legal pads inside. A breath catches in his throat, and he snatches them out.

With a painful glance at Laura, he grabs his clothes off the bed. He climbs to the main floor, drops the clothes and puts his pistol down. He dresses quickly. His clothes are still damp, but he doesn't care. He watches the stairs as if Laura will come into view at any moment.

He struggles with clinging damp socks, but finally shoves his feet back into his shoes and fastens his holster. There's a sense of relief as he drops the Walther onto his hip. With a quick swing, he shoulders his whole pack and glances at the empty stairs. The new wound on his back blazes from the pressure of the pack. Sam winces, but lifts his rifle and darts through the kitchen.

Once outside, he straddles the bike and tightens the pack as close as possible. The bullet graze settles into an ache. He twists the ignition and sighs with relief as the bike comes to life. Snapping it into gear, Sam darts away. The engine sings up through the gears, and he's putting as much distance between him and the Lookout as he can.

Part 6

Aspen

1

Soft light filters through the closed blinds of the bedroom. Mark lays on his back with Ariel tucked up next to him. One arm wraps around her, drifting back and forth across her back. They're half-awake.

The door opens suddenly, and Danny steps into the room.

"Is there hiking in Switzerland?" he asks.

"And… we're up," whispers Mark.

Ariel snickers into his chest and sits up.

"Yes," she smiles at Danny. "They have lots of hiking in Switzerland."

"The same kind of trails?" Danny asks.

"Well, I'm sure they are a bit different. But it will be beautiful," Ariel assures him.

"I'm going to miss my hike."

"Do you want to go hiking today?"

"Yeah. Can I take my waterpack?"

"Of course. We can all take our packs and have lunch at the top," she say as she looks at Mark.

Mark finds his smile. "Yeah. Let's do it."

Danny smiles, big and broad.

"Let us get ready, okay?" Ariel says. "Then we'll pack up and go."

"Awesome," Danny says as he darts out of the room.

Ariel drops back down beside Mark and puts her head on his shoulder.

"We're all going, huh?" Mark whispers.

"What'd you want to do with your Sunday?"

He squeezes her close, his hand drifting down her back again. She kisses his neck.

"Later," Ariel smiles and sits up. "Come on. He actually wants to go for once."

***

Soon the three of them are rolling through Aspen in their golf cart. Mark drives, with Ariel beside him and Danny in the back. Mark is on the radio.

"Tomorrow's fine," he says.

He listens, the radio connected to an earpiece only he can hear.

Ariel watches him. Danny plays with the end of one of his pack straps, trying to keep himself occupied. They pass the house where Danny goes to school and push farther into the neighborhood. They wind their way up into the high side of Aspen. The houses get more unkept.

"I agree. You should take everything you can," Mark continues.

After a few switchbacks, they come to the large titanium wall. It splits right through the backyards of two homes. Mark pulls into one overgrown driveway and turns off the cart.

"That's a lot, Tom," Mark says as he waves Ariel and Danny to climb out. "No. If you think you need them, that's fine. Get me your list, and I'll call them all myself."

Ariel watches him from just beside the cart.

"No. I'll do it tomorrow morning. You can leave by lunch."

He smiles at Ariel. She cocks an eyebrow, impatient.

"I gotta go. Copy that."

He pulls the earpiece out of his ear and climbs out of the cart.

"I'm sorry. That's all for today."

"You have to go in, don't you?" Ariel asks.

"No. I'm really done." He looks at Danny. "You ready?"

Danny nods and smiles. Mark pulls a pistol from under the seat of the golf cart, checks the chamber and the magazine, and then shoves it into a holster on his belt.

"Let's go."

He leads them right between the houses and through the pines to a door in the wall. Barely larger than one man, it looks like a typical emergency exit in any building project.

He lifts the radio. Thinks, then offers it to Danny.

"You know what to do?" he asks.

Danny's eyes go wide. He snatches the radio in excitement. He looks to his mom, and Ariel nods at him. He lifts the radio and thumbs the transmit button.

"Authorized exit. West door," Danny says.

Mark draws his pistol, pushes the door open and steps through. He looks both directions, still holding the door. Then he waves Ariel and Danny through.

Danny holds the radio with both hands and looks to Mark expectantly. Mark nods.

"All clear," Danny says.

Mark lets the door close behind them. The latch clunks shut, and then the metallic whine of electric locks follows.

Danny hands the radio back to Mark. Mark nods up the hillside. "Go on. You can lead," he says.

Danny starts up the hill. Ariel watches him and then looks at Mark.

"What?" Mark asks.

"You got awfully generous all of a sudden."

"I know you want him to enjoy it."

He puts his pistol away and extends a hand to her. She takes it, and they start up the hillside behind Danny.

***

Less than twenty miles away, Sam sits on the bike at the mouth of a neighborhood. He's tucked under a tree and watching the blank main road just ahead of him. This is the same intersection he saw from the Lookout. All he has to do is turn right and head south for Aspen. He imagines someone staring down at him through the telescope. He thinks of Laura lying dead in the bedroom, and the breath catches in his throat.

The moment he moves, he'll be visible. He takes a quick look behind him. Then a longer look ahead.

He twists the throttle and pushes off. The sound of the bike rattles through the silent town as he blurs into the intersection and turns southbound. The road is two lanes each way, with a handful of abandoned cars pushed to both shoulders years before.

Feeling very exposed, Sam twists the throttle to the stops and climbs through the gears. He wishes he had a helmet, but can't bring himself to slow down.

***

On the mountainside, Danny leads up a grassy slope. In the winter this tree-cleared swath is a ski run for their dwindling tourist traffic. He takes a sip from the waterbag in his small backpack and looks back at his mom and Mark. They walk side by side, taking big strides in the tall, wild grass.

Farther up, Danny comes to a well-cut trail across the mountain. Fresh tracks can be seen from mountain bikes and hiking boots. Danny turns uphill on the diagonal track and continues toward the top of the ridge. Mark and Ariel climb up behind him.

As they crest the top, the wind picks up. Danny looks at the peaks beyond, and then turns to look back down on Aspen. Ariel goes to her son and takes in the views with him. Mark looks too, but only for possible threats. His hand is on his pistol as he steps beside Ariel. She puts her hand on his, and he relaxes. He gives her a quick smile.

They watch a private jet taxi to the end of the runway. The sound of its engines carries on the wind. At full throttle, it accelerates down the runway and gracefully lifts. The jet passes over the silver walls at the end of the runway and gains quickly as it streaks up the valley.

"Is that the one we flew?" Danny asks.

"No, that's Ambassador Hellmanzik's plane," Mark says.

"Germany?" Ariel asks.

"Yes. Same kind of plane, Danny. Good job."

They watch it bank east and climb higher. The sound of the engines dies away, and on the next gust of wind there's a new sound.

"Can we—" Danny begins.

"Quiet!" Mark interrupts.

They all listen for a moment. The sound of an engine can be heard on the wind. It revs through the gears, screaming faster. It's the distinctive sound of a dirt bike.

Mark knows nothing in Aspen sounds like this.

"We need to go," he says.

"But I wanna climb the next peak!" whines Danny.

"Not today, little man," Ariel says.

"That means never," Danny pouts.

"I'm sorry, Danny," Mark says.

"What about lunch?"

"We're going."

"We'll make it up to you," Ariel offers.

Mark pulls the radio from his belt and flicks it on.

"Tom. Copy this?"

Mark herds his family back down the hill as he listens.

"Copy that," Tom crackles back.

"We've got incoming. Sounds like a dirt bike. Have the sentries check in."

"Can you see it?" Tom asks.

"Audio only. Inbound from Carbondale," Mark says.

"Copy that. We'll spot it," Tom answers.

The downward slope has them nearly running now, descending toward the wall.

***

Backing off of full throttle, Sam weaves through a pair of cars in the road, strategically placed to slow anyone approaching. Seeing more up ahead, he jumps the curb and begins driving through the overgrown grass on the shoulder. If Aspen has lookouts like Grand Junction, he knows he's already been seen. If not, the bike is loud enough for him to be heard. He needs to dump the bike, but wants to get as close as possible.

As he accelerates down the shoulder, he sees a private jet pass overhead and bank out of the valley. He wonders about the last time he even saw a plane.

Up ahead he catches a glint of silver. He pulls into the middle of the road again and stops. Even from a distance, he can tell this is a Shining City wall blocking the road. After all the days and miles, he's seeing Aspen for the first time.

He wants to drive straight toward it. He knows he can't. The plan he's been forming since he left California still feels like the only way inside the city. He struggles with the thought of asking for Ariel, and pleading with her to come inside. A part of him still believes they have something. Most of him knows it would be suicide.

Resisting the urge to move straight for the city, Sam floors the bike and charges westbound up into the foothills again. He makes as much noise as possible before killing the engine and climbing off. Then, he waits.

***

At the small western gate, Mark closes the exterior door behind him. When the electric lock slides closed he exhales and grabs his radio.

"We're in," he says.

"Copy that," Tom responds. "We've spotted the rider. He was bound for the main, but just turned into the foothills. Glad you're back in."

"What do you know?"

"Too far away to get a good look at him."

"Okay."

Mark steps between the houses to find Ariel and Sam sitting in the golf cart. Sweat stands on their skin from the run, and they look spooked.

"It's okay," he says. "Nothing to worry about."

"I'm sorry," Danny says.

"For what?" Mark answers.

"I just wanted to go for a hike."

Mark looks at Ariel; she raises her eyebrows, hoping he can navigate this. Mark sits in the back seat of the golf cart, next to Danny.

"Danny. Bad people roam around outside the walls…. That's not your fault."

"And not everyone outside the walls is bad," Ariel interjects.

"True. We have to be careful, but we don't need to be frightened," Mark says.

"Why aren't there walls in Switzerland?" Danny asks.

Mark and Ariel look at each other, wondering if they've ever discussed this.

"Well," Ariel begins, "the people there have jobs, and they get along and don't steal from each other."

"So there's no bad people?"

"There are bad people everywhere," Mark says. "But outside America, they…"

They're struggling to explain. Ariel wonders where Danny is going with this. "What are you worried about, sweet boy?"

"Can I go for long hikes there? I hate the wall. I like the forest. Do I have to worry about bad people ruining hiking for me in Switzerland?"

"No. You can do all the hiking you want," Ariel smiles. "Plus skiing and sledding, and probably lots of biking. No walls to keep you in, just lots of mountains."

"Okay," Danny says quietly. "Can we go home now?"

Mark puts a hand on the back of Danny's neck and squeezes. "Sure, Danny."

When he climbs into the front, Ariel switches to the back seat. As they drive away, she extends her hand on the seat next to Danny. He takes it. She squeezes three times. Danny squeezes back, four times.

Ariel smiles as she watches the houses blur by.

2

Dixon rolls through the forest on Sam's old ATV. He slows as he reaches the turn-off for the Lookout and stares down the road. He turns the ATV onto the road, gets some momentum on the gentle grade and kills the engine. Freewheeling, he descends, watching and listening.

Soon he catches glimpses of the house's roof through the pines. He brakes the ATV to a stop and locks it in place. Climbing off, he pulls Sam's old shotgun from one of the fender holsters. He can hear rustling in the bushes just ahead. Slowly, he walks toward the sound.

As he approaches, Dixon can see ferns and dense brush pulling and thrashing below the road. Growls and wet grunts filter up through the leaves. He steps to the edge of the road, just above the noise, and can see the backs of coyotes moving over something.

He cocks the shotgun — an abrupt metallic interruption. The coyotes startle and look up at him. Dixon levels the shotgun at the closest one, waiting. The coyote snarls. Dixon looks past it to the body they are fighting over. He recognizes enough of the clothing to know it's Aaron.

BA-BOOM! The shotgun shatters the forest stillness as Dixon perforates the closest coyote. The rest of the pack scatter through the undergrowth. He steps down through the ferns for a closer look. He covers his mouth in disgust.

Back on the road, Dixon closes in on the house with the shotgun leveled. He reaches the back door, pauses, then steps inside in a rush. Shotgun panning, he wavers as he looks over the bloody kitchen. The smear across the floor leads to the bullet-dented refrigerator.

"Laura!" he yells.

No other sound in the house.

With big strides, he crosses the kitchen and sweeps the open living room and lookout station. Then he crosses to the stairs, passing a discarded robe on the floor.

"Laura? Sam? It's Dixon. I'm coming downstairs."

He descends quickly, leading with the shotgun as the downstairs comes into view. Now a smell catches him. He recoils at first, then steps into the master bedroom.

Laura lies face up between the bed and the balcony. She's surrounded by a dried stain of her own blood. The stench overwhelms the room. Dixon covers his mouth and nose with one hand as he steps closer.

He stands over her and looks down, shaking his head. Then he scans the room and sees the broken pieces of the sat phone. Two used wine glasses and a dirty plate sit out on the balcony.

Walking to the balcony, he slides the glass door open. He stands at the railing and looks down into the thick brush and ferns a full story below the house. The mountainside slopes away, and the forest is quiet.

Back inside, he recoils from the smell again as he lays the shotgun on the bed. He squats beside Laura's body and slides an arm under her legs. It takes a moment to slide the other under her shoulders through the dried blood and muck beneath her. He stands with a grunt, turning his face from the smell. But it doesn't help.

In quick strides, he steps out onto the balcony and up to the railing. He tips Laura's body toward the forest and lets it fall. He steps back into the room, refusing to look as crashing and tumbling sounds rise from below.

He hopes the coyotes come back soon.

"I'm sorry, Laura," he whispers.

Dixon steps over the blood stain and looks at the pieces of the shattered sat phone. He pulls his own sat phone from his belt and turns it on. He hopes the one in Grand Junction is on as well.

Keying the programmed number, he waits.

"I need him," he says when the line is answered. "Yes. Right now."

Holding the phone with one hand, he picks up the shotgun and goes back upstairs. Curtis comes on the line.

"What is it?" Curtis says.

"The Lookout's been trashed," Dixon says. "Aaron and Laura are both dead."

Dixon stands in the middle of the large upstairs living room.

Curtis stands in his office talking into a large speakerphone station. Lawrence is in the office, listening. Curtis waves him out. Lawrence darkens, but goes.

"What happened?" Curtis growls.

"Don't know for sure," Dixon says. "Looks like he shot them both. Probably got the drop on Aaron. Laura… it must have been an argument."

A mixture of sadness and rage brings tears to Curtis' eyes.

"Did you get him?" Curtis asks.

"I'm sorry, Curtis," Dixon says.

Curtis sits on the edge of his desk, looking at the shelves of books that fill his office. He takes a deep breath.

"Any movement from Aspen?" he asks.

"I'll be watching," Dixon says.

"I know you will," Curtis says. It sounds like a threat.

He ends the call.

Dixon hangs his sat phone back on his belt and goes outside to retrieve the ATV and his supplies.

***

The sun has set, and the light is fading. The dirt bike lies on its side, abandoned under a tree. A set of obvious footprints leads away from the bike and higher up the hillside. A quarter-mile closer to Aspen,

Sam descends out of the trees, taking careful steps. He stops, looking toward the bike in the near-dark. Then he continues moving lower.

When he reaches the roadside, he's standing in full darkness. He looks up at the flour dusting of stars overhead. The moon won't rise for a few hours. He moves quickly across the road, glancing toward Aspen to see a warm glow inside the unlit walls. Reaching the other side, he runs into the trees. There's a chance someone saw him, but he's a man on a mission now.

This side of the road flattens with the valley. Sam turns toward Aspen and begins a wide perimeter march. He keeps a steady pace, going for almost ten minutes and then stopping. He searches in the darkness until he finds a dense stand of pines. He unloads his pack and sets up his simple camp.

He eats a cold meal from a can, sitting without light and listening for any sound. Part of him expects to be discovered at any moment. The scrape of his spoon on the can sides seems amplified in the silence. Somewhere behind him, he can hear the small skittering of an animal. But he never hears the crunch of anything large.

As the moon rises, Sam climbs into his sleeping bag. He leans up against a trunk and barricades himself in the center of the cluster of pines. His Walther is in reach of one hand, the rifle in reach of the other. He needs to sleep, but in the excitement he wonders if he can.

Hours later, Sam awakens with a jerk. He's slumped against the tree and the wound in his back throbs. It hurts to sit up, and he grimaces as he works the stiffness out of his neck and shoulders. He grabs the Walther and listens anew. He doesn't hear anything moving. Peering east through the trees, he can see the blue light of dawn on the horizon.

With a slow breath, he tries to relax. For the first time in days, he pulls his notepad out of his pack and digs out a pen. The pages are kinked from their handling, and holding them makes him think of Laura.

> *Nothing will confuse you more than lust and love and sex. You'll meet someone and they'll draw you in. Sometimes right away. Sometimes over time. You'll feel a pull toward them that's nearly*

overwhelming. I felt a twinge of it when I first met your mother at a birthday party. The more I talked to her the more my attraction grew. By the time we got married I couldn't see the lines between lust and love and sex, but I knew there was no one else I wanted but your mom.

Over time it faded away. It was hard to see at first, but I know even you could tell before I was taken.

Don't believe anyone that says there's only one person for you. Or that attraction makes things easy.

Being with one person builds a life of shared experience that's unlike anything else you'll ever find. But there's a crippling amount of work involved. People don't like to say this, but you could be happy with any one of a dozen people you'll meet. You just have to dedicate yourself to making a life. It might not seem romantic. It probably sounds like hard work. It is. Luckily there's a cause and effect to a long relationship. The work helps you understand it, and make it better. Attraction is the part that gets you in trouble.

There will be people you can't escape even though you know they're bad for you. Something in them will entice you anyway. I think it's the last bits of our animal instinct wanting to breed and conquer. That probably sounds terrible, but it's the best way I can describe the feeling. It's unthinking. It's a craving turned to action.

Be careful who you have sex with. I'm not talking about diseases or perception, or anything you normally hear from parents. I heard all of that from mine, and they completely missed the biggest things to look out for.

Right now you might think sex is weird or disgusting, but that will change. Once you discover it for yourself you'll be obsessed, and you'll do almost anything for it. That will make you vulnerable. You will get manipulated. Don't be a victim of it. Don't make anyone else a victim either. Know that who you have sex with is your decision. All the great that comes with it is just for you and that person. And any consequences are yours too. Own it all.

Sex is like that velcro that fastened your shoes when you were small. It links things, but doesn't make it permanent. A bad relationship can stumble onward held together by only sex. When sex is good, it's hard to see everything that's wrong.

Don't for a moment think sex and love should be avoided. They should be embraced. Chased. Hang on tightly when you have someone. Make an effort to keep them looking at you the way they will the first time you have sex. It's one of the most magical things you'll ever encounter. I hope you get to experience it.

I rarely recognized the escapist magic of sex. No matter how terrible everything else might have been, those moments were some of the best of my life. So many times I let my expectations or baggage cloud the otherworldly moments of making another person scream in pleasure or losing your own control at their touch.

It makes it all the worse when things end. There's a ripping, just like the velcro, but it never really goes back together. And even when you know it should be over, the only memories that will surface are the ones that tell you reasons to stay.

When it ends, you may do something terrible. Leave with respect if you can. But there will be times you'll look back and wonder if what you did was the actions of someone else. That guilt may never go away. I hope you can learn from it.

No matter what, love deeply.

For all the pain and struggle it will cause you, love and sex are worth the effort. Don't hide yourself away. Take every chance for those moments of rapture. Try not to leave carnage in your wake.

Sam stops writing and looks up at the first rays of sunlight in the trees. He can't shake the image of Laura dying on the bedroom floor.

He shudders and puts the pad and pen back in his pack. Listening to the forest, he waits and scans the trees in all directions. Satisfied he's alone, Sam stands up out of the sleeping bag and begins to shove it into his pack. After another glance around, he holsters the Walther, lifts his rifle and begins picking his way through the pines.

He walks for hours, approaching Aspen in a wide arc. At one point he drifts too close to the wall, and he can suddenly see it towering over the trees. Heart racing, Sam eyes the blank structure, feeling drawn to it but knowing he can't be seen this close. He searches the top for guards while forcing himself deeper into the forest. He never sees anyone before he's gone again.

Cutting wider now, he rounds the corner of the structure and begins walking almost directly south. He keeps a steady distance from the wall, catching glimpses through the trees. The entrance he's looking for will be in a large clearing. After all this time, being discovered before he's ready would destroy his chance to break in. They might be watching the forest, but no one will be watching his way inside.

3

Dixon stands at the large telescope in the Lookout. He checks the distant intersection again, then goes to the large TV. Behind it, he finds a coil of cable and unwinds it toward the telescope. One of the cables is a power cord he plugs in near the telescope. The other is a video cable that he plugs into a box near the eyepiece. He connects them and steps away.

Dixon flips on the television, and the telescope image is now displayed on the large screen. He drops the remote on the end table and goes to the kitchen.

He stares at the bullet dent in the bloody door. He can't avoid it. He should clean it, but can't imagine how much time that would take. Dismissing the carnage, he opens the fridge and grabs a beer as if this were his vacation home.

Returning to the living room, Dixon flops down on the couch, sips his beer and waits.

***

In Aspen, Mark steps inside a huge warehouse. All around him sit large, intimidating vehicles and people loading gear. He walks past two jacked-up Wranglers beside the cab of a two-trailer gasoline hauler. The big cylindrical tankers are filthy, and the rig is so long it nearly touches both sides of the warehouse.

"You don't have to see me off, honey," Thomas laughs as he sees Mark approach.

Mark smiles and steps beside Thomas into a circle of well-armed men and women.

"I missed you already," Mark smirks as he eyes everyone. "Thank you all for going on this retrieval. It may be our last one for a while, so we all need this fill."

The group around them nods and shrugs.

"How far can you go?" Mark asks Thomas.

"I'm hoping Glenwood Springs still has some. If I can only fill one, I'll split them and send it back, with Eli."

"How?"

"The dually," Eli says as he points. Mark follows the man's thin finger to see a large pickup with a fifth-wheel tow disc in the bed.

"Otherwise, we'll start pushing east," Tom continues. "I'm sure Denver Airport has a stash. They had a pay station last time."

"Let's hope they still do."

"If not, I guess we're pushing to Cheyenne. Won't have fuel to drive any further without the fill. By that point we'll probably be half a convoy anyway."

"Be careful," Mark says and offers his hand. Thomas gives him a hard shake.

"Don't blubber. I get to go for a nice drive. You still have to run the place."

They trade knowing smiles, and Thomas walks to one of the Wranglers. All the trucks start up, rumbling diesel clouds into the rafters of the warehouse. Someone opens the huge roll-door in the side of the building.

Tom's Jeep rolls out first, with the other close on its bumper. The semi chugs into motion, brakes releasing, and the huge wheelbase takes a wide turn out of the warehouse to settle in behind the Wranglers. The dually follows, with Eli driving, and two huge, armed men are in the cab.

Mark watches them go. He almost feels sorry for anyone that challenges them.

***

Outside the walls, Sam stops just before a gap in the trees and listens. He can see the wall to his right, cutting across an open clearing and continuing into the trees on the other side.

There are piles of ash in the clearing. They form a circle around a central hub of untouched wild grass. It looks as if a ferris wheel were laid on its side and buried to form a frame, leaving symmetrical piles around the central circle. Sam can see the newest pile is taller than a man, and the smallest is just a dark scar on the earth. The smell of sulphur and smoke linger in the air.

Sam knows he's in the right place.

He slinks back into the forest and takes off his pack. He seeks out a stand of trees with a good view of the clearing but blocked from the wall. Setting his pack down, he sits and watches the clearing for a long time. No animals wander through. A light wind makes the only sound.

Sam has no idea what day it is. He knows he could wait here a week before anything happens. Still, he can't help but stare at the clearing.

***

At the Lookout, Dixon almost misses the convoy. He comes out of the kitchen to see the dually truck leave the frame on the TV. Dropping his plate on an end table, he snatches up the TV remote and runs over to the telescope.

As he puts his eye to the eyepiece, the clearing is empty. He turns to the TV and fumbles with the remote, punching the rewind button, then trying another combination before hitting rewind again. Finally, he finds the right sequence, and the image on screen rewinds. He doesn't know how this system works, and remembers fighting with Curtis and Lawrence over whether it was necessary. Now it feels like it saved his life.

Hitting play again, Dixon watches the Jeeps stop at the southern end of the intersection. They split, each taking one edge of the road. The massive two-trailer semi rolls up between them, and the three vehicles make their way across and out of the picture. Then the dually pauses at the southern end, waits nearly ten seconds, then powers through. Just as it leaves the frame, Dixon rewinds it again.

He plays and pauses the recording now, stepping through it slowly. At each pause he examines the frame, counting the people in the truck cabs. He rewinds it again, and counts again.

Satisfied, he picks up the sat phone and calls Curtis.

***

Sam chews on some jerky and looks around the forest. The stand of trees he's hiding behind has enough space in the middle for him to sleep sitting up. He listens for a long time, straining to hear water flowing to the east. Then he opens his pack and counts the food inside. He has enough to stay here for at least a week before retreating for more.

Suddenly, he's surprised by a hydraulic hiss. He crouches and looks into the clearing.

A line of fencing rises into view. It surrounds the perfect circle of untouched grass in the middle of the clearing. Twelve-foot high fence posts come to a stop, with thick cables stretched between them. The fence creates a perfect island surrounded by the piles of ash. The wild grass sways as the fence electrifies.

Sam can hear the power surge, even from far away. He grabs his pack and starts for the clearing. He's pulling on the straps as he breaks into a sprint. Running headlong toward the electrified fence, he smiles. His idea is going to work.

As he approaches, Sam tries to figure out which of the ash marks in the earth looks the smallest. The closer he gets, the more they look the same. He runs toward the two that look the oldest, and hopes.

The electric fence arcs and sparks, ionizing the air. Sam can feel the change as he reaches two of the piles. He stops, his breath heaving in and out. He scans the top of the wall but can't see anyone. Still gasping, he watches the fence.

Inside the electrified circle, the center lifts out of the ground, a dense layer of dirt ascending in a perfect wall before a metal platform comes into view. It keeps rising, revealing a large metal cylinder underneath, like a massive curved elevator door. The cylinder rotates, turning toward Sam to reveal an opening full of smoking ash. The open section spins to a stop in line with the pile to Sam's right.

The section of fence in front of the ash drops into the ground. Sam crouches, feeling a wave of heat hit him like a wall. He waits, hoping he'll have enough clearance. The ash pile is pushed out of the cylinder in a trough, sliding across the open ground as giant pistons push it forward. Super-heated ash tumbles and rolls toward Sam and past the opening in the fence.

Sam holds his breath as the wall of ash slides past him. He watches the gap between the edge of the pile and the first post of the fence. It's half his size, but he waits, trying to endure the heat. He drops his pack off his shoulders and holds a strap in one hand.

Then the back wall of the trough slides outside the fence, the pistons fully extended behind it. There's a gap less than two feet wide. Sam lunges forward, diving his body sideways through the opening. His pack catches an arc of electricity as he tugs it through. The surge makes all Sam's hair stand on end.

He tumbles to the ground, inside the fence but behind the trough that pushed out the ash. Sam clambers to his feet and runs beside the pistons into the opening of the cylinder. The trough begins to retreat behind him.

Slamming into the center of the structure, Sam presses himself as flat as possible against the wall. The pistons keep compressing. The back wall of the trough closes in on him. He pushes his pack close to the structure beside him and flattens himself out. He even sucks in his chest and stomach. This is going to be close.

The pistons don't slow down until the last second, and the trough wall comes to a sudden stop as it presses into Sam's chest. He moans as the heat from the metal burns his chest through his shirt. He tenses instinctively, burning the tip of his nose on the metal, then snapping back again.

Then the pistons relax, sliding out six inches and releasing Sam. He gasps for breath, alive and terrified. He can feel the entire platform descending again, taking him underground and snuffing out the faint light from gaps in the structure. There's an abrupt stop; and Sam stands in silence and total blackness. He can move away from the wall, but there isn't enough space to turn.

Now Sam can feel rotation as the trash trough spins back to its center point. There's a groan as it comes to rest, and the sound trails off to silence again. Sam strains in the dark for any new sounds. For a moment, he thinks he can hear the muffled voices of two men yelling instructions at each other. He waits. The sound doesn't come again. He wonders if he imagined it. He hopes he's that close.

Dropping his pack to the ground, he fumbles into the top pouch with one hand. Finding his headlamp in the darkness, he pulls it out and flips it on. The tiny amount of light seems blinding until his eyes adjust. He pulls the headlamp on and looks around.

To his left, the compressed pistons are folded in a web of joints between the back of the trough and the main wall. To his right, the gap runs parallel to stop at a concrete wall with a metal access door in the middle. Sam smiles, drags his pack and moves toward the access door.

Sam pushes on the back of the door with one hand. He drops his pack and turns as best he can to push with both hands. The door doesn't move. It's so solid, he can't even tell which way it would open. He's trapped.

Sam takes a deep breath, trying to calm his racing heart. This tiny area is all he has until he can get the door open. Looking back at the pistons, he sees the hoses and wiring laced through them. Determined — and fighting claustrophobia — Sam slides back toward the pistons. He grabs the closest bend of hose and wires and traces it back to the connection point in the wall. To his relief, they are plugged into the wall for easy service and replacement.

Sam struggles to pull a cable free, only able to reach it with one arm. Blindly, his fingers search for plastic hooks or catch pins in the plug. The base feels like a metal sleeve, and he spins it with all his strength. His efforts become frantic and desperate. Finally the sleeve twists, and one hose pops free, sending hydraulic fluid spewing out. Sam recoils from the hot liquid, slamming the back of his elbow on the opposite wall and turning his hand numb in an instant. The liquid splatters his feet and arms, still hot enough to hurt but not boiling.

Drenched, burned and still reeling from his numbed arm, Sam shuffles away from the pistons and back to the access door. He sags against the wall, his body held up by the tiny space. He hopes it won't be long before someone comes to fix the hydraulics. He fears it will be days.

4

A crowd of people gathers inside the double gates of Grand Junction. Most are security forces, well-armed and serious. Others move among them, apprehensive and mostly unarmed. Curtis rounds the corner in a UTV, knobby tires thrumming. He brakes to a sudden stop, rocking the vehicle on its suspension. Every working, gas-powered vehicle in town sits around him. The golf carts are parked together nearby, useless for this trip.

Curtis stands on the seat of the UTV, rising up above the roll cage. Everyone around him goes quiet and looks his way. He waits for every face to stare back, and then pauses for effect.

"I know many of you are nervous," he says. "We talk about how dangerous it is to leave the city, and it truly is. But we have an opportunity today. The thing we've wanted. Waited for. Thought would never come. Our chance to have everything we dream of, and the things the Shining Cities keep for themselves. If we work together, it's all ours today.

"Follow the lead of our security forces. If you don't have a gun, stay with those who do. Whatever you have, prepare to use it. The people from Aspen will not hesitate to hurt you. Hit them first. We have strength in our numbers.

"Whatever happens. Don't be afraid. Don't stop. Think about what you can gain for your families and yourselves. This is our moment to shape the world, and make it ours!"

He drops into the seat and motions for the gate to open. The inner gate slides to the side, and Curtis lurches forward in his UTV, weaving through others. They start the engines of motocross bikes, a panel truck, a large panel-backed UTV, the armored UTV with a .50-caliber mounted on the roof, and a collection of scooters and mopeds.

The outer gate opens, and Curtis blasts through. The group follows in a stretched-out line. They exit west and turn down a side street, headed north. Curtis slows as the road widens, letting the group converge. By the time they turn east for Aspen, they are moving as a mismatched pack.

***

At the Lookout, Dixon starts Sam's old ATV and accelerates away. He turns toward Carbondale, just as Sam did, but then finds a side road and turns north again. Climbing up through the gears, he hopes the screaming engine can't be heard in the valley. If this road goes where he remembers, he'll end up just ahead of Curtis and everyone else from Grand Junction.

***

On the road, Thomas looks in the side mirror of his Wrangler at the semi rumbling just behind them. He glances at the other Jeep, flanking the semi on the other side. Then he lets his eyes scan the edges of the road.

Enrique, the small, thin guy riding shotgun, grips his pistol with both hands and rebalances the rifle across his knees.

"You're gonna give yourself a heart attack," Thomas says.

"You think they're out there?" asks Enrique.

"Someone's always out here," Thomas answers.

Enrique stares at the roadside. He touches the rifle again.

"It's okay," Thomas says. "No need to go off. Just look for the unusual. The things that seem out of place or unexpected… they're that way for a reason."

"By then it's too late."

"No. It would take an army to make a dent in us — and no one out here can agree on dinner, let alone strategy. There's no point in seeing danger in everything. You'll drive yourself crazy. There's enough shit in the world, deal with your part when it comes."

He reaches out and puts his hand on Enrique's pistol.

"Seriously. Put that away until you need it. You're gonna blast out the roof."

Enrique holsters his pistol. Thomas checks his mirrors again. He sees the dually bringing up the rear and wishes he had one of the more seasoned guys who ride with Eli.

In the dually, Eli watches the semi and Wranglers rolling through another intersection. He pauses the truck, then follows again.

Moses, the huge black man in the back seat, speaks up in a low rumble. "We make a big fucking target doing this."

"No worse than last time," Eli says.

"Yeah, and that went so well."

"Think we can make Denver before dark?" asks Trevor, the old military guy in the passenger seat.

"I'm hoping we get lucky in Glenwood Springs. Denver's a shithole," Eli says.

"As long as they've got gas," Trevor says.

"Have to fight them for it," Moses sighs.

***

In Aspen, Danny walks out of the school house and up to the golf cart sitting in the driveway. Other kids climb into other carts and dart away as he settles in beside his mother.

"How was your day?" Ariel asks.

"Boring," Danny says.

"Only one more week," Ariel says as they pull away.

"I know," he says and then sighs. "Can I just skip school until I leave? I'm not learning anything anyway."

"You have to go to school."

"You're sending me away to school! Why can't I play this week?"

Ariel blinks back a quick wash of tears. Danny doesn't see them, and she collects herself.

"Please?" Danny pushes the issue.

"Maybe we can do some things together before you go?" she asks.

"Sure. I guess so."

"Well, let me talk to Mark about it, and maybe we can do some field trips."

"Outside the wall?" Danny asks with a mix of excitement and fear.

"I can't promise, but we'll see."

They close in on their house near the center of town. It's a pristine brick and log home with a perfect lawn.

Ariel pulls into the drive and stops the cart. Danny jumps out and hurries inside. Ariel follows, watching him bound through the front door. She's caught again by the thought of him going somewhere unknown.

***

In the trash chute, Sam jerks awake. He's slumped down between the two close walls, his heels and back on one wall and his knees and forehead touching the other. Everything hurts as he tries to stand up straight.

Then he hears the chiming sound of tools and keys beyond the door. Fully awake now, he shuffles closer to the door as he hears hinges turn.

The door swings open toward Sam's face, and he grabs it. A startled Hispanic man looks back at him.

"Fucking hell!" the man yells and jumps back from the doorway.

"I need your help," Sam says. He starts to pull his body through, not waiting for an invitation. He's sore and tired, still pulling his pack with one hand, but trying to clamber out anyway.

"No!" the man yells. "I'll have to shoot you."

"Just listen. Listen. Please!" Sam pleads as he falls out of the thin chamber and into a cool, wide industrial hallway. His pack tumbles out behind him, landing broadside on his chest and almost knocking him out.

The man backs away as if Sam were toxic. He looks terrified, and Sam hopes he doesn't actually have a gun. Sam tries to shake his head clear as he pushes the pack off of him. He can feel the Walther on his hip, and knows his rifle is strapped to the outside of his pack. He doesn't want to use them.

"The hydraulics aren't broken, just unplugged," Sam spits out as fast as he can. "I needed someone to open the door.... I belong here. Please, I can prove it."

The man stands out of reach, his eyes searching Sam and his gear.

"You're a marauder," he says as he notices Sam's guns.

"No... I'm a traveler. And I can help you."

"How did you survive the crusher?" the man asks.

"I know where to hide. I used to build them."

"That doesn't mean you belong here."

"You're right. But I have something you need." Sam sits up, leaning against the wall. "I've got some titanium?"

"If you had titanium you wouldn't be hiding in the garbage," the man says.

"You always need it down here, right? Things to fix and no titanium left."

"Who the fuck are you?"

"I'm Sam," he says, trying to stay friendly and not frantic as he pulls the top of his pack open.

"Stop that! You're a fucking terrorist!" The man starts to back away again.

"Wait!" Sam pleads as his arm dives into the pack and pulls out the titanium femur he's carried since his parents' house.

The man stops, shocked.

"Here," Sam says quietly as he sets it on the ground. The metal bone rings softly as it touches the floor.

"Holy. Shit," the man whispers. "That's a fucking bone, man!"

"I know. It was my father's. Pure titanium."

"You took his leg?!"

"He was already dead. It's all I have left. The rest of my family is here."

The man steps closer and picks up the bone.

"Damn, man. You're one sick fucker."

"Please. Take it. Just let me back inside with you. I'll do any job."

"Sam, right?" the man asks as he holds the bone. "I'm Julian."

"Thank you, Julian."

"But understand I cannot help you."

"What? My family is in there! They will verify me, I'm certain."

"No," Julian shakes his head. "You don't get it. There's an ID system on all the doors. Unless they override them, you have to have your code."

"I know computers. Show me the terminal, I can make myself a code."

"That's not possible. The system is very confusing."

"I was a programmer in the old world. I can figure it out."

Julian squats down. Still holding the titanium bone, he looks at the tattered desperate man sitting in front of him.

"I will show you the door. And I will go through it. If you can get through the system, then I will help you. If not, I'll come down here tomorrow and bring security with me. They do have guns."

He starts to walk down the hallway, daring Sam to follow.

"And I'm keeping your bone."

***

In the forest, Dixon accelerates downhill, the tires of the ATV bouncing in a blur over the rough dirt road. Up ahead he can see the pine trees of the mountains thinning. He blasts out into the open, skirting the edge of a field long overgrown. Suddenly, he locks his brakes and slides to a stop in a cloud of dust.

The sat phone rings again, now clear over the idling engine. Dixon pulls it from his belt.

"I'm almost there," he says as he connects.

"Good," Curtis answers. "We're still on I-seventy."

"How's the traffic?"

From his seat in the UTV, Curtis glances back at the swarm of vehicles and smiles.

"Not bad." He looks forward again as they navigate around a burnt hunk of car lying sideways across three lanes. "Just a bit of stop and go."

"I'll update you when I get to seventy."

"Confirmed. See you soon."

Curtis ends the call and looks down the lanes of freeway ahead of them. The road winds through the valley and follow the river. It's beautiful, and for a moment it almost seems normal. The convoy rolls on. Soon they can see another jumble of abandoned cars ahead.

***

In the tunnels, Sam moves in a painful shuffle and can't keep up with Julian. He sees Julian step up to a thick plexiglass door in the middle of the hallway. He pulls a keycard from the lanyard around his neck, touches it to the reader, and the door slides open. Sam tries to close the distance, but the door slides shut so fast it almost clips Julian as he steps through.

Sam falls into the door. He drops his pack and looks at the seams on all sides. No way in. He gazes up at the corners of the doorway and sees a security camera staring back. Startled, Sam shrinks away. Then he notices Julian just beyond the doorway, watching.

"Who's watching these?" Sam asks as he points at the camera.

"Probably no one," Julian answers. "Nothing ever happens down here."

Sam goes to the keypad and studies the interface. The pass reader is big and flat, and Sam guesses it doubles as a finger-print scanner. He lays his palm flat on the surface, and a quick scan follows.

"Access Denied" appears in the center of the small screen above the scanner.

Sam leans in closer, prying at the plastic under the screen. A rectangle pops off the corner, revealing a diagnostic cable inside. Sam looks back at Julian.

"Will you still help me?"

"I told you," Julian says, shaking his head. "I can't get you past the checkpoint."

"Can you bring me a computer? Or a tablet?"

"I knew you couldn't do it!"

"This is just a reader. It doesn't have any buttons or a keyboard.

There's no way to interact with this. I can use any laptop. I can make a tablet work. Please!"

Julian looks at Sam and then at the titanium femur. He smiles, shakes his head and walks away. Sam begins pounding on the door, pleading for help. But Julian keeps walking.

5

Curtis peers down the road ahead through binoculars. In the distance, there's a man sitting on an ATV in the middle of the freeway.

"Sir?" his driver says, seeing the man and slowing.

"It's okay," Curtis answers. "That's Dixon."

The driver speeds up again, and Curtis climbs out of his seat to stand out of the roll cage. He smiles as they close in, finally coming to a stop just in front of Dixon. The rest of the group slows and stops behind him.

"You made good time," Curtis says.

"We can hit them before dark," Dixon says.

"No. We only get to surprise them once, and darkness will help us. You know where we're going?"

"Yes. But we'll have to dump the vehicles a little ways out. I heard you guys coming for nearly five minutes."

"Okay. We'll follow your lead. Catch us up," Curtis says.

Dixon climbs off Sam's old ATV and walks past Curtis to the middle of the huddled vehicles.

"We're hunting a dual-tanker rig. It has four support trucks, and I believe they're all armed."

The unarmed members of the group trade glances.

"They'll cut us in half," Leonard says.

Murmurs pass through the group.

"I won't lie to you," Curtis says. "Some may be wounded. Maybe even killed. But they can't stop us all, and we'll surprise them."

"Then what?" Leonard asks. He's seen too much to be easily swayed.

"Then," Lawrence speaks up from near the back, "we'll have keycard access to Aspen and a huge battering ram. They'll have to let us in."

The whispers continue. Some are more hopeful.

"Quiet," Dixon says. "Follow me. And when I say to park and walk, no exceptions."

He climbs onto his ATV, starts the engine and leads them down an off-ramp to the street below.

***

In his windowed office, Mark rubs his face in frustration and looks across the desk to his assistant Brooke. She's sitting with her laptop open and scrolling through a spreadsheet.

"Yes, safety is almost thirty percent," Brooke says. "Twenty-eight point six."

"Why do they feel unsafe?" Mark asks.

"The responses began to change once the National Guard left."

"Are we sure it's not just a bunch of disgruntled travelers? They're used to Europe."

"Maybe. But since surveys have been required for visas, the trend's been clear."

"What's the second highest?" Mark asks.

"Luxury amenities. Especially food," Brooke answers as she traces a finger across her screen.

"Well, I can't get them everything they are used to back home. And I can't make the National Guard come back."

"I know," Brooke nods. "Do you want to keep going?"

"Jackson thinks more advertising is going to help. Remind all of Europe to come shoot and play cowboy."

"It might help. But if people don't feel safe, it won't get the travel numbers back."

"Okay. Can we get some uniforms for everyone that works security? Even for those in maintenance."

"That's not going to go over well with those people."

"I know," Mark sighs. "But our visitors have no idea how many of us keep this place running. If everyone's wearing a uniform, we'll seem like an army."

"I'll get a time frame and a cost breakdown."

"Thank you," Marks says as she stands and leaves.

***

Still trapped in the underground hallway, Sam slouches against one wall. His pack is just out of reach, but he looks like he can't move. His eyes are glazed, and he stares at nothing. He's all alone and convinced that if Julian comes back, this bare hallway is where he'll make his last stand.

So close.

He's exhausted. The elation of finally reaching this city has gone and been replaced with an overwhelming sense of defeat.

The sound of footsteps rises from the stairs just beyond the clear door. Sam watches and slides his hand up to draw his Walther.

Julian descends into view. He's still holding the bone. Behind him, another man appears. He's holding a gun.

Sam scrambles to his feet and points the Walther with both hands.

"No, no, no!" Julian yells at Sam. "Put the gun down!"

The other man points his gun at Sam. Julian puts himself in the middle.

"I have a pad for you," Julian says as he pulls a tablet and patch cable from his coveralls. He walks over to the keypad and prepares to open the door.

"Step back," the man with the gun demands. "Way down the hallway."

"Please," Sam says, lowering his gun. "I just want a chance to get in."

The man keeps aiming, but his tension eases.

"We're giving you that," Julian says. "You just can't be right on top of the door when I open it."

Sam retreats down the hallway.

"Keep going," the man with the gun says.

Sam backs away even more, much farther than he could run and make it through the door. Then he pulls his rifle, drops his pack and lies on the floor behind it. Using the pack as a sandbag and the top as a brace, he aims at the door with the rifle.

"Okay. Don't shoot me, Sam," Julian says.

"Tell your friend that," Sam says.

"This is Roger," Julian says. Roger glares at him.

"Don't tell him my name," Roger hisses.

Julian shrugs.

"Yeah, okay," Roger says. "It's not going to matter."

He steps closer to the door, letting Sam see him.

"Here's how this is going to work," Roger begins. "We all started somewhere. I remember what it's like to fight for your place here. And Julian thinks you deserve it."

Now he lowers the gun and stares back at Sam.

"We're going to drop the pad on your side. You've got one day. After that, you're either through the door with an ID, or I have to come down here and kill you."

Julian scans his card, and the door slides open. Sam resists the urge to run for it. He knows he'd never make it, and Roger would shoot him for trying. Julian slides the tablet through the opening just before the door shuts again.

"Good luck," Julian says.

Sam gets up from the pack and walks over to the tablet. Roger watches him from the other side. Picking up the tablet, Sam smiles at Julian and then looks at Roger.

"Thank you," Sam says, his hope alive again.

"You've got no chance," says Roger. "It's a proprietary system. The woman that coded it is some kind of genius."

Sam looks up, surprised. "A woman coded the security system?"

"Yeah. And no one can beat it.... You think you're the first to try?"

Roger grabs Julian by the shoulder and pushes him toward the stairs.

"I just wanted to shoot you," Roger continues without looking back. "But that titanium bought you this chance."

Roger pauses and looks back over his shoulder. "You're a sick man, cutting up relatives," he says.

Sam looks at the tablet and patch cable hanging off the side. He fumbles with the plug connection, excitement building. It plugs perfectly into the port under the touch pad.

"See you tomorrow, Sam," Roger threatens as he climbs out of sight.

The tablet scrolls lines of code as soon as Sam turns it on. When the lines stop updating, Sam scrolls to the top of the page and begins reading the code. As he does, he can't help but smile. This coding structure looks familiar.

* * *

Years earlier, Sam and Ariel sit side by side, both coding in their living room. They're young and infatuated with each other. Coding is almost a kind of foreplay.

"Done," Ariel says, triumphant.

"No way," Sam says.

She hands him her laptop. "Speaks for itself," she says.

Sam takes the computer and scans the code.

"This is wrong," Sam says. "You can't string these together like this…."

"You might not, but it'll work."

"That's like saying English works backwards."

"Believe me, you will," Ariel says with perfect Yoda cadence. Sam shakes his head.

Now underground in Aspen, Sam looks at the code on the tablet and knows it's Ariel's work.

"Believe you, I will," he says under his breath.

6

Thomas' men scan the streets of Glenwood Springs. Weapons ready, they stand by their vehicles, peering down the empty lanes. The shadows are long in the late-day light and creep across the cracked parking lot of the gas station. The entrances and exits are blocked by the two Wranglers and the dually. The double-tanker semi sits amid the pumps, hoses filling the back tank from all sides.

Inside the run-down office, Thomas stands across the counter from Ted, a filthy and wiry man. A stack of playing card-sized gold plates sits between them.

"Let me come with you," Ted says as he picks up the gold.

"You know I can't do that," Thomas says.

"They're not going to refill me. No reason to stay."

"Has your status changed?" Thomas asks.

Ted spins the dial of an ancient safe. It opens, and he shoves the plates inside. He slams the door with a clang and spins the dial again.

"Don't give me that shit," Ted says as he turns back. "There's people down there that don't belong. How'd they get in?"

"You know what I'm going to say. Their IDs check out. I don't worry about where they got them."

"Everyone else is throwing out the system."

"You mean Tahoe," Thomas corrects him. "They can do whatever they want. We're staying with IDs."

Ted leans across the counter and looks around like he's about to share a secret.

"There's a guy in Denver making them. Good ones too. I'll give you back your gold to give me a ride."

"We're not a car service. You find your own way," Thomas says as he turns for the door.

"What the hell am I supposed to do, walk?" Ted asks.

Thomas shrugs. "I can't help you. But I promise if you come to Aspen with an ID that checks out, we've got jobs for you."

Thomas steps outside and up to the pumps. Each one has passed a couple thousand gallons in the last two hours. One has stopped at 2206. He climbs the tank and pulls the nozzle from the top, dropping it off the side with a clang. Turning slowly, he scans the streets for any other movement. With sunset approaching, he knows it's past time to go.

"We're done here," he says to his men.

The driver of the semi starts putting away nozzles as Thomas tosses them down. Two others disconnect the tanker trailers.

Thomas climbs down from the tanker and walks toward Eli's dually.

"Just the one?" Eli asks as Thomas approaches.

"We've cleaned him out. He's begging to come with us," Thomas says.

"That's not good."

"Yeah. There's no refill coming. You take that one back, and we'll press on to Denver."

Eli looks at the sunset. He doesn't like this.

"I know," Thomas says. "Let's move."

Two blocks away, Curtis stands at the second story window of an old office building. He stares through his binoculars toward the gas station.

"See," Dixon says from beside him. "They're splitting up."

"You're right," Curtis answers. "How do you want to do this?"

"Follow the full tank. It'll be dark soon. We'll hit it as it leaves town."

Curtis lower the binoculars and smiles.

***

Roger sits at his desk with a huge book in front of him. He leans back in his chair, focused. Inside the book is a yellowed porn magazine. The gun he pointed at Sam sits on his desk, forgotten. Cooling ducts pass overhead, and electrical boxes make up the back wall. It could be any dark, forgotten office anywhere in the world — before or after the crash.

"What should I use this for?" says Julian as he enters, startling Roger, who slams the book shut.

"Jesus, man. What the hell?" Roger snaps at him.

"Sorry," Julian says. He looks at the book on the desk and smiles. "Am I interrupting?"

"What? What do you need?"

"The titanium. What do you want to patch first?" Julian asks.

"Check the work orders. Find something that gets seen a lot. The classy folks will want things to be pretty."

"What about that chunk on the south wall?"

"It's not enough to fill it, and no one sees it anyway."

Julian turns to leave, then stops.

"Still nothing…?" he asks.

Roger looks up at him again, then toward a ladder in the corner that drops through the floor.

"The stowaway?" Roger asks, thumbing toward the ladder. "He's not going anywhere. We'll finish him tomorrow."

He picks up his book again. Julian looks at the ladder, then at Roger.

"Go on," Rogers says. "Make things pretty."

Underground, Sam works on the tablet, the screen lighting his face. He tries another combination of keystrokes, his fingers tapping the screen rapidly. He looks up at the light on the keypad. It goes green.

The plexiglass door slides open. Sam stares in elated surprise. Then he panics, knowing the door will close in seconds. He drops the tablet, letting it swing, as he dives for his pack. The door begins to slide closed as he turns and shoves the pack at the opening. The door slams into the pack, stopping but trying to push through.

Upstairs a light goes red on a wall panel, and a quiet but insistent alert begins to ping. Roger looks up from his book, annoyed. His eyes go wide as he realizes which door the alarm represents. Tossing his book aside, he types keystrokes to bring up that security camera.

On screen, Sam grabs the tablet, unplugs it and steps over his pack to squeeze through the door. Then he grabs the pack and pulls it toward him with a tug. The pack slips out of the doorframe, and the plexiglass door clamps shut.

Sam lies on his back, his pack on his chest. He pants. And smiles.

Roger looks at the security camera. "Holy shit," he says, and stands for no reason. He looks around, confused, as if someone should be there to tell him what's next. Grabbing the gun on his desk, he looks at the ladder.

"You okay?" Julian asks as he steps back into the room.

Roger looks at him, startled. Julian tenses, suddenly alarmed.

"What's going on?" Julian says, staring at the pistol.

Roger points at the ladder. "He did it."

Julian smiles. "No way."

Roger chambers a bullet in his pistol and starts around the desk.

"Wait," Julian says as he steps closer. "Now you're going to kill him?"

"What do you want me to do?"

"He earned it, man! We've gotta find a place for him."

"Doing what?"

"I don't know," Julian says. He looks around the office. "There's plenty of stuff to do around here. What's something you hate?"

"Bushes," Roger says. Julian stares at him, confused. "Trimming the fucking bushes into boxes and circles. I hate that."

"So give it to him," Julian says as he points at the ladder.

They both glance at the ladder, then at each other. They hear a sound from below as Sam begins to climb the rungs. They look at the ladder again.

Sam climbs his way into view — dirty, exhausted and barely able to fit through the opening while wearing his pack. He collapses onto the floor of the office and looks up at the two men.

"Thank you," he whispers as he pulls the tablet out of his pack. Then he sees the gun in Roger's hand.

"How'd you do it?" Roger asks.

"My wife did the programming," Sam answers.

Roger looks at Julian. Julian shakes his head.

"What?" asks Sam.

"She's not your wife," Julian says.

"I know she's here," Sam says, his voice gaining strength.

"You don't understand," Roger says. "If she's your wife, then you can't be here."

Sam looks at the gun, then up to Roger's uncertain face.

"Okay," Sam says. "Maybe it wasn't my wife. I told you I was a programmer before all this."

"We don't need a programmer," Roger says.

Sam feels his only chance slipping away. "What do you need?" he asks.

Julian smirks at Roger.

"A gardener," Roger says.

"I can do that," Sam says.

Roger looks over at Julian.

"We could use the help," Julian says.

"I'll do anything. Please."

Roger drops the gun on the desk and snatches the tablet from Sam.

"Don't make me regret this," he snarls.

7

Thomas dials his sat phone as he looks in his rearview mirror at the semi getting up to speed behind him. His half of the convoy heads east on Interstate 70, bound for Denver. His Jeep is in the lead, with the other following the single tanker.

The phone rings twice, and Eli answers.

"How's the load?" Thomas asks.

"Doing okay. Taking it slow," Eli says.

He's driving the dually truck and pulling the full tank behind him. The engine growls loudly.

"Transmission temp got really hot initially, but it's settling out now that we're moving," Eli says.

Thomas looks east as he drives, watching the late-day light turn the mountains gold.

"Alright. Don't stop until you get to Aspen."

"Will do," Eli says. "Good luck in Denver."

Eli kills the call and opens the cavernous center console. He drops the sat phone into the bottom and closes the lid.

"Mom checking up on you," jokes Trevor from the passenger seat.

"You know how she worries," Eli says with a smile.

With a heave, the dually shifts to a higher gear. The transmission whines, and they accelerate again.

"This thing gonna make it?" asks Enrique from the back seat. He's still gripping his pistol as if it were a lifeline.

"We'll be…" Eli starts to answer but stops himself. The road ahead is completely blocked by abandoned cars. Among them sit two UTVs. The entire roadblock wasn't there when they came by hours earlier.

"Who the hell did that?" Trevor wonders aloud as he chambers a round in his AR-15. He rolls down his window and leans out, weapon first.

Eli lifts off the gas and goes for the brake.

"Don't slow down," Trevor says as he ducks back inside. "We'll blast right through it."

Eli eyes the roadblock and then hits the gas again. He dives his hand into the center console as Trevor leans back out.

CRACK! Trevor snaps back against the doorframe, and his gun falls to the passing pavement. The loud boom of the shot follows. Eli recoils, jerking the truck as Trevor falls back into his seat with half his face gone.

Enrique screams like a terrified child and pulls the trigger on his pistol. The round blasts through the roof above him, raining shrapnel down.

Figures pop up from behind the roadblock. Too many to count, and many of them armed. Eli thinks he sees a rocket launcher on one shoulder. He puts both hands on the wheel and buries both feet into the brakes. The tires screech while the nose dives.

"Don't stop!" Enrique bellows.

"Fucking shoot them!" Eli yells back.

Enrique looks around the cabin as if this were a revelation, then he rolls down his own window. Leaning out quickly, he aims at the roadblock and empties his pistol magazine as fast as he can. Sparks and ricochets pepper the roadblock as the figures duck behind it.

The dually shudders to a stop mere feet from the block, and Eli dives his hand back into the console for the sat phone.

A shot splinters off the driver's window, shattering it inward. Eli recoils again, pulling a .45 up in one hand and the sat phone in the other. He catches a glimpse of people approaching the passenger side as he turns back toward his window.

"Enrique, right side!" he yells as he turns to see three people approaching his own door.

Eli perforates the first man in the chest, gore spraying the one behind him. The second man stumbles, distracted by the carnage, but the third raises a shotgun at the cab. Eli fires again as he ducks away. The shot hits the attacker in the leg, tipping him forward and sending buckshot into the cabin and down the driver's door.

A dozen bloody pockmarks form on Eli's large shoulder.

Enrique hefts his own AR-15 from the floorboard and kicks open the rear passenger door. He steps out onto the running board and sprays a line of bullets into the closest person. A middle-aged woman with a tiny pistol drops like a sack. Behind her, a tall elderly man brandishes a bolt-action rifle. Enrique sprays toward him as the man reaches the truck. The line of bullets catches the old man across the chest, turning him as he pulls the trigger. The rifle bullet blasts into Enrique's shoulder instead of his head.

Eli almost presses the call button before a man jumps onto his running board and wallops him in the face with a bat. He doesn't have time to realize this is the weapon he thought was a rocket launcher. The man pulls the door open and drags Eli outside. The sat phone goes tumbling across the pavement as Eli tries to land on his feet.

Enrique guns down two more people before a bullet cuts through his neck. He stops, gurgling, as the closest attackers pull back in horror. Tipping forward, he falls from the truck, his trigger finger flinching out three more stray shots at the pavement right before he hits face first.

Dixon walks up from the roadside with a smoking rifle. He looks at Enrique on the ground and Trevor in the cab. He resists the urge to smile at his work. Seeing Curtis moving toward the driver's side, he follows.

Eli lies on his back on the ground. Four attackers stand over him, each pinning one limb. Jesse, the tall blond guard, aims a pistol at Eli's chest.

"It's okay, Jesse," Curtis says as he steps up to Eli.

"Hello," he says to Eli as if they are friends. Eli just glares back at him.

"You seem like a fine soldier," Curtis begins. "But I hope you're also a smart man. I'd like your help."

Dixon arrives, and Eli's eyes find him and his rifle.

"You killed my friends," Eli spits at Dixon.

"A necessary action," Curtis says, stepping into Eli's view of Dixon. "You don't have to join them if you'll help us."

"Go to hell."

"We're there already," Curtis says. He pulls a pistol from the holster on his belt and flips the safety off. "You've been living in luxury, like all the worst things never happened. All we want is our piece of your world."

He leans down and begins checking Eli's pockets. Eli tries to pull himself free, but the four people on his limbs just push down harder.

Finding a keycard in Eli's shirt pocket, Curtis raises it triumphantly. The crowd around them mutters as Lawrence steps through. Curtis hands the card to Lawrence, who eyes it carefully.

"Any more?" Lawrence asks.

"That's the only one," Eli says.

"Come with us," Curtis says.

"You're never getting inside the walls," Eli says. "They'll see you coming for miles."

"Curtis!" calls a tall blonde as she rounds the dually. "I found another one."

She hands the keycard to Lawrence, and he compares them.

"Where was it?" Curtis asks.

"The guy in the front seat had it," she says with a grimace from the gore.

"You lied to me," Curtis says to Eli. Eli struggles again, but Curtis lowers his pistol and fires.

Everyone jumps back as Eli's body jerks and goes limp.

"Clear the road!" Curtis orders. Everyone around him springs to action except Lawrence, Dixon and Curtis.

Dixon walks over and picks up Eli's fallen sat phone. He checks the "Recent Calls" screen and sees only the call from Thomas.

"He almost got a call out," Dixon says as he steps back to Lawrence and Curtis. "But I can guarantee they'll be back tomorrow anyway."

"It won't matter," Curtis says with confidence. "By the time they get back, we'll be inside."

"We should go now," Lawrence says.

"I'm anxious as well, but it's gotten too late," Curtis says. "The darkness only offers us initial surprise. I agree with Dixon. We should regroup in darkness and infiltrate in the morning."

***

Inside Aspen, Sam gazes into a huge storeroom as Roger holds the door open.

"I know it's not the best," Roger says.

Sam stays put, waiting. Roger shrugs and steps inside, then Sam follows.

"This is the stuff we have to have, but no one wants to store. Streetlight bulbs — never even thought of those 'til I came here. Replacement parts for the mowers. All the stuff you used to find once a year at the back of a hardware store. All here now."

Sam marvels at the rows and rows of shelves. The scale of the room becomes clear as they walk deeper. This must have been a warehouse before the crash, and now it's packed to every corner.

Roger pulls coveralls off a shelf as they pass. He tosses them to Sam without looking.

"See if those fit," Roger says. "You at least need to look like you belong here."

They reach a back corner without any shelves. Sam sees a cot and a camp chair. An industrial sink stands against the wall. Roger goes to the sink and turns the faucet.

"Cold water only," Roger says. "Bathroom's back out in the hallway, sorry about that."

"Am I a prisoner?" Sam asks.

Roger bristles and steps close.

"Ungrateful little bastard, aren't you," he growls. "A lot of us have spent a few nights slumming it down here. You want a parade?"

"I'm sorry," Sam says. "I'm just trying to understand what you expect of me."

"I get that you're smart. I'm impressed that you hacked your way through the door. And Julian seems to like you for some unknown reason. But now I've got a bunch of documents I have to create so I don't get fired while you're shoved out the first door they can find. I expect you to stay here until we tell you otherwise."

Sam sets his pack down and goes over to the bed. He sits on the edge and pulls off his boots.

"Julian will be here about five in the morning. He'll take you on a work detail. If you're working all day, no one will ask you questions. By tomorrow night I should have everything in order."

"Thank you," Sam says.

Roger just waves a hand at him and walks away. Sam listens to his footsteps across the huge room and then the sound of the door opening and closing. He's all alone again. But he's inside Aspen.

***

Far beyond the walls and out in the darkness, Curtis and his makeshift army sit around a fire ringed by the dually and the mismatched collection of UTVs and motorcycles. They're at the mouth of a neighborhood just off the main road to Aspen.

Dixon patrols the edge of the group, his back to the fire. He peers out into the darkness, looking for any movement.

"If we'd only found one key, we would have gone directly," Curtis explains to the group. "But with two keys, we have an advantage."

"We hope," Lawrence interrupts.

"Yes," Curtis says, eyeing Lawrence. "We lose the element of speed, and they may expect something happened to their convoy. But if we were infiltrating right now, in the dark, we'd be limited to the main gate. At first light, Dixon and a small group will find another door. While the rest of us go in the front, they'll come in from the rear."

Dixon speaks up as he paces. "They expect people to come to the front gate. And they're expecting this tanker to need access. We lose the surprise of darkness, but gain another access point."

"*If* the cards work other doors," Lawrence interjects again.

"True," Curtis admits. "It is a risk. But I'm proud of each of you for taking it with me. Tomorrow will change our lives forever."

***

Mark and Ariel sit side by side in bed, both on their laptops. He looks over at the sat phone on his nightstand.

"If you look at that one more time I'm going to get jealous," Ariel says.

"It is quite attractive," Mark says.

"Just call them. Find out where they are," Ariel says.

"One of them should have been back by now."

"Not if they went to Denver," Ariel says. "You told me that before they left."

"Yeah. I know."

"So stop it," Ariel says. She glides a hand under the sheet and across his upper thigh. "Think about something else."

"Now I am," Mark smiles at her.

"Sorry," she says. "I'm still in work mode. Did you see there was a glitch today?"

"No. Where?"

"Down in engineering. One of the doors did a reboot."

"Is that a problem?"

"Doubt it. But I'll give them a call tomorrow."

"I thought you were letting Danny stay home tomorrow?" Mark asks.

"I was going to, but now he wants to go to school. His friends are asking him to."

"His friends?" Mark asks.

"Yeah. Apparently getting ready to leave has made everyone his best friend. I don't get it. They're seven-year-olds with more drama than twelve-year-old girls."

"You're a good mom," Mark says.

"My days are ending," Ariel responds. "I need to make the most of them."

8

Sam snaps awake. He grabs his headlamp from the floor and flips it on. The beam casts long, tangled shadows as he pans it across the huge warehouse space. Something woke him up, but now there's only silence.

He sits up, adrenaline still surging. The edges of a dream fade from his mind but leave him with fear. His heavy breathing slows, but his mind still races. He's wide awake now.

Sam puts on the headlamp and pulls his notepad and pen from his pack.

> *Most people in the debt program were parents. We'd talk about our kids a lot. Many of their families even visited. I remember seeing dads with kids your age and wondering if you were anything like them.*
>
> *One guy, his name was Fred, used to tell me I was missing the best part. His boys were teenagers, and he liked seeing them but said he wished they were six again. According to him all six-year-old boys think their dads are superheroes.*
>
> *You were three when I left, and just starting to find me more interesting than your mom. I could play anything with you and it would seem like your favorite game. No matter how much I dreaded spending the time, you would smile as if I'd made your day.*
>
> *I remember how much I hated the stupid games.*
>
> *But your laugh was the most amazing thing.*
>
> *Sometimes I'd tickle you just to make you laugh. It sounds almost wrong to say that, but when*

your crying or whining really started to grind on me, I'd make you laugh just to salvage a bit of my sanity.

I remember when you were an infant, you were crying so hard and I couldn't make you stop. Your mom was asleep, and I was bleary-eyed and angry that you were wailing again.

It wasn't your fault, you were a baby.

I squeezed you. We'd been told that squeezing was supposed to calm you. But this was too much, it was the biggest squeeze I could manage. I squeezed with all my strength because in that moment it made sense to my sleep-deprived brain.

You didn't stop crying, but I have no idea how I didn't hurt you.

What if I'd hurt you?

I couldn't hold you for a week after that. It scared the hell out of me that I'd tried to hurt you just to get some sleep.

If you ever thought I was great, I didn't deserve it. I'm a bad father. I've missed out on what's supposed to be your most amazing time. And I look back to see how terrible I've been for you at every turn.

I'm here. In Aspen. And I hope and pray you and your mom are here. I need to know you're safe and you have a family.

If you're happy. If you're better off without me. I'll go away.

I don't want to hurt you anymore.

You deserve a dad you can look up to. Every kid needs a superhero, especially now.

I miss you. I want the best for you.

I will only fail you.

Sam sits for a long time now, rereading these last few lines. He's in a warehouse where he doesn't belong. He can't shake the feeling this whole journey has been a huge mistake.

***

Across town, Ariel lies awake. The clock changes to five AM. She knows in the next hour Mark will wake up and obsess over the safety of the convoy. Then she'll have to get up and keep Danny moving toward school. But for now, with the faintest blue in the windows, there's nothing to do.

She rolls over and looks at Mark: stubble on his face and mouth-breathing. But he looks peaceful. She slides an arm across his chest. He stirs and welcomes her as she slides close.

"I love you," she says.

He mumbles a response. She smiles.

"You're a good man, Mark," she says a bit louder.

"Wha?" he says, not really awake.

"You're good to me. You've been great for Danny. Thank you," she says.

"You're… welcome. What's going on?" Mark asks as he blinks himself conscious.

Ariel thinks of the hitchhiking and struggles they had to endure to get here. The nights she couldn't sleep because someone might attack them on the road. The relief she felt getting to Aspen. Meeting Mark has been a gift she didn't earn.

"I love you," she says again, like a fact he needs to learn. "I realize I never felt protected with Sam. I didn't know I wanted that until I met you. I feel safe with you."

"Thank you. I'm glad," Mark mumbles, rubbing his eyes with his free hand.

Ariel props herself up on her elbow and looks at him. He stares back, trying to see what's coming next.

Her hand glides down his chest and under the waist of his boxers. Mark's eyes go wide as she caresses him. She pulls his boxers lower and straddles him. Sitting up, she pulls her nightgown over her head and tosses it away.

"Do you want me?" she whispers.

His hands slide up her thighs.

"Completely," he says.

Ariel slides and takes him in. Mark roils beneath her as she rocks her hips.

***

Outside the walls, Dixon walks through the makeshift camp. He wakes Jesse, the big young guard, and Hugo, a grizzled Latino with a lifelong history of brawling. The two men try to shake off sleep as Dixon corrals them to a UTV.

The start of the engine wakes most of the rest of the camp, but Dixon doesn't wait or apologize. They roll out, leaving the camp behind.

"Good morning, everyone," Curtis says as the sound fades. "Mr. Dixon has gone ahead to find an alternate entrance. The rest of us should be ready to move in about an hour. The sun is nearly up."

***

In the warehouse, the sound of the door wakes Sam this time. He sits up and stares down the rows of shelves as Julian comes into view.

"Buenos días," Julian says.

"Good morning," Sam responds.

"We have a job for you," Julian says. "If we get you to it before most people are awake then no one will question it. If they see us training someone new, it will raise suspicions. Until we have your ID cards, you should speak to no one. We must go."

Sam gets up and reaches for his pack.

"No, no, no," Julian says. "You can't take that. Your coveralls, and that's it. I'll get you a baseball cap to hide your face."

Sam pulls the coveralls over his ratty clothes while Julian steps away. He looks at his pack. Leaving it makes him anxious. He knows he can't take his rifle or journal. Hearing Julian's footsteps returning, he grabs his Walther from its holster and shoves it inside the coveralls and into the back waistband of his pants.

Julian comes back into view as Sam zips his coveralls closed. Sam takes the baseball cap from Julian and pulls it down low on his head. Julian glances at Sam's belongings beside the cot.

"Sleep well?" Julian asks.

"No," Sam answers.

"You will tonight. Come on."

They exit the warehouse just before sunrise. Julian slides into the driver's seat of a John Deere Gator with an open bed. Sam notices a leaf blower, trimmer and a plastic storage tub in the back as he climbs into the passenger side.

Julian cranks the engine and wheels the tiny utility truck toward the center of town. Sam marvels as they drive through clean streets and businesses seemingly untouched by the crumbling world outside. The main street gives way to houses as they climb up the hillside. The lawns and homes look impeccable. For Sam, this feels like time travel.

They turn down another street, and Sam notices the lawns aren't as well kept. It's the level of mess that would enrage a homeowners' association in the prior world, but still looks better than anything outside the walls.

One block down, Julian pulls into the driveway of a corner lot and kills the engine.

"This is you," he says as he pulls the leaf blower out of the back. He points Sam toward the hedge trimmer. "See the trees and bushes on this block?"

Sam looks. Nearly every house has some sort of landscaping in the yard.

"Yeah," Sam says, uneasy.

"They all get cut back twice a year. Try to make them look symmetrical. Don't worry if you cut them way back — it'll be a while until we're back here."

"The whole block?" Sam asks.

"Three blocks that way," Julian says as he points. "It's a shit job, I know…. We've all done it."

Julian returns to the Gator and grabs one end of the tub. He motions for Sam to help him, and they strain to lift the heavy tub and set it on the ground.

"What's this?" Sam asks.

"Your batteries," Julian says, opening the lid to reveal rows and rows of batteries. "They're interchangeable, and they should last you all day. Do all the cutting, then blow it out, or do it house by house…. I don't care. Doubt you'll finish today anyway."

Julian climbs back into the Gator and starts the engine.

"Wait a minute!" Sam says. "What if I need something? Food. Or I have to pee?"

"The corner houses are kept empty… except for the school, that's at the end," Julian explains. "They're unlocked, and set up as public places. Pee all you want."

He shoves the Gator into reverse, and it beeps as he pulls out of the driveway. A light comes on in the house next door. Sam bristles and pulls his cap lower on his head. As Julian vanishes around the corner, Sam turns and looks to the far end of his task: three blocks away, by the school.

Sam pulls a battery from the tub and loads it in the trimmer. He shoves another into the leaf blower. Then he puts four more into pockets on his coveralls. The weight sags and misshapes the pockets, but they hold. He lays the leaf blower over one shoulder, then picks up the trimmer and begins walking the three blocks.

Part 7

A New World

1

Thomas pulls his Jeep under a peeling sign that reads "Denver | West Gate." The national guardsman holding the gate salutes as he passes. Thomas gives a half-hearted, two-finger salute and looks in his rearview mirror at the semi. Full of fuel, the semi bucks and strains as it climbs up the gate ramp and onto the freeway. Ahead of them, the open lanes of Interstate-70 stretch west.

"I fucking hate that city," Leroy says.

"At least they got it under control," Thomas replies.

"Kill enough people, and folks start getting in line," Leroy says as he looks in the side mirror.

The trailing Jeep also clears the gate, and the three-vehicle convoy gets up to speed.

Thomas lifts his sat phone from the center console and starts a call. It rings.

At his home in Aspen, Mark stands in the master bathroom, brushing his teeth. The sat phone rings on the counter beside him, and he hurriedly spits and rinses.

"Thomas!" Mark answers.

"Miss me?" Thomas asks.

"Starting to wonder, yeah," Mark says. "Where are you guys?"

"We just left the West Gate. Headed your way."

"Sorry you had to go all that way."

"Probably be this way from now on," Thomas says. "Did you get Eli unloaded already?"

Mark looks into the mirror, confused. He doesn't know what to say to that.

"Mark?" Thomas says into the long silence.

"I thought Eli was with you?"

Thomas takes his foot off the gas, coasting and looking over at Leroy.

"What's up?" Leroy wonders.

"Say again, Mark. Eli hasn't gotten back yet?" Thomas asks. Leroy's eyes go wide.

"We haven't seen him. Where is he?"

"He headed back from Glenwood last night. He was overloaded, but should have been there before midnight."

Mark and Thomas both look around, minds racing.

"Hang up right now, I'm calling him," Mark says.

He kills the connection and scrolls on the sat phone to a new number. He starts the call and waits. He hears a single ring and a CLICK.

"NOT AVAILABLE" shows on the phone screen. Eli's phone could be turned off or destroyed. Mark runs through the house, buttoning his shirt as he goes. He's glad Ariel and Danny have already left for school and don't see his panic. He grabs a radio off the kitchen counter, bolts out the front door and jumps into his golf cart. Engine whining, he heads for the front gate.

***

Outside the walls, Curtis sits on the passenger side of the dually truck as it trundles south toward Aspen. The sat phone sits on the seat beside him, turned off. He looks in the side mirror at the cluster of UTVs following closely. An intersection approaches, and they slow the dually. The truck's brakes strain under the weight of the trailer.

The UTV with the gun mount pulls up beside them, and they roll slowly together. Lawrence stands on the passenger seat, the map in his hands fluttering.

"This is our turn," Lawrence says. "We'll be close enough to see you."

Curtis nods.

Lawrence drops back down into the passenger seat and motions to a side road. His driver turns the UTV, and the rest follow. Two short blocks later they turn back south, parallel to Curtis in the dually, but hidden on a tree-lined access road.

Curtis listens for the sound of Lawrence and the UTVs, but can't make it out over the sound of the dually. He smiles.

***

In the streets of Aspen, Ariel and Danny sit side by side in her golf cart as they roll toward the school. Danny gestures with his hands as he tells a story.

"And I said since I was the only one going away, I should get to read the book. And Taylor said that wasn't fair because he'd never read it. I told him and Ethan I could read it to them, but Ethan said he wasn't a baby and never wanted to hear it again."

"This is over a book?" Ariel asks.

"Yeah. It's a snake book. There's even this picture of a *bored constructor* trying to sqeeeeeeeeze this guy to death." Danny grins and hugs himself to signify the squeeze as he draws out the word.

"A what?"

"It's this snake that wraps around you and keeps squeezing until…"

"Oh, a boa constrictor!" Ariel says, finally understanding.

"Yeah."

"You said *bored constructor*, which I kinda like… but it's actually BO-uh con-STRIC-ter," Ariel smiles at him as she sounds out the words.

"Are they mean?" Danny asks.

"I don't know."

"You've never seen one?"

"No."

"Oh," Danny says, surprised. "You said people had everything in the old world. I figured you had them."

"Maybe someone did, and I didn't know it." She smiles at Danny. "Mostly though, we had everything but snakes, okay?"

Danny shrugs his shoulders and looks ahead.

Ariel shakes her head as she rolls down the last block before the school. She sees other parents converging, some walking and some in carts. There's a man from maintenance blowing leaves and trimmings out of a nearby yard, but he keeps working as parents pass. She can't place who it is, but with his back to her it's hard to tell.

"Well, if you get the book today, will you share it please?" Ariel asks.

"I don't want it today anyway."

Sam recognizes Ariel's voice over the whirring of the trimmer. His entrenched memory of it cuts through everything else. He turns as they pass and watches them stop a few houses down outside the school.

Danny climbs out of the passenger side. He's nearly twice as tall as Sam remembers.

"Bye, Mom!" he calls as he waves and heads up the walkway.

Sam marvels at the strong, sharp movements of his son. The awkward toddler in his memory seems like a different person.

Ariel navigates her cart around the other kids and parents and sets off in a different direction. Sam watches her, trying to be discreet. With a clear view of her profile — even from a distance — she's unchanged and wonderfully familiar. She drives out of sight, and Sam stands frozen.

They're here.

***

Across town, Mark pulls to a stop at the security center, a bland industrial building a block from the main gate. He bolts through the front door and passes a few surprised security personnel reporting for work.

Without stopping, he steps into a darkened room of monitors.

"Anything?" he says to Gavin, the mid-twenties guy behind the desk. Gavin turns, and they pick up a conversation midstream.

"Clear on every entrance," Gavin says. "Main has no traffic at all, but I don't have the range of a rifle."

"Has Jackson reported yet?" Mark asks.

"Just arrived. You're welcome if you want to go."

"Show me the lookouts," Mark says.

Gavin flips four screens to display images from inside the lookout towers. The two smallest rooms sit empty. The two larger rooms have two men each. The one marked "Main" has a third man attaching a large scope to the top of a rifle.

Mark raises his radio and hits the transmit button.

"Whoever's assigned to Northwest and East towers better get your asses in there now."

On the "East" monitor, a disheveled man in his forties charges into view and drops into the chair. He nods at the screen and keys a microphone in front of him.

"East here. Sorry. What am I looking for?"

"Anything that shouldn't be there," Mark says, trying to keep from yelling. "The job hasn't changed."

He glares at the monitor labeled "N.West." The room is still empty.

"How long has this been going on?" Mark asks Gavin.

Gavin shrugs. "I dunno. Most of the time the person here is doing the looking. We don't really turn the cameras inside much. I never see anything."

"That's why we have the lookouts," Mark growls. He starts toward the door. "Tell me when Northwest reports in."

With hurried strides, he leaves the room and dials his sat phone.

Rumbling down I-70, Thomas sees it ring. He nods at Leroy, and the big man glances at the semi and Jeep behind them.

"Is he there?" Thomas says as he answers.

"Nothing yet," Mark says as he starts his golf cart and turns for the wall. "I've got Jackson placed at the main gate."

"Jackson?" Thomas says. "I hope you don't have to shoot anybody."

"He's the best we have," Mark responds.

"For an elk hunt, sure. His spotting is insane, but—"

"I just need eyes right now." Mark stops at a set of stairs beside the main gate. He's out of the cart and heading up. "Did you know we've had empty lookouts?"

Thomas looks around at the untouched forests and empty road ahead. "Since the Guard left, it's hard to keep people showing up. It's boring work."

Mark stops on the stairs. He thinks how spoiled they were while the National Guard protected the Shining Cities. Though he's tracked the downturn in tourism, how many other things have slid into complacency? Aspen is more at risk than he realized.

Ending the call, he climbs the last few steps and enters the main entrance lookout station.

"What do you have?" he asks as he approaches Jackson.

Jackson pulls back from his scope, and looks at Mark with gray eyes. He's still dressed in his mix of backcountry and cowboy. He doesn't seem alarmed.

"Saw a rabbit at about 3,000 meters," Jackson says slowly. "Thought it was a big rat at first, but then he flipped his ears back up. A squirrel family is stockpiling next to the center divider about 900 meters from the gate. And I'm no tree expert, but I think that old blue is going down soon."

Mark picks up binoculars from the desk and stares down the road to the huge blue spruce standing next to the road about a half-mile away. He scans up and down the road. Then he looks over the treetops, but there's nothing to see.

He wants to yell at Jackson, but knows it's no use. He wishes Thomas were here and not hours away. Mark solves problems and can manage almost anything, but he's not a strategist.

2

Dixon walks quietly through the forest carrying an AR-15. He's descending from higher up the hillside and closing slowly on the western edge of Aspen. Jesse follows a few steps behind, carrying Sam's old shotgun. Hugo brings up the rear, brandishing another AR-15.

Dixon leans against a tree, peering around it at the edge of the city. The other men hide behind their own trees.

"Hundred yards south," he whispers to them. "You see it?"

Jesse peers around, baffled.

"Got it," Hugo says.

"Don't know," Jesse says.

"Stay close. Stay high until we're right on top of it," Dixon says.

They step quickly between the trees, moving parallel to the wall. If someone were studying the cameras on this side, they could catch a glimpse of something moving in the trees. But no one is looking here.

***

On the main road, Curtis grins in the cab of the dually. Ahead of them is the Shining City wall and main gate. As the truck rumbles forward, the wall slowly takes over their view. He knows they are being watched. He sits still, wearing the clothes the passenger had been wearing. He's even holding his gun.

In the lookout station, Jackson stares at the dually through his scope.

"Hard to tell if there's anyone in the back seat," Jackson says. "Looks like Eli's driving, and I think that's Trevor in the passenger seat."

"Are you sure?" Mark asks as he stares through the binoculars.

"No," Jackson says. "I don't know what he looks like all that well."

Mark sighs. He scans the monitors around the room, wishing to see something. In a quick glance, everything looks quiet except for the

Paper Father

dually coming toward the main gate.

"Gavin, do you have eyes on any other movement?" Mark asks into his walkie-talkie.

"Nothing other than the fuel," Gavin responds.

Mark lifts the binoculars again. He's staring at the cab of the dually.

"Are those bullet holes?" he asks Jackson.

"Yeah," Jackson says. "Must've had a bad night."

"They lost their escort," Mark breathes.

The dually rolls closer. Jackson keeps staring at the cab, his crosshairs on the driver's chest.

Mark steps out of the lookout station and onto the deck. He's directly on top of the wall now, overlooking the road and main gate below. Peering through the binoculars again, he thinks both men in the cab look like strangers.

Then he stops and listens. The light breeze carries another engine noise, higher and more frantic than the big dually. He can't tell where it's coming from.

"Defense stations!" Mark says into his radio.

He bursts back into the lookout station.

"Everyone!" he yells at the people in the station. Then he raises the radio again: "Everyone to defense. Right now."

"You want the alarm on?" Gavin asks through the radio.

"Did I confuse you?" Mark yells back.

A distress siren warbles to life, winding up to a full-blast shriek.

In the forest, Lawrence and his swarm of ATVs and UTVs crank their engines and close in through the trees.

On the road, the driver begins slowing the dually as it nears the closed gate.

"Here," Curtis says as he pulls the card from his shirt pocket. The driver nods, downshifts and then grabs the card from Curtis.

The dually strains as it slows to the covered gate and stops.

Above them, Jackson steps to the edge of the railing on the observation deck and points his rifle down at the cab. Taken as a whole, the truck is littered with bullet holes, and he wonders what happened to the team.

"Shoot them!" Mark yells.

"They're our guys!" Jackson answers.

"No, they're not," Mark says as he pulls the pistol from his belt.

The driver leans out of the dually and inserts the card into a reader. A small screen blinks a single green flash, and then the huge door to Aspen begins to open.

Above them, Mark begins unloading his entire pistol clip into the roof of the dually. He can't see the entire cab as it tucks under the gate opening.

Curtis yells in pain as bullets smack into his side of the cabin. One shatters his right shoulder in a spray of blood. Another sizzles by his ear and ricochets around the cab, spidering the windshield from the inside.

The driver pops the clutch and accelerates, pulling the dually inside the city like a Trojan horse.

On the wall, Jackson spins toward the sound of approaching engines and sees UTVs and ATVs closing in. His uncertainty with the dually is gone. He knows these are strangers.

Sighting quickly, Jackson pulls the trigger, snapping one ATV driver out of his seat and into the dirt. The riderless ATV smacks into a tree, and two others slow down to find a way past.

Jackson chambers another round without ever taking his eyes off the scope. Another driver goes down, his ATV hitting a third and tossing its rider into a tree.

One engine screams very close: a four-seat UTV has broken the perimeter.

***

Across town in the Engineering center, Ariel runs to Roger's desk and looks at his monitors. The alarm siren screams loud enough to nearly drown out all other sound. She yells at him anyway.

"What's happening?"

Roger points at the screen with a green outline of Aspen's perimeter wall. A red dot blinks at the main gate. Ariel doesn't believe it until Roger pulls up the front-gate camera footage on a monitor.

Inside the main gate, the dually continues forward. People are descending from the wall security station. They fire at the dually, but the men inside fire back.

Then a UTV pushes through the gate on the bumper of the gas tanker. A man stands up in the back and sprays automatic weapon fire in all directions.

Bullets ping and ricochet off the gas tanker. For a split second, everyone on both sides takes cover. Wild firing around the tanker seems like a very bad idea. Though people stop crouching, they now aim cautiously. But the tanker keeps moving.

An ATV with two men follows the UTV inside. The door begins closing, but as Ariel stares at the monitor it seems eternal.

Then she sees a new dot appear on the perimeter screen.

"Where's that?" she yells at Roger over the sirens as she points at the new dot.

Roger pulls up the image, from a grainy camera on the west gate. Ariel recognizes it immediately. This is the gate they've used to go hiking, and it's two blocks from Danny's school. She grabs Roger's pistol off the desk and runs out of the utility station.

***

Just inside the west gate, Dixon steps out into the street and looks around. Hugo lets the side door close behind him and returns the keycard to his pocket. Jesse looks frantically between both men but keeps his shotgun trained at the ground.

Dixon raises his AR-15 and motions for the men to follow. They begin a quick step down the sidewalk, scanning with their weapons as they move. The sirens blare all over town, but there's no one anywhere near them.

Two blocks away, Sam hunkers down in an empty corner house, peering out a window toward the school. He ran inside when he heard gunfire coming from the main gate. He suspects this invasion is led by Curtis, but he can't believe they got far enough to even have a firefight.

***

At the main gate, Lawrence slumps in his UTV seat, a gun pointed to his head. The driver is dead, and their vehicle crashed into an inner retaining wall. Blood oozes from Lawrence's side, but he grits his teeth and glares at the armed security men around him.

The dually has turned a corner and gone out of sight. He can still hear gunfire somewhere in the distance. Lawrence wonders how far Curtis will go.

"It's all going to burn," Lawrence says.

"You can't do shit," the security guard says as he tightens his grip on the pistol.

"You've got a rolling bomb in the middle of your city," Lawrence hisses with a smile.

The reality of this seems suddenly to dawn on the guards. Most turn and run, climbing into golf carts as if they were assault vehicles. The man holding the gun to Lawrence looks away, his focus shifting.

Lawrence bats the arm away and lunges forward. He unsheathes a knife in his sleeve and stabs it deep into the guard's side, right between the panels of the man's body armor.

The guard pulls away, gasping for breath and trying to recover. Lawrence starts to climb out after him, reaching for the man's pistol.

Then Lawrence's skull cleaves in two, a bullet entering the top of his head and exploding out his left ear with a softball-size chunk of gore. The force tugs Lawrence like a rag doll before he drops to the pavement.

Above him, Jackson lowers his rifle and looks down at the fallen guard.

"Man down!" Jackson screams to no one. He eyes the guard still alive below him, and ignores Lawrence and the other citizens and strangers lying dead around him.

Then a yell rises from outside the wall, and Jackson spins to see a mismatched group of nearly twenty people rushing the gate. He runs to the railing as he reloads his rifle. The group has nearly reached the wall when he gets the first one in his crosshairs.

The overweight man with a bat spins as the rifle bullet catches him in the upper chest. He gurgles and stumbles, falling to the earth. He isn't dead yet, but Jackson searches for another target.

Aspen's main gate remains open, suspended in mid-closure by debris and crushed UTVs from the raiding party. More of Curtis' group crawl through the opening and exchange their makeshift weapons for real ones among the corpses.

***

Ariel careens her golf cart through town. She hears gunfire from the main gate. Near the city center, she looks north one block and glimpses the dually crashed into a store, with men all around.

She continues across town.

***

Near the west gate, Dixon has slowed to a walk, his eyes still sweeping as his gun barrel follows.

"What are we looking for?" Jesse asks.

"High ground," Dixon answers.

Jesse looks back the way they came. The mountainside looms up over the wall, much higher than their current location.

"Keep moving," Hugo says, tugging on Jesse's shirt as he passes.

The kid turns to follow Hugo and sees Dixon crouching just ahead. They drop into ready positions behind him.

Dixon opens the sat phone and dials. It rings and then disconnects.

"We're on our own," he says to Hugo. "We take this, and we hold it."

Jesse looks at the sign in the yard two houses away.

"A school?" Jesse asks.

Dixon jumps up and runs for the door, his AR-15 leading the way. Hugo hops up and goes with him. Jesse follows, reluctant.

Across the street, Sam sees Dixon approach the school from the far side. Sam stands up, no longer hiding as he stares out the large window in disbelief. Dixon motions to someone behind him, and Sam sees a large Hispanic man come into view. While Dixon closes in on the front door, the Hispanic man goes around the side.

Then Sam recognizes Jesse, following slowly as Dixon climbs the stairs. Dixon slams his shoulder into the front door, and it gives. As Dixon disappears inside, Jesse runs after him.

Sam turns away from the window. Then he looks out at the school again. He stands frozen for a second, eyes darting. Dropping his gun, he pulls all the heavy extra batteries from the pockets of his coveralls. Then he steals another look at the school. Jesse has gone inside, and nothing looks out of the ordinary from the street.

Sam snatches his gun from the floor and sprints out the back door of the house.

***

In the center of town, Mark pulls open the passenger door of the dually to find Curtis looking back at him. A large gash bleeds from Curtis' hairline and down over one eye. He smiles at Mark, blood in his teeth.

"Boom," Curtis sputters as he tosses a grenade out of the cab and over Mark's shoulder.

"Grenade!" Mark yells as he watches it fall. One of the men behind him leaps on top of it, and the whole group freezes. As seconds pass and Mark looks away, Curtis reaches painfully for his fallen gun.

The grenade doesn't explode. Dud or distraction, Mark doesn't know. He turns back to Curtis and sees him trying to raise the rifle. Without thinking, Mark smacks Curtis in the face with the butt of his pistol. Curtis slumps in the passenger seat, unconscious.

3

Sam moves through the backyard of the corner house to the alleyway behind. He looks across the street to the school. He sees Hugo round the far corner, moving out of sight on his perimeter sweep of the building.

Crossing the street in a crouched run, Sam loads a round into the Walther and flips off the safety. He leaps up the back stairs of the schoolhouse and stops against the door.

Carefully Sam turns the knob. He's relieved to find it unlocked, and he cracks it slowly. He can hear a frantic mix of kids' voices inside, and the occasional adult telling them to be quiet and calm.

"Against the wall. Single file. Now," Dixon says from the other room.

Sam recognizes Dixon's voice as he steps inside the back door and looks around the small kitchen. The frightened children and the clunk of Dixon's boots sound close in the next room. Moving toward the kitchen doorway, Sam grabs a kitchen knife.

Carefully, Sam holds the knife out and uses the side of it like a mirror. It all looks like a mix of blobs, but one of the blobs moves closer.

"Don't move," Dixon says to the room. He sounds very close now.

Sam steps into the room, leading with the pistol and looking for a target. Dixon turns toward him in surprise. He's mere steps away from the kitchen. Sam aims fast as Dixon brings his rifle around.

Sam pulls the trigger. The bullet catches Dixon in the neck, spewing flesh and chunks from the edge of Dixon's body armor. He tries to recover. Sam takes better aim.

Both of them fire, Dixon spraying bullets into the floor and doorframe as Sam hits him just below his left eye. Dixon's head snaps back, and his legs fold under him. His AR-15 clatters to the floor as his body follows.

Sam catches a glimpse of Jesse standing across the room. The young man holds Sam's old shotgun with uncertainty. He looks at the mob of young faces between him and Sam. Jesse hesitates.

Sam retreats to the kitchen, snatching Dixon's AR-15 as he goes. Jesse yells out for Dixon. Sam ignores him and turns the rifle on the back door. It swings open as Hugo climbs the stairs in a rush. Sam aims and pulls the trigger on the AR-15.

Bullets spray the kitchen walls, moving toward the back door opening. They rattle across Hugo's chest as the two men lock eyes. Hugo fires his own rifle, and Sam feels a trio of bullets snapping through the baggy sleeve of his coveralls. One round punches through the meat of his underarm, and another blasts a chunk from his left side, tearing a piece off his lat just a few inches from where Laura shot him. Sam recoils in pain, his aim failing as it drops to his side.

Hugo falls back against the doorframe, blood blooming from bullet wounds on his arms, torso and face. His body armor repelled the direct chest shot, but the entry hole in his forehead turns him into a twitching, tumbling zombie.

Sam watches Hugo convulse as his body slides down the doorframe to the floor of the kitchen. Dropping the AR-15, Sam returns to the Walther and lets his left arm dangle.

"Jesse?" Sam asks aloud as he peers back into the main room.

"Why'd you have to shoot him!" Jesse yells back in near hysterics.

"I didn't have a choice, Jesse," Sam says. "He was pointing a rifle at children!"

"He wouldn't have shot anyone," Jesse says.

"My son's in there," Sam says. Then he instantly regrets it.

"Yeah?" Jesse responds, his voice turning colder. "Which one is he?"

Sam looks at the floor, hating his own stupidity. Then he rounds the corner in a rush.

"Drop the shotgun," Sam says as he points the pistol across the room at Jesse. He doesn't know if he can hit the guy from this far away. He knows the pistol will be much better than the shotgun at this distance. But between them stands a room full of kids.

"You ruined everything!" Jesse yells as he starts across the room.

Sam tightens on the trigger. Jesse raises the shotgun.

A gunshot blasts from the front door, and Jesse stumbles. Then Sam sees Ariel step into view and adjust her aim. Jesse tries to turn to see his new attacker, but she fires again. Jesse hits the floor, already dead.

Sam drops the Walther and puts his hands up before Ariel can even aim toward him.

"On your knees, asshole!" she yells at Sam.

He kneels, but looks at the kids huddling in the room. His eyes urgently scan the faces.

"Danny," Sam says. "Are you okay, buddy?"

Stunned silence follows. The kids look at each other.

Ariel crosses the room, her pistol pointed at Sam's head.

"Don't shoot him," one of the teachers blurts out. "He saved us!"

Ariel stops, looking at the teacher and then at Sam.

Sam sees Danny step forward. He looks frightened and confused, but he steps out of the crowd.

"Hey, buddy… there you are," Sam says.

"Da—" Danny starts and then looks at his mom.

"Sam?" Ariel says, her voice a mix of disbelief and anger.

"Hi, Air," Sam says as he looks up at her. She stops cold at her nickname.

"Daddy?" Danny says now, his eyes locking on Sam's face.

"Yeah," Sam says. "It's me."

"I thought you were dead," Danny says as he takes another step closer.

Sam looks at Ariel and then at his son.

"I thought he was," Ariel says to Danny.

"You're thin, Daddy," Danny says, confused.

Sam laughs at that and stands slowly. Ariel keeps the pistol aimed on him.

"It's been a long trip, buddy," Sam says and stares at Ariel.

She catches his stare. "That's enough," Ariel says. "You're coming with me."

***

Hours later, Sam sits in a run-down house with minimal furniture. He's alone on the threadbare couch and unloading his pack in front of him. His guns are gone. His gold is missing. In the top pouch he finds his handful of pens and a blank legal pad. His journal is gone.

Sam sits back with a frustrated sigh. Restless, he gets up and goes to the front door. An armed stranger stands on the porch. Sam walks back into the living room and scans the room. There's an odd triangle against the ceiling in one corner. Sam slides the couch against the corner. Then, standing on the arm, he reaches up, grimacing from pain, and grabs the edges of the triangle. With a pop, the cover comes loose, and he sees the camera mounted underneath.

Tossing the triangle away, he waves at the lens. Then Sam climbs down and walks through the house, noting the similar triangles in every room. He's in another prison cell.

***

A few blocks away, Mark stands in the living room of an even more derelict house. Curtis sits across from him in a folding chair. There's dried blood on Curtis' face from the gash at his hairline, and his right sits lifeless across his lap.

In spite of his injuries, Curtis smiles.

"Your people didn't even bother to fix me up," Curtis says.

Mark looks over his shoulder at Jackson and Gavin, who stand silently watching.

"You're alive," Mark says.

"Hell of a place you're running here," Curtis responds.

"A lot of our citizens are dead. You're not my first concern," Mark says.

Curtis finds a big menacing smile at this.

"Sorry about your little utopia. Welcome to the real world," Curtis growls.

"You didn't accomplish anything but get your people killed."

"I showed your world isn't perfect. And I proved you've got no idea what the fuck you're doing."

"What was your plan? If you'd taken over Aspen, then what would you have done?"

"Balance the scales. Give everyone a portion of what you're hoarding in here."

Mark crosses his arms and smirks at Curtis.

"Maybe give yourself an extra portion?" Mark says.

"I would be fair," Curtis answers.

"Right," Mark scoffs.

They stare at each other for a long moment. Curtis tries to maintain his defiance.

"What happens to Grand Junction now?" Mark asks. He watches a hint of surprise pass across Curtis' face. "We know you're Emanuel Curtis. We know you've been in charge there for a while. I just can't figure out how you got so many people to think you had a plan."

"You don't deserve what you have here," Curtis spits at Mark.

"Is that why you tried to hack our security?" Mark asks.

Curtis does a double take at this accusation.

"We used your keycards," Curtis says.

"No. I mean the man in the trash tunnels," Mark continues. "What was he supposed to do?"

Curtis looks stumped.

Mark pulls out his phone and shows Curtis a picture of Sam. He watches the recognition on Curtis' face turn to anger, and then menace.

"Is he alive?" Curtis asks.

"You know him?" Mark asks.

"Yeah. He's a good soldier. Probably did a number on your systems, I bet." Curtis finds his smile again.

"Something like that," Mark says as he turns for the door.

***

The front door of Sam's house opens, and Mark steps into the entryway. Sam stands up from the couch.

"Has anyone told you the charges yet?" Mark begins.

"No one's told me anything."

"Sit down," Mark says. Sam does.

"We're charging you with unauthorized entry, terrorist invasion and murder," Mark threatens.

"I'm not a murderer," Sam says. "I killed three intruders."

"You're an intruder!" Mark says.

"I didn't come here to hurt anyone. Or take anything. What do you think they were going to do?" Sam asks.

"We would have handled it."

"They were targeting children. I saved my son. And how many others?"

"You don't know that."

"I know they would have done anything for their leader. They think none of you deserve this. They wouldn't have spared children. Imagine if they had them as hostages," Sam says.

Mark offers no response, only glares.

"I did what had to be done," Sam says.

"What if you'd injured one of the children?" Mark asks.

"I knew what I was doing," Sam says. "You should be thanking me."

"You aren't supposed to be here."

"I paid my debt. And since I got out I've been shot, stabbed, hunted, beaten, starved and manipulated. I was safer in prison! I've come halfway across the country to get to my family. I nearly died every day. So, if you're going to kill me for wanting to be with my son, then you're just the same as everyone else I've met. At least I know he's alive and well. Do what you will."

Mark looks at Sam for a long time.

"Curtis says you're here with him," Mark says.

"He's a good liar," Sam says.

Mark keeps looking at Sam.

"How'd you two meet?" Mark starts again.

"I stopped in Grand Junction for a last round of supplies. They tried to recruit me."

"So you just happened to show up on the same day?"

"The day before, actually," Sam says. "I'd have been here a week ago, but they took my ATV."

"Curtis says you've been with them for a year," Mark lies. "According to him, you were vital in planning the attack."

"Do you believe him?" Sam asks, unconvinced.

"And Ariel says you really are her husband," Mark admits. "But that doesn't make you one of us."

"One of us?" Sam says with a smirk. "Most of Curtis' bullshit springs from comments like that. All he cares about is who's on what side…. I'm surprised you two aren't getting along."

Mark glares at Sam. Then he turns for the door.

"I can't prove who I am, because you stole it," Sam says.

Mark stops and looks back over his shoulder.

"You have my journal. I've been writing on it since I left California. If you'd bothered to read it, you'd know."

Mark grabs the door and slams it behind him.

Sam drops back on the couch.

He looks around the room and settles on the camera. His only companion.

"He's fucking her, isn't he?" he asks the lens. "You have mics in here? Can you answer back?"

He gets up and begins to pace. "Don't tell me."

***

Ariel sits on the couch with Danny tucked in her arms. His eyes are red and full of tears. Ariel stares off at nothing, her own eyes red from crying.

"You're really sure," Danny says. Not for the first time.

"Yes," Ariel confirms again, hoping it's the last time.

"So he didn't die?" Danny asks.

"I guess not," Ariel says.

Danny pulls away from her and looks back. He throws his hands up, his emotions taking over again.

"You told me he died!" Danny yells, as his voice breaks and tears stream down his cheeks. He wipes his face, jerking his hands across his cheeks in angry swipes.

"I know. And I'm sorry," Ariel says.

"Why can't I see him now!" Danny demands more than asks.

"Because he broke into the city. He's not supposed to be here."

Danny considers this. Ariel can see his emotions changing as he thinks about the consequences.

"Is Mark going to kill my dad?" Danny asks, almost whispering.

"No, sweetheart," Ariel answers as she wraps him in a hug again.

"Are you lying?" Danny asks.

Unseen over Danny's shoulder, Ariel closes her eyes. She wonders how long he'll doubt her.

"Danny," she says as she sits up and holds his face, "I promise you. I won't let Mark kill him."

Danny hugs her now. It's desperate and needy.

"I want to see him," Danny pleads.

4

Mark walks out of Aspen's broken front gate as Thomas brakes the huge semi to a stop just outside.

"What the hell happened?" Thomas asks as he leaps down.

"Full attack from Grand Junction," Mark answers. "Curtis and his men took the dually and used it."

"We saw the roadblock," Thomas says. "Leroy is collecting the bodies."

Mark nods, hating that image.

"We've almost got things cleared enough to get you inside," he says to Thomas.

"How bad is it?" Thomas asks.

"I don't know yet," Mark admits. "They did damage, but we got 'em."

They walk up to the gate. Thomas looks up to see Jackson watching, rifle in hand.

"You okay?" Thomas yells up at Jackson.

"Lots of dead bodies, boss," Jackson says back.

Mark and Thomas step through the main gate, the door mostly open and the debris pushed into piles on either side of the road.

"It'll be tight, but I think I can get through," Thomas says. "We've gotta get that fuel inside."

"Then I need you with me," Mark says. "I'm no good at interrogations."

"You've got prisoners?"

"Curtis," Mark says and watches Thomas' face turn to anger. "The other… I don't know."

"What?" Thomas asks, sensing Mark holding back.

"There was an attack on the school," Mark says. "We're still sorting it out."

"Where's Julie?" Thomas asks, suddenly on edge.

***

Sam looks out a window of the little house and sees a woman standing on the porch. He recognizes her as the teacher from the school — the one who told Ariel not to shoot him.

"I don't care what your orders are," Julie says.

"Gimme a break, okay," the guard says. "I don't know anything about this guy. He's dangerous, and no one's supposed to see him."

"You have a gun. If he tries anything, shoot him."

She grabs the door and turns the handle. The guard grabs her hand.

"You gonna shoot me?" Julie says, not backing down.

Sam backs away from the window and watches the door. Julie swings it open, and they stare at each other in the entryway.

"Don't try anything, asshole," the guard says as he points his gun over Julie's shoulder.

Sam raises his hands, showing what they all know: he's unarmed.

"I'm Julie," she says.

"I'm Sam," he answers. He lowers his hands again. "You're the teacher?"

"You're Danny's father," she says. It's not a question.

Sam nods. "You believe me?"

"I was there. Danny made it clear." She looks at him in silence, studying him. Then she turns to the guard standing behind her.

"You go watch your little cameras and leave us alone."

"Julie, seriously. I can't let you do this."

"Call my husband. Call Mark if you want. They should be here anyway. Go on."

She pushes him out the door and closes it behind him. Then she motions toward the couch in the living room. Sam sits, and she takes the chair facing the couch.

"I wanted to thank you," Julie says. "You saved a lot of kids today."

"I'm sorry they had to see that."

"The world is hard now. Scary. They're pretty protected here, but they'll learn it sometime."

Sam just looks at her. Then looks at the camera. Julie follows his eyes.

"I'm not trying to trap you, Sam," Julie attempts to assure him. "Danny talks about you. He's got a lot of memories. I've probably heard them all at least twice. Other days, he doesn't say a thing."

Sam looks at the floor.

"How long's it been since you saw him?" she asks.

"Almost four years," Sam says, still not looking up.

"Well, be glad you got here when you did. In a few weeks, he would've been gone."

Sam looks up suddenly, confused.

"He's headed for boarding school in Switzerland. It's pretty common these days if a family can afford it."

"Mark," Sam says as he puts the pieces together.

"He's been good to Danny," Julie assures him. "But a boy needs his dad."

"I missed my chance," Sam says.

"You're here now. And if you hadn't been, there's no telling what might have happened. Seems to me you timed things pretty well."

She's looking at him, almost suspicious.

"What?" Sam asks.

The front door swings open, smacking on the hinges. Thomas strides in, leading with a drawn pistol.

"Julie," he says as he steps up behind her chair. "What the hell is going on?"

Sam looks past Thomas to the guards standing in the doorway.

Julie gets up and steps to her husband. She puts her arms around him and pulls him close. He hugs her back with one arm, while still pointing the pistol with the other.

"You okay?" Thomas asks.

"Yes," Julie says, fragile. "But I think I almost wasn't. I'm glad you're back."

"What are you doing in here?" Thomas asks as Julie stands straight again.

"This is Sam," Julie says with a smile. "He just might be the hero of the day."

***

Mark walks into Curtis' house. Curtis has cleaned up and looks almost normal, except for his limp and bandaged arm.

"Still don't know what to do with me?" Curtis asks.

"I can think of a few things. But we're still sorting out the facts," Mark says.

"Facts can be tricky things," Curtis says with a smile.

Mark reveals Sam's journal from behind his back. He drops it on the floor in front of Curtis.

"Tell me about this," Mark says as Curtis picks it up.

"Oh, are you buying this?" Curtis asks. "He said you would."

"So, you've seen it?"

"It's these scribblings that keep him controllable. I've seen the whole thing… musings about some journey he never took and some family he never had. Kinda sad really."

"What's your goal here?" Mark asks.

"I've already done it."

"Getting captured?"

"I've got you and your delicate flowers wandering around terrified. No idea what's true. That's more than I could hope for."

"When we kill you, is that mission accomplished?"

"Oh, you're going to kill me now? No trial? That doesn't seem very *civilized*."

"I could have shot you in the street," Mark threatens. "And the more you give me bullshit answers, the more I wish I did."

He grabs the journal from the floor and walks out.

***

Mark sits at his desk. Ariel sits on the other side. He looks past her to the sunlight fading on the peaks.

"How is he?" Mark asks.

"He's been crying a lot. He's not sure what to believe," Ariel sighs. "He knows I lied to him. And he wants to see his dad."

"You told me he was dead," Mark says.

"Yes. I did. Because there was no way he could survive prison. And even if he did…" she trails off, shaking her head at the impossibility of the situation. "I didn't think there was any chance he'd find us. You've heard the stories out there — no one goes cross-country!"

"And it's really him?"

Ariel nods. "He's gotta be forty pounds lighter, and a lot harder. But it's him."

"How'd he get in?"

Ariel can't look at Mark now; this really hurts to say. "He hacked the terminal in Engineering. Got through my security."

"How's that possible?"

"He knows my style. No one else could have done it."

"Where'd he enter?"

"Through the trash compactors, I think."

"Something else that's not supposed to be possible."

Mark's staring at her now. It's not friendly.

"What?" Ariel asks.

"Did you help him do this?"

Her face falls, incredulous. "No. Absolutely not! I had no idea he was here. I nearly shot him at the school…. Ask Julie."

"I did," Mark says quietly. "She said the same thing."

Ariel folds her arms, vindicated and now angry.

"I'm sorry," Mark says. "I'm just trying to figure out how all this happened."

He opens a drawer of his desk and pulls out Sam's journal. He slides it across to Ariel.

"This is Sam's. He says it proves he's not with the attackers. Tell me what you think."

***

The sun has set in Aspen. In spite of the scars and rubble around the entrance, the main gate is closed again. All across the city, people work to return it to normal. The semi pulls the first tanker into the large warehouse beside the other one. At the dually crash sight, a group labors to get the huge truck righted and out of the storefront it decimated.

In the Engineering facility, Roger copies and edits security footage, putting together a visual timeline of the attack on the city. Julian feverishly builds a similar reel showing Sam moving through the city. There's footage of them both talking to Sam. He fears what that will mean when others see it.

Sam sits alone in his guarded house. He glances at the cameras again, wondering if Roger is watching him right now. Then he wonders who else might be watching. He wants to write, and knows that someone in town has his notepad. He thinks of what they are reading and how they will judge him for it. He digs in his pack and finds the second pad, unused but curled at the edges. He digs further for a pen and finds one. Then he starts walking through the house to find somewhere, anywhere, he doesn't feel like he's being watched.

> *I saw you today for the first time in nearly four years. You're so much taller than I imagined. You're a boy now, not just a child. I recognized your face, your eyes are the same, but I got a glimpse of the man you'll become.*
>
> *Seeing how big you are made the time very real. I've missed so much it makes me hurt.*
>
> *Nearly every day in prison I thought about seeing you again. I created a thousand ways it could happen, and debated the best way to do it as I traveled.*

Paper Father

I never thought you'd first see me with a gun in my hand. Or have to connect your father's return with a murder right before your eyes. What must you think of me now? I want to talk to you and try to explain it. But I doubt they'll let me anywhere near you.

I knew the men I killed. Not well, but well enough to know they were misguided and serious. It's hard to say if they would have hurt you to get what they wanted. But I couldn't let them try.

Please forgive me for endangering you. Please know I'm more than a man with a gun.

The look on your face when you realized who I was. The tall intelligent boy you are right now. That's a gift I never thought I'd get.

Live well. And know that I love you.

Sam sets his pen down as he sits in the corner of the small kitchen. There's a camera directly above his head, but he's so tucked into the corner that it looks right over him. He glances down at what he wrote, knowing someone will read this before Danny. He wonders if he just wrote his confession. Could his thoughts be his death sentence?

He wonders again who might be reading all his prior entries.

***

Ariel sits in a huge chair in her living room. She has her feet curled under her and a glass of wine in her hand. Sam's journal sits in her lap, and she turns another page to read another entry. She's read halfway through. Resigning herself, she looks down at the pad and wipes a tear from her eyes, angry they are even there.

"Mom," Danny says from behind her.

Ariel flips the pages closed and turns to look at him.

"I can't sleep," Danny continues. His eyes are red from crying.

"Come here," she offers as she sets down the pad and wine and opens her arms. Danny crawls up in her lap. She wraps him in a hug.

"You thinking about today?" she asks, knowing he must be.

"Would those men have really hurt us?" Danny asks.

"No, Danny, I—" she starts.

"But you shot one!" Danny interrupts.

He's looking at her now, his eyes wide awake and studying her face. She thinks about all the lies she's told in the name of keeping him safe.

"You're right," she says. "I did. And honestly, honey, I don't know what they would have done. They were with the people who attacked the city. They hurt a lot of people. And killed some. I did what I thought would protect you."

"Like Dad did," he says, stating it like a fact.

"I guess so," she answers. "I didn't know that's who he was at first. But I'm glad he was there."

"Me too. I've missed him."

"I know you have, honey. I'm sorry you had to see him that way."

"What's going to happen to him?" Danny asks, looking at her again.

"I don't know," she says, and sees the disbelief in his face. "I really don't. But Mrs. Julie was there, and she's telling everyone how he protected all of you. That's a good thing."

"Can he live here too?" Danny asks.

This hits Ariel full force, stirring questions she's been avoiding. Sam is in Aspen and must be faced.

"That's not up to me, Danny."

"But you're his wife?"

"Yes. I am," she says this to herself as much as to Danny. It feels strange to admit. "I'll have to find out."

"Can I see him?"

She wants to tell him it's impossible. She wants to lie and say no one can see him. But she can't lie to him about this, not after today.

"I need to see him first," Ariel says.

Danny nods slowly. He can see in her face that this won't be debated.

5

Mark climbs out of his golf cart and starts toward Curtis' house as his cell phone rings. He sees Ariel's name on the face. He stops walking and answers.

"Everything okay?" he asks.

"Danny's not sleeping. Where are you?" she answers.

"I'm about to talk to Curtis again."

"Tonight?"

"I can't let it linger. We've got to give people something by tomorrow," he says as he looks around. The guards on the front porch look back at him as he stands in the yard. "Plus," he continues more quietly, "we still haven't collected all the bodies."

"Will you be home tonight?" she asks.

"I doubt it. I'm sorry."

"Anything I can do?"

"Did you read his journal?"

"I've started. Some of it's pretty hard for me."

"I didn't think of that," he says, no longer pacing in the yard. "So you think it's legitimate?"

"I think he really came across the country for me, if that's what you're asking," she says, more harshly than intended.

"Okay. I understand," Mark says, sounding frayed. "That's good to know before I go in here. Try to get some sleep, you and Danny both. I gotta go. Love you." He hangs up before she can respond and climbs the stairs into the house.

Thomas is in the living room. Curtis has a fresh bruise rising around one eye.

"Tom," Mark says with concern. "What are you doing?"

"Oh," Curtis says with a pained smile. "You're here to play the good cop now?"

Mark ignores him and pulls Thomas out of the living room. Thomas leaves reluctantly, staring back over his shoulder at Curtis.

"Tom," Mark says, getting his attention. "Talk to me."

"He claims he didn't know about the school," Tom says in an angry whisper.

"Didn't know?" Mark asks. "He claims to know everything."

"Says it was a… 'rogue element,'" Tom says. "Even says it was all Sam's idea."

"Did you hurt him?" Mark asks, serious.

"Not enough," Tom admits.

"Go home," Mark says. "Seriously. One of us has to sleep. What's Julie doing?"

"I don't know," Tom says as he starts for the door. "She's got our kids staying with friends. Said she might go see Ariel."

"Good," Mark smiles. "I hope she does. Get some sleep."

Tom steps out of the house. Mark lets the door close and then turns to Curtis.

"What happens to the Junction?"

Curtis looks back at him, silent and surprised. This was not a question he expected.

"They'll be fine," Curtis says.

"You told me this was your strike force," Mark presses. "Judging by the mix of vehicles, I'm guessing it's everything you have. And most of it running on fumes."

"You have no idea," Curtis shrugs.

"That's why I'm asking," Mark continues. "If you were expecting to win, then they'd be told to follow in a few days. But you don't seem that concerned that you lost. Or that your men are dead. Or that you're going to join them."

"If you kill me, they'll rise up and burn this place to the ground."

"Scary," Mark admits. But he's not scared. "You going to send up some smoke signals later? Are they coming when the clock strikes twelve?"

"There are thousands of them, well trained and waiting."

Mark leans against the far wall. He eyes Curtis' hands cuffed together and chained to the chair leg.

"I don't believe you. I suspect they're lost without you. No supplies. No vehicles. And no leaders."

"Nice story," Curtis says.

"Curtis," Mark sighs and sits on the arm of the ratty couch. "The Junction has been our closest hostile city for over a year now. We've been watching you just as much as you've watched us."

"Bullshit. My scouts would have seen you."

"Maybe," Mark admits. "But they'd have a hard time identifying which planes took photos and which ones were just leaving the area."

"What are you wanting me to say?" Curtis asks.

***

A few blocks away, Ariel steps through the door of Sam's house. He snaps awake and sits up as she marches across the room toward him. Rubbing his eyes, he tries to clear his head.

She stares at him, arms crossed and eyes blazing. "You have no right to be here."

"I fought halfway across the country to be here!"

"You think I didn't? You don't know what I did to get here!"

"I could guess."

"I earned my place here. My son is safe."

"Our son."

"You've missed out on half his life. What happened today doesn't prove a thing."

"He knows me."

"You don't know him."

"I'm his father."

She scoffs at that.

"It's not like I walked away," Sam says. "You know I did it for us."

"You left us! We shouldn't have had all that debt."

"It was *our* debt! Someone had to pay for it!"

"We all paid for it."

Sam looks away. She's right about that. The last few years have cost them all something.

"Is Danny okay?" Sam asks, concerned and trying to change the subject.

"Other than watching his absent father kill people right in front of him?"

"I didn't shoot them all," Sam says while looking right at her. He sees color rise in her cheeks as her own victim comes to mind. She looks away.

"You have no idea how much you've fucked this up for us," she scoffs.

"We're safe and well cared for. Danny's thriving."

"So why send him away?"

"Julie told you," Ariel says, realizing she must have.

"Does he want to go?"

"He's seven. He doesn't know what he wants."

"Can I see him? I'll ask him."

"No," she says.

Sam just looks at her. His eyes scan all the way to her feet and then back up to her face. He can't help himself. He's really seeing his wife for the first time in nearly four years.

Ariel sees him staring and shakes her head in frustration.

"Do you get how serious this is?" she asks. "Why did you do this? You broke in!"

"I heard stories about people being shot on sight at Aspen."

"That's not true."

"Well, I couldn't take the chance," he says. "And the guys in maintenance thought I could help."

"Yeah. That's never going to happen again." She laughs. "When Mark's done with them, they'll be lucky to maintain a coffee maker."

"And what about the coding?" Sam asks, knowing it was Ariel's work.

"No one else would have gotten through."

"You're probably right," Sam says. "But can you convince anyone else of that?"

She starts to say something but stops. Disgusted, she turns and walks out.

Sam sits on the shabby couch. He rubs his face in frustration, letting his hands linger over his eyes. He has no idea what Curtis is saying about him, or what Mark will do to him.

After a while he lies down again.

He doesn't hear the kitchen door open later. Someone enters from the back of the house and moves through the shadows. The figure steps up close to the couch, standing over Sam in silence. There's a gun in his hand.

"Get up," Tom says.

Sam recoils, popping awake and pulling into a corner of the couch.

Tom flicks on a side-table light. Sam stares at him wide-eyed, his glance darting to the gun.

"This is for you," Tom says. He sets the gun down on the end table and waits for Sam's eyes to come back to him.

"I sent the guard at the back door home for the night. The door's unlocked."

Sam sits up very straight, both feet on the floor and his hands at his sides. He stays away from the gun, convinced this is a trap.

"Curtis is in a house like this. Two blocks south," Tom continues. "That back door is clear too."

"If anyone sees me leave this house, they'll kill me," Sam says quietly.

"You snuck in here just fine, I bet you can do it." Tom squats down to Sam's level. "Unless you really are with him."

"Your wife believes I'm not."

"So finish what you started." Tom picks up the gun and tosses it on the couch next to Sam. "Do us both a favor."

Then he walks back out of the house, flicking the light off as he passes.

Sam sits in the dark, shuddering.

***

When Mark walks through the front door a few hours later, Sam is awake. The gun still sits on the couch next to him, but Sam's arms are stretched out along the back. Mark stops in the middle of the living room and stares at him.

"Hey, Greg!" Mark calls over his shoulder.

The man on the front porch steps into the house and approaches them. Seeing the gun, he snaps his rifle up and aims at Sam. Sam lifts his hands off the couch, palms up in compliance.

"Where'd you get a gun?" Greg demands.

Sam looks at the floor.

"Has he had any visitors?" Mark asks. Greg shakes his head. Mark walks over to the couch and picks up the pistol. He flips it from one hand to the other. He knows this gun.

"Never mind, Greg," Mark nods him toward the doorway. Greg lowers his rifle, unsure, but he leaves anyway.

As the door closes, Sam looks at Mark. "Did I pass your test?"

"What test?" Mark asks.

"If I kill Curtis, and anyone in town kills me, then you've got all your problems solved."

"Curtis will get a trial. We have a justice system here," Mark says. "But Tom nearly lost his wife today. He knows you could do it. It would prove you're not with him, and we'd be saved the trial."

"I'm not a killer," Sam says.

"There are dead bodies that suggest otherwise," Mark says.

Sam looks away. "I'm not going to do your dirty work."

"So what was your grand plan?"

"I'm not here to cause problems. I just wanted to put my family back together."

"Your son doesn't know you. Your wife doesn't want you. Your family doesn't exist anymore."

"They didn't know if they'd ever see me again. But I'm here now."

"And what? You're all going to hold hands and skip off into the sunset? You have nothing to offer, and you're here illegally. I can have you killed. You'll be gone again."

Sam looks at the floor. He knows Mark is right. He has nothing to offer and nothing to bargain with for his freedom.

"Everything I had was in my pack," Sam sighs. "Everything I did was to get to my family."

He looks up at Mark now. "You have it all. Do what you will."

Mark stares back at Sam for a moment. Then he goes to a nearby chair and sits heavily.

"What do you know about the Junction?"

"Not much," Sam admits. "Curtis is their dictator, and you only see what he wants you to see."

"Can they survive without him?"

"A lot of people out there are scared and want to be told what to do. Curtis is good at it. Without him, someone will step into the role."

"Do you think they'll attack again?"

"If they get desperate enough, yes. But I doubt they have any more weapons."

"So why do you think he did it?"

"He fashions himself as a savior. Live or die, he's a hero."

Mark studies Sam.

"He says you're a murderer," Mark says.

Sam looks away again.

"You killed your lover," Mark continues.

"His lover. She tried to kill me to prove her loyalty."

"Self-defense, huh?" Mark says. He doesn't believe it.

"I've done a lot of terrible things, Mark," Sam says in a near whisper. "Worse than I ever imagined in prison. And every one of them could have been done to me. Maybe in here, behind these walls, you still have laws and justice. But not out there."

"We're a lot like the old world," Mark admits. "But I'm not running a prison. You won't be allowed to stay."

"Are you going to kill me?" Sams asks.

"No," Mark says as he stands.

"If you send me out there without anything, I'll die anyway."

"You could have taken this," Mark says as he holds up the gun. "That tells me you're not stupid, and you're probably telling me the truth."

Mark moves for the door. He doesn't look back.

"What about Curtis?" Sam asks.

Mark stops at the front door. He opens it and looks at Sam. "He won't be staying either."

He steps outside into the early morning and pulls the door closed behind him.

Sam can hear him walk to the driveway and then whine away in his golf cart.

6

Sam's journal sits on a pristine kitchen counter. Most of the pages have been turned. Ariel refills her coffee mug and sits in front of it again. She's been awake for a while.

She reads one of his more desperate recent entries, and she stops. The fear of failing as a father is right in front of her, but she can't reconcile it with the Sam she knew.

Ariel's mind drifts to a family walk they took when Daniel was six weeks old. She remembers them struggling with the massive plastic stroller, and Sam finally getting it ready to place Danny inside. They fought about the sunshade — the words lost in her memory, but the anger still clear. They walked around the park, saying nothing to each other.

It was their first family outing. Sam's unhappiness was palpable, like heat from an open oven. Ariel resigned herself to the fact that at least they were doing something as a family. She found a weak hope in the moment, but feared the future.

The father who wrote the entries in front of her is the man she had hoped Sam would be. If he hadn't traveled halfway across the country, she would have never believed these thoughts came from him.

When the debt system collapsed, she'd spent days in bed. A crushing depression overtook her, and Sam was left to care for her and parent alone. As the news solidified and the Rec prisons were set up, Sam had tried to explain his leaving to Danny. Ariel had been no help. She remembers seeing Danny and Sam in many quiet conversations and long, snuggling hugs. Now she wishes she'd known what he'd said.

Their marriage was over before he left for prison. Looking back, she realizes so much of what Sam said and did went ignored on their last days together. He tried to leave things well. She played the part of a grieving wife, but in truth she couldn't wait for him to go. Danny was her responsibility, and she hadn't cared what Sam intended.

Now, she wonders if the things Sam wrote were being said before he was gone. She flips another page of the pad and hears the back door open.

Mark steps into the kitchen and lets out a long exhale. He slumps as he steps close and folds himself around her. She squeezes him, her head on his shoulder. They stay this way, silent and holding each other, before Ariel finally speaks.

"Do you have to do the meeting today?" she asks.

"Yes. People lost family. They want blood. I can't have Curtis here another day," Mark says.

"What about Sam?" she asks.

He steps back and looks at her. He sees the open journal.

"Do you think he was with Curtis?"

"No," she says. "He had to go through Curtis to get here. It seems suspicious because they arrived at the same time, but I don't think they are connected."

Mark flips through the pages of the journal.

"Is he dangerous?"

"Not to Danny and me. I don't know beyond that."

"Was he dangerous before?"

"Not at all," Ariel says with a marvel. "I'm amazed he survived. He's not the same."

"He can't stay here."

Ariel looks at Mark, and then at Sam's journal. "I know."

Mark stares at the pages. His eyes are heavy.

"You need some sleep," she says.

"The meeting isn't 'til noon.... I've got a few hours," he says.

"Danny's still sleeping. When he wakes up, I'm taking him to Julie's."

Mark walks toward their bedroom. "See you at noon?"

"No. I've got to get the system purged," she says. "You know my vote."

Mark stops and looks back at her. She smiles at him. He nods, exhausted, and goes to bed.

***

In the engineering center, Ariel sits in front of the surveillance computers. She's alone this morning, having taken over Roger's shift so he can attend the trial. She scrolls through lines of code, looking for any other possible back doors. Her mind drifts to Sam's journal. It's in the shoulder bag at her feet, tempting her.

She stops scanning code and closes the work window. With a few keystrokes, she pulls up the camera feeds around the city.

A few mouse clicks more, and she's looking at Sam.

He sits on the couch. He rubs his face and digs the sleep out of his eyes. Standing, stiff and tired, he walks over to the front window and looks out. There's a bored man still keeping guard. Shaking his head, Sam walks into the bathroom.

Ariel watches Sam step off-screen and knows she could switch cameras. She sits for a moment, finger hovering over the mouse. Then she pulls up a grid of every camera in the house. Clicking each tiny window, she turns them all off. One by one, the thumbnail screens go black until the whole house is offline.

Ariel looks around as if she's being watched. She knows there will be a fight over this. With a deep breath, she closes the workstation, grabs her bag and leaves the security center.

Across town, residents are already appearing at the high school auditorium. They pull on the locked doors. The meeting may be hours away, but it's the biggest gathering in years. Some are coming for retribution, some just looking for a show.

Ariel arrives at Sam's house. The guard stiffens as she steps out of her golf cart and starts toward him.

"What's up, Ariel?" he asks.

"I'm surprised to see you here," she says.

"Short straw. Somebody's gotta watch him," he says.

"Weren't you on the wall during the attack?" she asks, knowing he wasn't.

"No, I was in the street with Jason Carney," he pauses at the name, reverent. "Poor guy."

She's standing on the porch with him. He still looks spooked.

"You should go to the meeting," she says. She rests her hand gently on his forearm and looks up at him in earnest. "I'll watch Sam."

"Is Mark okay with that?" he asks.

She nods, unable to voice the lie.

"You're sure?" he asks.

"I've got this," Ariel assures him.

"Take this," he says and hands her a pistol.

With a reluctant smile, she takes the gun. He walks away, still uncertain.

"Take my cart," she offers. "You'll have to come back here and relieve me anyway."

"Nah, I'll walk," he says. "You sure you're okay here?"

"I was married to him. This is easy," she says.

He starts walking away. Ariel watches him go. He looks back once before rounding the corner out of sight.

Ariel exhales, amazed the guard actually left. She looks at the gun in her hand and starts around the house. Peering around each corner, she confirms there are no other guards.

Then she unlocks the kitchen door and enters the back of the house.

Sam stands across the kitchen in the doorway to the living room. He stares at Ariel as she closes the door behind her.

"Are you here to kill me?" he asks.

Ariel looks at the pistol in her hand again. She sets it on the counter by the door.

"No," she says as she takes her bag off her shoulder. Sam watches her pull out the curled pages of his journal.

Sam looks up at the camera in the corner of the kitchen.

"Don't worry," Ariel says. "There's no one watching."

"How do you know?"

"My system, remember?"

"Does Mark know?" Sam smirks.

She scoffs, frustrated already. It's easy to find anger with Sam.

"I can't believe you're here," she says.

"Me either," Sam says.

"What is this?" she asks, holding up his journal.

"What do you mean?"

"It's not you," she says. "You're not this father."

"I've been in prison!"

"Before that. He idolized you, and you hated it."

"I didn't know how to deal with it."

She shakes the journal at him, saying, "And now you do?"

"I'd like to try."

"You should be dead."

"Sorry to disappoint you."

"I don't mean that," she softens. "I'm amazed by it." She flips the journal pages. "And this… I don't know the man that wrote this." She looks up at him again. Sam can't tell if the tears in her eyes are from anger or sadness. "I wish the guy that wrote this had been my husband. I wish Danny could have known him. But words scribbled on a page aren't enough."

"Tell me what I need to do," Sam says.

"You can't do anything," Ariel says. "You can't stay here."

"Can I see him?" Sam asks.

"Why?"

"Because I didn't think I ever would. I should have died a dozen times trying to get here."

Ariel walks across the kitchen, close to Sam. She looks at him. His thin face. His sun-scorched arms. His small waist.

"I was sure you were dead. Maybe in prison. Maybe killed after you got released. I tried not to think about how, but I was sure you wouldn't make it."

She pushes him aside and steps into the living room. She drops the journal on the coffee table beside the new one Sam has started. Looking at Sam, she sits on one end of the couch and motions for him to join her.

Sam walks over. He looks down at her, but doesn't sit.

"You're a better man than I thought you were," Ariel says. "Stronger. And a lot more concerned about us."

"I was always concerned about you," Sam says.

She holds up a hand. She's just getting started.

"I had days. Sometimes weeks. When you were around, but I could tell you were hating it. Hating that you were a dad. Hating that I wasn't better to you."

"I never—"

"Shut up," she says. There's fire in her eyes, and Sam needs to let her finish.

"That's how it felt. And in those moments I had to accept that at least you were there with us, even if you didn't want to be."

She holds up the legal pad, putting it between them.

"You never shared any of this with me," Ariel says, trying to keep her voice from breaking. "Maybe it came from being away from us. Maybe it's part of your trip. But I wish I'd seen it before."

Sams sits on the other end of the couch.

Ariel reaches a hand out toward him. Sam looks at it, wanting desperately to touch her.

"I'm glad you're alive," she says at last.

He takes her hand. She squeezes it once.

He squeezes her hand. Once. Twice. She pulls it away just as he starts a third squeeze. The anger is back in her eyes.

"What was your plan once you got here? Did you think we'd just walk out the front gate and live happily ever after out there?"

"No. But there are places we could go."

"You're not even supposed to be here! I'm risking my place just being with you."

"You are my wife."

"Yes. Technically."

"What the hell does that mean?"

She folds her arms. The motion feels more final to Sam than anything she could say.

"There's no one around to enforce a marriage anymore. Or anyone who'd bother to verify a divorce…."

Sam looks at her for a long time.

"That's what you want?" he asks.

"I wanted to send you papers when you were inside, but there was no system or infrastructure for that."

"You could have come to see me," Sam says, and she looks away. "You never came to see me."

Her eyes turn back to him now. Teary, but defiant.

"I was taking care of our son. I was making sure we had a future. You left us with your parents."

"I left you with family."

"And how are they now?"

"Dead," Sam says flatly. Ariel softens a bit.

"I'm sorry. I didn't mean to…"

"No, you were right to go. You would have died if you stayed. And I can only imagine what you did to get here."

He looks at her, unblinking. She looks back. A whole argument passes silently between them.

"I'm here. And so is Danny. I gave him a good life."

"Mark's good to him?" asks Sam, with a mix of heartbreak and hope.

Ariel looks away before saying, "Yes."

Sam gets up. He paces. "You're right. You did it. You have the money and access you always wanted. Nothing to worry about, right?"

"I did what I had to do," she says and nods at his journals. "Just like you."

"I bet you keep Mark happy, too," Sam says with a bite. "He keeps buying you things, and you keep opening your legs."

She bolts to her feet. "I built the system that keeps Danny safe. And I met someone who actually loves us."

Sam steps closer. "I loved you both. I just got tired of always getting the worst of you."

"Maybe if you'd been the man you think you are, we'd have stayed."

Sam hangs his head. "You're right. I was bitter about you. And I was a bad father to Danny. I'm sorry. I want to fix it."

"It happened. It can't be fixed."

"We could try."

"How? You don't have anything. You have nowhere to live."

"There are other cities."

"I live here. With Mark."

"Do you love him?" Sam asks.

Ariel blinks. Sam pounces.

"That's a no."

"I do."

"You love him like you loved me. Only when it gets you things."

Ariel slaps him. Sam doesn't flinch. They've done this before.

Ariel starts for the door. Sam wants to stop her, but knows he can't.

Suddenly, she turns back and snatches up his legal pad.

"You really want him to read this?" she asks as she flips through the pages dramatically.

"If he's never going to see me again… yes."

"So it's his then. And I get to decide what to do with it."

Shoving it back in her bag, she steps to the kitchen door and outside before Sam can respond.

He stands there, stunned. She controls his future with Danny in every way. Dropping heavily into a chair, he looks up at the closest security camera and sighs.

7

Roger sits at the security station in Engineering, looking at the screens in confusion. The cameras in Sam's detention house appear to be offline. He scrolls through them individually, seeing all microphones and recorders are off as well.

"Ariel?" he calls out, letting it echo through the building.

No answer. But he didn't expect one. She isn't here.

Ariel had agreed to oversee security so Roger could go to the trial. He wouldn't be here except Mark sent him back to retrieve the recordings of Curtis' capture. Now he's seeing the cameras turned off and Ariel gone. He doesn't want to tell Mark, but he's in enough trouble already. He'll share anything to save his job. He raises his phone.

"Roger?" Ariel calls as she enters the station. "What are you doing here?"

He jumps, his phone clattering to the desk.

"Uh… I was… Mark sent me back for the recordings," Roger explains.

Ariel enters the room and sees him sitting behind the monitors. She hides her surprise and starts for the desk.

"Did you turn off the cameras in Sam's detention house?" Roger asks.

No point in trying to hide it, Ariel thinks as she rounds the desk. She sees the cameras in the house highlighted on the monitors.

"Yes," she says. Her fingers clatter over the keys, and she clicks the mouse on all the windows. One by one, the cameras come back online.

"Private conversation," she says.

They both look at the monitors. Sam is in the kitchen of the little house, filling a glass of water from the tap.

"That water's terrible," Roger says.

They both watch in silence as Sam walks around the house.

"So," Ariel says finally, breaking the tension. "Are you staying here, or going to the trial?"

"I'm just here 'til I find files for Mark," he says.

"Is Julian coming in today?" she asks.

"Not 'til noon."

"Alright. I'll be here until he takes over," she says as she drops into the other chair.

Roger looks at his phone, and then at Ariel.

"When I leave, you're going to leave again," he says.

"You'll be at the trial. Everyone will see you there," she says.

"What are you going to do?" he asks.

"It'll all get recorded, I promise," Ariel says with a smile.

Roger doesn't feel comforted, but he smiles back. They both look at the copy status bar on one of the monitors. Silence passes as the last few seconds of the copy finish, and the window closes. Roger pulls the USB stick from the computer and stands in a rush.

"I'm gonna tell Mark," Roger says as he walks toward the door.

"I know," says Ariel as he leaves.

She waits for the door to close. The clock on the wall says ten-thirty. Mark will be leaving the house and heading to the trial. There will be people expecting him for a final review, and he won't divert from that no matter what Roger tells him. She has time, but not much.

***

Across town, Mark stands in their kitchen drinking his coffee. He looks out into the empty back yard, his eyes unfocused and distant as he thinks about the trial ahead. His bald head is freshly shaved, his shirt tucked in at his thin waist, and a side holster presses his small pistol into his ribs. He doesn't normally wear the gun, but it felt appropriate when he got dressed this morning. He sips the coffee again.

Glancing at his TAG Heuer watch, he quickly puts the cup in the dishwasher and takes a look around the room. The house is pristine and quiet with both Ariel and Danny gone. Everything is in its place.

Mark picks up his suit coat from the back of a chair and slips it on. He rolls his shoulders as he looks in the hallway mirror, uncomfortable. Reaching inside his jacket, he rearranges the pistol. It looks as obvious as it feels.

Sliding out of the jacket, Mark drapes it over a chair and then peels off the shoulder holster. He puts the holster and the 9mm inside it on the end of the kitchen counter, grabs his sport coat and leaves.

***

Ariel logs into a new program on the security system. Under the words "Intercity Chat" she types her credentials and hits enter. A map of the US comes into view, and then dots appear over every Shining City. Some of the dots are green, others red. Aspen's dot is green, online, and Ariel knows it's the first time in over a year.

"Intercity Chat" was built alongside the cities themselves. It was intended as a safe and encrypted way for each of the refuge locations to communicate, share resources and understand what was going on in different parts of the country.

Unfortunately, with supplies running short and each city having its own agenda, it soon became unreliable. As some of the cities failed or were overrun, there were those who believed the system was being used for reconnaissance and even outright coups.

As the years passed, Mark became increasingly concerned with Aspen's safety and uniqueness. He tasked Ariel with disconnecting the city from the system.

Now this security station remains the only place with a link to the service, and using it is supposed to be approved by the city council.

Ariel clicks on the green dot for Tahoe and opens a new message window. Flurries of old and archived chats fill other topic windows, but she ignores them and types a new direct message. She hits send. And waits.

***

Roger enters the high school auditorium. Residents of all ages mill about in the lobby, wondering in and out of the auditorium even though the main event is over an hour away. He opens a door marked "Authorized Personnel Only" and climbs the stairs to a small control booth.

Mark and Thomas look up at him. Roger stiffens, fearing Thomas might tackle him.

"Did you get it?" Mark asks.

"Yes," Roger says as he holds out the USB stick. "He's a bit away from the closest camera, so I don't know if the audio will be good enough."

"Can we test it?" Mark asks, turning to a dark corner of the booth.

Craig, a tall, thin teenager, steps into view and takes the memory stick. After plugging it into the booth's computer, he changes some cables and pulls the video up on a monitor.

The footage begins to play, showing Mark standing over the dually with his back to camera. Curtis can be seen in the cab of the truck. Wind noise rustles by. Other than hearing a difference in Mark's voice and Curtis' near whisper, the words are too low to make out.

"That's useless," Mark says.

"I don't know," Thomas offers. "It shows restraint on your part. I would've killed him on the spot."

"That might have been easier," admits Mark.

"You'd be here either way," Thomas says. "In this version you look like the compassionate, levelheaded leader."

"How are we going to explain the bruises?" asks Mark.

"Tell 'em I did it."

"You did do it!"

"That's why you say that," Thomas says. "And then people that think you went too easy on him will side with us too."

Mark studies the image on screen.

"Alright, don't add that to the presentation," he says to Craig. Then he turns to Roger. "Thanks for trying."

Mark looks out of the small windows of the booth to the auditorium below. People are already claiming seats. He turns and looks at Thomas. "Go get him."

***

Ariel reads a response from Tahoe, and types a rapid follow-up. She waits, staring at the clock and hoping the trial will run long. Tahoe responds again in the direct-message window.

"Finally," she says aloud. "You're not complete assholes."

She looks around the security station, searching for the printer. Standing, she looks deeper into the room but still can't see one. Ariel smiles to herself, wondering the last time anyone here printed anything. Giving up, she returns to the computer and clicks on an attachment sent by Tahoe.

A document opens, showing an overly elaborate coat of arms intertwined with word "Tahoe" in the banner at the top. The lines below look more like a diploma than a message. Ariel hits print and listens.

She hears a printer squeak to life somewhere down the hall. Jumping up, she follows the sound.

8

Curtis steps out of his detention house. Ankle shackles keep him moving at a slow shuffle, and two large guards flank him, their hands gripping his arms. Thomas leads them to a waiting multi-row golf cart. Curtis looks up at the sunlight, his broken nose still red and crooked. His upper lip cracks with new blood as he smiles.

"Beautiful day," Curtis says.

"Enjoy it while you can," Thomas says.

One of the guards ducks Curtis' head as they get into the back bench of the cart. Thomas starts the cart, and they whir away.

Two blocks away, Ariel wheels her own cart into the driveway of Sam's house. She waits, holding her cell phone.

Inside, Sam pulls back a blind and looks at her sitting out front and staring at her phone.

Then he hears another cart approaching. He can't see it clearly until it parks beside Ariel. Seeing the two people inside makes Sam recoil from the window. He's instantly sweating.

Ariel gets out of her cart and walks over to Julie and Danny sitting together.

"Hey, sweetie," Ariel says to her son.

"Hey, Mom," Danny replies as his eyes drift past her to the house.

"Thanks for bringing him," Ariel says to Julie.

"I'm glad you're doing this," Julie says.

"Really?" Ariel says, needing encouragement.

"Whatever happens, they need this opportunity," she says.

"Danny," Ariel says to her son, "you don't have to do this."

Danny keeps looking at the house. "I know," he finally says.

"Okay," Ariel says and extends a hand toward him. "Let's go."

Danny climbs out of the cart and takes his mother's hand. She looks over her shoulder at Julie.

"I'm right here if you need me," Julie says.

Ariel smiles at her friend and walks hand in hand up to Sam's house. When she drops Danny's hand to unlock the door, he looks up at the two cameras aimed at the porch.

"Are we allowed to do this?" Danny asks.

Ariel uses the keys to unlock each latch. "I have the keys, see?"

Danny nods as she swings the door open. She steps inside and extends a hand back to Danny.

"Sam?" she calls into the house. "Where are you?"

Sam shakes; he can feel his arms twitching involuntarily. He holds himself, arms crossed over his chest. With deep controlled breaths, he tries to calm down.

"I'm in here. The living room," he calls from the single armchair farthest from the door.

Sam holds his breath as Ariel steps into view. A second later, Danny stands in full view, hand in hand with his mom and just across the room from him.

"Hi, Daddy," Danny says.

Breath explodes out of Sam as if he's come up for air. "Hi, buddy," he gasps. He smiles as tears form in his eyes.

"Are you okay?" Danny asks.

"Yeah, buddy," Sam says as he uncrosses his arms and wipes his eyes. "It's great to see you."

"Why are you so thin?" Danny asks.

"Well. I've been traveling a long time and not eating much."

"You're too thin, Daddy."

"You don't like it?"

"You don't look like you," Danny says.

"But you know it's me, right?"

Danny nods vigorously. He lets go of Ariel's hand and steps closer. She tenses but stands her ground. Sam puts both his hands on his knees, fearing that any sudden move will send them running from the house. He wants to hug his son.

"We learned about the outside in school," Danny says.

"Yeah? What did you learn?"

"We learned about the bad people that want to hurt us. And to never go outside the walls by ourselves."

Sam nods. "There are some bad people out there. And good ones."

"Did the bad people hurt you?"

"I got hurt a few times," Sam says. "But I got helped too."

"Are you going to live here now?" Danny asks. Sam looks to Ariel for a second and then balls his fists.

"I don't think so, little man," Sam says. "I don't belong here."

"Then why did you come?" Danny asks.

"I came for you. And your mom. I wanted to know you were okay."

"Mom said you died."

Sam and Ariel trade a look.

"I know. That's what she thought," Sam says.

"You're not the ghost of my dad? Or a zombie?"

Sam smiles. "Nope. I'm real."

Sam slides out of the chair and onto his knees. He lifts one hand toward Danny, palm up and open.

"It's really me," Sam says.

Danny looks at his mom. She inhales and bites her lip. Then she nods and says, "Go on. If you want."

Sam keeps his hand out, expecting Danny to take it. His son looks at it and then at him.

In a burst, Danny closes the distance and wraps his arms around Sam's neck. Sam catches a cry in his throat and closes his arms around Danny.

Then the tears come, heavy lines down each cheek. Sam gasps, trying to maintain his composure but failing.

"It's okay, Daddy," Danny says.

"I love you, buddy," Sam says.

"I missed you, Dad. I'm glad you're not dead."

"Me too, Danny. Me too."

They talk for over an hour — Danny asking questions about Sam's travels, and Sam retelling his adventures. But he avoids sharing anything from Grand Junction to Aspen.

Over time they move from the floor to the couch, and Ariel settles in the armchair. She watches Sam and Danny, noting how many hand gestures they share. A stranger could see this conversation and know these two were father and son.

"No way!" Sam says excitedly when Danny tells him about his ride in a

Gulfstream.

"Yeah, it was awesome!" Danny responds.

"I've never been in a private jet," Sam says. "You're a lucky kid!"

"But you've ridden on a plane, right?" Danny asks.

"Many times. But they were always the big ones with lots of people," Sam says. "And this was before I went away. I've barely seen a plane since I got out."

"We see them all the time," Danny says with pride. "Mark says we have the best airport in America."

Sam can see Danny's admiration when he mentions Mark.

"That's probably true, bud-bud," Sam says. "Aspen was always a great place. I'm glad you like it here."

"It gets kinda boring sometimes," Danny says.

"Boring! With planes flying overhead and beautiful mountains all around?" Sam teases.

"I've seen it all," Danny says, a bit sad. "I wanna go outside more. Mark tries to take us, but it's bad."

"Well. In Switzerland you'll have lots of mountains to run around in," Ariel says.

"Yeah. I guess," Danny replies.

"And new friends," Sam adds.

"But I'll miss you again," Danny says.

Sam feels that hit him, but tries not to show it. He looks at Ariel, and she finds a tiny smile.

"You're gonna miss your mom the most, I bet?"

"Yeah, but I've seen her. I haven't seen you," Danny answers.

"We're catching up now! What else do you want to know?" Sam asks.

***

In the auditorium, Mark stands at the podium and speaks to the audience. Curtis sits silently in a chair on the stage facing the room. He's still shackled. He grins as he scans all the faces staring at him. None of them smile back.

"…resulting in thirteen injured and nine killed," Mark says, finishing a wrap-up of the charges against Curtis.

"Kill him!" someone calls from the back of the crowd.

"Well, that's the question," Mark says as he rounds the podium. He's standing next to Curtis, and gives him a look before looking back at the audience.

"As you all know, we don't have a jail," Mark says.

"This whole place is a prison," Curtis says.

"You tried awfully hard to get in," Mark says.

"You're all soft and pampered. We came to show you the real world. Maybe now you'll last a little longer!"

Mark ignores this and takes another step toward the crowd.

"We need a vote," Mark says. "We can let him go. Banished outside the walls without provision. With only the clothes on his back."

Murmurs rise from the crowd. No one seems to like this idea.

"We can keep him. But that also means we'll have to pay our guards to watch him and keep him fed."

"He doesn't belong here!" someone else shouts.

"Or we can execute him for his crimes," Mark says flatly.

People lean together in the crowd, sharing their thoughts with each other. Curtis watches them. He snorts, almost chuckling.

"This is a public vote," Mark says. "Hands high, and each one counted."

"You call this justice?" Curtis says.

"It's democracy," Mark answers.

"It's mob rule," Curtis says.

A hand goes up in the back.

"We're not voting yet," Mark says. "I'll list each option, and we'll get a count."

The hand drops, but the person stands. It's a tall, thin woman with dark eyes and gray streaks in her ponytail.

"What about the other one?" the woman asks.

Nods of agreement and supporting comments ripple through the crowd.

"The other trespasser," Mark says with a sigh. "Sam…"

"Yes," says the woman. She speaks with a fearless finality. "Are we voting for him as well?"

"We've determined he wasn't with Curtis and his attacking force," Mark says.

"That's a lie!" Curtis barks. "He was our scout. Great man and a hell of a killer."

"That's enough," Mark says and nods to Thomas. Thomas steps close. Mark turns to Curtis. "We believe you should see your sentencing, and people should see you. But another outburst, and we're going to gag you."

"We are voting on this man's punishment," Mark says to the crowd as he points at Curtis. "No other matters."

The woman sits again. Mark can see her smoldering.

"All those in favor of banishment," Mark calls.

A few hands go up, staccato half-hearted lifts.

"Keep them up until we have a tally," Mark says.

"That's twelve," Mark hears from backstage.

"All those for detainment?" Mark asks.

A single hand comes up from the back, perfectly straight. The woman looks at Mark and then at Curtis as she holds her hand in the air. "If we're keeping one of them, then let's keep them both," she says.

No other arms are raised.

"All those in favor of execution," Mark says and sees hands rise all over the room. It isn't unanimous, but the vote is overwhelming.

"Rich assholes," Curtis says as he looks out at the hands. Thomas promptly gags him for speaking. Most of the audience stare at him as their vote is counted.

***

Ariel stands by the door of Sam's detention house, her arm outstretched to summon Danny outside. Danny lingers in the living room, looking at Sam.

"It's okay, Danny," Sam says. "I'll see you again."

"You promise?" Danny asks.

Sam looks past Danny to Ariel at the door. She tilts her head, not quite a nod, and Sam knows it's a maybe.

He kneels in front of his son.

"No. I can't promise," he says. "But your mom and I are going to do everything we can to get us more time together."

"Mom, you have to talk to Mark!" Danny says to Ariel. "He'll let us. He can find Dad a place to stay!"

Ariel nods, knowing there's no way to explain all of this to Danny. "I will. Come on. Now."

"You gotta go, bud-bud," Sam says quietly.

Danny looks at him, eyes locked on his father's. Sam realizes how much the face looking back is a younger version of his own.

"Love you, little man," Sam says.

Danny hugs his dad. Sam wraps his arms around his little frame, holding him close.

"Mark will fix it," Danny says. The trust in his voice hurts Sam to hear.

Danny breaks away and goes for the door. Sam is still on his knees when Ariel pulls the door closed behind them. His shoulders slump, and he needs a hand to steady him as he stands.

When he reaches the window, Ariel has already turned onto the street. Danny sits in the passenger side of the other cart with Julie. He looks down at nothing as the cart backs up. Sam waves, but Danny doesn't see it. Then they round the corner and are gone.

Sam is alone again. Tears come, slowly at first, and he blinks them away. Then he's weeping, head in his hands with tears falling through his fingers. He shakes with sobs, unable to control himself. Sam gives in to it, and cries until exhausted.

When he recovers, he reaches for his notepad.

> *I think I've just gotten as close to you as I'll ever get. You're amazing. A little man already. I've missed so much I can't recover.*
>
> *Thank you for calling me Dad. I don't think I deserve it, but in these last few years I've wanted to. I guess I'll always be your Dad, but I won't get to be your father.*
>
> *I wish you great friends. Not the ones that get you into trouble and make a terrible idea sound*

fun (though there's greatness in that too), but real friends that challenge you when you need your ass kicked, and love you when your world crumbles.

I hope there are men in your life you can look up to. Whatever mentors you find will let you down, they won't be perfect. But let older men tell you what they've learned. Take their painful lessons and stand taller.

Never be afraid to ask for help. Or learn something new, or admit that you are wrong.

My guess is you'll be right a lot. Don't use it as a weapon.

This journal is probably the best of me. I hope you get to read it. And if there's even one piece of wisdom in these pages I will have done all I hoped.

I love you, Danny.

Dad

9

Mark shakes the hand of another townsperson, and they step away. He looks around the auditorium and finds only city staff. He sighs with relief, and then sees the woman with silver-streaked hair.

"Elizabeth," Mark greets her as she steps closer. She looks at him for a beat.

"Mark," she says flatly. "Have you killed him yet?"

"Of course not," Mark says. "We've only just finished."

"Are you going to do it?" she asks, almost daring him.

"I…" Mark is unsure what to say. "We will—"

"If you're going to condemn a man, you should at least be responsible for killing him," Elizabeth says.

"I appreciate you sharing your perspective," Mark musters.

"Don't placate me, Mark," Elizabeth snaps. "You still haven't addressed the other one."

Mark looks at her, offering nothing.

"When's the meeting to decide on him?"

"It's not quite the same," Mark begins. "He saved lives. And he's willing to go."

"So that's it? You're a dictator now?" Elizabeth spits.

Mark folds his arms and looks at her. Elizabeth stands even straighter as she notices.

"My role… as administrator," Mark says slowly, "is to make a safe place for us to live and an inviting place for others to visit. We're not a country. We're a members-only club. You can vote. You can have your say. But I have to consider what everyone thinks and keep up our reputation."

"Your reputation," Elizabeth says. "Killing Curtis will change that quite a bit, Mr. Administrator! And executing one while another walks free will certainly cause confusion."

"All the records will be made public," Mark says. "And the rules on entry violations are pretty clear."

"An entry violation?" Elizabeth scoffs. "A gunman in the elementary school."

"Your objections have been noted and will be on the record," Mark says as he nods toward a nearby staffer typing the minutes on her laptop.

"When I come back here next summer," Elizabeth says over her pointing finger, "I'll make sure you're not here."

"Have a safe trip to your island," Mark says, actually succeeding in keeping a straight face.

Elizabeth turns and steps out in slow, regal steps. She never looks back.

Mark watches her leave the hall. He looks over at the minutes reporter. She raises her eyebrows as her fingers sit poised over the keyboard. Mark motions a cut across his neck. She closes her laptop.

"I don't know how you do it," Thomas says from behind him.

Mark turns to his friend with a shrug.

"Can we take a vote on her?" Thomas continues.

"Where's Curtis?" Mark asks.

"East side. Compactor zone," Thomas says.

"Let's go," Mark says as they head for the doors.

***

Sam sits at the kitchen table of the detention house. His pen hovers over his additional legal pad. He wonders if Ariel gave the other one to

Danny.

> *I don't know how often my Dad thought he was failing. Did he leave our conversations convinced he'd made things worse only to realize I'd only seen the best in it? He always seemed certain. No matter how old I was, he was convinced he had the answer and could give me wisdom. Even when I found a different way, he stood his ground.*
>
> *I always thought it was a mix of ignorance and stubbornness. Maybe it was fear. Or uncertainty. Maybe he didn't want to seem weak and wavering.*
>
> *Danny. I talk to you again and I feel unsure of everything. But, somehow the worst of me didn't connect with you and my failures seem forgotten.*
>
> *Then I realize I'm the new thing, the long-lost toy, and I feel more like a grandparent or crazy traveling uncle than your father. How soon would you get bored of me? How long until I'd let you down completely?*
>
> *I got here. I've seen you. And I'm powerless to do anything but hope for more moments together. Supervised visits like a man on parole. To have you smile and hug me may be more than I deserve. But I wish for more. I suspect it's all I get.*

He stops at a noise from the back porch. The locks are being spun.

Sam stands, pad in hand, and looks at the door as Ariel steps through, holding his backpack.

She dumps the pack on the floor.

"I think I found everything," she says, winded. "You'll have to repack it."

She still hasn't looked at him. Sam picks up the pack. It feels familiar.

"Where am I going?" Sam asks.

"West gate. I can get you to Danny's school again. The gate is a few blocks away. We'll have a window, but it won't be much. Once outside, get to Tahoe."

"Why? That's back where I started," Sam says.

"In the top of your pack there's an official entry letter," Ariel says in a rush.

Sam opens the top and pulls out the sheets Ariel printed earlier that day.

"Keep them hidden," she says, pushing the pages toward him.

Sam puts the printouts in the back of his pad and shoves it and the pen into the pack. Ariel stands in the doorframe, looking both ways in the afternoon light.

"What about my guns?" Sam asks.

Now she looks back at him. "You know I can't do that," she says.

"Then I'll die out there," Sam says.

"You'll die in here," Ariel responds.

"What about Danny?" Sam asks.

"Come on," she says, ignoring the question and stepping outside.

Sam follows her into the alleyway between the house rows. Tall fences block them from being seen. He sees Ariel climb into the driver's seat of a John Deere ATV with a pickup bed.

"Hide in the back," she says.

Sam climbs under the cover of the bed, his pack beside him. They are moving before he's even settled. He knows she could take him anywhere, and he'd never know until it's too late. He lies on his back with the canvas flapping near his face. He hopes when he climbs out it won't be the end.

***

Among the patches of burned grass outside the walls, Curtis stands handcuffed and looking off into the distance. Mark stands behind him with Jackson and Thomas. The center island is raised, with the incinerator open.

"Curtis," Mark says, quiet.

Curtis turns around, looking past Mark to the walls of Aspen behind him.

"No last meal? No gallery of angry family members looking for *justice*?" Curtis spits out the last word, making awkward air quotes with his cuffed hands.

"You heard what the city decided," Mark says.

"And you are nothing but a servant of the people," Curtis mocks.

Thomas draws his pistol and aims it at Curtis.

"Why is he still talking?" Thomas asks. "Haven't we had enough of his bullshit?"

Curtis smiles at Thomas. "It's beginning already. You're being second-guessed. How long until you're out here in handcuffs?"

Mark puts his hand out toward Thomas. His friend looks over, surprised.

"Where's yours?" Thomas asks.

"At home," Mark answers, his hand still out for the gun.

"Safety on, one in the chamber," Thomas says as he hands the pistol to Mark.

"I did what you could never do," Curtis begins again. "I broke into your bubble and set things in motion which—"

BLAM!

Mark shoots Curtis in the head. His body falls backward, landing in a heap.

"Put the body in the incinerator," Mark says as he hands the gun back to Thomas. "Tell me when the next disposal cycle is complete."

Mark leaves Thomas and Jackson staring at each other. He doesn't look back.

***

Sam settles his pack on his shoulders. He looks down the alleyway behind the school. His eyes drift to the back door where he charged in only days before.

"Two blocks west, straight down the alley," Ariel says. "The alarm is off. Hit the crash bar on the door. And get as high into the mountains as you can."

"What happens to you?" Sam asks her.

"Mark will understand," Ariel says.

"Will he protect you?" Sam asks.

"You need to go," she says as she climbs back into the ATV.

"Tell Danny goodbye for me," Sam says.

"Sure," she says, and they both know it's a lie.

"Then give him the journal," Sam says.

"He's too young," Ariel says as she drives off.

Sam watches her turn the corner. Then he looks west down the alleyway.

***

Mark and Thomas stand in the security center with Roger seated at the console. They watch security footage of Ariel entering Sam's detention house.

"That's it," Roger says. "All the cameras were off on the inside." He points to the multiple windows showing a black feed.

Mark looks at Thomas. "How long was she in there?" Mark asks.

Roger scrolls through footage and finds where Ariel exits the house.

"About a half-hour," Roger says. "Then she comes back here."

Roger jumps through various camera feeds, showing Ariel buzzing through town in her golf cart.

"That's when I saw her, and…"

The camera feeds from the house return and fill the multiple black windows.

"Then it goes black again later and stays black, but…" Roger nearly talks to himself as he scrolls through footage, "this happened."

The cameras show two golf carts in front of the detention house. Mark sees Ariel in the first one. Thomas steps forward, looking at his wife and Danny in the other one.

"I wanted you both to see it," Roger says, almost apologetic.

"Thank you, Roger," Mark says.

Mark starts for the door. Thomas goes with him. Both of them shell-shocked.

***

Mark enters their house through the kitchen, the same way as any evening. Most of the lights are off, and he walks past the bare kitchen counters in search of Ariel.

He finds her in the front room with a glass of wine in her hand. Mark stops and stands across the room. She won't look at him.

"Is Danny here?" Mark asks.

"He's upstairs. Asleep," Ariel answers. "It's late."

"It was a long day," Mark says. "For you too."

"What happened with Curtis?" Ariel asks.

"He's dead," Mark answers flatly. "And Sam should have been with him."

Ariel looks at him. He steps closer.

"Why'd you do this?" Mark asks.

"He's my husband," Ariel replies.

"You turned off all the cameras, Ariel. I have no way to defend you when the questions come."

"You'll have to trust me," Ariel says.

"What'd you do in there?"

"We talked. I convinced him to go."

"Did you fuck him?" Mark asks.

Ariel jumps to her feet as if stung. "What? No! Why would I do that?"

"As you said, he's your long-lost husband," Mark says, almost mocking. "He's come halfway across the country for one last fuck."

"I'm with you! I don't care about him!"

"So why sneak around and risk everything to smuggle him out?"

"For Danny," she says.

"Bullshit," Mark counters. He steps closer again, his anger climbing. "Did you think for a minute what this will do? I'll have to resign. There will be calls to banish you."

Ariel looks at him, surprised. "He saved people's children!" she yells at him.

"He's an intruder. And you let him go. That's all they'll see."

"You have to make them see," Ariel says. "That's what you do."

"I can't help you!" Mark yells. "I don't know that I'll get to stay. And I certainly can't guarantee Danny's boarding school."

Ariel goes wide-eyed. "But you promised me—"

"That was before all of this!" Mark catches himself and lowers his voice. "We looked like one of the last sane places in America before a few days ago. When this reaches our contacts in Europe, there's no telling what the consequences will be."

Ariel looks at him, stunned.

"I'll fight for it," Mark says quietly. "For all of us. But because you let Sam go—"

"I didn't go anywhere," Sam says from the shadows.

Ariel recoils. Mark turns, on alert.

Sam steps from a dark corner with his pack on his back and Mark's gun in his hand.

"Ariel tried to get me to leave," Sam says as he steps closer. "But without a weapon, I'm dead."

He looks at Mark, tracking him with the gun.

"How'd you get that?" Mark asks.

"You left it on the counter," Sam says. "A loaded gun… with a kid in the house. My kid."

Sam spins the gun in his hand, turning the handle toward Mark.

"You should be more careful," he says to Mark. "And you should know that my wife thinks the world of you. My son too."

Sam raises the gun handle toward Mark. "I'd like my own guns. And then I'll go."

Mark reaches out toward his pistol, tentative. He wraps his fingers around the handle, and Sam lets it go.

"That's twice I could have killed you if I wanted to," Sam says.

Mark points the gun at Sam.

"Really?" Ariel says. Mark looks at her and lowers the gun.

Sam pulls folded sheets of legal paper out of a pocket and holds them out toward Ariel. She takes them, and Sam turns back to Mark.

"Do what you will," Sam says to Mark. "Just take care of them."

10

Just before sunrise, while Mark puts Sam back under house arrest, Ariel opens the pages Sam gave her.

> *Danny*
>
> *I have to go. I don't know if I'll ever see you again, but I hate to leave you here. These people around you act like they have all the answers - they talk as if they know what's going on in all the parts of the world. Their words show force and confidence, but in truth, they're paranoid.*
>
> *The whole privileged world is terrified of anything hard. And they jump to believe the worst about those around them.*
>
> *I've seen things and survived trials I never imagined. I have more scars from the last few months than my entire lifetime before. I want to think it's made me better. I hope it has.*
>
> *But I know I'm not frightened. Cautious, yes. Being wary and taking stock in the unknown is valuable. And yet, when I hear "no one does that" I remember it only takes one person succeeding to make the impossible attainable.*
>
> *Don't settle for fear. Don't wall yourself up in this world of privilege and believe it's all you need.*
>
> *Maybe it is best for you to be overseas. I hate the thought of you being alone over there, but at least you won't be walled up here letting everyone's paranoia rot your sense of wonder and adventure.*
>
> *Be well. Take chances. If you focus on the*

negative you bring it about. Focus on the things just out of reach, the distant goals that make you smile.

You can be more than anyone has ever told you. But achieving it will take more work than you've ever done.

I Love You, Bud Bud.

Ariel looks up and out the window to see the orange tips of sunlight hitting the tops of the peaks. Mark still isn't home. She won't get any sleep until Sam is gone.

***

As the day begins, the incinerator rises into view outside the east wall. It disgorges a load of ash and pushes it to the far edge of the waste area.

At the main gate, Mark looks at the notification on his phone. He reads, then nods.

"Open the gate," Mark says as he looks up to Jackson on the wall. The main gate parts, and he turns to Sam standing beside him.

"No deviations," Mark says. "Straight down the main road for a mile. If you double-back or turn off before that—"

Sam interrupts with a point toward Jackson. "He gets to shoot me."

Mark nods. Sam looks up at Jackson and sees the man give him a "no hard feelings" shrug. Thomas walks up with Sam's Walther and rifle. Sam puts on the pistol holster and straps the rifle to his pack.

Slowly, he hoists the pack onto his shoulders. As he pulls the straps tight, he winces at the pain in his side from his latest injuries. He looks up again. Jackson has raised his rifle.

Sam nods at Jackson and then turns to Mark. "Can you still get Danny into that school?"

"I don't know. Depends on if I keep this job," Mark answers.

"Thankless job," Sam smirks and starts walking.

"Where will you go?" Mark asks.

"Back to California," Sam says without stopping or turning back. "It's the only thing I know."

Then he stops in the frame of the gate and turns around. He points over his head toward Jackson, who can't see him until he moves again.

"Tell him not to shoot me when I turn west," Sams says.

"Go all the way to the first crossroad, and we won't have a problem," Mark responds.

"Enjoy your world. Enjoy my wife," Sam says as he starts walking again. Then over his shoulder he adds, "Thanks for not killing me."

The gates close, and he walks alone down the centerline of the main road.

Mark climbs to the lookout platform and stands beside Jackson. Thomas joins them.

They watch Sam walk. A steady cadence with no stumbles or missteps. He stays perfectly on the centerline. It quickly becomes boring.

"You want me to shoot him?" Jackson asks.

"No," Mark says. "If he really goes, we'll really let him."

Thomas looks at Mark and then at Sam in the distance.

"Did they even say goodbye?" Thomas asks.

***

At the first crossroad, Sam stops. He looks both ways, then straight ahead.

Cautiously, he turns around to face the city. He waves over his head.

Paper Father

On the wall, Jackson watches through his scope. "Now he's waving," he says.

"I see it," Mark says as he peers through binoculars.

They watch Sam turn west off the road and quickly out of sight.

"You're gonna have a hell of a time explaining this," Thomas says.

"See you at the auditorium," Mark says as he heads down the stairs.

A mile away, Sam continues up the dilapidated road and toward the pine forest. His pack feels heavy but familiar. He sees a few discarded ATVs and bikes from Curtis' group and wonders if any of them could help him.

"Daddy!" comes Danny's voice from the nearby trees.

Sam stops suddenly. He looks toward the voice and sees Ariel and Danny sitting in an electric cart on the end of a dirt road.

"What are you doing here?" Sam asks, amazed.

"Mom said we had to get away from all the cameras," Danny answers.

"I'm so glad you did," Sam says. "But you've gotta go back — you're gonna get in trouble out here."

"You're not in trouble anymore, are you?" Danny says.

"No. I guess not," Sam says.

Ariel climbs out of the cart and lifts a small backpack from the back. Sam watches her walk to Danny and hand him the pack. He puts it on as she crouches in front of him. Danny hugs her and cries.

Sam looks on, baffled.

"Tahoe will take you both," Ariel says to Sam with tears in her eyes.

"No. He should go to Switzerland," Sam says.

"Even if he can, he doesn't want to go," she says as she pulls back from Danny. She stands and looks at him for confirmation. Danny gives a teary nod.

"We talked about it," she continues, looking at Sam. "He wants to be with his father."

Ariel leads Danny by the hand and passes him to Sam. Danny looks up at his father as he grips Sam's palm.

"I can't do this," Sam says to Ariel.

She kisses him, a good bye and good luck gesture.

"You can," she says. "I've got pages and pages of proof. Now you have to do it."

"What happens to you?" Sam asks.

"I'll be okay. I built the security system, remember?" She smiles through tears as she steps into the golf cart.

Sam drops down to Danny's level.

"Are you sure you want to do this, bud-bud?" Sam asks. "We'll be walking a lot. Maybe riding if we're lucky. But we're sleeping outside and hunting for food. It's not like what you've had."

Danny actually smiles at this. "You'll protect me, right? And show me how?" he says in a be-brave tone.

Sam starts to say something, but it catches. He smiles, tears in his own eyes. "Yeah. Of course I will, little man."

Ariel turns the cart around and stops. She holds up Sam's notepad over her shoulder. He can see the wrinkled pages.

"I'm keeping this," she says. "Tell him yourself."

And then with a whir, she begins rolling away. She can't bring herself to look back as she bounces down the road. She hopes Danny won't cry out for her, because she knows she'll change her mind.

Sam stands and watches her go.

He feels Danny's hand slide into his again.

Instinctively, Sam squeezes the little hand three times. I. Love. You.

Danny squeezes back. Four times. I. Love. You. Too.

They turn for the forest.

For Tahoe.

The End.

Author's Note

"Paper Father" was a long time in the making. I first had the idea when my wife and I found out we were having a boy. As a screenwriter, I instantly thought of the story as a film and quickly wrote a few opening scenes. Sam arriving at his parent's home, meeting Hollis, and winding up in the panic room were all a part of the initial creation.

By the time my son was born we knew we were leaving Los Angeles, and I started thinking about the story as novel. Moving to the mountains, starting a new job, and nurturing a start-up business on the side took up all the time I had outside of being a husband and father. Moments for writing were few and far between, but I never gave up on the idea.

For a while I intended to have this book completed by the time my son reached Danny's age. The age of seven came and went, as my side business became my only business and grew further into a TV show, podcast, and catalyst for travel. The story of Sam and his journey to be a father changed as I worked on it, becoming broader and adding moments as I slowly got it down.

I finally finished the first draft of this book while over the Atlantic, flying to Europe for my business. My wife and son were far away, which connected me with Sam. My son was nearly ten, which made me feel like I'd taken far too long to tell this story.

And yet, I think the slow telling helped the end result. I'm ecstatic to finally have others experience Sam's journey. Thank you for reading.

Todd Deeken – Park City, Utah. Fall 2020.

Acknowledgements

I must thank my wife and son for stretching me to be a better man than I would be on my own. And giving me personal experience as a husband and father so I can take it, tweak it, and create.

Thanks to my sister who stepped up to edit this book, noting issues and fixing my tendency for wrong words.

And a big thank you to my handful of early readers who helped me get out of my head and figure out what worked and what didn't.

Finally, to the audience of Everyday Driver who continually asked about the status of this book. I hope it was worth the wait.

Todd Deeken has been telling stories and having outdoor adventures his entire life. He wrote multiple short stories as a teenager, and moved to Los Angeles in his twenties to pursue screenwriting. After fourteen years, more than a dozen scripts, and many solo camping and climbing adventures throughout California, Todd moved to Park City, Utah with his wife and son. He built the well respected car review show "Everyday Driver" and never stopped writing. Fatherhood and time outdoors delayed this novel, but allowed Todd to pull parenting moments into the fictitious world he was creating. Paper Father is his first novel.

ToddDeeken.com
EverydayDriver.com

Made in the USA
Columbia, SC
11 May 2021